Piano Competition:
The Story of the Leeds

PIANO
COMPETITION:

The Story of the Leeds

*Wendy Thompson
with Fanny Waterman*

ff

faber and faber

LONDON · BOSTON

First published in 1990
by Faber and Faber Limited
3 Queen Square, London WC1N 3AU

Phototypeset by Input Typesetting Ltd, London
Printed in England by Clays Ltd, St Ives plc

A CIP record for this book is available from the British Library

ISBN 0–571–16072–7

To all the pianists who have played at Leeds

Contents

List of illustrations

between pp. 80/81 and 176/177

Acknowledgements

The authors would like to thank all those – past competitors, jury members, managers, critics and many others in the music profession and at Leeds – for generously granting interviews for the purpose of this book. Wendy Thompson would also like to thank Fanny Waterman and Geoffrey de Keyser for their generous hospitality during her visits to Leeds and for permitting her access to their personal archives; and Mrs Françoise Logan, Honorary Administrator of the Harveys Leeds International Piano Competition, for supplying press cuttings and other information from the Competition's archives. In addition, she would like to thank her family – Christopher and William – her colleagues, and Helen Sprott of Faber and Faber for their patience, encouragement and support during the writing of this book.

Every effort has been made to contact owners of copyright material reproduced in this book. The authors and publishers apologize for any omissions, and would like to acknowledge gratefully the following for permission to reproduce material:

The Royal Academy of Music (letter from Sir Henry Wood to Fanny Waterman, Chapter 1); The Trustees of the Britten–Pears Foundation (letter from Benjamin Britten to Fanny Waterman, Chapter 2, © The Trustees of the Britten–Pears Foundation, not to be further reproduced without written permission); Rudolf Serkin (letter to Fanny Waterman, Chapter 9); Murray Perahia (letter to Fanny Waterman, Chapter 9); Anthony Phillips (private letter, Chapters 9, 17).

New Statesman and Society (extract from Hans Keller's article 'The Piano Cup', Chapter 4); by courtesy of the *Yorkshire Post* (extracts from reviews and interviews by Ernest Bradbury, Robert Cockcroft and others, in Chapters 2, 4, 6, 8, 10, 12, 14, 16, 18); extracts from 'Triumph for Briton in Leeds Piano Competition' by Godfrey Barker, 'British Winner' by Robert Henderson (Chapter 14), 'Notes of Discord' by Alan Blyth, and 'Inevitable Choice for Leeds' by Michael Kennedy (Chapter 18) all © the *Daily Telegraph* plc; extracts from reviews by *The Times* Special Correspondent, 30 October 1966 (Chapter 4), William Mann, 21 September 1969 (Chapter 6), Joan Chissell, 18 September 1972 (Chapter 8) and 15 September 1975 (Chapter 10), Hilary Finch, 21 September 1981 (Chapter 14), 24 September 1984 (Chapter 16), and 28 September 1987 (Chapter 18), all © Times Newspapers Limited, 1966, 1969, 1972, 1975, 1981, 1984, 1987); the *Financial Times* (extracts from reviews by Dominic Gill in Chapters 12 and 16); the *Jewish Gazette* (extract from article by Rabbi J. Apfel, Chapter 2); the European String Teachers' Association (extracts in Chapter 9 from the ESTA 'Report on Competitions', available from Alfred Russell, 89 Barons Keep, Gliddon Road, London W14, price £1.50, pp. included); Gerald Larner (extracts from reviews in the *Guardian*, Chapters 6, 8, 10, 16, 18); Sir Thomas Armstrong (extract from *Sunday Times* article, 'Young Virtuosi at the Piano', 29 October 1963, Chapter 1); Bryce Morrison (extract from review, 'A Triumph for Donohoe' in the *Daily Telegraph*, Chapter 16).

For some information in Chapter 3, the authors are indebted to the article 'Leeds' in *The New Grove Dictionary of Music and Musicians*.

The authors also wish to acknowledge the *Yorkshire Post*, Judy Tapp, Jack Perkins, John Lyles, Sophie Baker, Frank Corr and Maxwell Roberts for permission to reproduce the photographs.

Foreword

If one reads through the list of prize-winners from previous Leeds Piano Competitions, it will soon become apparent that many of the greatest pianists of the world today have survived the ordeal of being competitors at 'The Leeds' and are among the finest artists of their generation.

We are all concerned that there appears to be the necessity for a young musician to enter and win a competition in order to become established on the international music map; but with the breakdown years ago of the patronage system which fostered great soloists of previous generations, the competition ladder remains the only fair and reasonable alternative.

The list of national and international engagements offered to the Leeds prize-winners is as great and prestigious as ever. We always hope that a young pianist will emerge with a touch which proclaims a master – with a fine technique, beauty of tone, musical understanding and integrity, rhythmic vitality, passion and the most important quality of all, that indefinable inspiration, artistry or magic. Many doors will have been opened by us; with these musical qualities and professional opportunities, it is hoped that they will remain open for ever.

Do the finest pianists always win first prize? This is a question I am frequently asked. My reply is that the jury, having listened to about a hundred solo recitals and six concertos in two weeks, has come to the conclusion in its musical wisdom that *this* competitor shall be proclaimed a winner. The real competition of a professional pianist's life now begins.

Winning first prize is only the first hurdle; from now on, the performer is not only compared with all other international prize-winners, but also with the greatest pianists of the day. The jury at this time has no access to a crystal ball which might reveal the future personal fortunes and misfortunes of the winner and how he or she will react to them. The jury never knows whether a winner possesses great reserves of physical and emotional stamina, and can cope with adverse criticism; whether nerves lower the standard of performance; how much intensive teaching has gone into the preparation of the competition programmes; and whether there is an over-dependency on the teacher. How quickly can a winner absorb and memorize new repertoire at the same time as travelling and performing all over the world? Does he or she enjoy travelling and being away from home and family? Only the passage of the ensuing months and years will give the answers.

I am often asked what qualities of character a musician must possess in order to become a great performer. I would answer only half jestingly: First, you must have *inclin*ation and *imagin*ation, backed up by *applic*ation, *concentr*ation and *determin*ation. Be prepared for *perspir*ation and at times *frustr*ation and even *tribul*ation. With *inspi*ration, you will receive *appreci*ation, *adul*ation, and *ov*ation!

I should like to record with deep gratitude my thanks to a great friend and colleague, Marion Thorpe, co-founder of the competition; to Geoffrey for his total support and constructively critical encouragement; to Harveys of Bristol, our most generous sponsors, who give without any strings attached.

To my patient and imaginative collaborator, Wendy Thompson, I offer my affection and respect. Without the willing and enthusiastic co-operation of Françoise Logan and numerous other supporters, neither this book nor, indeed, the Harveys Leeds International Pianoforte Competition could ever have happened.

Fanny Waterman

Chapter One

Fanny Waterman

Unable to sleep one summer night in 1961, a Leeds piano teacher, housewife and mother of two young sons, woke her husband and said, 'Why don't we start an international piano competition?' Most men would have uttered some soothing platitude and gone back to sleep. But Geoffrey de Keyser, a GP accustomed to being woken in the night, gave his wife's unusual proposal his considered attention. 'It won't work here in Leeds,' he said. 'You need the resources of a capital city.' 'I'll show you,' said his wife.

Just two years later, the first Leeds International Piano Competition was launched. Controversial from the beginning, it has attracted both praise and a fair measure of criticism from the musical world and the media. But the fact that in 1990 it celebrates the twenty-seventh anniversary of its foundation with the tenth triennial competition, and has taken its place alongside the Tchaikovsky, the Chopin and the Rubinstein Competitions in the top league of such international events, is largely due to the energy, optimism and vision of one woman – known affectionately in Leeds as 'Field Marshal Fanny', or 'the human dynamo'. 'We understand that she is hooked into the national grid and provides part of the Leeds lighting system', said one admiring former Arts Council chairman.

Fanny Waterman was born on 22 March 1920, in Albert Grove, Leeds, the largest city in the West Riding of Yorkshire. Her father, Myer Waterman, was a Russian Jew who had emigrated to England. He went first to London, where he trained as a jeweller at Hatton Garden, becoming an expert diamond-mounter. Myer Waterman never forgot his humble origins: he often recounted to his own children how, in order to earn a few copecks, he and his young sisters used to climb the rickety ladders of the local synagogue in the freezing cold to close the shutters; and when his father died, the family was too poor to afford a coffin, so the children carried the body to its grave wrapped only in a sheet. Myer's own children,

Harry and Fanny, grew up aware of this past privation, and were schooled from the start to make their own way in the world.

Myer's wife, Mary – also of Russian Jewish origin, but of English birth – came from a cultured, artistic background. Her father had abandoned his wife and children to become a painter in Paris, a shock from which the family never really recovered. After their marriage, Myer and Mary settled in Leeds, a northern industrial city with a reputation for encouraging the entrepreneurial spirit (Michael Marks had set up his famous 'Marks' Penny Bazaar' – later to develop into the chainstore Marks and Spencer – on a trestle table in the market there in 1884), and where there existed a solidly established Jewish community of several thousand people, mostly employed in the clothing trade and other light industry. Myer Waterman soon found a niche in Leeds, where he opened his own jeweller's business.

Encouraged by both parents, Harry and Fanny showed early musical promise, he on the violin, and she on the piano. At only eighteen months, Fanny was already beginning to pick out the popular tunes of the day. But no really first-class piano teacher was then available locally: Fanny's first teacher kept her piano in the kitchen, and left her small pupil plodding diligently through 'In a Monastery Garden' and 'Tiptoe through the Tulips' while she attended to the more important things in life – baking and washing up.

At the age of eleven, Fanny Waterman entered the Chapel Allerton High School for Girls. The headmistress, Nora Henderson, used to deliver daily homilies at morning assembly which made a great impression on the young Fanny: her own life has been guided by a set of brief but telling aphorisms, for which she is famous. The school's motto was '*In minimis fidelis*', an incomplete quotation from St Luke, which translates roughly as 'He who is faithful in the things which are least, will also be faithful in those which are great'. This attention to detail – caring about the small, but nonetheless important things in life – has been one of Fanny's own guiding principles.

As the most promising pianist in the school, she was asked to play for morning assembly, and despite being Jewish she quickly learnt many Anglican hymns, ancient and modern. 'But at first I wasn't too popular with the other girls, until I realized that if I was to be invited to their parties, I had better stop talking about Bach, Beethoven and Brahms and meet them on their own terms.' To that end, Fanny learnt to play all the popular songs of the thirties, and from then on, found herself socially in demand. Although academically bright, she was, on her own admission, not much given at that stage in her life to hard work. 'My mother often reduced me to tears by saying, "The trouble with you is that you only want to enjoy yourself." It wasn't until I got married that I realized that she had been absolutely right.' Fanny attributes her subsequent success to a combination of hard work and the simple enjoyment of life's pleasures.

Meanwhile, her musical education continued under a series of unsatisfactory teachers. In October 1935 she and her brother took part in the sonata class at the Blackpool Music Festival. The adjudicator was Herbert Howells, whose notes are revealing:

. . . they were brother and sister in movement, as well as
otherwise . . . Fanny more settled then Harry in early stages. She
treated the piano like a box of toys, inviting Harry to gaily join in
the fun. . . . She shaped things . . . the decisive and gifted work of
the pianist . . . was constantly giving her a superiority of interest.

Harry was never to achieve the musical heights of his more talented sister. He eventually became a successful solicitor in Leeds, marrying Fanny's duet recital partner, Rene Selig. Their three children, David, Wendy and Ruth Waterman, all showed exceptional musical talent, and two have become professional musicians.

Fanny left school at seventeen. The music critic Herbert Thompson heard her play privately, and recommended her to Myra Hess. Hess replied that she was too busy to take on any pupils, but in turn passed her on to her own former teacher, Tobias Matthay – 'Uncle Tobs' to his many pupils. So for the next two years Fanny travelled regularly to London for private lessons at 94 Wimpole Street, at four guineas an hour – a huge sum in those days. 'My father used to give me £5 for each lesson, including 10/6d for the rail fare. "A man can keep a wife and family for a week on what I'm giving you," he would remind me.' It certainly was a drain on the family's meagre income. Business in a luxury trade was difficult during the Depression, and the Watermans still lived in a small terraced house. But Myer Waterman preferred to find money for lessons than for clothes or trinkets. 'We were always reminded that the fostering of talent, together with respect for family life, were of far greater importance than the possession of material goods.'

Fanny's innate musicality blossomed under Matthay's guidance. He realized that she had a natural technique, and concentrated on the interpretative side: phrasing, rubato, pedalling. Her small hands would always limit her choice of repertoire, so Matthay encouraged her to concentrate on a small but vitally important group of works – by Mozart, Beethoven, Schumann and Chopin – which are, after all, still the core of the piano repertoire, and which have since influenced her choice of set works for the piano competition. But this intensive training had a lighter side too. An admiring newspaper report from 1939 records Fanny's performance at a Leeds 'Varsity Rag Revue':

Our petite piano player [she is only 5' 2"] and oh boy, can she play! Can tackle anything from 'Tiger Rag' to a Chopin waltz. Uses a water-cooled piano with asbestos hammers. Her music is of the type which, as the poet said, 'washes from the soul the dust of everyday life'.

A year later Fanny gave a concert at Wakefield in aid of the Red Cross, at which she played the Mozart D major Sonata, K.576: 'She has a real talent and the right technique for Mozart, a clean crisp touch, a sparkling tone, and a sound knowledge of pedalling . . .'

By this time she was starting to give lunchtime recitals at the City Museum in Leeds with great success (one performance packed an audience of 550 into a hall seating 400). In February 1941 she gave the opening concert of the Leeds Symphony Orchestra's season in the Town Hall, playing Mozart's A major Concerto, K.488. It was the first time she had played with an orchestra – and she survived a trauma which could have completely demoralized anyone less self-assured. 'Miss Waterman', reported the *Leeds Mercury*, 'is a gifted pianist and her delicacy of tone and fluency showed to advantage in the Mozart A major Piano Concerto. The Andante was beautifully expressed, and in the Presto, soloist and orchestra combined in a brilliant performance.' But shortly after the concerto began, the sustaining pedal stuck, and had to be taken apart and screwed back together again, while Fanny waited nervously in the wings. 'After this', the report continued, 'Miss Waterman gave a sparkling performance, crisp in figuration and clear in melodic outline.'

In May 1941 Fanny won the Mathilde Verne scholarship, worth £50 a year, to the Royal College of Music, where she studied with Cyril Smith. He taught her to read her scores accurately – 'I was rather lazy about notes' – and her lessons were a great success. 'She has done excellent work and has made enormous progress', Smith reported at the end of her first term. The blitz was then at its height, and Fanny's parents were understandably worried about their daughter's safety in wartime London, so Fanny found digs in Oxford, where a friend was President of the Union, and travelled up to London for her lessons. She concluded her first year at the RCM by giving her first BBC recital at a matinée concert, making her London 'début' at the RCM playing music for two pianos with her fellow piano scholar and future sister-in-law Rene Selig, and carrying off the Hopkinson Silver Medal and the Borwick Prize for excellent work.

Then, in August 1942, she was selected to join her fellow RCM students Colin Horsley and Joan Baker in a performance of Bach's Triple Concerto in C at the Promenade Concerts (which by then were being held at the Royal Albert Hall, the Queen's Hall having been bombed the previous year). A note at the bottom of the programme supplies a telling reminder of the conditions under which London audiences continued to turn out for such concerts: 'In the event of an Air Raid warning, the audience will be informed immediately, so that those who wish to take shelter, either in the building or in the public shelters outside, may do so. The concert will then continue.' (!)

A few days after the concert, Fanny received the following letter which she still treasures:

63 Harley House
W1
August 23rd 1942
Dear Miss Waterman
I am sorry it was not possible for me to come round to thank you personally for your excellent performance of Bach's Triple Concerto No. 2 last Wednesday evening, at my Promenade Concert at the Royal Albert Hall. The ensemble was fine, & thanks to the keen interest you all took in the Concerto and the amount of time you gave to its rehearsal, the work created a deep impression.
Many thanks
Sincerely yours
Henry J Wood

Fanny remained at the Royal College of Music for another year, during which she formed a regular two-piano partnership with Rene Selig, by then a Chappell Gold Medallist. In January 1943 they took part in an 'Aid to Russia' concert; and in her last term at the college, Fanny won the Challen & Sons Gold Medal (the last time it was awarded) and the Ellen Shaw Williams Prize for piano. But her studies came abruptly to an end when she was called up for war service, and was given the choice of the Women's Land Army, or teaching! After one term at a school in Eltham, near London, she discovered a natural affinity for teaching. She left the RCM in the spring of 1943, armed with outstanding testimonials from Cyril Smith ('a brilliantly gifted pianist and musician who will be a source of inspiration to her pupils') and from Harry Stubbs, who praised her 'outstanding musical facility and a really discriminating mind . . . I have every confidence that as a teacher she would acquit herself with distinction.' Fanny returned home to Leeds and applied for several posts, including that of piano teacher at her old school, Chapel Allerton, where she was welcomed back with enthusiasm. She also continued to give recitals around the country where her interpretation of Mozart and Bach were singled out: 'Miss Waterman's performance was model Mozart playing, full of freshness, depth and charm,' wrote one local critic.

But another powerful interest besides music had by then entered her life. Back in 1941, when giving a recital in Leeds, she had been introduced to a young London medical student – also a keen music-lover – called Geoffrey de Keyser. He was greatly taken with the brilliant young pianist from the provinces; and by the time Fanny returned to Leeds in 1944, neither party could accept a prolonged separation. On 16 August 1944, the young couple were married at the Beth Hamedrash Synagogue in Leeds.

Their partnership has been an exceptionally close and happy one. Fanny Waterman constantly pays tribute to her husband's loyalty, devotion and sound common sense, which have continued to give her the emotional warmth and security to which she was accustomed in childhood. For his part, Geoffrey de Keyser has consistently supported his wife's multifaceted musical activities, helping to organize the piano competitions (in which he has always played an active part, as platform announcer, programme editor and general trouble-shooter); travelling with her all over the world in her role as international juror; and offering advice when needed in her business dealings; while at the same time maintaining his own career as senior partner in a busy medical practice. In return, Fanny has always laid great stress on the importance of a stable domestic life: she is a marvellous cook and hostess, and firmly believes in the importance of a comfortable and attractive home. The success of this policy may be seen in Woodgarth, the de Keysers' elegant Victorian home in a leafy suburb of Leeds, from where each pursues an independent career but a common interest.

But for the first few years of marriage, things were not so easy. Geoffrey was struggling along on a hospital doctor's tiny income, while Fanny divided her time between a small hospital flat in Ashford, Kent, where Geoffrey was a registrar, and her parents' home in Leeds, where she continued to teach and to develop her solo career. In November 1944 she was again invited to give the opening concert of the Leeds Symphony Orchestra season, under the conductorship of Harold Mason, playing Mozart's D major Concerto, K.537. Her performance, according to the local Press, had now assumed 'breadth, more poise and a complete assurance. Not only did Miss Waterman dash off the two fast movements with breathtaking ease, but her playing in the Larghetto revealed a sense of poetry fully commensurate with her technical skill.'

The same year, she formed a violin-and-piano duo with another local musician, the violinist Rosemary Rapaport. Together they gave many concerts at music clubs and societies all over the north of England and at Toynbee Hall in London's East End. This 'ideally comfortable' partnership in the central works of the sonata repertoire (Beethoven, Mozart, Brahms, Franck) gave Fanny a lifelong love of chamber music, and influenced her decision to include a chamber section in the piano competition. 'Taking part in chamber music is an essential part of any pianist's all-round training, even if he or she intends to pursue a solo career.'

Fanny's own career as a soloist flourished at a national level in the immediate post-war period. In December 1947 she was invited to make a BBC broadcast from Leeds (her first from her home town) and its success led to a repeat recital broadcast on 7 March 1948. Having been taken on by the London agent Ibbs & Tillett, she also began to get more concerto dates – on 2 October 1948 she played the Mozart D major Concerto (the *Coronation*) with the Yorkshire Symphony Orchestra and Maurice Miles, and two months later she played the same piece with the BBC Northern Orchestra under Charles Groves for a Manchester broadcast. The BBC also offered her several more recitals which demonstrated her versatility in a wide range of music from Bach to the twentieth century: in February 1948 she gave a Bach recital for the Third Programme, followed by another broadcast which included music by Chopin, Granados, Déodat de Sévérac and Rimsky-Korsakov. On 7 April 1949 she broadcast a performance of the Beethoven Second Piano Concerto with the BBC Northern Orchestra and Groves; and in 1950 she took part in a series of concerts in Leeds commemorating the 200th anniversary of Bach's death, during which her performance of the Bach D minor Concerto elicited praise for its 'artistic perception of the tonal values recognised by shapely phrasing and excellent rhythm'.

The birth of her first child, Robert, in 1950 finally ended Fanny Waterman's career as a concert pianist. Her husband had completed his army service in Egypt, and the couple settled permanently in Leeds, he as a GP in a practice in Morley; and she at first as a full-time mother. A second son, Paul, was born in 1956; both he and his elder brother took up the violin rather than the piano, studying with the distinguished Leeds teacher Eta Cohen, and both were selected to play in the National Youth Orchestra. Robert later decided to pursue a business career, while Paul, now married to the Bulgarian violinist Vanya Milanova, has followed his mother's example, becoming a successful violin teacher in London, and publishing a series of best-selling violin tutors. He and Vanya have a daughter, Carmella; while Robert also has two daughters, Alexandra and Gemma.

During the 1950s, while her children were small, Fanny Waterman decided to concentrate on teaching as a new career, something she could do from home. Many ex-performers would have considered that second-best, but Fanny threw herself into it with her customary enthusiasm: she felt she had discovered her vocation. Together with her great friend Marion Harewood, she later encapsulated her teaching methods in a series of piano tutors for young people published from 1967 onwards by the newly established London firm of Faber Music Ltd (Benjamin Britten's publishers). The first of these, *First Year Piano Lessons* (later reissued as *Piano Lessons Book 1*) has become a major bestseller of its kind.

What is the secret of Fanny Waterman's success as a teacher? The essence of her beliefs is distilled in the book *On Piano Teaching and Performing* (Faber, 1983), in which she declares that 'the three aspects of musical training which I believe to be of paramount importance are: learning to be a craftsman, learning to be a musician, and becoming an artist . . .' The mastery of technique – all aspects of finger control, tone production, pedalling, 'the perpetual challenge of how to make the piano sing', perfect co-ordination between the hands, and a host of other technical details – will, says Fanny Waterman,

absorb the pianist from his first lesson to his last performance . . . Craftsmanship, or 'technique', cannot be created in a vacuum. I have never been able to accept that there is a dividing line between technique and the two other aspects of training – musicianship and artistry. With these we enter a limitless and elusive field where each individual's imagination and personality have an essential role to play.

My approach is to help the pupil to explore the artistic essence of the work and to strive for his ideal interpretation. No amount of 'technique' in the sense of a precise and faultless rendering of the notes, velocity, bravura, etc. will produce a fine interpretation. Only when practice is combined with study of the meaning of the music will it lead to an artistic performance . . .

How does a pianist equipped with technical virtuosity and musical sensitivity blossom into an artist? This third and vital stage is impossible to teach. Artistry is the one quality which, I believe, is innate, and therefore cannot be taught but only stimulated.

One vital ingredient of Fanny Waterman's success as a teacher of young pupils is her ability to express a complex technical concept through a simple yet effective analogy – for instance, by comparing the degrees of tone production obtainable from a single piano key, if depressed in various ways, to the degree of bounce achieved by a rubber ball when dropped at different speeds. 'If it slips gently to the ground, it will produce much less noise than if it were bounced with vigour.' 'Fanny has great imagination and vitality', recalled her famous pupil, Michael Roll, 'in the way she can transfer musical into pictorial ideas'. When working on the intepretation of major works with older pupils, she dissects the piece into its tiniest component phrases.

The opening phrase of a piece, or even just one chord (the opening of Beethoven's Fourth Piano Concerto, for instance), might absorb a whole lesson. I will try the passage myself several times in different ways, and together the student and I discover the approach he likes best. He, in turn, will try the passage several times and the process of exploration and discovery is continued until he has clarified his interpretation for himself . . . As part of the process of exploration, I will comment on details such as the balance between the hands, singing the top note of the chord, polyphonic clarity, the unobtrusive emergence of one chord from another, the mood of the passage, and so on. Besides playing, I will also demonstrate by singing, conducting, explaining, making up words to fit the music, capturing the mood with a quotation from a piece of poetry, even dancing, if necessary (*On Piano Teaching and Performing*).

'I cannot imagine how much time – and money! – went into the opening phrase of the Schumann Concerto,' recalls Paul de Keyser, of the time when his mother was coaching Michael Roll for the Leeds competition.

By 1960, Fanny had established a reputation as one of Britain's leading private piano teachers through a string of extraordinarily gifted youngsters. Among them was her own niece, Wendy Waterman, who played a Bach concerto at the Royal Festival Hall at the age of ten; Kathleen Jones and Nicola Gebolys, who both played concertos at the Proms, with Walter Susskind and Sir John Barbirolli respectively, at the ages of fourteen and fifteen; Allan Schiller, a brilliant young Leeds pianist who played at the Edinburgh Festival at thirteen, made his London début at the Royal Festival Hall two years later, and then went on to make solo appearances with the Royal Liverpool Philharmonic and the Hallé Orchestras before leaving Leeds to continue his studies at the Moscow Conservatory; and Michael Roll.

The son of an *émigré* Viennese doctor and his wife, Michael showed exceptional musical promise at a very early age, and began piano lessons with a local teacher at four. When he was six he went to Fanny Waterman. 'I was that terrible thing, a child prodigy.' At eight, Michael gave a recital in the Art Gallery in Leeds, then played the first movement of a Mozart piano concerto with the CBSO, appeared on television with Victor Borge, and in 1959, aged twelve, made his début at the Royal Festival Hall with the National Youth Orchestra under Sir Malcolm Sargent in the Schumann Concerto. 'The Schumann was one of the first concertos I learnt,' says Roll:

It's a terribly difficult piece in every way. Then I found the cadenza 'a little bit tricky' – now I find it horrendous! But Fanny and I worked it out together. We had a very intense kind of relationship. Fanny was born with good ears and good taste. We believe in the same kind of piano playing, so I was never working with her against the grain. Her influence was very powerful, but sometimes I felt that I wanted to play a particular passage my way. Fortunately I was able to answer her personality with my own. I would certainly never have been able to play Mozart, for instance, as I do, without her guidance.

While still a schoolboy, Roll went on to play concertos with the Hallé, Royal Liverpool Philharmonic, Bournemouth Symphony and London Symphony orchestras, but despite his precocious talent, he intended to keep music as a hobby and follow his father into the medical profession. The first Leeds International Piano Competition changed all that. Michael Roll remains perhaps Fanny's best-known pupil, although she has since taught pianists of the calibre of Paul Crossley, Jonathan Dunsby, Robert Bottone (now Head of Music at Winchester), Terence Judd ('who, had he lived, would have been one of the world's greatest pianists'), and, more recently, Benjamin Frith, another outstandingly talented young pianist who shared the second prize (no first being awarded) in the 1986 Busoni Competition, and went on to share first prize in the 1989 Rubinstein Competition. Frith has studied continuously with Fanny Waterman for twenty-two years, from the age of ten:

For me she's the complete piano teacher. I have total faith in her musicianship. She can teach artistry, rhythm, tone, technique and interpretation – all are inseparable. Having lessons with her is like a juggling act – first of all she points out one thing that's wrong, so you go back and put it right, and then a few moments later you'll be concentrating on something else, and she'll remind you of the first thing again, and so on. It concentrates the mind amazingly, and makes you so alert and aware. Also, she's not too proud to do all the boring groundwork; many fine teachers can't be bothered with taking people from the beginning, but Fanny takes you through all the early stages of learning right up to the finer artistic points of playing concertos. Her method is based on thorough preparation.

The first time I went to her, there was a girl playing a Beethoven sonata. The lesson was full of theatre – it was so alive.

She's a very forceful person – there's not much point in arguing with her at the time – but musically, I've rarely disagreed with her. She sometimes makes me angry, but it's a good thing, it ignites me. I like a challenge, and Fanny is a challenge. She would never lead you up the wrong path. She teaches you how to make the piano sing. All her pupils have a wonderful singing tone – it singles them out at any level. She has taught so many prodigies, turned out so many wonderful pianists. The fact that not all of them have gone on to make great careers is something else. People are people, and not many are cut out for a pianist's life. Being a pianist is also to do with whether you like travelling on trains, whether you want to have time for your private life.

Jonathan Dunsby, at thirty-seven the youngest professor of music at a British university department (Reading), studied with Fanny for thirteen years, from the time he was eleven, through his undergraduate and postgraduate years at Oxford, until he won a Harkness Fellowship to Princeton University. Despite his academic commitments, he is still an active performer, both as a soloist and in partnership with Vanya Milanova. 'I was rather successful in my mid-teens', says Dunsby,

broadcasting and winning competitions. I won the Commonwealth Competition at twenty-one, and while I was at Oxford I got the bronze medal at Geneva, and a special prize at Munich. I started to win things very quickly after going to Fanny – she obviously did something to my playing in a short space of time. She trained me so thoroughly that even when I was going through career crises like any other teenager, it would have seemed silly to go to any other teacher. I think her success lies in the thoroughness of the way she works. The British music education system is very lackadaisical compared with the continental – and Fanny has managed to transfer the Russian approach to studying – the same intensity and concentration that you need to train athletes – to England. She has an unbelievable ear, the most incredible hearing – you can't get away with anything. She is like a great conductor in her total aural control. And with very young children, she has a great gift for conveying ideas, and an instant empathy with them.

What few people realize, because she gave up playing in public herself for her own good reasons, is that Fanny herself is a great pianist. Ninety per cent of her teaching is verbal, but there always comes a moment when she will sit down and play – and you are hearing a great pianist. She has a fabulous technique, and she can teach you to make the kind of sound on the piano that Rubinstein or Pollini or Ashkenazy can make. It's an immaculate, beautiful, Russian sound. And she can also teach that sort of distinctive rhythmic vitality that Toscanini had on the rostrum. I don't think it matters if you learn interpretation from the example of a great teacher. Of course fine teaching is about trying to bring out the best in the individual, but few young teenagers have the necessary artistic conviction to produce fine playing entirely unaided – they learn it through the apprentice system.

I consider Fanny Waterman to be the doyenne of the piano playing world. If you judge a musical culture by its great teachers, then Fanny has a major role to play in our culture. Over the last twenty years there hasn't been a British piano teacher to match her reputation. But she has ensured that others can take over from her.

Paul Crossley, now one of Britain's most important specialists in contemporary piano music, studied with Fanny Waterman for six years:

She couldn't have been a better teacher. I learnt all my basic technique from her. She had a very analytical approach: everything was taken apart, both from the vertical aspect – how to balance chords so that you can sing any note – and on the horizontal level, how to shape a phrase, how to listen to yourself when you are matching up notes, which can't be done unless you hear the sound of each note; and – a unique feature – absolute concentration on what you do with your feet, which Fanny always says is just as important as what you do with your hands.

What she never did was to impose any musical idea on me. She treated one as a musical adult. If she was teaching a Beethoven or a Schubert sonata, she would only do the first movement, or even only half a movement, the idea being that if you hadn't got it by then, there wasn't much hope.

'A great teacher doesn't overteach,' says Fanny Waterman. 'He or she should teach a pupil to think independently, and then cut the umbilical cord.'

But despite her own successes, by the early 1960s Fanny began to feel considerable disquiet at what she saw as the complacent attitude of far too many British musical institutions and teachers. Compared with the Soviet Union, the USA and some European countries, teaching standards in the UK were low, and professional British pianists were, she felt, consistently failing to match up to the level of their overseas contemporaries. This view was strongly corroborated by the then-Principal of the Royal Academy of Music, Sir Thomas Armstrong, who was on the jury of the 1962 Tchaikovsky International Competition in Moscow. In the aftermath of the first Leeds competition, Armstrong wrote an article in the *Sunday Times* (29 September 1963) in which he said of the current generation of British pianists:

There are certain levels of advanced technical skill which we seldom seem to reach. The astonishing facility that some European and American players display can be positively repellent if associated with poor musicianship; but there comes a point, even with the finest musical imagination, where technique proves to be a decisive factor. Without it, the player cannot do what he wishes to do, and what his imagination dictates . . . No country can be expected to produce many talents of this order [Michael Roll]. We have them in Great Britain, but it is clear that we need to carry our young instrumentalists to a higher technical pitch at a much earlier age. They ought to have reached at fifteen the level that they generally attain, after a struggle, only at twenty-three. This is a matter which vitally concerns all who care for music and education.

It was this disquiet which led Fanny Waterman to formulate the idea of an international competition that would put Britain on the world map so far as piano playing was concerned, and give young pianists, in particular, a goal. The problem was – how to fund and run such an event . . .

Chapter Two

The First Competition: 1963

The morning after her sleepless night, Fanny immediately telephoned her friend the Countess of Harewood to enlist her support. Marion Harewood had first met Fanny at a tea-party at the home of Lady Parkinson, a friend of Marion's mother-in-law, the Princess Royal, in the winter of 1955; and Marion had later asked Fanny if she would accept David, Marion's eldest son, as a pupil. Since then a firm friendship, based on common interests and mutual admiration, had sprung up between them.

The first two problems to be solved were how to raise sufficient finance for such a large-scale event, and how to attract a jury of international calibre. In both areas Fanny's tireless crusading zeal and formidable powers of persuasion, together with Marion's social and musical contacts, proved invaluable. A wealthy local businessman, Jack Lyons, quickly agreed to donate £1,000 towards setting up the competition, while his wife contributed the same amount as the first prize. An obvious potential source of support was Leeds City Council itself. Then, as now, a Labour administration was in charge, and the councillors duly met to consider the request. Half of them disliked the idea of supporting an event that could be considered 'élitist', while the others felt that the competition should be wholly council-funded, without outside patronage. With such fundamental lack of agreement in principle, the motion was at first rejected; whereupon Jack Lyons announced his intention of withdrawing his original generous offer. After several stormy sessions, Leeds Corporation eventually decided to match Lyons' personal donation of £1,000, while further offers of financial support came from the Leeds Triennial Music Festival (at that time under the artistic directorship of the Earl of Harewood) and from the Arts Council of Great Britain. A second prize of £500 was offered jointly by two local businessmen, Charles Tapp, owner of a large printing firm, and Norman Wilkinson; Granada Television Network, while not covering the event itself, offered a third prize of £250; and fifteen further prizes of £50 each for the second stage runners-up were donated by local businessmen, banks and private individuals. The balance of the money needed to fund the first competition – which cost some £8,000 – came from local fund-raising efforts, such as concerts, coffee-mornings, and the anticipated box-office takings from Finals Night, which was to take place in the imposing Victorian splendour of Leeds Town Hall.

To cope with the administration, a competition committee was set up. Its composition was the subject of some debate. It seemed logical that Fanny Waterman and Marion Harewood should be joint chairmen, but one of Jack Lyons' conditions for donating such a substantial sum was that he should chair the committee. Since Marion's social position was clearly an incalculable asset, and a triple chairmanship looked unwieldy, it was agreed that Fanny should act as vice-chairman, with Marion and Jack Lyons as joint chairmen. This arrangement lasted for six years, until Lyons' retirement, whereupon Fanny and Marion assumed the joint chairmanship.

The other members of the committee – fifteen in all – included three Leeds City councillors, the Earl of Harewood, Mrs Lyons, Geoffrey de Keyser, Canon Fenton Morley, the Vicar of Leeds, Lady Parkinson, Charles Tapp, James Denny (Professor of Music at the University of Leeds), and other notable local names; while the executive administration was handled by a sub-committee of six, under Marion's chairmanship. Its members were Fanny Waterman as deputy-chairman, Cecil Mazey (a retired manager of the Leeds branch of the National Provincial Bank) as competition manager (he was also the competition's first treasurer, and later, its administrator), Professor Denny, Maurice Hare of Leeds Grammar School, Charles Tapp and Joan Valentine, a former schoolfriend of Fanny's, whose assistance over many years was to prove invaluable to the competition.

The competition was fortunate to establish itself under the patronage of the Princess Royal, sister of George VI, mother of the Earl of Harewood, and Chancellor of the University of Leeds. Princess Mary, who lived at Harewood House, took an active interest in local affairs. She agreed to present the prizes at the first piano competition, including a gold medal bearing her portrait for the winner, and although she died in 1965, each successive Leeds winner has continued to receive the Princess Mary Gold Medal. The competition's first president was the Lord Mayor of Leeds, with the University's Vice-Chancellor, Sir Charles Morris, and the Vicar of Leeds as vice-presidents.

The University of Leeds was closely involved from the start. Fanny Waterman was a personal friend of the University's Vice-Chancellor elect, Sir Roger Stevens, and his wife, who was a good amateur pianist. One of the major disadvantages of trying to operate a major competition involving up to a hundred pianists in Leeds – as opposed to London – was its lack of a conservatory, with facilities for practice and accommodation, not to mention a first-class recital hall. The University was partly able to remedy this deficiency by offering the use of one of its student halls of residence, Tetley Hall, for purposes of accommodation during the competition; and its Great Hall, which, with its quality concert grand, could be used for the earlier rounds. To solve the practising problem, the organizers drew on unlimited resources of local goodwill, scouring the city to find families possessing pianos of a sufficient standard, and who would be prepared to accept into their homes an influx of young people – many of them speaking little or no English – who wanted to practise up to six hours a day. More than eighty such families and individuals responded to the appeal.

The next step was to get the competition itself under way. A date having been fixed (13 to 21 September 1963), handsome printed brochures advertising the new competition were sent out to all music colleges and conservatories both in the UK and abroad, inviting applications from young pianists – professional and would-be professional – aged under thirty. The competition was to be in three stages, the first two to be held in the Great Hall of the University, and the third – when three finalists would play a concerto with the Royal Liverpool Philharmonic Orchestra, conducted by John Pritchard – at Leeds Town Hall. All would be open to the public.

Fanny and Marion personally selected the repertoire, based largely around the kind of works they themselves loved and had played. The first stage, in which all competitors were to participate, offered a choice of one work from a limited selection by Beethoven – three sonatas, Op.53, Op.31 No.2, and Op.57 (the *Appassionata*) – Bach, and Chopin. 'If you can't play the classics, you're not a pianist,' Fanny's teacher Tobias Matthay used to say. Twenty competitors would then go through to the second stage, in which candidates were invited to put together a short recital drawn from each of four categories. The first category contained substantial works by Mozart, Beethoven, Chopin, Schumann and Brahms; the second, virtuoso pieces by Liszt, Debussy, Ravel and Albéniz; the third, works by four twentieth-century composers, Bartók, Prokofiev, Stravinsky and Schoenberg; and the last, a compulsory piece written specially at Marion's request by her great friend Benjamin Britten. *Notturno*, or *Night Piece*, is a delicate, atmospheric work of subtle beauty, demanding great control of pedalling and interpretative skill – an ideal piece to sort out the musicians from the mere technicians.

The last stage of the competition offered three finalists a choice of ten concertos; Mozart's K.466 in D minor, K.503 in C or K.595 in B flat; the last three Beethovens, the Schumann, both Liszts, and the Tchaikovsky B flat minor. No twentieth-century concerto was included.

Meanwhile, thanks to their international contacts, Marion and Fanny had assembled an impressive array of international names for the jury, all carefully chosen across a breadth of specialist interests. Sir Arthur Bliss, Master of the Queen's Music, and then aged seventy-two, had agreed to be the first chairman, with the distinguished musicologist, critic, radio producer and broadcaster Hans Keller as vice-chairman. Keller, whose stimulating and provocative articles – on topics ranging from functional analysis to football – consistently enlivened the pages of the British musical Press, had, like Marion Harewood, been obliged by the *Anschluss* to abandon Vienna for London, where he had at first worked as an orchestral violinist and played viola in the Adler Quartet.

In early 1963 Marion visited the Soviet Union with Britten, and she discussed the new competition with Madame Furtsova at the Ministry of Culture. As a result, the great Soviet pianist and teacher Jakob Flier, himself a veteran of international competitions and a specialist in the Romantic repertoire (especially Liszt and Rakhmaninov) was able to sit on the first jury. Another Russian-born pianist, Nikita Magaloff (by then a Swiss national) offered a particular insight into the music of Chopin; while Géza Anda, the celebrated Hungarian pianist, specialized in Mozart, Bartók and the Romantic repertory as a whole. The distinguished Austrian pianist and musicologist Paul Badura-Skoda offered an expert approach to the Classical repertoire, while France's Yvonne Lefebure, herself a former child prodigy, and then a professor at the Paris Conservatoire, was particularly versed in early twentieth-century French music, especially Debussy and Ravel.

Apart from Sir Arthur Bliss, the British jury members consisted of John Pritchard – then musical director of both the Royal Liverpool Philharmonic Orchestra and of the LPO, and a noted champion of contemporary British music – and Clifford Curzon, Marion's former mentor, and also a great friend of Fanny's. Like her, Curzon (a pupil of Schnabel) had made his own début at sixteen in the Bach Triple Concerto under Sir Henry Wood. Renowned for his beautiful tone, Curzon began his career as something of a contemporary music specialist, but later became better known for his performances of the Classical repertoire. The other two members of the 1963 jury were the Polish pianist and teacher Barbara Hesse-Bukowska, herself a second-prize-winner in the 1949 Chopin Competition in Warsaw, and Paul Huband of the BBC. 'One wanted to get pianists one admired and enjoyed listening to and whose judgement one could trust,' says Marion. As always, there were some disappointments: Rudolf Firkušný, the American pianist of Czech birth and a former pupil of Janáček, at first accepted the invitation to join the jury but subsequently found at short notice that other engagements prevented his coming to Leeds.

What qualities would this distinguished jury be looking for? From the outset Fanny and Marion determined that the emphasis in their competition would be on musicianship, not on the kind of flashy technique that had already given some competitions a bad name. Beauty of tone was Fanny's top priority, followed by musical integrity, rhythmic vitality, and artistic imagination.

In order to recognize and isolate the competitors who could demonstrate all these qualities, the jury members prepared to submit themselves to a gruelling schedule: eight days of listening solidly for at least nine hours a day – without financial remuneration. The response to the Leeds invitation had been substantial: 105 competitors originally applied from 30 different countries; but by the time the programme was printed there had already been several withdrawals. Ninety-four names from 23 countries were officially listed (but several of these failed to show up at the last minute). Of the competitors accepted, by far the greatest number (37) came from Britain, 13 from the USA, six from France, five each from Poland, Russia and Australia, three each from New Zealand and Portugal; two each from Cuba and Hungary, and one each from Rhodesia, Austria, Bulgaria, Colombia, Canada, Lebanon, Spain, Sweden, Norway, Israel, Argentina and China. Surprisingly, there were only two from Germany. The oldest competitor was twenty-eight, the youngest seventeen. A decision was taken – with hindsight, an unsatisfactory one – to admit all comers: 'such is the quality that we have decided it would be fairer to hear them all', explained Fanny, optimistically. In the event, some kind of selection process was later to prove essential. One flamboyant young man modestly placed a rose on the piano before beginning his recital – sadly, his pianistic skills failed to match up to his talent for presentation – and one young lady's rendering of the *Waldstein* Sonata in the style of a café-concert reduced the jury to helpless fits of giggles.

Looking back, it was easy to see that mistakes did occur in the planning stages. One such hiccup was the lack of a properly formulated marking system. Fanny and Marion – with touching naïvety – thought that such a distinguished panel of internationally experienced jurors would prefer to evolve their own system, rather than have one thrust upon them. But juries, like any other *ad hoc* body of individuals, are prone to internal squabbling, and the result was temporary chaos. 'You must formulate your rules,' said Nikita Magaloff, a veteran of many similar disagreements. The system that finally emerged was based on 'one person, one vote', rather than giving marks out of twenty-five per performance, which commonly obtains in other competitions. Each juror is asked to write down the names of the competitors he or she would like to hear in the second round, and the lists are compared. Out of twenty 'places', fifteen or so names will tend to be the same, and a re-vote is taken on the remainder. The same system is used throughout the other stages of the competition, until the final round, in which each juror is asked to name his/her preferred winner of the first prize, then of the second, the third, and so on, so that each prize is voted for separately. Although, as with every other major competition, the result has rarely been unanimous, the major controversies tend not to concern the first prize, but the remaining placings.

It was also decided that the first competitor to arrive at Tetley Hall would be invited to draw the name of the person who would then be the first to play, and the others would follow alphabetically. This playing order would be maintained throughout the successive rounds (rather like a show-jumping contest), until the final, in which musical considerations would determine the order of play.

While the 1963 jury, in the luxurious surroundings of the Queens Hotel, was trying to reach agreement as to how to start, the competitors began to arrive in Leeds, and were whisked off to Tetley Hall, where they were to be fed and accommodated. The hearts of the organizers missed a beat when the five-strong Russian contingent including Jakob Flier, plus three Poles and the Polish juror, Barbara Hesse-Bukowska, failed to arrive as expected at Leeds City Station. But the Russians had caught a later train, and eventually, to everyone's relief, the Poles turned up too. At Tetley Hall, an efficient army of helpers prepared to demonstrate the hospitality for which Yorkshire is famous, including a series of civic receptions and excursions for the competitors and jury members. Several visits to Harrogate, Wharfedale, Harewood House and York had been planned, but had to be hastily cancelled (not without embarrassment) as it soon became clear that the competitors were far more interested in practising, when they were not actually competing, than in taking scenic tours.

At ten o'clock on Friday 13 September, Fanny Waterman's former pupil, twenty-year-old Allan Schiller, sat down at the Steinway grand in the Great Hall of Leeds University to begin his performance of

Bach's *Italian* Concerto. The first Leeds International Piano Competition was under way. It began and ended in controversy. The second stage was to be held on Thursday and Friday 19–20 September, which unhappily coincided with Yom-Kippur, the Jewish Day of Atonement. Orthodox Jewish opinion was enraged, particularly since two of the local entrants, Schiller and Michael Roll, were Jewish, and would be behaving reprehensibly if they were required and agreed to take part, according to Rabbi J. Apfel in the *Jewish Gazette*:

If the co-chairman and vice-chairman [both Jewish] attend, then that is their own concern entirely. For myself, I think it would be terribly wrong . . . if Jews attended this concert, or Jewish artists participated. Jews everywhere would derive more spiritual comfort and guidance by attending their places of worship in the company of their co-religionists than by sitting in a concert hall on these two days . . .

However, as Fanny Waterman was quick to point out, this was not the Leeds International Jewish Piano Competition. On the evening of Wednesday 18 September, Sir Arthur Bliss faced a tense gathering of competitors at Tetley Hall to announce the list of the fortunate twenty who would go through to the second stage. 'Do not think you have failed,' said Sir Arthur to the disappointed contestants. 'Failure is not a word that an artist uses. Think of this contest as a great stimulus. You can regard this as a most valuable experience in the course of your careers.' The list of semi-finalists, ironically, included both Schiller and Michael Roll, along with three other British competitors, Martin Jones, David Wilde and Philip Jenkins, three Russians (Alisa Mitchenko, Ekaterina Murina, and Vladimir Krainiev, aged nineteen – whose name throughout the competition was misspelt as Krainov), four French (Sebastein Risler, Dominique Merlet, Marise Charpentier and Irene Pamboukjian), three Americans (Robert Guralnik, Michael Rogers and Armenta Adams), Woijciech Matuszewski from Poland, Sergio Varella-Cid from Portugal, Ruslana Antonowicz from Austria, Patsy Toh from China and Zsuzsanna Sirokay from Hungary. It was clear from the start that the Leeds competition was to be no respecter of reputations. The list of first-round casualties included the American Marilyn Neeley, a gold medallist in the 1959 Geneva Competition, and the only woman at that time to have reached the finals of the Van Cliburn Competition; John Barstow, who was to become one of Britain's most prominent players and teachers; Eileen Broster, who had made her Proms début with the LPO in 1961; Brenda Lucas, John Ogdon's wife, who had already played at the Edinburgh Festival and the Wigmore Hall, and the nineteen-year-old John Lill, whose impressive London début in Rakhmaninov's Third Concerto under Boult, followed by his Festival Hall début in the *Emperor* Concerto in the spring of 1963 had generated a great deal of publicity. 'It was a big surprise not to be placed,' says Lill, who went on to take first place in the 1970 Tchaikovsky Competition. 'It certainly left a nasty taste in the mouth.'

But by and large, the standard of British entrants in particular was appalling. 'Every time an English pianist appears on that platform,' said Sir Arthur Bliss, 'I want the floor to open and swallow me up.' Of the five British survivors, David Wilde – at twenty-eight one of the oldest competitors – had by far the most impressive record, with several major international prizes including joint first in the 1961 Budapest International Liszt–Bartók Competition, and joint second in the 1962 Rio de Janeiro Competition; while twenty-three-year-old Philip Jenkins had won the Daily Mirror National Competition Prize in 1958.

Of the second-round Russians, Alisa Mitchenko, a student of Flier at the Moscow Conservatory, had won first prize at the sixth International Festival of Youth and Students in Moscow in 1957, and fifth prize in the 1960 Queen Elizabeth of the Belgians Competition. Her stablemates, Vladimir Krainiev and Ekaterina Murina, were both still students at Moscow and Leningrad respectively. Three of the French semi-finalists had won international prizes (Dominique Merlet had already given several BBC recitals), while Patsy Toh and Wojciech Matuszewski were both prize-winning veterans of several major competitions, including Geneva.

Local attention naturally focused on the two Leeds survivors, both pupils of Fanny Waterman. Although Flier was on the jury and one of his own pupils was competing, Fanny felt that the situation was sufficiently delicate to warrant her keeping well out of the limelight. She stayed mainly at home, coaching her sensitive seventeen-year-old prodigy. Michael Roll had only just left school that summer, and had enrolled at Leeds University to study medicine. One of his great passions was football, and to Fanny's dismay, he much preferred to kick a football around the de Keysers' garden with their eldest son Robert, rather than practise his competition pieces. Only a week or so before the competition began, Michael had still not learned the compulsory test piece, Britten's *Notturno*. On hearing that he intended to give up a whole Saturday afternoon to attend a Leeds United match, Fanny burst into tears. 'You'll disgrace me, Michael,' she said, and offered to refund the £10 entrance fee for the competition.

On Tuesday 17 September, Roll had played his qualifying piece, the *Appassionata* Sonata. Fanny spent much of the day coaching him down to the last detail. Then she and Geoffrey took the boy down to the Great Hall of the University. 'It was like taking a soufflé out of the oven,' said Fanny. 'He had risen to perfection.' Sir Arthur Bliss reportedly wept; Clifford Curzon said it was the finest performance of the piece he had ever heard. 'I was walking along the street the next day', recalls Michael Roll, 'when I was stopped by Yakob Flier, who said [here he mimics a strong Eastern European accent], "Roll! *Appassionata* – very good!" ' The *Appassionata* has remained one of the works with which Roll is closely identified. 'Then I played it as if in a single breath – in one continuous line,' he recalls. 'That has been very hard to recapture. In fact, I recorded it just after the competition, and it wasn't perfect, it felt a bit flat.'

In the second stage, Roll again chose to play a Beethoven sonata, Op.111. 'That was an outrageous thing to attempt at seventeen – but I play it better now than then.' On Friday evening, the anxious contestants were again summoned to hear the jury's decision. Five were singled out for honourable mention: Wilde, Murina, Mitchenko, Varella-Cid and Matuszewski. But in view of the magnificent standard of playing, said Sir Arthur Bliss, four finalists, rather than the proposed three, had been chosen. They were the Frenchman Sebastien Risler, a twenty-seven-year-old black American from New York, Armenta Adams, Krainiev, and Michael Roll.

The distinguished guests who filled Leeds Town Hall, which was decked with the flags of all the competing nations for the final evening, included the Princess Royal (who was to present the prizes), the Earl and Countess of Harewood, the Lord Mayor and Lady Mayoress of Leeds, Mr and Mrs Lyons, the Bishop of Ripon and his wife, Sir Roger Stevens in his capacity as the new Vice-Chancellor of Leeds University, Sir Thomas Armstrong, Principal of the Royal Academy of Music, and, of course, Fanny Waterman and Geoffrey de Keyser. John Pritchard took his place on the platform with the Royal Liverpool Philharmonic Orchestra, and the final began.

The first to play was the American girl, Armenta Adams, whose fresh and sincere approach, rather than her technical skill, had impressed the jury in the earlier rounds. She elected to play the Schumann Concerto, always a difficult choice – since it requires fine-tuned interpretation rather than technical brilliance. The pressure of the event proved too much for her: she took the first two movements far too slowly, and then suffered an unfortunate memory lapse in the last (which, according to Sir Charles Groves, often proves a stumbling block). The Frenchman Sebastien Risler offered an accurate but unexciting performance of Beethoven's Third Concerto. Then it was the turn of the young Russian, Vladimir Krainiev, whose mercurial temperament and irrepressible sense of fun had won him many friends. Joan Valentine remembers him, completely undaunted by the occasion, doing handstands all down the hall during a break in one of the earlier rounds.

Krainiev enjoyed every minute of the Leeds competition. A student at the Moscow Conservatory, he had had to enter several national competitions which qualified him to enter an international one.

It was a long road to Leeds. But I have fantastic memories of the competition – it was a really musical experience, with an interesting and unusual programme. I never expected to get to the finals. I just desperately wanted to get through to the second round, because everyone in that round got a £50 prize. I was mad about Van Gogh at the time, and I had seen a beautiful book of Van Gogh illustrations, which cost 21s. It was my dream to be able to buy it. So once I got into the second round, I knew I would get my £50, and I didn't pay any attention to the jury – I just played the way I wanted. It was a great success.

Krainiev's impressive second-round recital had consisted of the Chopin B flat minor Sonata, the Prokofiev Sonata No.3, Debussy's *L'isle joyeuse*, and the compulsory Britten *Notturno*. In the final, he chose to offer the brilliant Liszt Concerto in E flat, a virtuoso *tour de force*, which roused the audience to transports of enthusiasm. 'Athletically speaking, he is very small,' wrote the *Yorkshire Post* critic Ernest Bradbury:

a wisp of a boy, with fair hair and a fidgety manner, moving his hands and pulling at his jacket or running fingers through his hair. But he seemed to be endowed with a fantastic strength and wrists of steel, almost baffling to his beholders. He found for Liszt the required vigour and vitality, its soaring disposition and brilliance in cascades of notes, but he has also learned to temper his effects with a lyrical warmth just this side of sentimentality.

'I usually found I wasn't afraid once I got on to the platform', recalls Krainiev,

but this time I was very nervous. I never dreamed I would be in the final, and I became aware of the audience for the first time. I wasn't at all happy with my playing. The Liszt concerto isn't very long, and it took me a long time to settle down. Fortunately I had played it in public before, when I was fifteen.

'I was very impressed with Krainiev,' says his rival Michael Roll.

'He's a barnstorming player of the flamboyant Russian school, and his performance of the Liszt was electrifying.'

Then came Roll's own performance. Like Armenta Adams, he had chosen to play the Schumann Concerto, but it was one he knew thoroughly, having already played it several times in public. (The critic Joan Chissell had written of his performance of the same concerto at the age of twelve: 'A pianist five times his age could not have given a finer performance'.)

Despite the enormous pressure on him, Roll's technique and interpretative skill proved equal to the occasion. 'For Schumann', observed Bradbury, '[Roll] had to find some languishment and tender poignancy, also stamina for the long closing sections of the first and third movements, when spectacle is not the reward.' Though Bradbury felt that Roll's performance was 'not always exquisite, since lines in the cadenza were blurred and the little rising conversational figure of the middle movement lacked something of spontaneity and charm', Martin Cooper of the *Daily Telegraph* felt that Roll gave 'a quite astonishingly mature account . . . technically in every way assured and masterly in detail, but even more in the natural authority of style. Faults of over-emphasis or occasional precipitancy betrayed the player's youth without seriously marring the quality of the performance. The *Guardian*'s critic Colin Mason concurred:

Krainov's [*sic*] sure-handed and aggressively self-confident performance of Liszt's E flat Concerto revealed a remarkable technical equipment and an undoubted basic innate musicality . . . whereas Roll's performance of his musically more difficult and revealing work, without getting quite to the heart of the lyrical Schumann, had a warmth and feeling that made his the more enjoyable performance.

From the applause, it was clear that the audience favoured Krainiev. The jury retired to consider its verdict and was out for over an hour. Sensing that Roll might win, Fanny Waterman was frantic with anxiety. Such a result could cause serious embarrassment, and might possibly compromise the entire competition. She asked Marion, as chairman of the committee, to intervene if necessary, and insist that the first prize should at least be awarded jointly to Roll and Krainiev. Marion made Fanny's views known to the jury, but the die was already cast. The first prize was to go to Roll, the second to Krainiev, the third to Risler and the fourth to Adams. It was not a unanimous decision, however. Roll thinks that eight out of the eleven jurors voted decisively in his favour, while one or two, including Nikita

Magaloff, would have preferred a tie, fearing that the youthful Roll might not stand up to the pressure of winning outright.

From the very beginning at Leeds it has been the custom for the competitors to be told the result ten minutes or so before they go on to the platform to receive their prizes – 'to give them time to compose themselves', according to Fanny Waterman. This compassionate but onerous duty falls to Geoffrey de Keyser. As he ushered the finalists on to the platform, Sir Arthur Bliss began his public summing-up of the jury's decision. But the mischievous Krainiev, behind the jury's backs, indicated the result to the breathless audience, holding up two fingers and pointing to himself, then one and pointing to Roll. It was not a popular result. As Fanny Waterman came on to the platform to congratulate the finalists, she was discomfited by the audience's cool reception. 'I think this result is very bad politically,' she said to Arthur Bliss. 'Politics shouldn't enter into music,' he replied.

Why was the Leeds audience so partial to the Russian, rather than supporting their own 'local boy'? It seems all the more strange considering the year – 1963 – with the Cuba crisis still fresh in people's minds. But Russian artists have traditionally received a warm welcome at Leeds (where there is, after all, a large expatriate Russian Jewish community), while conversely, British artists have always been highly acclaimed in Moscow. 'The British are the last people to praise themselves,' says John Lill. 'British pianists seem to have done better abroad – especially in Moscow – than at Leeds; look at John Ogdon, Terence Judd, Peter Donohoe, Barry Douglas.'

Feelings certainly ran high. While the winner was being photographed, one woman from the audience asked Gerald MacDonald (then Head of BBC North) whether he agreed with the jury's verdict. 'Yes', he said, whereupon she scratched his face! Over the next few weeks, the columns of the *Yorkshire Post* resounded with continuing debate over the respective merits of the winners, and the jury's decision. Sir Arthur Bliss felt obliged to defend the verdict publicly in a letter to the *Yorkshire Post*. The final decision, he said, was made on 'purely musical and pianistic considerations, based on all three stages of the competition' and 'uninfluenced in any way by any other matters'. Ernest Bradbury (whose opinion of Roll and Krainiev was based not on their performances on Finals Night itself, which he was unable to attend, but on repeat performances at a winners' concert given the following afternoon with the Royal Liverpool Philharmonic under Charles Groves) detected more than a 'faint whiff of humbug' from those who accused him of lacking patriotism when he declared Krainiev to be the superior player. Fortunately, the one thing that

Fanny Waterman dreaded – that the competition would be pilloried in the Press on the grounds that the winner was her own pupil – seemed largely to be passed over. 'I was both excited and terribly embarrassed by Michael's victory,' she says. 'I met Rudolf Serkin in Edinburgh a few months later, and he thought it was unbelievable, like something out of a novelette, that a British schoolboy should measure up to a fine young Soviet pianist.'

Meanwhile, the winner himself was facing a personal crisis. Flushed with his unexpected and unhoped-for triumph, Michael Roll declared to the Press that he still intended to enter Leeds Medical School as planned. But 'I shall keep up my piano playing' he told the *Yorkshire Post*:

It has always been a toss-up between music and medicine. It has been a great problem. I always wanted to be a pianist, but the cautious side of me told me not to. There is too much stress and strain involved in a career as a concert pianist. There isn't very much security in this country: music is really a luxury. It isn't so much that I want to be a doctor but I shall feel sorry if I don't try. If I graduate, I shall probably work for my father. I may reconsider my decision then.

And the £1,000 prize money? 'I would like to buy a car. But we'll have to see. I'm putting the money in the bank.'

Michael's parents supported their son's decision, particularly his mother, who very much wanted to see him in a secure profession. 'He must do what he wants,' said Dr Roll. But his decision infuriated many people, particularly Mrs Lyons, one of the competition's influential patrons, who had donated the prize money 'to encourage serious musicians', and several members of the jury. 'Coming as it did on top of a world success,' said John Pritchard at the time, 'it was a bit of a blow to the adjudicators and the patrons, seeing their cash used to fit a boy for a medical career.'

'Michael Roll has a God-given gift,' said Sir Arthur Bliss. 'Hearing him play the great Beethoven sonatas was one of the musical impressions I shall always retain.'

Alarmed by this barrage of criticism, Michael Roll and his parents retreated behind closed doors for a conference. On the Sunday evening, Michael publicly announced that he had changed his mind: he was definitely not going to study medicine. 'I feel after what the jury said to me – they usually discourage young pianists, but they encouraged me – that I must try a musical career.'

Mrs Lyons was mollified. 'The boy has great gifts. His decision to be a doctor had been a great blow to all concerned.' Dr Roll admitted to *Yorkshire Post* reporters that in the aftermath of the competition, Michael had been

depressed and bewildered. The talent which none of us had dared to look fully in the face was out – in public. Michael is our only child. We want to protect him from a strenuous and nerve-racking sort of a life . . . But now comes this remarkable achievement and complete acclaim from established musicians. That must have some effect . . . Michael came to feel that he owed it to a lot of people and himself. If you have an exceptional gift, it is wrong to discard it.

Looking back now at that momentous decision, Michael Roll remains disarmingly modest about his achievement:

My good fortune was my age. I didn't know what was at stake. I just went and tried. Ten years later, it would have been much more difficult. That weekend was a difficult one – I remember it more powerfully than the competition itself. I had felt generally comfortable until the final. Then I was under more pressure . . . I was 'brought up short' by winning. I was really just being stubborn saying, 'I'm going to be a doctor'. I had lots of conversations with Curzon, Anda, Flier – they were all very supportive. I felt Pritchard was rather unhelpful, saying, 'Well, if you can't face it, you shouldn't do it.' I stuck to my guns for a day. But it was very disturbing to have to make such a major decision in such a short space of time. I was led to believe I was in the international limelight.

So on the Monday morning, Michael Roll rang up the Dean of the Medical School, and told him that he was not going to enrol there afer all. 'Great,' said the Dean. 'I hope you make a wonderful success of your career.' Roll continued to study with Fanny for several more years, consolidating his repertoire and undertaking several engagements as a result of his Leeds win – though by no means as many as are now offered. 'There wasn't the media attention in 1963. I was signed up immediately by a top agent and got a handful of major engagements.' These included a BBC broadcast of the *Appassionata* Sonata and of Britten's *Notturno* (its broadcast première), and concert appearances the following year at the Leeds Triennial and the Edinburgh festivals. Benjamin Britten, who became one of Roll's most ardent supporters, immediately engaged him for the Aldeburgh Festival, writing to his proud teacher:

September 23rd 1963

My dear Fanny Waterman,
May I congratulate you on the astounding and well-deserved
success of Michael Roll? I am sure that a lot of it is due to your
remarkable and tactful guidance of his talent – it cannot be easy to
handle a gift of that size, & I think you have done it wonderfully.
I hope he decides to make piano-playing his career – but I do
understand his reluctance! . . . especially when one thinks of the
careers of other prize winners. But I am sure with you to guide him
he need have no fears. When I suggested him playing at the
Festival next year I had no idea he would win the competition
(having felt the Russian boy was a certainty). The invitation of
course still stands – but I expect he will get other and bigger offers
now, & we may have to be passed over if, indeed, he accepts any
of them! Perhaps you would be kind & find out for us what he
would like to do – we shall quite understand if he has bigger fish
to fry!
   It was a great pleasure to meet you again, & I do congratulate
you on the real success of the competition.
With best wishes
Yours sincerely
Benjamin Britten

Chapter Three

Why Leeds?

At first glance, Geoffrey de Keyser's misgivings about the feasibility of establishing a major international musical event in a northern industrial city more given to whippet-racing and football than the pursuit of culture might have seemed justified. In 1963 Leeds came fairly low down the list of British cities in which music and the arts flourished: unlike Birmingham, Manchester, Liverpool or Newcastle, it could boast no resident orchestra, no opera company and no music conservatory. But it did have a fierce sense of civic pride, fostered in the Victorian era when its great captains of industry and commerce – Joshua Tetley in the brewing business, the printer Alf Cooke, Michael Marks, founder of Marks and Spencer, Montague Burton in the clothing trade – were busily establishing Leeds as a thriving metropolis with a strong sense of community and social responsibility; a spirit embodied in its magnificent municipal buildings, of which Cuthbert Brodrick's Town Hall, with its imposing neo-Classical façade, is the finest.

But even before the Piano Competition put it on the musical world map, Leeds was by no means a cultural wilderness. There has always been a strong choral tradition in the West Riding of Yorkshire, both Methodist and Church of England, fostered originally among workers in the textile industries. Leeds Parish Church, rebuilt in the mid-Victorian era, maintains a choir of an exceptionally high standard (it is the only English parish church which has a sung service every day of the week, and whose choir regularly makes recordings). In 1842 Samuel Wesley was appointed organist there: he and his successors William Spark and Robert Burton did much to improve and strengthen the musical life of the community.

In September 1858 Queen Victoria visited Leeds to open the new Town Hall, and to mark the event the citizens of Leeds decided to hold a music festival under the direction of William Sterndale Bennett. Sixteen years elapsed before another such festival was held; but from 1880 onwards, it was decided that similar events should take place every three years. For the first twenty-one years of its existence, the Leeds Triennial Festival was directed by Sir Arthur Sullivan, who drew together a chorus of enviable quality, and who commissioned new works from major international composers of the day, including Dvořák, Massenet, Humperdinck, Parry, Stanford and Elgar (whose *Caractacus* was premièred at the 1898 Festival). Sullivan also introduced to Leeds audiences the works of great masters of the past – the English Madrigal School (then in the process of being rediscovered by Canon Edmund Fellowes) and the choral works of Bach, Handel and Mozart. When Sullivan retired, he was succeeded by Charles Stanford, and then by a series of well-known conductors including Thomas Beecham and Malcolm Sargent: the latter gave the première of Walton's *Belshazzar's Feast* at the 1931 Leeds Festival.

But by the mid-1950s, the Festival was in deep financial trouble. In 1953, for the first time in its history, there was no festival chorus: instead, separate concerts were given by the choral societies of Leeds, Huddersfield and Sheffield. The Festival made a loss of £6,000, and the committee resigned. This was not good enough for the burghers of Leeds. Led by Sir Linton Andrews, the indignant editor of the *Yorkshire Post*, they decided that a festival must be held in 1958 to celebrate the centenary of the Town Hall's opening. Lord Harewood was invited to become director: a new choral work, *The Vision of Judgement*, was commissioned from Peter Racine Fricker, and Otto Klemperer was invited to conduct. Unfortunately he had recently sustained an injury to his hand, so Jascha Horenstein was called in at the last minute. Opening with a performance of Beethoven's *Missa solemnis* and ending with a concert attended by the Queen and the Duke of Edinburgh, the 1958 Festival restored some of Leeds' wounded pride. Since then, the Leeds Festival has continued to be held regularly, with the core of its repertory centred on the strong Yorkshire choral tradition, and on the excellence of the local choral societies, including the Leeds Philharmonic Society and the Leeds Guild of Singers.

After a promising start, orchestral and instrumental music in Leeds fared less well at first in terms of local support. The first documented public concert in Leeds took place in September 1726 in the Assembly Room in Kirkgate; and from 1772 onwards the responsibility of co-ordinating such events in Leeds – in particular a series of subscription concerts – fell to the organist of the parish church. In 1795 the incumbent of that post, one David Lawton, first introduced the piano concerto to local audiences at a concert held in the recently opened New Music Hall. Just over thirty years later, in accordance with the prevailing philanthropic spirit of the time, an Amateur Society was formed to ensure that concerts would continue on a regular basis, in an attempt to cultivate 'a more extensive taste for music'.

However, after the opening of the Town Hall, it was felt that its large and grandiloquent organ would make an admirably cheap substitute for orchestral concerts, dispensing with the necessity of maintaining a resident orchestra in the city. Meanwhile the Leeds Festival continued to draw its orchestral players from the pool of London professionals. But fortunately for Leeds, the parish organists had more ambitious plans; and two series of popular Saturday night concerts – originally intended to bring culture to the labouring classes but, in fact, largely enjoying the support of the wealthy bourgeoisie – were instigated at the Town Hall and the Coliseum respectively. Early this century, these stimulated the formation of a resident ad hoc professional orchestra, first known as the Leeds Symphony Orchestra, and from 1928 onwards as the Northern Philharmonic Orchestra. In 1947 the short-lived Yorkshire Symphony Orchestra (with which Fanny Waterman gave several of her early concerts) was formed at the instigation of the Labour-controlled Leeds City Council, at an initial cost of £15,000. It lasted only eight years, before lack of funds and rivalry with the nearby Hallé Orchestra brought about its downfall. 'This is a black day for Leeds,' said the conductor Norman Del Mar on the night of its final concert.

Its place was temporarily filled by the Wakefield-based West Riding Orchestra, formed by the forward-looking Head of Education, Alex Clegg, to give concerts at local schools, and by another professional, chamber-sized group, the Yorkshire Sinfonia, run by Harry Tolson. Both orchestras drew most of their players from the personnel of the disbanded YSO, with the addition, in the Yorkshire Sinfonia's case, of London-based players such as the members of the Delmé Quartet, and the trumpeter John Wallace. Funded by a mixture of local authority and Arts Council support, the Yorkshire Sinfonia began to cover the county, playing for local choral societies and at the Leeds Festival, and making a few recordings. But eventually, in 1979, it too was obliged to disband for lack of funds.

Even though Leeds had lost its resident symphony orchestra, it was not to be deprived of concerts. The city had always been 'on the circuit' for visiting artists – Paganini and Liszt played there in the nineteenth century; and Fanny Waterman remembers being taken to concerts as a child to hear the greatest performers of the day: Paderewski, Rakhmaninov, Kreisler, Heifetz, Schnabel and Cortot, among others. Even during the last war, while people's minds were otherwise occupied, concerts by Solomon and the indefatigable Harriet Cohen brought a few hours of artistic relief. In 1935 the Vienna

Philharmonic Orchestra, conducted by Bruno Walter, gave a concert at the Town Hall, in a programme of Schubert and Wagner: the C major Symphony, the Prelude and *Liebestod* from *Tristan*, and the *Wesendonck Lieder*. It was attended, the *Yorkshire Post* critic remarked, by a 'rather sparse but enthusiastic and youthful audience'. And after the demise of the YSO, Leeds City Council provided a substantial annual sum of money to continue the tradition of orchestral concerts at Leeds. Visiting orchestras and artists were invited to take part in an 'International Series of Concerts' for local subscribers. Now under the aegis of the council's Leisure Services department, this series continues to thrive: the 1989/90 season includes concerts by the Moscow Symphony and Cracow Philharmonic orchestras, the Royal Liverpool Philharmonic, the RPO, CBSO, Bournemouth Symphony, Hallé and Northern Sinfonia, in programmes ranging from Bach's *Brandenburg* Concertos to Schoenberg's *Gurrelieder*. Almost all these concerts are consistently sold out.

And while, in the 1960s, a report entitled 'A Policy for the Arts in Yorkshire' deplored the fact that 'a vast and populous county like Yorkshire cannot maintain one professional symphony orchestra, while the neighbouring county of Lancashire can maintain two – the Hallé and the Royal Liverpool Philharmonic' and noted that 'there are pockets of great activity, some of them most adventurous . . . but for all this, involving as it does tens of thousands of Yorkshire people every year, there is no perceptible pattern, no sharing of talents, no phasing of activities and no co-ordination between one community and another', these glaring deficiencies have largely been remedied in the past three decades by two musical events of outstanding importance in Leeds. One is English National Opera North's adoption of the city as its permanent base in 1978, under the inspired leadership of David Lloyd-Jones. This has not only served the whole of Yorkshire with a young, enthusiastic opera company offering an unbroken series of brilliant and much-praised productions, but has also provided Leeds with a first-class professional resident orchestra, the English Northern Philharmonia. The other is the Harveys' Leeds International Piano Competition, which gave Fanny Waterman the opportunity to galvanize the local community into concerted action towards a recognizable artistic goal.

Leeds City Council has always had an uneasy relationship with the piano competition. When asked for money in the first instance, the council failed to agree on a philosophical basis for funding the event (see chapter 2, p. 14). After the initial injection of £1,000 into the first competition, the council has subsequently only provided relatively insignificant amounts – until 1990. Mike Palmer-Jones, formerly director of Leeds Leisure Services with responsibility for the music programme (including the Town Hall concerts and a recital series at Temple Newsam, a nearby stately home), would welcome a closer relationship:

When the competition started, the Lord Mayor of Leeds used to host a lunch for the jury, and we're hoping to resurrect that. For years the city council only gave small amounts of money to the competition because it knew that it was in good hands and on a secure financial footing. Some years ago it looked as if the council would take a closer role – it paid for a seconded officer to help with the administration – but it didn't work out. By 1987 we had drifted apart, but I feel we are coming closer again now, and I'm very glad. For the 1990 competition, the council has agreed to give £20,000, since we wish to see the jury paid in line with other international competitions, and I hope that there will be from now on a much closer connection between the competition and the council.

It's true to say that the Harveys' Leeds International Piano Competition has carried the name of Leeds far and wide, especially in the USA and behind the Iron Curtain. Owing to the vision of Fanny Waterman and Marion Thorpe, Leeds now has one of the premier competitions in the world – possibly the top one. I have very great admiration for Fanny Waterman – I applaud all that she is doing. Leeds is very lucky that she was born here. My only regret is that there is no really suitable venue – the acoustics of the Town Hall are bad. But we all appreciate that and we shall try to rectify it.

Much has been said and written about the unsuitable acoustics of the Victoria Hall, whose High Baroque interior – redecorated in the 1970s from the original designs in 'authentic' multicoloured wedding-cake style, incorporating a frieze bearing such stern Victorian maxims as 'Industry overcomes all things', 'Goodwill towards men', 'Honesty is the best policy', and (most appropriately for a building which houses not only the piano competition, but also the city's magistrates' courts) 'Judge not, that ye be not judged' – provides such an impressive setting for the final stages of the competition. While the Great Hall of Leeds University seats between 550 and 600, the Town Hall can in theory accommodate about 1,600 (more like 1,200 at a symphony concert, depending on the size of the orchestra). For piano recitals or chamber music concerts, baffle boards have to be erected round the back of the stage, cutting off the chorus seats, and thereby reducing the accommodation by up to 400 places. The most expensive seats are in the front rows of the gallery, where the jury normally sits during the finals. 'There's a loss of detail in the gallery seats – the sound is very dead,' says Geoffrey de Keyser (who himself subscribes to the Saturday Night Concert series). 'Also, there are few amenities or facilities backstage – it's very bad for orchestras. It's dirty and decrepit. We badly need a new concert hall.'

'It has a reverberant acoustic, superb for big choral events,' says Sir Charles Groves, who has conducted there many times. 'The details are as clear as anything, and there's a wonderful spaciousness. It is too reverberant for a solo piano. But if the sound doesn't come over in a piano concerto, it's the pianist's fault. When we moved to the Grand Theatre in 1975, everyone complained that the acoustic was dead.' ('Probably the only acceptable place in the hall from the acoustic point of view is the conductor's podium,' says Geoffrey de Keyser.)

The Town Hall had never been considered wholly suitable for the purposes of the competition, and Fanny Waterman has now directed her formidable energies towards persuading the citizens of Leeds that a new concert hall is essential. There are two problems: money and location. The great virtue of the Town Hall is its central position; it is one of the finest buildings the visitor sees on emerging into the town centre from Leeds City Station. Clearly any new large-scale concert hall could not occupy such a commanding or convenient position.

At the present time, the future of the Town Hall itself looks uncertain. Within the next three years, the magistrates' courts are due to move to new premises further down The Headrow. At the moment, the half million pounds or so required to maintain the Town Hall each year is mostly paid by the Home Office, but once the courts have moved, the city council will become entirely responsible for its upkeep – a prospect it does not relish. Several schemes for its future use have been devised, including turning the entire building over to a major arts, conference and recreational centre; but the council has yet to decide its fate. Jon Trickett, the council's Leader, is determined that the Victoria Hall should continue to fulfil the role it has played for 150 years in the musical life of Leeds. 'I have no fixed ideas about what should happen when the magistrates move out, but one thing I do want to see is the continuance of music in the Town Hall.'

Chapter Four

The Second Competition: 1966

Despite the musical controversy it engendered, the first Leeds International Piano Competition was widely held to have been a great success, and plans were immediately put in hand for a follow-up, to be held three years later. The administrative committee – now consisting of Marion Harewood and Jack Lyons (Chairmen), Fanny Waterman (Vice-Chairman), Cecil Mazey (Manager and Treasurer), Charles Tapp (Publications Director), Curtis Ward (Secretary), Maurice Hare and Joan Valentine – enlisted the support once again of Leeds Corporation and the Arts Council of Great Britain, together with the University of Leeds and the Yorkshire Arts Association. The President of the second competition remained the Lord Mayor of Leeds, with the Vice-Chancellor of Leeds University, Sir Roger Stevens, and Canon Fenton Morley as Vice-Presidents.

Once again, the combined efforts of Fanny and Marion secured a formidable array of talents for the 1966 jury. Its chairman was to be William Glock, a former piano pupil of Schnabel, whose multi-faceted career in music embraced criticism (he initiated and edited the music periodical *The Score*), music education (he founded the Dartington Summer School in 1948, remaining its Director until 1979), and music administration. Since 1959 Glock had been Controller of Music at the BBC, in which capacity he proved a tireless champion of contemporary music. Glock's imaginative and innovative programme planning had breathed new life into the Proms, and he was responsible for introducing many great artists, including Pierre Boulez, to British musical life. He received a knighthood in 1970.

Glock's friend and BBC colleague Hans Keller once again agreed to act as vice-chairman, while further intellectual weight was added to the jury by the great French teacher Nadia Boulanger, then seventy-nine years old, but with all her formidable critical powers still intact. In 1937 Mlle Boulanger had become the first woman ever to conduct a symphony orchestra in Britain, at a Royal Philharmonic Society concert.

Pianists on the 1966 jury were represented by Gina Bachauer, a former student of Cortot and Rakhmaninov, who spent six months of every year touring the USA, and whose musical strength lay in the late nineteenth- and early twentieth-century repertory; Annie Fischer, the celebrated Hungarian pianist, a former student at the Liszt Conservatory in Budapest, where she won the Liszt Prize in 1933, and whose large repertory extended from Bach to Bartók – although she was particularly admired for her subtle and stylish interpretations of Mozart, Beethoven and Schubert; her compatriot Béla Siki, whose playing was becoming widely known through recordings; Maria Curcio, a well-known Italian pianist and teacher; Rudolf Firkušný, a former student of Schnabel, and a champion of works by his native Czech composers such as Janáček and Martinů, as well as the standard Mozart–Brahms repertory; Nikita Magaloff, who had served on the 1963 jury; and Lev Oborin, then a professor at the Moscow Conservatory where his pupils included Ashkenazy, and himself a former first-prize-winner of the Chopin Competition. Marion Harewood was a personal friend of Lev Oborin, whom she had met when he played at the 1962 Edinburgh Festival, then under the artistic directorship of her husband.

Also invited were André Tchaikovsky, the Polish pianist whose international concert career had taken him throughout Europe, the USA and the Far East; and Carlo Zecchi, another former Schnabel pupil, who had also studied with Busoni. Both these pianists subsequently withdrew, owing to the pressure of other commitments. Instead, Fanny and Marion invited the American performer and writer Charles Rosen, a highly intellectual pianist whose thoughtful interpretations of Bach, Mozart and Beethoven were noted for their stylistic purity. Rosen was also a forceful advocate of the twentieth-century classics, and a much-admired writer on music: his book *The Classical Style* (Faber, 1971) has itself become a classic.

Such was the 1966 jury – one of unparalleled intellectual and musical distinction, but also a collection of lively and forceful personalities. It was not an easy one to control, and tensions quickly surfaced.

The 1966 competition offered its winners a first prize of £750, donated by Mr and Mrs Charles Tapp, plus the Princess Mary Gold Medal; a second prize of £400 (The Dominic Crosfield Prize); an anonymously offered third prize of £200; five semi-final prizes of £100 each, four offered by the Northern Arts and Sciences Foundation and one by Lord Savile; and twelve second-stage prizes of £50 each, offered by a variety of local businesses and individuals. Although the prize-money was in fact less than had been offered in 1963,

Fanny and Marion had secured an impressive list of potential engagements for the winner(s), including a Prom, a concert with the LSO at the Royal Festival Hall, concerts with the Scottish National Orchestra, the Royal Liverpool Philharmonic, and at the Leeds Triennial, Aldeburgh and Edinburgh Festivals; a BBC broadcast recital and a television appearance, and a date at the Robert Mayer concerts. It was the prospect of engagements, not the prize-money, which was to make the Leeds competition so attractive to international competitors.

For the 1966 competition, Fanny and Marion decided to widen the repertoire requirements, especially in the first stage. Whereas in 1963, competitors had been obliged to play one of three Beethoven sonatas, either the *Italian* Concerto or the E flat Prelude and Fugue by Bach, and one of four études by Chopin, now they were given rather more choice. The pieces in Group 1 again included a choice of three Beethoven sonatas, but in addition, the same group also offered the Bach E minor Partita and the Haydn E flat major Sonata, Hob.XVI No.52. As before, a Chopin piece was compulsory, but this time none of the études was required. Instead, there was a choice of one of four ballades, the F sharp minor Polonaise, Op.44, or the C sharp minor Scherzo, Op.39. The final group consisted of virtuoso studies by Liszt, Debussy or Dohnányi.

The second stage too, was very different from 1963. Then, the competitors had played four works, one taken from the standard Classic/Romantic repertory, one from the virtuoso late Romantic/early twentieth-century repertory (Liszt, Debussy, Ravel, Albéniz), one from the later twentieth century, and the Britten *Night Piece*. In 1966 only two works were required at this stage. Group 1 consisted of large-scale sonatas by Mozart, Beethoven, Schubert, Weber, Brahms, and the Schumann Fantasy in C, Op.17; while Group 2 was drawn entirely from the big twentieth-century repertoire: the *Danse russe* from Stravinsky's *Petrushka*, Prokofiev's Toccata in D minor, Op.11, Bartók's *Allegro barbaro*, Schoenberg's Op.33a and b, and Messiaen's *Fantaisie burlesque*.

Of the twenty competitors who took part in this stage, eight would then be selected to perform an 'own choice' recital at Leeds Town Hall (an extra stage), and three finalists would perform a concerto with the Royal Liverpool Philharmonic Orchestra, under Charles Groves. This marked the beginning of a long and successful collaboration between Charles (now Sir Charles) Groves and the Leeds competition: he has so far conducted the finals of five of the nine competitions. Once again, the choice of concertos was kept to a manageable number – two of the previous three Mozarts (K.466 and K.595) were retained, together with the last three Beethovens; the Schumann and the Tchaikovsky No.1 also stayed, while the two concertos by Liszt were replaced by the Brahms D minor and Chopin's Second in F minor.

One major step forward in 1966 was the interest of the media. BBC Radio decided to record the semi-finals, with the intention of transmitting the recitals on the Music Programme, and undertook a live transmission on radio of the winners' concert from Leeds Town Hall. Gerald MacDonald, then Head of Music for the BBC's Northern Region, told the *Yorkshire Post*: 'The Leeds competition has already achieved such international distinction that we have geared our TV and radio resources towards furthering its ambitions of promoting the talents of the young successful aspirants.' Unlike most radio broadcasts of concerts, when the programme is fixed in advance, the radio producer faced extra problems when covering a concert in which the programme would not be known until the last minute. 'We, together with the RLPO, have to be in readiness to prepare orchestral works, which will open and close the programme, and also to fit these into a time-limit concerning the broadcast concert's schedule,' explained Macdonald.

In addition to the radio coverage, an up-and-coming young producer with BBC Music and Arts, John Drummond, intended to make a television documentary about the Leeds competition. Television cameras would be present throughout, and competitors would be interviewed and filmed at all stages, not only while they were playing. 'This,' said MacDonald at the time, 'should be a major breakthrough in the presentation of music on TV.' John Drummond termed his programme an 'eavesdropping documentary' – of the style which has, of course, become commonplace since. But then, especially in connection with an arts event, it was both bold and innovative. 'This approach makes for spontaneity and a completely natural result,' said Drummond:

This competition is a great challenge. We aim that the film will reach a terrific climax on Saturday and that all the excitement and tension will be revealed through the eyes of the cameras. This is yet another attempt by BBC TV to give a new and vital slant to music, and we are finding the Leeds artistic atmosphere invigorating. Maybe we shall discover another Schnabel or another Horowitz.

John Drummond's 65-minute documentary 'Great Expectations' ('a film about brilliant, attractive young people') launched the Leeds International Piano Competition on to the nation's television screens in October 1966, achieving mass viewing for an artistic event which had previously only been equalled by the Last Night of the Proms, and by Ken Russell's controversial dramatized composer-biographies. The BBC then entered it in the documentary section of the Prague International Television Festival, where it won the production award. Its enormous success certainly boosted Drummond's own reputation (he is now Controller of Radio Three, having formerly run the Edinburgh Festival after leaving television), and turned him into something of a local hero in Leeds. He has attended several Leeds Piano Competitions since, and feels very protective towards them: 'One feels very tender towards these outstanding young musicians, and the atmosphere is very warm and supportive.'

To avoid the embarrassing first-round performances of the 1963 event, of which some under-trained British pianists had been particularly culpable, the 1966 competition held a preliminary audition session for the British entrants in London, at which candidates who were clearly not up to standard were weeded out. Even so, the 1966 competition attracted 91 entrants from 35 different countries, ranging from as far afield as Uruguay, Lithuania and Japan. Fifteen were British (less than half the number who entered the 1963 competition), and although the 1966 competition was to prove disappointing for British pianists, many of those who entered have gone on to establish solid careers in the UK at least, an indication of the potential strength of the native entry.

As before, the arrival of the four-strong Russian contingent caused great excitement. This year it comprised three men, Aleksei Nasedkin, nineteen-year-old Semyon Kruchin, Igor Khudolei, and one girl, Viktoria Postnikova, together with their interpreter and adviser, Sergei Dorensky. Professor Dorensky, a former college centre-forward, was known to be a great football fan; and Fanny Waterman arranged for him to meet Don Revie, then manager of Leeds United. To his great delight, Dorensky found himself invited to see a Leeds United match against Everton.

Of the original 91 entrants, 26 withdrew before the competition started, and approximately 10 more simply failed to appear at the last minute. The competition opened, therefore, on Thursday 22 September with 57 of the original applicants. One of the late arrivals was the French girl, Laurence Allix, who had been drawn to open the competition's first round: she finally turned up, worried and exhausted, at midnight on Wednesday, having encountered travel problems. The organizers decided to allow her time to rest and practise, postponing her appearance until the afternoon session – something which does not always happen at other competitions.

(Peter Donohoe recalls an incident at a more recent Tchaikovsky Competition in Moscow, when a cellist was unfortunate enough to break a string during her first-round recital – and that was the end of the competition as far as she was concerned.)

As always, the first round of the competition proved the most gruelling for the jury. Rudolf Firkušný was suffering from toothache throughout, and was feeling thoroughly miserable. Nadia Boulanger, easily bored by indifferent playing, astounded her fellow jurors by composing intricate canons whenever she felt that a particular competitor did not merit further attention. 'It's awful to listen to bad playing,' lamented Gina Bachauer. William Glock, the chairman, had to miss much of the first round, since he was deeply involved with the BBC's forthcoming celebration broadcasts for Roberto Gerhard's seventieth birthday. Under such circumstances, it was perhaps not surprising that 'cliques' began to form among certain sections of the jury.

On the Monday afternoon, the list of twenty competitors who would go through to the second stage was announced, and the unlucky losers were invited to meet the jury to discuss their performances. Not a single British pianist had reached the second round. This major blow to national pride after Michael Roll's triumph in 1963 was seized upon by the Press, causing the organizers some disquiet. Fanny Waterman herself went to the Queens Hotel to discuss the situation with Glock, who was at one time rumoured – incorrectly – to be on the point of resignation, for different reasons.

The second-round pianists included all four Soviet competitors; two Americans, James Tocco and Michael Ponti; two Czechs, Peter Toperczer and Emil Leichner; Jean-Rodolphe Kars from Austria; Rafael Orozco from Spain; Laurence Allix from France; Cynthia Barrett from Jamaica; Roujka Tcharakchieva from Bulgaria; Gellert Modos from Hungary; Edison Quintana from Uruguay; Domenico Canina from Italy; Dov Kalid from Israel; Verda Erman from Turkey; Chung Lee from South Korea; and José Contreras from the Philippines. Of these, ten (instead of the intended eight) were selected to give a semi-final recital. Three out of the four Russians got through, as did Orozco, Kars, Tocco, Tcharakchieva, Toperczer, Allix and Barrett. The final result might have been very different had not Toperczer fallen victim to one of those accidents of fate which would not be utterly disastrous at a concert, but which, happening in the vital round of a competition, can potentially alter the course of a career. Toperczer was the first semi-finalist to perform in the Town Hall. Shortly after he began, the jury, who had become accustomed to the sympathetic acoustic of the University Great Hall, decided to move from the balcony down to the middle of the stalls, where they thought they would be better able to assess the performance. So Toperczer was asked to stop, wait, and begin again. Then, during the slow movement of Beethoven's Sonata, Op.2 No.3, the atmosphere was rudely shattered by the sound of fire-engine bells outside. Undaunted, he continued, only to have the fire-engines augmented by alarm bells ringing inside the hall itself. Eventually, William Glock stopped him once more and explained that his recital would have to be delayed until the disturbance could be identified. Apparently the Town Hall heating system had suddenly gone into overdrive, alerting the fire brigade. Though a false alarm, the combination proved too much for the luckless competitor. When asked to repeat his recital the following day, he declined.

John Drummond remembers Aleksei Nasedkin's performance of the *Hammerklavier* Sonata in the semi-final round: 'He thought he was Gilels.' And Gellert Modos, a Hungarian pianist who failed to get into the semi-finals, played the Liszt Sonata 'brilliantly. It was the real thing'. Rafael Orozco, who had played a stunning *Gnomenreigen* in the first round, and a combination of Brahms and *Petrushka* in the second, chose the Mozart A minor Sonata, two pieces from Albéniz' *Iberia*, and Prokofiev's Second Sonata for his semi-final recital. Postnikova selected the Liszt Sonata, a Schubert impromptu, and a prelude and fugue by Taneyev.

Once again, the jury decided to admit more competitors to the final than had been originally planned: five instead of three. Since there was only one final concert, this meant that not everyone could play a complete concerto. All three Russian semi-finalists – Postnikova, Nasedkin, and Kruchin – were through. With one accord, each elected to play the Tchaikovsky Concerto, as did the Austrian Jean-Rodolphe Kars. Only one finalist, Rafael Orozco, offered a different concerto – the Brahms. This posed problems for the organizers, the conductor, and for John Drummond's documentary. 'It wasn't much musical fun,' says Drummond. 'But the Russians were expected to concentrate on their national repertoire.' The organizers' solution was to divide up the Tchaikovsky Concerto: Nasedkin and Kruchin each played the first movement, while Postnikova and Kars supplied the second and third. That way, there were two complete performances of the Tchaikovsky, separated by the first movement of Orozco's Brahms.

By this time, rumours of a split in the jury were beginning to circulate. Throughout the competition, it had been noticeable that the jury had divided itself into two wings. There was little doubt that a certain element of sexual politics had begun to emerge – several of the ladies were lobbying vigorously for the handsome young Spaniard Orozco ('a tiger' according to Gina Bachauer, a 'bullfighter' according to Glock); while another faction, headed by Glock himself and robustly seconded by Hans Keller, was in favour of the blonde Russian, Viktoria Postnikova. 'Orozco's playing had great life,' says William Glock, 'but I felt it lacked the subtlety of Postnikova's. Nasedkin was the Russian favourite [and, incidentally, Nadia Boulanger's too], and I felt Kruchin was good but prosaic.' Charles Rosen personally supported the young Austrian Jean-Rodolphe Kars, whom he felt showed great promise, but who had never played a concerto with an orchestra before.

Of the performances in the finals, the special correspondent of *The Times* commented that Orozco played the Brahms with

superb keyboard mastery and all the passionate, emotional commitment one might legitimately expect from a Spaniard – but also with enough rhythmic licence to make us hope that before accepting the large number of engagements that follow in the wake of his award, he will quickly learn when it is judicious to put a composer's wishes before his own.

Of Kruchin's and Nasedkin's performances, the same critic felt that both were artistic extroverts, with Kruchin the more individual of the two. Kars he found inexperienced, but 'for sensitivity to musical as well as tonal values, he could be hailed as an embryonic Cortot'. The last to play was Postnikova, who, according to *The Times*, 'contrived to make this music sound as beautiful, fresh and exciting as if she were introducing it to the world for the first time'.

The jury retired to consider its verdict – and was out for two hours. Tension mounted inside the hall, as the audience waited for Marion Harewood to present the prizes. Eventually, an emotionally battered William Glock emerged to announce the result. The winner was Rafael Orozco, with Postnikova and Kruchin sharing joint second place, Nasedkin third, and Kars fourth. The jury had virtually been unable to reach a decision. William Glock and Marion Harewood had spent the last five minutes trying to dissuade Hans Keller from publicly annnouncing his resignation, to express his disapproval of the result.

In his speech to announce the winner, William Glock (who privately thought – and later publicly declared – that the result was 'based on a dreadful lack of artistic judgement') paid tribute to the 'quite outstanding performances' which had been heard during the competition as a whole, and stressed that the jury's decision had been based on the playing throughout all four stages. 'We are looking for a strong musical character and a mastery of the keyboard. I don't say we have discovered a genius . . . that will depend on how the prize-winners develop. But it has certainly revealed some great talents.'

As in 1963, Ernest Bradbury attended the winners' concert, given the following afternoon with the RLPO under Charles Groves. Both Rafael Orozco and Viktoria Postnikova were invited to play their complete concertos. Bradbury commented on Orozco's 'calm, cool, almost rational reading' of the Brahms, which 'lifted it on to a plane of extraordinary experience. Yet', continued Bradbury, 'if his manner seemed detached, it was from the first phrase musically committed. He brought a deal of warmth and sonority to the slow movement, found the requisite stamina for the finale, and was always able to suggest the breadth and sweep of Brahms' more demanding phrases.' Postnikova, Bradbury found, 'had all the crisp and nimble delicacy required for Tchaikovsky's work, showing finger-work of great brilliance in the second part of the opening movement and again, superbly, in the scherzo movement.' Though in Bradbury's opinion Postnikova had the easier task, since the Tchaikovsky is such a favourite with audiences, 'she showed musical perception of an uncommon order, and played poetically and sensitively in the more delicate regions of the concerto's second movement.' Having found himself at the centre of the 1963 controversy when he questioned the jury's decision in print, Bradbury wisely refrained from expressing an opinion as to the relative merits of the major prize-winners.

Who was right? Of all the 1966 finalists, none has really pursued an absolutely top-class international career. Jean-Rodolphe Kars abandoned the piano to become a Trappist monk: Aleksei Nasedkin is now a professor at the Moscow Conservatory, while his younger compatriot Semyon Kruchin managed to fall foul of the Soviet authorities, apparently by applying for an exit visa, and was not allowed out of the USSR again. He is rumoured to have spent twenty years or so in internal exile, but is now teaching in Moscow. Viktoria Postnikova was luckier than some of her compatriots: she was allowed to fulfil some of the engagements in the West which resulted from her participation in Leeds. She appeared at the Proms the following year, and has regularly played in Britain and other parts of Western Europe since.

Rafael Orozco, who was taken under Maria Curcio's wing after the competition, got off to a good start with a career in Britain: the personal intervention of Gina Bachauer enabled him to postpone his threatened period of compulsory military service in Spain in order to fulfil the engagements resulting from his win at Leeds, and for a while he lived in England. Now he lives in Rome, and only occasionally plays in the UK. His manager Terry Harrison thinks that the controversy over the result, in particular 'the stance publicly adopted by the BBC members' adversely affected Orozco's chances of a major post-Leeds career. 'Rafael is very sensitive,' he says, 'and what happened after he won in 1966 made a big difference to how he developed. The talent is there, but he was unfairly criticized and hounded by some sections of the musical establishment, which diluted the impact of his success at Leeds.'

Hans Keller was never one to take defeat lying down. Shortly after the competition, much to the annoyance of the organizers, he published a short article in the *New Statesman* (7 October 1966) in which he vented his wrath at the result, saying that it was a matter of urgency to formulate a critique of artistic competitions. While giving Rafael Orozco due credit for his 'natural gypsy musicality' and for making his sharply characterized *Gnomenreigen* sound 'almost a better piece than it is', Keller made no bones about his preference for Postnikova's playing:

With intensely restrained intensity, with breathtaking poise between extremes of contrasting emotion, with an originality of insight that made every phrase, even every Tchaikovsky phrase, sound brand new, with a sense of sound and sonority, a range of colour that owed nothing to sound effects and everything to well-defined, yet spontaneous, sound sense-making – in short, with continuous inspiration and mastery, this 22-year-old [*sic*; Postnikova was actually twenty-four] girl gave a performance which showed where music came from: that it was neither entertainment nor duty, but an urgent communication inexpressible by any other means, so urgent as to be, for those who had ears to see, a matter of life or death. At this point, the verdict of the jury became perverse: Miss Postnikova is a supreme artist who composes while she plays, and damn all competitions and second prizes.

Whatever the course of Viktoria Postnikova's subsequent career, her playing at Leeds must surely have reached truly Olympian heights to merit such a tribute from one of the keenest and most penetrating minds in music criticism. Keller went on to complain of the 'inartistic side of artistic competitions', in which someone of Postnikova's standing has to emerge 'beaten'. 'Don't let sport penetrate art' urged Keller; and he warned of the dangers inherent in such competitions, which can serve 'to promote great talent – but only if we remain constantly aware of their dangers and counteract them'. The way to do this, according to Keller, was to remove the 'overweight of

44

instrumental expert opinion from the jury. A piano competition should not be judged chiefly by pianists, however distinguished, because their verdict will subtly be influenced by technical considerations at the expense of ultimate musical values.' Such a jury, argued Keller, however carefully selected, 'will not be able to resist the sporting aspect, the question of who is "best".' Keller ended by advocating sharing the prizes equally among the leading talents, so that no 'winners' and 'losers' emerge. His own, staunchly maintained view was that 'above a certain level, you're not "better" or "worse", but *different*, and it's the difference that makes you interesting.'

Chapter Five

Marion Thorpe

Despite Fanny Waterman's immense personal talent for organization, there is little doubt that the Leeds Piano Competition would have experienced great difficulty in getting off the ground without the committed involvement of Marion Thorpe, then Countess of Harewood.

A professionally trained pianist, Marion has spent her life surrounded by great music and musicians. She was born in Vienna in 1927, the only child of the distinguished Austrian musician and editor Erwin Stein, a pupil of Schoenberg. 'My father's musical circle was that of the so-called "Second Viennese School", which was dominated by the powerful figure of Schoenberg,' recalls Marion Thorpe. 'I only met Schoenberg when I was very small. He had moved to Berlin in 1926 and I only remember him on one or two of his visits to Vienna.'

Erwin Stein met his wife Sophie in 1920 at the Darmstadt Opera House, where he was conducting. She was then a widow, with a son and two stepsons, and Stein took up lodgings in her house. After their marriage, they returned to Vienna, where Stein conducted a choral society, and became artistic adviser to Universal Edition – then the major European publisher of contemporary music. One of his last tasks there was to make a vocal score of the third act of Berg's opera *Lulu*, left unfinished at the composer's untimely death in 1935. 'Berg was a close personal friend of the family,' recalls Marion. 'He was enormously tall and dark and handsome and as a small child I remember being rather frightened of this lofty figure looming high above me, although he could not have been a kinder man, and was, I believe, very fond of me.'

Marion's own musical tastes were formed in the rich cultural life of pre-war Vienna. As a child, she was often taken to the opera, where her father carefully selected the repertoire which he considered suitable on musical and moral grounds for an eight- to ten-year-old. *The Magic Flute* was deemed appropriate, while the more *risqué* stories of *Figaro, Don Giovanni, Carmen* or *La Bohème* were not. But, as Marion says, 'what better start than the glorious music of the *Flute*. I fell in love with the music, with Mozart, with the fairy-tale characters. They haunted my imagination, and for a time I even tried to make up operas myself on those lines.'

Another life-long passion has been the music of Mahler, whose symphonies and songs Marion came to know from her earliest years. 'Mahler influenced my father's "ethos" and understanding, not only through his compositions, but also through his performances of other composers' works,' recalls Marion. In the early years of the century, Erwin Stein used to attend many rehearsals and performances at the Vienna Opera, where Mahler was the musical director. 'My father would absorb every nuance of Mahler's musicianship in his legendary interpretations of Mozart, Wagner, Beethoven and others, and all this was the basis of his own musicianship.' Erwin Stein made a chamber music version of Mahler's Fourth Symphony for the Schoenberg circle's Verein für musikalische Privataufführungen (Chamber Music Society for Private Performances); and Marion and her father used to play through the Mahler symphonies (and many other scores) four-handed on the piano.

Marion began piano lessons as a child. But in 1938, when she was eleven, the *Anschluss* forced the Steins out of Austria. Erwin Stein was offered a job as music editor with the firm of Boosey & Hawkes, the British agents of Universal Edition, and in September 1938 he left for London. Marion and her mother followed on via Berlin, where they wanted to visit relatives. Just as they got there, the Munich crisis blew up, and for a few days they did not know if war would be declared, and whether they would be allowed to leave. 'It was very dramatic,' Marion remembers. 'But fortunately, nothing happened then, and we got out.'

Once in London, the family settled down to live on Erwin Stein's modest salary; but in 1940, after the fall of France, he and many other refugees were interned on the Isle of Man for some months. Marion and her mother had to manage on a £3 weekly allowance from Boosey & Hawkes. They spent the whole war in London. Marion had won a scholarship to Kensington High School, which for one term was evacuated to Oxford. All the girls were thoroughly miserable, and were highly relieved to return to London, despite the risks. And indeed, on the night of 11 May 1941, both the school, in St Alban's Grove, South Kensington, and the much-loved Queens Hall were destroyed by the Luftwaffe's bombs.

During her schooldays Marion had continued her piano studies, and on leaving she entered the Royal College of Music, where she studied with Kendall Taylor. After two terms she left, and after a period of study in Brussels she went privately to Franz Osborn, who developed her technique. She was unsure then whether or not she wanted to try to become a concert pianist, but she was greatly encouraged by Clifford Curzon: 'He was my mentor. I never had lessons from him as such, but he encouraged me to become "professional", so to speak, and I could always turn to him for advice.' Long telephone conversations with Curzon could be devoted to the fingering of a particular Mozart passage. Marion's other great hero of the piano was Arthur Schnabel, whom she first heard play in the Albert Hall: 'Listening to Schnabel, I felt that here was musicianship of a new dimension coming from the keyboard. He seemed to embody all I was striving for, and all that I believed in where tempo, phrasing, subtle rubato, musical breathing and shaping were concerned.' Marion hoped to study with Schnabel – but it was not to be.

During the war, Marion was introduced to the other great musical love of her life. Boosey & Hawkes put on a series of concerts at the Wigmore Hall which gave a platform to contemporary works, many from the Boosey & Hawkes list. At these concerts, Marion first heard the music of Benjamin Britten, who had recently returned from America with Peter Pears, and had begun work on *Peter Grimes*:

I shall never forget the thrill, delight and excitement at first hearing such works as the *Michelangelo Sonnets*, the *Serenade*, the *Hymn to St Cecilia*, the *Ceremony of Carols* – each a masterpiece in its own right. I hardly ever missed a first performance of Britten's works, and often heard him try them out beforehand on the piano at home.

The Steins became close friends of Britten and Pears, and after a fire in their flat, Erwin, Sophie and Marion moved into Britten's maisonette in St John's Wood, an arrangement of shared London houses which continued for several years. There was, however, one disadvantage – Marion felt too inhibited to practise the piano when Britten (a fine pianist) was around, and so Clifford Curzon offered to pay for a practice studio for her. But the rewards were enormous – she was able to observe at close quarters the preparations for the first performance of *Peter Grimes*, which opened at Sadler's Wells Theatre just after the end of the war on 7 June 1945. 'I still remember the amazement we all felt,' she recalls. 'Suddenly, here was a fully fledged British opera composer. The war was over, the world had opened up, and now a musical victory had been won. It was the beginning of a new era.' Marion was so excited by the preparations and rehearsals at home and in the theatre, that she insisted on attending the dress rehearsal of *Grimes* – which meant playing truant from a piano exam at the RCM. 'Clifford Curzon did not forgive me for a long time.'

It was through the connection with Britten that Marion's life was shortly to undergo a dramatic change. The success of *Grimes* prompted Britten and Pears to set up the English Opera Group – a small touring company dedicated to the performance of contemporary British operas by Britten and others. The company decided to make as its permanent base the small Suffolk coastal town of Aldeburgh – by then Britten and Pears' home, and itself the inspiration for *Grimes*. In June 1948 Marion and her parents attended the first Aldeburgh Festival, at which Britten's chamber opera *Albert Herring* was performed. The Festival's president was George Lascelles, seventh Earl of Harewood, a keen music-lover and a great admirer of Britten's music. At a party after the Festival, the Earl was introduced to Marion, and some time later, after a performance of Berg's *Wozzeck* at the BBC, Lord Harewood asked her to marry him. Since he was a member of the Royal Family (his mother was the Princess Royal, sister of King George VI), the King's permission had to be obtained, together with the approval of Queen Mary, the Earl's grandmother.

On 29 September 1949, Marion Stein became the Countess of Harewood at St Mark's Church, North Audley Street. The wedding was attended by every member of the Royal Family, and the reception was held at St James' Palace by invitation of the Princess Royal. In honour of the occasion, Benjamin Britten wrote a wedding cantata, *Amo ergo sum*, to be performed during the service. Peter Pears and Joan Cross were the soloists, and the composer conducted.

Two years earlier, George Lascelles had succeeded to the title of Earl of Harewood, and to the magnificent family seat, Harewood House, a few miles north of Leeds. From the time of their marriage, he and Marion divided their time between Harewood and London, where they bought a house in Orme Square. Lord Harewood had begun writing opera and ballet criticism for the *New Statesman* and other periodicals, and in 1950 he founded the magazine *Opera*. In 1951 he became first a director, then administrative assistant, of the Royal Opera House; and was for some years Managing Director of the English National Opera.

Marion found that her new life put an end to her hopes of a concert career. Her first son David, was born in 1950, followed by a second, James, in 1953 and a third, Jeremy, two years later. Although she had given a few public concerts, and, a few months before her marriage, she had played the piano in *The Little Sweep* (part of *Let's Make an Opera*) and the cantata *St Nicholas* at the 1949 Aldeburgh Festival, she now relinquished the idea of a professional career.

'I got so far, and let it go. I don't regret it – I don't think I would have had the nerve to be a performer.'

In the mid-1950s, Marion heard some of Fanny Waterman's most talented pupils (including Allan Schiller and Michael Roll) at a charity concert in Leeds Town Hall: 'They were quite astounding.' Through a mutual friend, Lady Parkinson (a fine amateur violinist and great patron of the arts), she met Fanny and asked if she would teach her eldest son. Fanny and Marion soon discovered many common interests. They played and broadcast piano duets together, and 'started to plot things' – including the Piano Competition. Marion's contacts in the international music scene proved invaluable in the assembly of the top-class jury, and in persuading local business people and dignitaries to subscribe to the competition. She was also instrumental in the selection of repertoire – her own musical tastes coincided with Fanny's, and between them, they devised a broad but central repertoire which has been one of the competition's strongest features. It was Marion's idea that each competitor should have to play a slow piece: Clifford Curzon used to say that the Mozart A minor Rondo should be made compulsory at every piano competition – 'he considered it so subtly difficult that it would soon weed out the non-starters' – and at first she strongly resisted the inclusion of Rakhmaninov and Tchaikovsky concertos for the finals: 'I don't think you can tell from these concertos what sort of musicians they really are.'

Marion was also responsible for commissioning the test piece for the first competition, Britten's *Notturno*. 'Britten wrote so little for the piano. He was going to write another piece – Variations – but he never got round to it. I think *Notturno* sums up the spirit of the Leeds Competition – it's an intimate, evocative work, designed to show up musicianship and imagination.'

Marion was closely involved in the first four competitions, and remained joint chairman until her resignation in 1983, since when she has had only sufficient time to attend the finals. She has since become a vice-president. Between the first and second competitions her marriage to Lord Harewood broke down: by 1965 the couple had separated, and they were finally divorced in 1967. Marion (known for the next six years as Marion, Countess of Harewood) bought a house at Thorpeness near Aldeburgh, while also continuing to live at her London home in Orme Square.

In March 1973 Marion married the Rt. Hon. Jeremy Thorpe, then Leader of the Liberal Party. Since then, her life has developed along different lines: she became involved with her husband's political activities and the constituency work in Devon, and found she had less time to visit Leeds. She has not played the piano in public for over ten years: the last time was when she and Fanny played at the funeral of Lady Parkinson.

Marion, like Fanny Waterman, is now a grandmother. Her eldest son David Lascelles, heir to the Harewood title, is now a prominent film and television producer; James lives in the USA, where he is a jazz musician, and Jeremy works for Virgin Records. Marion's stepson, Rupert Thorpe, is currently making a name as a photographer.

Marion Thorpe is now trustee and acting chairman of the Britten–Pears Foundation, set up after Britten's death in 1976. 'The work involved is fascinating, diverse and widespread,' she says:

It embraces a variety of activities connected with Britten's works, such as recordings, performances, publications – as well as the running of the Britten–Pears Library, where the bulk of Britten's manuscripts are housed. It branches out into the activities of the Aldeburgh Foundation, which apart from the annual June Festival, also promotes other concert series throughout the year, and administers the work of the Britten–Pears School for Advanced Musical Studies at Snape.

Marion was also instrumental in forging one very fruitful link between the Leeds Piano Competition and the Aldeburgh Festival:

After Murray Perahia's success in Leeds in 1972, we got to know him, and he expressed enormous admiration for Britten and Pears, whom he had heard in recital in New York. I invited him to Aldeburgh, and introduced him to Ben and Peter. A warm musical friendship developed, and when, a year later, Ben's health no longer permitted him to perform, Murray took on his role, so to speak, and accompanied Peter in recital.

As a result, Murray Perahia became a artistic director of the Aldeburgh Festival (a position he held until 1989), where he performed and planned many fine concerts both as soloist and chamber music player.

'The Leeds Piano Competition played a very big part in my life up to 1972,' says Marion Thorpe. 'Although there are now other interests and activities which concern me, I naturally regret no longer being involved in it. But music continues to play a major role in my life and work.'

Chapter Six

The Third Competition: 1969

The third piano competition, held from 11–20 September 1969, once more attracted a jury of international standing under the chairmanship of William Glock, who made it a condition (after his experiences in 1966) that 'no woman under the age of eighty should be on it!' Nadia Boulanger, at eighty-two, was deemed eligible and re-invited, but was unable to attend; so her compatriot, the former child prodigy pianist Youra Guller, then aged seventy-four, was invited to replace her. Glock was also prepared to admit Gina Bachauer again, although she missed the minimum age-limit by nearly a quarter of a century!

No such stipulation applied to the male members of the jury. Nikita Magaloff and Béla Siki once more agreed to sit; as did Clifford Curzon, who had been on the 1963 jury. The new members included the distinguished American violinist Szymon Goldberg, a pupil of Flesch, who had led the Berlin Philharmonic in pre-war years before touring widely as a soloist and in partnership with the pianist Lili Kraus. For the past fourteen years Goldberg had been musical director of the Netherlands Chamber Orchestra, with which he had often visited Britain, and in the year of the 1969 piano competition, he decided to settle permanently in the UK. Also new to the jury were Peter Gould, representing the BBC; Ivan Moravec, a Czech pianist and professor at the Prague Academy, whose repertory focused on Chopin, Beethoven, Brahms and the early twentieth-century French school; Raymond Leppard, the English conductor and harpsichordist, who had become widely known in the sixties for his inventive realizations of Baroque operas by Monteverdi and Cavalli, and who was among the first British performers and conductors to investigate the concepts of Baroque performance practice; and the Soviet representative Lev Vlasenko, a professor at the Moscow Conservatory, and a replacement for Yakov Zak.

By 1969 Jack Lyons had decided to step down from the Chair of the committee, leaving Marion Harewood and Fanny Waterman as joint-chairmen. The Administrative Committee had been enlarged by two further members, and Anthony Tapp had joined the other three honorary officers as Music Librarian. The Executive Committee of the competition had also been enlarged to twenty-four members, as local support for the competition grew.

To ensure the continuance of this support, an association of the Friends of Leeds International Pianoforte Competition had been formed in March 1967, with the aim of maintaining interest during the three year gap between competitions, providing a solid base of financial support, and ensuring that a committed core of supporters would be available to help with the competitions themselves. Under the chairmanship of Lady Parkinson, the Friends quickly acquired a membership of 400. Between 1966 and 1969 they held many fund-raising events in and around Leeds, including recitals by James Tocco, and Peter Toperczer (the unlucky 1966 semi-finalist whose recital was ruined by a series of unfortunate accidents), a major recital at St James' Palace by the 1966 winner, Rafael Orozco, a Christmas party, and a 'Brains Trust'-type competition, chaired by Geoffrey de Keyser. All this activity meant that the Friends were able to hand over £1,000 towards the costs of running the 1969 competition.

This competition offered its winners three main prizes of £750, £400 and £200 respectively, five semi-final prizes of £100 each, and twelve second-stage prizes of £50. As before, the competition relied heavily on the generosity of individual donors and local businesses for its fund of prize-money; but this time it offered an impressive list of engagements spread over the remainder of 1969 and 1970, ranging from several BBC broadcasts on radio and television, a Prom appearance, a recital in the QEH and a concert in the Festival Hall with the London Philharmonic Orchestra, a six-concert recital tour of the north-east sponsored by the Northern Arts Association, appearances at the Aldeburgh, Bath, Edinburgh and Harrogate Festivals, concerto dates with the BBC Northern Symphony, the Royal Liverpool Philharmonic, the London Mozart Players, and a London concert sponsored by Victor Hochhauser, many smaller recitals around the country, and, for the first time, engagements abroad including a concerto date in Tel Aviv and recitals in Prague and Belgium. Furthermore, after the enormous success of John Drummond's 1966 television documentary, the BBC had agreed to record all the semi-final stages and the final concert both for radio and television. Highlights from the semi-finals would then be shown on the penultimate evening of the competition; and the finals (and the prize-giving ceremony) were to be shown in a 50-minute *Omnibus* programme on the evening after the competition. In addition, the BBC agreed to produce a gramophone record of selected performances from the competition.

This was the kind of media coverage which the organizers had hoped for; and the prestige of the final was to be further enhanced by the news that Her Royal Highness the Duchess of Kent, Chancellor of Leeds University since 1966, had agreed to present the prizes. The Duchess, formerly Miss Katherine Worsley of Hovingham Hall near York, was herself a great music-lover and a long-standing member of the Bach Choir, and took a keen interest in the promotion of the arts in her native county.

The repertoire for the 1969 competition was chosen on the same basis as for the previous two; but once again, the selection of 'set pieces' was enlarged to allow competitors more freedom of choice. There were to be three stages: in the first, competitors had to offer one of a number of prescribed pieces by Bach, Haydn, Mozart and Beethoven; a Chopin scherzo or impromptu, and either one of the *Paganini* studies by Liszt, or a Debussy étude.

Twenty competitors would then be admitted to the second stage, which comprised two works, one drawn from a group of major nineteenth-century works by Beethoven, Schubert, Schumann, Brahms and Musorgsky, and the other a twentieth-century work drawn from a choice of seven, by Bartók, Britten, Hindemith, Messiaen, Stravinsky, Tippett or Webern. Eight semi-finalists would then play a recital programme of their own choice; and the three finalists would then, as before, go on to play a concerto with the Royal Liverpool Philharmonic Orchestra, conducted by Charles Groves. The list of concertos was also larger than in 1966: it included five by Mozart, all five by Beethoven, the Schumann, the Chopin No.2, the Brahms No.2 and the Bartók No.3 – the first twentieth-century concerto to appear on the list. After the experience of 1966, when four out of the five finalists had chosen the Tchaikovsky, the organizers decided to leave it out.

Seventy-six competitors from almost thirty different countries applied. The English entry – again as a result of the preliminary auditions – was down considerably. Only twelve native pianists applied, among them Paul Crossley, a former pupil of Fanny Waterman, who was at that time studying in Paris with Messiaen and Yvonne Loriod on a government scholarship, and who had won the 1968 Messiaen Competition; John Bingham from Sheffield, who studied at the Moscow Conservatory and was a finalist in the Busoni Competition at Bolzano and in the Clara Haskil Competition in Lucerne; Philip Jenkins, who had entered the first Leeds competition; Howard Shelley; and Martino Tirimo. There was one Scottish competitor, Christopher Elton, and a contingent of four from the Republic of Ireland. There was a nine-strong French entry, including Georges

Pludermacher, a veteran of the 1963 Leeds competition, and winner of the third prize at Lisbon in 1968; Henri Barda, a semi-finalist at the Van Cliburn Competition, and Anne Queffelec, a first-prize-winner at Munich in 1968. Only six Americans entered in 1969; four Russians, including Emil Gilels' twenty-one-year-old daughter, Elena; and three Brazilians: Vicky Adler, a semi-finalist at the Rio de Janeiro competition, J. C. Assis Brasil, a 1967 medallist at the Barcelona Competition, and a first prize-winner at the 1968 Vienna Competition, and Arthur Moreira-Lima, a former student at Moscow, who had won second prize in the 1965 Chopin Competition.

From the start, all eyes were on the single Romanian entrant, twenty-three-year-old Radu Lupu, also a former student at the Moscow Conservatory (of Neuhaus, Richter's teacher), and winner of the 1966 Van Cliburn Competition. Lupu, who had a reputation for being temperamental, was already an experienced concert artist, having made his Carnegie Hall début after his Van Cliburn win; and had recently played all five Beethoven concertos on two successive evenings in his native Bucharest.

The youngest entrant, Geoffrey Tozer, was only fourteen but he had been performing in public since the age of nine, and was already something of a television and radio personality in his native Australia. A Churchill scholarship enabled him to come to Leeds. 'I really wanted to play in front of this wonderful jury in Leeds,' he told the Press. 'Winning isn't everything, but it would be rather nice.'

By 1969 the organizers of the competition had become accustomed to the usual spate of last-minute withdrawals and non-appearances, and in fact, only fifty-six pianists actually arrived at Tetley Hall. This particular competition was characterized throughout by a remarkable spirit of camaraderie among the young contestants: when they were not playing or practising, they were playing table-tennis or drinking together at the local pub in the evenings. National rivalries were forgotten. One Hungarian competitor, Annamaria Krause, found to her horror that she had learnt the wrong piece for the compulsory first stage. 'When I got to Leeds', she said, 'I discovered that I had been practising the wrong work. I had been learning the Mozart Fantasy in C minor, K.475, when it should have been K.396.' She appealed to the organizers to allow her to play the piece she had learnt, but the rules could not be bent. Immediately, her Russian rival Elena Gilels offered to help her learn the other piece (which of course had to be played from memory), and they sat up for most of the night before Miss Krause's scheduled appearance. To her surprise and relief, Krause was one of the twenty contestants admitted to the second stage. 'I played as well as I could and was very happy not to be out of the competition at that stage,' she said. 'I was terribly tired afterwards. It was a very big effort of concentration.'

Through too were Elena Gilels and her three Soviet compatriots (Vadim Sakharov, Yuri Slesarev and Boris Petrushansky); Adler and Moreira-Lima; Pludermacher and Queffelec; two Czechs, Martina Maixnerova and Daniela Varinska; Stefan Wojtas from Poland; László Gyimesi from Hungary; Jung Ja Kim from South Korea; the Malayan Dennis Ean Hooi Lee, the Belgian Christian Parent, Lupu, Tozer, Betty Yang from China, and a single Briton, Richard Simm, a student at the Royal College of Music.

Both Lupu and Tozer chose to play Bartók's *Out of Doors* suite in the second round, and one of the most memorable moments of the competition came when several of the other contestants, arriving back at Tetley Hall one evening, found the Van Cliburn winner listening to the fourteen-year-old practising the Bartók, and giving him some helpful hints. 'It was a pleasure to listen to him,' recalls Lupu, twenty years later. 'He was a boy with colossal talent, not just for music. He needed some support, so I listened to him.'

'We had a nice time,' recalls Georges Pludermacher:

It was a very friendly atmosphere, being all together to eat, and getting to know everyone. I was glad to meet artists from different places. I made good friends with the people from the Moscow Conservatoire – Boris Petrushansky and Vadim Sakharov; and Radu Lupu and I spent a lot of time at Tetley Hall playing four-hand reductions of Beethoven symphonies.

'There was a very friendly atmosphere' says Lupu. 'With one or two exceptions, everyone supported each other, and went to hear each other. There wasn't the nastiness you sometimes get. I felt it was a great help.'

Anne Queffelec went in for the Leeds against the advice of her teachers in France, who felt that she might diminish the impact of her first prize in the Munich Competition the previous year. 'But I don't regret it at all,' she says:

I thought it would be a good opportunity to listen to other young artists from different countries, with different approaches. I didn't enter in a spirit of rivalry, but in order to learn new things in a different country. I love England, and I wanted to go to a good competition with a good jury. The programme was very interesting too – it gave me the chance to play the pieces I loved. There was a very warm atmosphere. Even now, many years later, I have good memories of meeting musicians from Poland, the USSR and listening to them. It was very rewarding – a shared experience. I didn't feel it was a combat at all. And there were so many wonderful players: I felt quite humble hearing them. I remember hearing Lupu playing the Haydn Variations in F minor. In the first ten seconds, I thought it would be impossible for anyone to play them better than that. There was such a feeling of quality – human and artistic.

Of the twenty second-round players, the eight selected to give a semi-final recital were three of the four Russians (Elena Gilels was eliminated in the second round), Pludermacher and Queffelec, Moreira-Lima, Lupu and Geoffrey Tozer. The standard, said William Glock, had been extremely high: 'We are going to have a very difficult time adjudicating in the final stages.'

Only at the semi-final stage did Radu Lupu show any signs of his allegedly 'difficult' temperament. He almost refused to play his recital, because a warm-up piano was not available in the practice room – it was at that time housed in the art gallery across the road from the Town Hall. But he relented, and delivered a superlative account of the four Schubert Impromptus and the 'Waldstein' Sonata.

After hearing the semi-finals, which also included fluent performances of *Gaspard de la nuit* from Pludermacher and of *Miroirs* from Anne Queffelec, the judges announced that, as had happened in both previous competitions, three finalists would not be enough to reflect the plethora of talent. They had chosen five: Pludermacher, Queffelec, Lupu, Moreira-Lima and the Russian Boris Petrushansky.

The critic William Mann attended the semi-finals, and in his later *Times* article, he singled out Sakharov's brilliant Liszt Sonata and his 'kinetic, human' account of Debussy's *Cloches à travers les feuilles* as outstanding. Tozer, he said, played Mozart, Beethoven and Bartók with 'unerring sensibility and flawless musicianship', but needed a few fireworks. Lupu he found 'exceptionally gifted in Schubertian poetry, perhaps wayward but refined and resourceful in nuance'; while Petrushansky's *Petrushka* he found vividly characterized, 'though his rip-roaring Schumann *Humoresque*' struck Mann as 'superficial and ill-controlled'. Anne Queffelec he thought a 'perfect French pianist, imaginative up to a realistic point, energetic but unmagical, urwilling to attempt the unknown or unenvisaged'. Pludermacher's rendition of Brahms' *Handel* Variations was, according to Mann, 'brilliantly characterised but uncohesive'. And Moreira-Lima made a 'brilliant, lovely mess of the Liszt Sonata' but 'played every tune and every rhythm, dramatic event, build-up and climax as if the continuance of the world depended on it'.

The announcement that there would be five, rather than three finalists, disguised yet another commotion in the jury room. When the votes for the three final places were cast, Fanny Waterman (who sat in at the jury sessions) and William Glock realized to their consternation that both Lupu and the Soviet Petrushansky had unaccountably been placed fourth and fifth, thereby disqualifying them from the final. To avoid public embarrassment, it was therefore proposed that all five should be admitted. At first the jurors were reluctant to change the rules. Fanny Waterman promptly declared that she would never organize another competition if someone like Lupu were to be excluded. 'Eventually, more and more people came round to my point of view,' she recalls; but Clifford Curzon, who favoured Pludermacher, stubbornly resisted. 'Even if my favourite falls down dead drunk under the piano tomorrow evening, I shall still vote for him,' he told Fanny Waterman, petulantly. But the combined persuasive powers of Fanny and William Glock won the rest of the jury over, and Lupu and Petrushansky were duly admitted to the final.

This brought its own problems. As in 1966, there was only one final night, and each pianist could only offer part of his or her concerto. 'If all five finalists played their concertos from beginning to end, the overall performances of the works would last over 160 minutes, not allowing for pauses between works, nor for an interval,' explained Marion Harewood to a critical Press.

Lupu, who had caused considerable alarm among his rivals from the start of the competition, when he was heard practising concertos while all the others were preparing their first-round pieces, recklessly offered the jury a choice of all five Beethoven concertos. 'Obviously in one respect I was out to impress someone,' he now admits, rather ruefully. 'Clearly I wasn't equally prepared for all of them!' In the end, he settled on the first movement of Beethoven's Third, because 'at the time I felt I could play that piece best' – 'like at a certain time of day I felt I would like a certain cake.' Pludermacher chose Brahms' Second (first and second movements). Anne Queffelec offered the last two movements of the Bartók:

At the time I didn't know about the acoustics of the hall. Afterwards several judges told me I should have chosen another concerto – perhaps Mozart. The Bartók didn't sound as powerful as it should. But I wasn't expecting to get through to the final anyway – I was very pleased to be in the company of such brilliant pianists.

Arthur Moreira-Lima chose the second movement of Chopin's Second Concerto, and Boris Petrushansky the first movement of Beethoven's Fourth.

The first to play on finals night was the Brazilian Moreira-Lima, with an imaginative and poetic slow movement of the Chopin, which William Mann found 'occasionally contrived', and the *Telegraph*'s Colin Mason felt 'had some dead patches'. Then came Boris Petrushansky. He had been unlucky enough to be stung on the index finger by a wasp earlier in the afternoon, requiring a pain-killing injection administered by Geoffrey de Keyser. Petrushansky's Beethoven, while 'masculine and individual', according to one critic, failed to arouse any great enthusiasm – he was 'too eager to prove too much', according to the *Guardian*'s Gerald Larner – while Georges Pludermacher gave a 'commanding performance' of the Brahms which Larner thought 'the most exciting and spontaneous playing in the whole evening'. Anne Queffelec, whose 'fine calculations in Bartók's third piano concerto were somewhat obscured by insensitive accompaniment from the Royal Philharmonic Orchestra' (Larner), had the misfortune to follow Lupu, whose 'playing of Beethoven's third piano concerto was an unbroken joy, grand, poetic, a vivid almost spectacular music-drama' (Mann). After Lupu had left the platform, Clifford Curzon, who had been so against the Romanian's admittance to the final at all, turned to Fanny Waterman with his hands together in prayer. 'Thanks be to God that I heard that performance,' he said.

The jury duly retired to consider its verdict, and came back with an almost unanimous result. 'There was no possible doubt whatever,' said Gina Bachauer afterwards. 'Such an overall agreement is unusual in competitions of the stature of Leeds – and most especially on this occasion when so many brilliant players were being heard.'

Lupu was awarded first prize, followed by Pludermacher, Moreira-Lima, Petrushansky and Queffelec. For once, there were few disagreements. 'Mr Lupu,' commented William Mann, 'is clearly destined to comfort and invigorate our lives for many years, whatever music he chooses to play. But', he added, 'musical competitions are harmful when they award exclusive judgements. This one at Leeds had the merit of bestowing praises on many good pianists who did not win first prize.'

As usual, the critic Ernest Bradbury assessed the winners in the wake of the competition. His 'loser' was Anne Queffelec, 'whose cantabile, poetic phrasing, colouring and sense of musical flow I would exchange any day for the brash and stormy Brahms of her compatriot, Georges Pludermacher.' Bradbury would also have placed Pludermacher behind Moreira-Lima, 'who restored notes to their own atmosphere, giving each an individual life. There were lightness of touch and sweetness of tone; occasionally, perhaps, a

slightly self-conscious assertiveness . . . but the memory of this playing lingers, its culture and refinement, and the lovely delicacy of
its figurations.' With Pludermacher's playing, Bradbury felt, 'music
becomes humanised, robust and very much aware of itself . . . but
there was little more than the cold, brilliant magic of technique.'
Petrushansky's playing, according to Bradbury, was prosaic, eclipsed
by that of the obvious winner Radu Lupu – 'now we really knew the
meaning of a pianissimo.'

Chapter Seven

The Key Board

'Leeds is the best-run competition' – 'we were so well looked after' – 'everyone was so friendly' – 'there was hardly any of the back-biting one encounters elsewhere' – 'I made some lifelong friends at Leeds' – 'I was wrapped in warmth'. Almost all the pianists who have taken part in the Harveys' Leeds International Piano Competition pay enthusiastic tribute to the organization (especially in comparison to some other competitions), and in particular to the kindliness, generosity and warmth of feeling they encountered, not only from the organizers, but also from the families to whose homes they were invited to practise. It is this spirit of open-handed hospitality from a whole community which has marked Leeds out from competitions that are held in the more impersonal atmosphere of a conservatory in a capital city, and which continues to encourage younger, or less aggressively competitive, entrants to submit themselves to the competition ordeal. One of the prize-winners at the 1987 event – who took part while undergoing a personal trauma that might have been expected to blight his recollection – was nonetheless able to pay this tribute to his experience at Leeds:

I have the fondest memories of Leeds. I enjoyed the competition – the atmosphere among competitors was cordial, and one got the special feeling that it is a community event. The whole city seemed to be involved – people open their houses to you – the competitors are welcomed. It's very beautiful. I, like others, have maintained lasting friendships with my hosts and drivers. It's quite unique. Fanny Waterman deserves credit for inspiring her whole city.

The organization of such an event, particularly where the required resources are far-flung, is a Herculean task, necessitating the co-operation of hundreds of people. And at Leeds nearly all the required time and labour is given voluntarily.

From the start, Fanny Waterman has been fortunate in securing the services of a core of devoted, loyal and tireless helpers. 'Someone once approached me, saying they would be interested in doing "a little job" for the competition,' she recalls. 'I replied that in this organization, there are no little jobs.'

The competition's first manager (later administrator), Cecil Mazey, was a retired bank manager who at first combined the roles of administrator and treasurer. Mazey was originally also involved with the administration of the Leeds Festival, but after two or three years, he relinquished that post to devote himself to the flourishing piano competition. 'Cecil had an immensely keen eye for detail, and an orderly mind,' says Geoffrey de Keyser:

Our budget was at first comparatively small, but Cecil was so meticulous that he made sure we never had an overdraft. It was he who negotiated with the university for the use of its facilities. I remember that in 1970 – the Beethoven centenary year – we organized three major recitals by the three Leeds prize-winners. It was my task to proof-read all the programme notes. I sent them off to Cecil for passing on to the printer – but then I got an urgent phone call from him. 'Geoffrey – you know I'm no connoisseur of music – but did Beethoven really write an *Erotica* Symphony?'

After Mazey's retirement in 1970, his place was taken for the 1972 and 1975 competitions by Edmund Williamson, Bursar of the University of Leeds. 'It was through the influence of Lord Boyle and Edmund Williamson that our relationship with the university grew closer,' says Fanny Waterman. 'From 1972 onwards, the competition acquired a main office in the university itself.' The next three competitions each had a new administrator – Edward Davies in 1978; Stuart Johnson, Chief Education Officer, in 1981; and Michael Barrett, formerly Pro-Vice-Chancellor of the university, in 1984. Fanny Waterman admits that she has not always had peaceful relations with all her administrators. 'You have to get on – it becomes a personal, intimate relationship, and one has to be good friends. Sometimes that doesn't happen.'

From 1987 the competition has been administered by Françoise Logan, the charming and efficient Swiss wife of a Leeds surgeon. Françoise, a graduate of the University of Leeds, first became involved with the competition in 1978, when the Swiss composer Marescotti was on the jury. He came from Geneva – Françoise's home town – and she was called in as an interpreter. She then became a part-time PA to Fanny Waterman, and in 1984 acted as deputy administrator to Michael Barrett, from whom she took over in 1987. Unlike her predecessors, she had no formal training or experience as an administrator. 'She's one of the best,' says Fanny

Waterman. 'She has every necessary attribute for the tremendous responsibility, and commands universal respect.'

The competition is run by a small executive committee, which meets every month throughout each three-year cycle. Its members are the chairman; the administrator; the deputy administrator, Robert Tebb; the treasurer, Paul Holloway; and Geoffrey de Keyser, its honorary executive director.

Robert Tebb, the chairman of a food distribution company, acts for Françoise Logan when she is not available, and is also responsible for the booking arrangements at the university and the Town Hall. He is also the jury officer – he looks after the jury from the minute they arrive to the minute they leave Leeds: 'We shadow them,' he says:

We meet them in the Queens Hotel, look after all their needs, and make sure they're always in the right place at the right time. Before each session, I lead them in with the chairman, and I write a daily news bulletin which the jury is given first thing in the morning.

Robert Tebb also acts as front-of-house manager at the Town Hall, where he is responsible for making sure that the arrangements run smoothly, particularly with regard to the BBC and the Royal party. The 1990 competition will be the fourth in which Robert Tebb has been involved: during the two weeks of the competition, he takes leave from his work and is constantly on call.

Paul Holloway, since 1983 the competition's treasurer, is the Senior Assistant Bursar of the University of Leeds. He handles the financial side, dealing with the Inland Revenue, the raising and investment of funds and the provision of budget forecasts for the committee and sponsors. As a member of the executive committee, his views are also sought on many issues such as the jury rules and the organization of recitals and concerts between competitions. Like Robert Tebb and other committee members, he is actively involved backstage during the competitions themselves.

Until 1990, all the competition's programmes and associated litera-ture were prepared and printed by the printer to Leeds University, Harry Tolson. 'We print separate programmes for the semi-finals and the finals,' he says. 'It's hectic when you have to produce a pro-gramme in twenty-four hours. You can't start until after the second semi-final, when the finalists have decided which concertos they're playing, and the order has been agreed with the BBC and the orches-tra.' However, the competition had to pay Leeds University for the use of its printing facilities. All the literature for the 1990 competition is being handled free of charge, on the initiative of Mr Michael

Ziff, through the generosity of Patrick Walter, managing director of Watmoughs' Financial Print Ltd, one of the competition's major donors.

'We have a small office in the university, which is the competition's official address,' says Françoise Logan:

We have an office manager, who deals with typists and so on, but the office is generally only open for three days a week. For the three months before each competition, it is manned full-time.

First, we produce a leaflet about the forthcoming competition, which gives details of repertoire and the names of the jury. Then we produce a brochure, in five languages, which is published exactly one year before the next competition. This gives more detail about the repertoire and the prizes and contains an application form. The applications start to come in around December, but the bulk arrive from mid-January to March. Then a selection committee – which includes Fanny, Geoffrey, and several eminent musicians including the Professor of Music at the university (currently Julian Rushton) and Joseph Stones, Director of the City of Leeds Musical College – sifts through the applications. Some people invent details – they say they won the first prize at a certain competition when they only got a top prize – not the first. All the references have to be checked. But in general, most people are honest. It's always the borderline cases that are so difficult to assess. Fanny hates rejecting anyone!

'One can't be too careful,' says Fanny Waterman. 'One applicant was turned down for entry to an international competition – not the Leeds – on the basis of a tape he sent. A few days later, the organizers received a letter saying, "You may like to know that you have just rejected Arthur Rubinstein!".'

The competitors have always been fed and accommodated at Tetley Hall, one of the university's halls of residence, a short drive from the city centre. Joan Valentine, who has known Fanny Waterman for sixty years, and has been one of the competition's staunchest supporters – even while maintaining her own former job as Principal of the College of St John at York – was originally in charge of the arrangements at Tetley Hall, where she helped to set up a smooth-running organization with the full co-operation of the Warden (currently Gordon Humphries, whose sense of humour and fluent Russian are much-prized assets).

Since Joan Valentine's retirement in 1984, Tetley Hall has been run by her former assistant, Mrs Anita Woolman, who has been involved since the first competition in 1963. In 1990 Mrs Woolman, a busy local magistrate, will in turn hand over the reins to her assistant, Mrs Elizabeth Arnold, whose husband, Olaf, is in charge of the transport arrangements.

'We lease Tetley Hall for the duration of the competition,' says Anita Woolman:

The competitors were formerly allowed to stay at hotels if they so wished – Murray Perahia, for instance, didn't stay at Tetley Hall – but we do prefer them to stay there. It makes things very difficult for the organizers if we don't know where the competitors are. They used to have to pay the cost of their own accommodation, but now it is subsidized by the Friends of the HLIPC. All competitors are paid for during the first stage: then if any who are eliminated wish to stay on, they may do so at their own expense. But if they are eliminated from the second round onwards, they can stay on at the Friends' expense.

'The Friends used to donate money towards the prize fund,' says Maurice Hare, their chairman, another active long-term supporter of the competition:

But we came to realize it wasn't such a good idea – one year we gave money towards a new Steinway for the winner – and it turned out he already had a good one. Then we noticed that some of the competitors were cutting down on meals – only having the odd fish and chips, and so on – and we realized it was because they were short of money. So we decided it would be a good idea if we could relieve their anxiety by funding their food and accommodation while they were participants. The first time, we provided £12,000. This year it will be nearer £17,000.

'There's a very good atmosphere at Tetley Hall,' says Anita Woolman:

It's like a good hotel, staffed by volunteers. Everyone wants to help. We have to discuss certain special arrangements relating to the nature of the competition with the Warden. For example, we have to have flexible meal-times. Most competitors prefer to eat after they have played – and if they're playing at an evening session, they may need to eat at 10 p.m.

The question of food is taken very seriously in Yorkshire, and unlike some international competitions, where the competitors occasionally complain of an inadequate diet, Leeds has always made sure that the demands of the digestion are fully satisfied. 'Every meal is difficult,' says Joan Valentine. 'There are always some people playing, others preparing, others wanting to attend the sessions.

Generally speaking, the competitors have breakfast and an evening meal in Tetley Hall, and we provide vouchers for lunch, which they can use in local cafés and restaurants, or at the university refectory.' Only one competitor actually seems to have disliked the food at Tetley Hall, where the caterers go out of their way to accommodate individual demands. In 1987 the American competitors wanted something sweet for breakfast, so sponge pudding and treacle was duly supplied; and in 1972, Craig Sheppard recalls complaining that the diet contained insufficient protein: 'The next morning there were two slices of black pudding on my breakfast plate. I managed to eat one – and after that I didn't complain again!'

The jury, of course, have special catering facilities. A team of local ladies has always attended to their needs. For the 1984 and 1987 competitions, a small sub-committee was set up, under the chairmanship of Mrs Betty Marcus, to handle these complex arrangements. 'When the jury members arrive at the Queens Hotel,' says Mrs Marcus,

they are presented with a basket of fruit. Then we make sure they are well supplied with refreshments in morning coffee-breaks and afternoon tea-breaks, and we arrange the menus for lunch and dinner at the university. During the early stages they are at the university from first thing in the morning until late in the evening. But by the semi-final stage, they are able to return to the hotel for lunch, and we bring in outside caterers for a buffet supper at the Town Hall. Then on finals nights, we sometimes have six different parties to be catered for, including the Royal party, the jury, the competitors, and any visiting VIPs. But Harveys have taken over the catering arrangements for the final reception.

'We have a highly detailed registration process at Tetley Hall,' says Anita Woolman:

It's rather like a customs hall. All the birth certificates have to be checked, and vetted, and the competitors compared with their photographs. Then we issue each with a competition pack – it contains all the information they need, about doctors, the nearest post office, brochures on Leeds itself, the rules of the competition, mints, barley-sugar, pencils, a pen – and a packet of tissues! We've tried to organize excursions for them – but no one wanted to go.

The first thing that everyone wants to know after registration is when can they get to a piano to practise, and when they will perform. At the Saturday evening briefing, which all competitors must attend, the order of play is decided – and it has to stand.

We've had no real complaints. But if a competitor hasn't arrived by then, he or she will be put at the end of the first stage. Louis Lortie arrived very late in 1984, and had to play right at the end.

'There has always been a marvellous spirit of camaraderie at Tetley Hall,' says Joan Valentine. 'There's a dais there with a small grand piano. You would often find a group of half a dozen competitors standing round it listening to one or another of them play, and making constructive comments. I was never aware of any animosity or jealousy.'

Vladimir Ovchinnikov, whose total dedication made such an impression on staff and fellow-competitors in 1987, was immensely heartened by the warmth of his reception – although he spoke no English:

It was my first visit to England, and I went there to work. I just concentrated on that. But it was important that we all lived together – Tetley Hall became a family place. It was a good working atmosphere, not frivolous. We were sent to various families to practise, and they all received us with great friendliness.

'There was a special atmosphere,' recalls Ian Munro, the eventual runner-up to Ovchinnikov:

There's something about everyone living together in a university environment. Our hosts were very pleasant, and the Warden, Gordon Humphries, was so helpful, and had a real sense of humour – he could puncture a tense atmosphere. When we weren't practising, we were playing table tennis, and we went to the pub every night. I'm a great fish and chips fan, and there was a fantastic fish shop at the end of the road. We used to bring in fish and chips, and eat them together in front of the TV. And it was fun meeting people in their homes. The pianos ranged from tinkle-boxes to beautiful Steinway grands. You never knew what you'd find.

One unique feature of the Leeds competition is that, in response to appeals from the organizers, local families offer their pianos – ranging from fine Steinways to modest uprights – for the competitors to practise on. During the first stage of the competition, as many as a hundred pianos may be needed more or less simultaneously, and making the necessary transport arrangements requires the precise planning of a military maneouvre.

'The first competition was touch-and-go,' recalls Joan Valentine:

Some people didn't turn up, and it caused some real problems. Peta Ransley had compiled a list of Leeds people who had pianos, and we appealed in the Press for more help. We managed that year, but it was clear that a more formal arrangement was necessary. The big problem was the weekends, when people were more reluctant to commit themselves. But once the first stage is over, things get easier, when there are only twenty or so competitors to organize. We try to guarantee each of them six hours' practice a day if they want it.

'The practice arrangements take months to compile,' says Anita Woolman:

We have devised a system of a huge booking chart, which changes every day. It's divided up into the districts of Leeds and its environs, and it shows piano availability in mornings, afternoons and evenings. We compile the details from forms sent out to the 'hostesses' – each one indicates when a piano will be available, whether she would prefer an English-speaker only, and whether she can provide meals or transport for the competitors if necessary. From that, we can compile an overall programme for practice arrangements. Some competitors – but not many – have their own transport. We have a transport officer, who draws up arrangements for ferrying the competitors to and from their practice pianos – some of which may be very distant – and down to the university for their performances. It always brings a train of troubles. Everyone has to be very precise about their movements – and it's no use if people are vague about time. In 1984 the whole complicated system nearly broke down altogether when many of the competitors fell ill with a mysterious virus. We had to abandon the plan and make last-minute arrangements, since we couldn't send anyone out to houses where they'd had the bug.

Betty Marcus was the competition's first transport officer. 'I started off with just one car – provided by the competition. But now, it needs a team of twenty or thirty drivers [many of whom are either non-working housewives or retired people, often Friends of the HLIPC]. I really enjoyed the contact with the competitors.'

Now Olaf and Elizabeth Arnold are in charge of these complicated arrangements. Olaf Arnold estimates that there are about 400 'movements' a day to and from Tetley Hall in the early stages of the competition:

Each competitor needs three practice sessions a day, and in between, he or she usually will want to return to Tetley Hall for lunch and supper. That's six journeys a day for around 70 competitors. It's chaotic at first, especially if someone is booked to go out to a distant district at 8.30 in the morning, and they don't wake up in time! We do sometimes lose them – we get a frantic phone call saying, 'I'm still out here in Pudsey – where's my driver?' Last time we devised a system of coloured chits relating to a map of Leeds, divided up into postal districts, on which each house is coded by number. That made it easier for the drivers to identify where they were to go. We also provide special posters for the people with pianos to put in their front windows – it's often difficult for the drivers to find houses in an unknown street late at night. Communication is a problem – I wish the cars were equipped with radio phones! The first week is always very difficult, and extremely tiring, but it does get easier. It helps enormously to have experienced drivers who know the ropes. We allocate the two best drivers to 'performance duty' – driving the competitors down to the university from Tetley Hall. That's the most important thing. After all, it doesn't matter too much if a competitor misses one practice session – but we make sure they all arrive in time for their performances! A competitor likes to know exactly when he or she will play, and can't be expected to rush on at a minute's notice.

In 1987 Elizabeth Arnold, who had been involved in the organiz- ation of the competition since 1981, took charge of co-ordinating the practice arrangements:

We always try to be scrupulously fair regarding the allocation of the best pianos. We make sure in the first round that the competitors who are the closest to their performances have a reasonable chance to practise on one of the 25 grand pianos which are available to us. Once each has played, he or she goes to the bottom of the pile, back on to the uprights. Most competitors are very co-operative – and we have found that the better the pianist, the less fussy he or she is likely to be. The Russians last time wanted to practise every minute of every day, but they were happy to use any piano. By the second round, of course, we only send them to houses with grand pianos, and if by the semi-final stage, they are becoming attached to a particular piano and a particular host or hostess, we like to encourage such a relationship to continue.

'Many close and lasting friendships have been formed between competitors and their hosts,' says Joan Valentine:

Viktoria Postnikova had nothing suitable to wear for the final in 1966, so her hostess bought her a long skirt and blouse. If a competitor feels really settled with someone, we try to arrange things so that they can continue going to the same person. Without the hostesses, the competition would be stuck.

In 1984 Ju Hee Suh and her mother were taken to Creskeld Hall, near Leeds, the home of Lady Stoddart-Scott, where there was a fine piano. 'I was knocked out by it,' Ju Hee recalls:

It was like a great big castle – it was so beautiful, and it had a wonderful piano. I kept hoping all through the first stage that I could go back there – and I was so relieved when I did. Lady Stoddart-Scott was so kind, and her hospitality was wonderful. Although she was an elderly lady, she cooked for me, baked me a cake. I couldn't believe how considerate she was. She never interrupted me when I was practising. My mother and I held a tea ceremony with her over a spirit lamp on her drawing-room carpet.

Another hostess who will never forget 1984 is Mrs Geoffrey Baskind. That was the year when she was introduced to Jon Kimura Parker, who came to practise at her home. Mrs Baskind's eldest son Richard had been a pupil of Fanny Waterman since he was seven. 'I was preparing for the first round,' recalls Parker,

and I arrived at this beautiful house. Richard Baskind let me in – he was only fifteen then – and he said he was a pianist too. So I asked him if he wouldn't mind listening to my first-round pieces. I started with a Mozart sonata. 'Not bad,' said Richard. I must say, I was quite taken aback. Then I found out he was a student of Fanny's.

'We were introduced to Jackie [as Jon Kimura Parker is known] early on, and it just clicked,' says Mrs Baskind:

We became great friends: I fed him well – and he really liked my apple pies. He has such a tremendous personality – we really felt he would win, because he can get through to the audience. We were absolutely thrilled when he did win – we went to the finals and the reception afterwards, and then we went down to London for his début there. Then we heard that Vancouver was having a a 'Jon Kimura Parker Day'. My sister lives in Vancouver, so I arranged to go over. There was a sold-out concert, and a reception. Vancouver just went mad. It was as if he'd won an Olympic gold medal. It was a tremendous year. Jackie has such an overwhelming, fabulous personality. He always comes to stay with us if he is playing, not just in Leeds, but anywhere in the north of England. Even if he's in Birmingham, he still makes an excuse to come and stay here. Now he has to have an apple pie every day!

'The first round of the competition used to take four days – but from this year, it will take longer,' says Joan Valentine:

There used to be about eighteen competitors a day in the first stage – it was really tough on the jury – but now the number is more like twelve, since each competitor plays a longer programme. We have tried to allow a free day between stages if possible. The second stage usually takes two days, and if the third involved a chamber music round, it took three. The Thursday before the finals is normally a free day for the jury, to allow time for rehearsals with the orchestra.

The first two stages of the competition take place in the art nouveau surroundings of the University of Leeds' Great Hall, situated in the old, red brick buildings which once constituted the Yorkshire College before its incorporation into the university. Behind the Great Hall is a long, narrow, rather dingy room where the competitors wait to go on. Maurice Hare is in charge of the Green Room. 'First of all,' he says,

all the competitors are brought down in shuttles from Tetley Hall, to try out the piano. Each used only to have exactly five minutes – but now we're trying to allow them ten. So we ask them to arrive two or three days before the competition begins. If people arrive late, it causes complications. Peter Donohoe didn't arrive until nearly the end of the first stage, and we had to arrange his warm-up between the afternoon and evening sessions.

On the day they are to play, each competitor is brought down by car from Tetley Hall, and must report to the green room 45 minutes before they are scheduled to play. Then he or she is taken for half an hour to a practice piano – either a grand in the main university building – or, if the competitor doesn't want to leave the building, we have an upright in a room sufficiently far away from the Great Hall – most are happy with that. Some don't want to be called until the very last minute, others prefer to have a drink before going on, comb their hair, and so on. Then Geoffrey de Keyser, the platform announcer, comes in and checks the competitor's programme and its timings. The competitor is identified by number, the pieces to be played by letters. These are put up on a board in the hall. Then the jury takes its place, Geoffrey announces the competitor's name and the pieces he or she will play, gives a signal, and we show the competitor through the door on to the platform. All the sessions are public: the audiences in the early stages were disappointing at first, but now the sessions are very well attended.

All the competitors are very tense before they play. The atmosphere in the Green Room is very quiet – we try to keep them calm. No one comes in, and there are only ever two competitors at a time in there – the one who's waiting to go on, and the one who's just come off the platform. Some just pace up and down – others sit in the corner with their Walkmen like stuffed dummies. They all have their little private foibles. One girl would only play if she could have a red piano stool. I remember one boy who perspired so much that he asked if he could be cleaned up after his first piece. Two of the ladies towelled him down, changed his shirt, and got him back on to the platform in two minutes flat! Only one girl has ever actually refused to go on at the last minute – and of course, we don't force people to play! But sometimes, we're not sure if they will play once they get on to the platform. I remember watching Junko Otake on the TV monitor in 1984 – she was ill in the second stage, and we thought she wasn't going to start. She just sat there for ages, hunched up in her black cardigan. Then she suddenly came to life.

After they've finished, there's a moment of silence, and then we receive them back in the Green Room. Then they can relax, and get rid of all the bad language if they want to. One or two are actually sick. The ladies here are very sympathetic – they calm them down. If they come back again, we remember what they liked, and try to have special little treats for them. There's an enormous sense of personal involvement. Often their drivers will take them to have coffee. Then they are either taken back to Tetley Hall, or, if they prefer, they can stay and listen to the other competitors.

On the two finals nights at the Town Hall, security is very strict when the Duchess of Kent attends. The competitors usually arrive by the side entrance, which is the quickest way to the artists' room. But sometimes, the people bringing the competitors have had great difficulty persuading the police to let them in at all! Occasionally they have had to resort to devious routes. The police wouldn't let Louis Lortie in, but fortunately the girl who was driving him knew a back entrance to the town hall, and managed to slip him in. Michel Dalberto gave us a fright. He was crazy about cars, and he insisted on driving himself down to the Town Hall. Shortly before the final was due to start, he hadn't appeared, and everyone thought he'd got lost. Then, fortunately, he turned up, as cool as a cucumber. Another competitor once turned up for the finals in

72

odd socks, and had to go back to change them. And Boris Berezovsky, in the last competition, turned up on the Saturday night in jeans! He'd played on Friday – so he thought he could wear anything. He didn't seem to realize that he'd have to go on the platform to meet the Duchess. We sent him back to change. And we couldn't get Ovchinnikov off the practice piano before his final. Simon Rattle was getting quite agitated, saying, 'Where is he?' 'He just wants another minute.' So Simon went down to the practice room, and said to Ovchinnikov, 'Come on, we can do it together!'

It's hard work, but we all do it because they're such marvellous young people. The Piano Competition is now the biggest single musical event in Leeds – it's overtaken the Festival. It has brought in international contacts, and has done so much for young musicians. For instance, wherever Noriko Ogawa [third prizewinner in 1987] goes now, she is greeted by friends. When people ask her how it is that she knows so many people everywhere, she says, 'I have so many friends because I was at Leeds!'

The citizens of Leeds are justifiably proud of the Piano Competition, which they all feel has 'put Leeds on the international map'. Denis Healey, a Leeds MP, spoke for many when he described the competition as 'one of the musical wonders of the world'.

'Fanny is responsible for the special atmosphere at Leeds,' says Joan Valentine. 'She has always evoked great loyalty and enthusiasm from everyone. She's always been prepared to turn her hand to anything that needed doing, and she can see a way to carrying her ideas through. No other competition could have been run entirely by voluntary support.'

Chapter Eight

The Fourth Competition: 1972

At the end of the 1969 competition, Fanny Waterman made an appeal for sufficient funds to enable the competition to continue. 'It is wrong that we should have to go begging for funds for an event of this calibre . . . In addition to the magnificent voluntary helpers, we do need an office and a number of secretaries.'

Another two competitions were to take place before the Leeds found a reliable sponsor: in the meantime, the burden of keeping the project afloat financially rested largely on the Friends of the Leeds International Piano Competition, who somehow managed to raise enough money to enable the 1972 and 1975 competitions to take place in the teeth of rapidly rising costs. Since the 1969 competition, the Friends' activities had included two dinners in the Senior Common Room of the University, at which Lord Boyle and Sir William Glock (jointly) and Richard Baker, the BBC newsreader, had been the speakers; a recital by Erich Gruenberg with Fanny Waterman herself at the piano; a lecture by Ernest Bradbury, a lecture–recital by Anthony Hopkins, and a profile of Beethoven by Joseph Cooper; in addition to a fashion show, a sherry-morning, and, in the Beethoven centenary year, three major Beethoven recitals at Leeds Town Hall, by the three winners of the Piano Competition.

The 1972 competition also received some financial help from Leeds Corporation and the University of Leeds, together with the Arts Council of Great Britain, the Yorkshire Arts Association, and a substantial donation from Sir Robert and Lady Dorothy Mayer. Furthermore, it acquired a permanent Royal Patron in the person of the Duchess of Kent, Chancellor of Leeds University, who has since lent it her continuing support, and has taken a very real interest in the post-Leeds progress of the competitors. As before, the president was the Lord Mayor of Leeds, while the six vice-presidents included Lord Boyle of Handsworth and Sir Roger Stevens, the Lord Savile, Sir Kenneth Parkinson (Lady Parkinson's husband), Stanley Burton and Charles Tapp.

Marion Harewood and Fanny Waterman – who in 1971 had been awarded the OBE for her services to music – remained as joint-chairmen of the Executive Committee, while the competition acquired a new administrator in Edmund Williamson, Bursar at the University, and a new secretary supported by an enlarged administrative sub-committee.

The chairman of the jury for the next three competitions was to be Edward, Lord Boyle, who in 1970 had been installed as Vice-Chancellor of Leeds University, and who was able to guarantee the competition the enthusiastic support of the university, and the use of its facilities. Formerly MP for Handsworth for more than twenty years, and a popular Minister for Education in the Macmillan government, Lord Boyle was greatly liked and respected by his former colleagues for his wide-ranging intellect, his honesty, and his kindly temperament: Harold Macmillan described him as a rare breed of politician: 'a man who had entered public life and was prepared to suffer its buffets simply for the good of the country, for the gradual improvement of society.' 'Each Vice-Chancellor brings a different approach to the position, and Edward Boyle had not only great experience of political matters, but a wide knowledge of cultural and educational affairs,' recalls his Pro-Vice-Chancellor, Professor Charles Whewell. 'He would always be able to bring some part of his experience to bear on a lecture.'

The possessor of an awesome memory, with total recall of facts and figures in many different fields, Edward Boyle exhibited a passionate enthusiasm for subjects as diverse as history, philosophy, cricket – and, his greatest love, music. Although he himself was an amateur music-lover, he came from a musical background (his father was a pianist and his mother a talented cellist). His own musical tastes were catholic, ranging from Monteverdi to Tippett, although Mozart was always his favourite composer. After his installation at the university, he quickly became a close friend of Fanny Waterman and Geoffrey de Keyser. 'Edward's knowledge of music, and piano literature in particular, was profound and professional, and made him an ideal choice as chairman of the jury,' says Fanny Waterman. 'His chairmanship added stature to the jury,' says Charles Whewell:

His political expertise enabled him to make a collection of talented individuals work together. He was a diplomat – he knew how to get the best out of people. And he had a formidable grasp of the repertoire. He also had the talent to listen very carefully and be completely absorbed in a performance.

Boyle was no mere figurehead. He insisted on being a voting chairman, with a casting vote if necessary. And he also took a close interest in the administration of the competition, regularly attending meetings, and assisting in the selection of repertoire. Before the start of the 1972 competition, he spent many hours studying the scores of the prescribed pieces, and listening to different recordings. His patience was legendary: Fanny Waterman recalls how he disliked using the bell to stop any competitor in the middle of a performance, however mediocre; and only once did he betray any exasperation, after a day when the jury had sat through eleven performances of the Third Prokofiev Sonata, seven of them in succession. 'I don't think I ever want to hear that piece again,' he remarked mildly.

He also took very seriously the responsibility of talking to the competitors afterwards, discussing their performances. Unlike many of his fellow jurors, he never needed to refer to his notes – having complete recall of not only what piece each had played, but their exact tempi, moods, tone, rubato, dynamics, and whether they had played the repeats. Not for him the *faux pas* of discussing a perform-ance of the *Appassionata* when the bewildered competitor had actually played the *Waldstein*.

The other members of the 1972 jury included Nikita Magaloff, Béla Siki, Raymond Leppard and Peter Gould, all of whom had served in 1969. Nadia Boulanger, invited at first as an 'honorary onlooker' in view of her great age (she was then eighty-four and losing her sight), insisted on taking an active part. The new members were the Polish pianist Artur Balsam, then resident in the USA; Ingrid Haebler, the Viennese pianist who specialized in Mozart; Geneviève Joy, a gradu-ate of the Paris–Conservatoire who specialized in contemporary French music, and was the wife of the composer Henri Dutilleux; Halina Czerny-Stefańska, also from Poland, a student of Cortot who had won joint first prize in the 1949 Chopin Competition; Charles Groves, who sat on the jury in his capacity as conductor of the finals; and the Romanian Valentin Gheorgiu. For the jury's convenience, eight new upright pianos were installed in their rooms at the Queens Hotel. Nikita Magaloff, who had an important recital just after the end of the competition, welcomed the gesture.

Once again, the Leeds competition attracted intense media interest: Kenneth Corden and his BBC camera crew were to film all the stages, especially the finals, for a seventy-five-minute *Omnibus* programme, to be broadcast the night after the competition, Sunday 17 September, since finals night itself unhappily coincided with the Last Night of the Proms. For the first time, the Leeds documentary would be in colour. Corden expressed the hope that the film would be 'brimful of artistic Olympian surprises . . . interesting to the normal viewer as well as to those with keyboard knowledge'.

The prizes offered to the 1972 winners were similar in cash terms to those of 1969: the Princess Mary Gold Medal and £750 (donated by Mr and Mrs Charles Tapp) for the first prize-winner; the George de Menasce Memorial Prize of £400 for the second prize; an anonymous £200 prize for the third; and five semi-final prizes of £100 offered by the National Westminster Bank, Lord Savile, Pierre de Menasce, Anthony Tapp and Ralph Yablon. Further donations to the prize-fund, as before, came from local individuals and businesses.

However, the list of engagements offered to the winner had expanded considerably: there were now some 45 dates, spread over the next two seasons, ranging from orchestral concerts – a Prom, a Royal concert with the Royal Liverpool Philharmonic in the Albert Hall, and concerts with the CBSO, RPO, Bournemouth Symphony, LSO, LPO, London Mozart Players, Northern Sinfonia, BBC Northern Symphony, Scottish National, Israel Philharmonic and Radio Philharmonic Orchestra of Amsterdam – to recitals all over the country, including the Bath, Brighton, Aldeburgh, Edinburgh, Harrogate and King's Lynn Festivals, and, most importantly, at the Queen Elizabeth Hall.

During the competition, which was to take place between 6 and 16 September, the contestants submitted themselves to four stages, rather than three. The first round comprised three works, rather than two (as in 1969). Group 1 offered a choice of sonatas by Haydn, Mozart and Beethoven; Group 2 prescribed a choice of works by Chopin; and Group 3, any Scarlatti sonata, any Debussy Étude, or any of the three Bartók studies, Op.18. Sixteen competitors would then go through to the second stage, where they had to play two pieces, one drawn from the virtuoso nineteenth-century repertory, and the other from seven major twentieth-century works.

The semi-final, in which eight competitors would take part, was for the first time divided into two sections: the first, an own-choice recital, the second, a choice of one of three chamber concertos – the Bach D minor, Mozart's K.449 in E flat, or K.414 in A – to be played with a section of the Royal Liverpool Philharmonic Orchestra, under Sir Charles Groves.

The final stage comprised the customary full-scale concerto – the choice of which was somewhat narrower in 1972 than in the previous competition. Only the last three Beethoven concertos were admitted, together with the Brahms No.1, the Chopin No.1, the Mendelssohn No.1, the Schumann, and Rakhmaninov's Third.

There was a large response to the 1972 competition, and for the

77

first time, the organizers were obliged to cut down the numbers. Of the original 188 competitors who applied, 95 were entered in the programme, of whom almost half had already won major awards elsewhere; but only 59 actually turned up to play. Again their nationalities, drawn from over different countries, ranged from Latin American to Greek. There were only six from Britain, including Penelope Blackie, Peter Hill and Christian Blackshaw, third prize-winner at the 1972 Casella Competition in Naples. Of these, only Blackie was admitted to the second round.

Among the pianists of other nationalities who successfully reached the second stage, Andras Schiff of Hungary and Mitsuko Uchida from Japan were both to achieve prominence in the 1975 competition. The others included the Israelis Daniel Adni and Carmen Or; the Lebanese Walid Howrani; the Brazilians Linda Bustani, and Cristina Ortiz (who had won the 1969 Van Cliburn Competition, was a pupil of Serkin, and already had a successful concert career in New York); Alegria Arce from Ecuador, who had been a finalist in the Leventritt Competition; Craig Sheppard from the USA, a flamboyant young pianist who had won the Young Musicians' Prize at the Busoni Competition, and had already made his New York début; Eugene Indjic, an American citizen of Yugoslav birth whose impressive list of teachers included Boulanger, Curzon, Rubinstein and Leon Kirchner, and who had taken the fourth prize in the 1970 Chopin Competition; Eva Bukojemska from Poland; Laszlo Gyimesi and Erica Lux from Hungary; Alberto Reyes from Uruguay, the American James Tocco, who had competed at Leeds before; his compatriot Alan David Marks; and the one Russian entrant, Marina Kapatsinskaya: the Soviet Union had virtually imposed a ban on its artists appearing abroad. Catherine Collard from France, winner of the 1969 Messiaen Competition in Royan, was eliminated in the first round.

Shortly before the competition began, Fanny Waterman had received a phone call from Irving Moskovitz in New York. 'Would you please book me a room at the Queens Hotel,' said Moskovitz. 'I'm coming over to Leeds, and I'm bringing the winner with me.' 'Really?' asked Fanny Waterman sceptically. 'Well, if he doesn't win, I want to be there to hear the pianist who beats him,' said Moskovitz. He was, in fact, bringing Murray Perahia, a small, dark, twenty-five-year-old American of Sephardic Jewish origin, who had studied with Jeanette Haien and at Mannes College in New York. Perahia had begun a concert career in the USA, but had never entered a major competition before. Nevertheless, his rising reputation preceded him: it was rumoured that several of his compatriots had hastily withdrawn when they heard that he was entering the Leeds. Craig Sheppard, who knew him well, confessed that his heart sank when he heard that Perahia was coming: 'I knew I would be in the position of having to try to win over someone I knew was better, and someone who was also a friend and colleague.' A couple of years before, Sheppard remembers,

three or four of us played at a private function in New York. Murray was in the audience – he had already made his New York début. I didn't play very well that evening. Afterwards, at about one in the morning, Murray sat down and played the Chopin Études. When we were in the taxi going home, I said to my friends, 'He made us look sick!'

It was originally the plan that sixteen competitors would be admitted to the second stage, but after hearing the first round, Lord Boyle announced that the number would be increased to twenty. Nikita Magaloff, who had served on all four Leeds juries so far, said prophetically of his exhausting but rewarding role: 'This year [the standard] is even higher, and artistically, I am certain we have the promise of once again the discovery of a major talent that could surprise the world.'

Perahia had been unwell during the first stage of the competition:

I was very sick – the University doctor had to look after me. They said it was a stomach bug, but I think it may have been nerves. But I didn't have to postpone any stages. I was very weak, but fortunately I didn't have to practise too much then – I had already done all the work. I just rested, and looked over the scores.

Needless to say, his name was among those of the twenty successful candidates.

Craig Sheppard had played the Chopin F minor Ballade, the Debussy Étude *pour les arpèges composés*, and Beethoven's Sonata, Op.31 No.1 in the first round. 'Fortunately, they only asked for the first and last movements of the Beethoven. I was so happy that they didn't ask for the second movement – by chance they skipped it.' In the second round, 'which didn't feel so good – it could have been my mood', he played the Liszt and Bartók sonatas. Murray Perahia, who had chosen a Scarlatti sonata, the Chopin Polonaise-fantaisie and Beethoven's Op.31 No.2 Sonata in the first round, went on in the second to play a rhythmically vital Bartók Sonata and a *Davidsbündlertänze* so deeply moving it literally reduced several members of the jury to tears. 'They went out holding handkerchiefs to their eyes,' recalls Fanny Waterman. 'It was one of those rare occasions when people are moved to tears in public – it's very embarrassing, but uncontrollable. I don't remember another occasion before or since when everyone was so moved.' Uchida also chose the *Davidsbündler-tänze*, which Gerald Larner thought 'more poetic and no less accomplished' than Perahia's. Carmen Or played the Schumann F sharp minor Sonata and the Prokofiev Third Sonata, which Cristina Ortiz coupled with *Gaspard de la nuit*, and Penelope Blackie with the Brahms *Handel* Variations. Both Blackie and Andras Schiff were eliminated at this stage.

Sheppard and Perahia went through to the next round, together with James Tocco, Eugene Indjic, Carmen Or, Daniel Adni, Mitsuko Uchida, and Linda Bustani. At this point, Ladbrokes 'opened a book' on the semi-finalists, offering 7–4 against the 'favourite', Murray Perahia, 5–12 against Sheppard, 5–1 against Uchida, 7–1 against Adni, 8–1 against Indjic, and the others at 10–1. Someone placed £1,000 on Perahia. Sheppard was furious when he found out: 'I felt like a racehorse.'

In the semi-finals, Perahia chose a Mendelssohn sonata to begin, followed by Chopin's B flat minor Sonata. Joan Chissell, who was covering the competition for *The Times*, commented on his 'stabbing intensity and exquisitely floating cantabile in the funeral march and its trio, besides haunted virtuosity in the finale', which more than made up for 'the disappointment of a rather lumpy scherzo'. One of the officials was so visibly overcome by Perahia's performance of the Chopin that it induced not tears, but a severe nosebleed. Sheppard, who played the Haydn C minor Sonata and the Three Pieces from *Petrushka*, impressed everyone with a 'dazzling and sensational display of virtuosity', according to Bryce Morrison, who heard it. 'I don't remember hearing *Petrushka* played better,' concurs Geoffrey de Keyser. But Joan Chissell considered that three other performances were outstanding – Carmen Or, Uchida's 'supersensitive Haydn and Schoenberg' and Linda Bustani's 'irresistibly effervescent Schumann Toccata'.

By this stage of the competition, the word had got around that there was a startling new talent in the making at Leeds, and several managers were beginning to swarm around Perahia. Fanny Waterman tried to put a stop to it: 'I felt it would demoralize the other competitors.' In defiance of the competition's rules that jury members were only allowed to speak to competitors at certain prescribed times, Nadia Boulanger came to see Murray Perahia after every round, to tell him how much his playing had touched her. 'I haven't been so moved in years,' she told him.

None of the semi-finalists made a good job of the chamber concerto, largely through exhaustion and under-rehearsal. Indjic played

1 Fanny Waterman as a child.

2 Fanny Waterman aged twenty-one.

3 Fanny Waterman and Geoffrey de Keyser on their wedding day in 1944.

4 (*Top*) Four of Fanny Waterman's most celebrated pupils: (left to right) Allan Schiller, Kathleen Jones, Michael Roll, Wendy Waterman.
© *Photo Press*

5 Shared moments: Fanny Waterman teaching the young Michael Roll.
© *John Searle Austin*

6 The founders of the Leeds International Pianoforte Competition: Fanny
Waterman and Marion Harewood.

7 (*Top*) Fanny Waterman and Marion Harewood with Benjamin Britten in 1963. © *Yorkshire Post*

8 Marion Harewood with the 1963 finalists: (left to right) Sebastien Risler, Armenta Adams, Michael Roll, Vladimir Krainiev. © *Yorkshire Post*

9 The winner: Michael Roll outside Leeds Town Hall after his triumph
in 1963. © *Yorkshire Post*

10 (*Top*) Michael Roll receives his prize from HRH The Princess Royal, while Sir Arthur Bliss and the Countess of Harewood look on. © *Yorkshire Post*

11 John Drummond, producer of the 1966 BBC TV documentary *Great Expectations*, talking to Charles Tapp.

12 The 1966 jury: back row (left to right) Hans Keller, Rudolf Firkušńy, Béla Siki, Gina Bachauer, Nikita Magaloff, Charles Rosen; front row: Lev Oborin, William Glock, Nadia Boulanger, Annie Fischer, Maria Curcio. © *Yorkshire Post*

13 The 1966 prize-winners with Marion Harewood and Fanny Waterman: back row (left to right), Rafael Orozco, Aleksei Nasedkin, Jean-Rodolphe Kars; front row: Viktoria Postnikova, Semyon Kruchin. © *Yorkshire Post*

14 (*Top*) Rafael Orozco receives his prize from the Countess of Harewood.

15 The first two winners of the Leeds competition: Michael Roll and Rafael Orozco in the garden at Woodgarth. © *Yorkshire Post*

16 The 1969 semi-finalists with Marion Harewood, Fanny Waterman and Cecil Mazey, the competition's administrator (centre): (left to right) Yuri Slesarev, Geoffrey Tozer, Georges Pludermacher, Boris Petrushansky, Anne Queffelec, Vadim Sakharov, Radu Lupu, Arthur Moreira-Lima.

© *Yorkshire Post*

17 Some members of the 1969 jury: (left to right) Nikita Magaloff, Gina Bachauer, Clifford Curzon, Youra Guller, Szymon Goldberg.

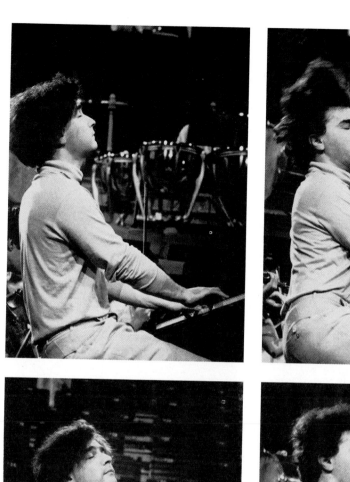

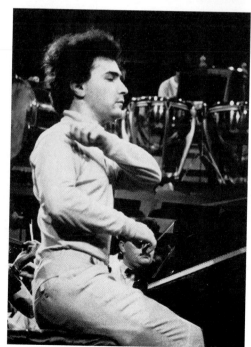

18–21 Radu Lupu in rehearsal at the 1969 competition.

22 (*Top*) Marion Harewood and Fanny Waterman at the 1969 competition.
23 Radu Lupu receives his prize from HRH The Duchess of Kent.

24 A competitor's eye-view of the Great Hall at Leeds University.

25 Some of the 1972 competitors at Tetley Hall drawing lots for the order of play, with Fanny Waterman and Marion Harewood. © *Yorkshire Post*

26 The 1972 jury at work: back row (left to right) Valentin Gheorghiu, Peter Gould, Geneviève Joy, Raymond Leppard, Béla Siki, Artur Balsam, Sir Charles Groves; front row: Mlle Dieudonné (aide to Mlle Boulanger), Nadia Boulanger, Lord Boyle, Nikita Magaloff, Ingrid Haebler, Halina Czerny-Stefańska. © *Judy Tapp*

27 Murray Perahia in rehearsal. © *Jack Perkin*

28 The 1972 finalists with Lord Boyle, the Chairman of the Jury: (left to right) Eugene Indjic, Murray Perahia, Craig Sheppard.
© *Yorkshire Post*

29 Awaiting the results, 1972.

30 Murray Perahia receives his prize from HRH The Duchess of Kent, while Lord Boyle and Marion Harewood look on. © *Yorkshire Post*

31 The Duchess of Kent with Nadia Boulanger after the award of Mlle Boulanger's honorary Doctorate of Music. © *Yorkshire Post*

a dull K.414; Sheppard a 'very mixed' K.449. 'Radu Lupu heard me play. He said, "The last movement was very good, but what happened in the first movement?" ' Even Perahia's performance of the same concerto gave little hint of his future as a great Mozart player. Ronald Crichton of the *Financial Times* thought the best performances came from Uchida, Tocco and Adni, none of whom survived to the final. The experiment was so disappointing that Fanny and Marion wisely decided to drop it in the next competition. 'It was just an idea which flew into my head – that hearing them play an intimate concerto would be an improvement, an added dimension,' says Fanny Wateman. 'But it was a very expensive experiment – we had difficulties with rehearsal time, and the contestants seemed to treat it as a less important stage. Even Perahia seemed to have got his concerto up just in time.'

Gerald Larner, writing in the *Guardian* at the semi-final stage, thought the competition 'not so exciting and the general standard not so high as last time', attributing it partly to the 'high proportion of American athleticism'. And indeed, it proved to be an all-American final – Perahia, Indjic and Sheppard – the only time that Leeds has ended up with the number of finalists originally prescribed. 'It was the only year in which the voting was so clear-cut that three finalists emerged and the rest came nowhere,' says Geoffrey de Keyser.

Craig Sheppard did not expect to get to the finals. 'I hadn't brought a dark suit – I didn't think I'd get that far. So I went to a shop and paid £44 for a suit.' Murray Perahia 'had no outcome in mind, though I thought I had talent, and I felt reasonably confident'. For the final, Perahia chose the Chopin First Concerto, while in complete contrast both Indjic (who played first), and Sheppard (who played after the interval) chose the Rakhmaninov Third. This was the first time since 1963 that the audience on Finals Night had been treated to complete concertos.

Joan Chissell felt that Indjic's Rakhmaninov seemed a little under-involved, although to her it was clear that the technical standard of the competition had been higher than ever. Perahia's Chopin exhibited 'glistening tonal delicacy', but suffered from a 'less than perfectly rounded reading, with several accidents *en route*'. Sheppard, she felt, gave a technically assured, exciting and flexible performance of the Rakhmaninov. Ronald Crichton thought that 'on the evidence of that evening alone, Sheppard's Rakhmaninov was the most satisfying performance, with stunning strength and brio', while Ernest Bradbury thought that his performance, 'robust, confident, integrated musically and generally very brilliant was . . . a severe challenge to the performance by Murray Perahia.'

81

But the final decision was not based on the concerto performances alone, and it appeared that this year there was little disagreement among the jury. 'When I think of that year, I can only see one name – it almost obliterates everything else,' recalls Fanny Waterman. Although it was not a unanimous decision, the first prize went to Murray Perahia, the second to Sheppard, and the third to Indjic, whom several critics felt should perhaps not have reached the final, given the strength of the competition. 'It was a great duel between Perahia and Sheppard,' recalls Charles Groves. 'Many people preferred the Rakhmaninov, and it was in the air that Craig should perhaps have won. But I think the decision was right. Fine pianist and artist as Sheppard is, Perahia is an outstanding musician and an exceptional artist.' Retiring by nature, Perahia himself found the implications of his success overwhelming. 'My first reaction was panic,' he recalls. 'How would I cope with it?' As he stepped on to the platform with Fanny Waterman at his side to receive his prize, he turned to her and said, 'Tell me, Miss Waterman, am I really a better pianist now than I was ten days ago?'

After the prizes had been presented, the Duchess of Kent conferred the honorary degree of Doctor of Music on Nadia Boulanger, whose eighty-fifth birthday it was that day. Fanny Waterman remembers her at that moving moment – a diminutive figure amid the flags and the lights, acknowledging the prolonged applause for one who had devoted her entire life to the nurturing of young musicians.

It was to be another year or so before Perahia returned to England to launch a brilliant career which has taken him into the top league of contemporary pianists. 'When they leave Leeds,' says Fanny Waterman,

they have their own characters, their own personalities to cope with. Getting on in a career depends on one's personality and reliability, quite apart from artistic qualities – many ingredients, many more attributes than mere pianistic skill go to make up a great artist. Nothing will ever tarnish Murray and his standards. He is a very special person.

Chapter Nine

Competitions

'We believe it is of the utmost importance for young artists to have the opportunity of hearing their musical contemporaries in an atmosphere of friendly rivalry, and we hope that the Leeds International Pianoforte Competition will provide a forum for competition of a truly "Olympic" standard.' (Foreword to the brochure of the 1963 Leeds International Piano Competition)

Over the past decade, the seemingly inexorable growth of musical competitions has stimulated a great deal of controversy among musicians. On the one hand, those who organize them – or have done well out of them – argue that winning a major competition is the only way to establish an international career by attracting the interest of a good manager and the media; while on the other hand, some musicians and teachers feel that the competitive spirit is entirely inimical to music: that while sporting achievements can be measured and compared in absolute terms, one artistic performance cannot necessarily be assessed as being 'better' or 'worse' than another.

Musical competitions, of course, have taken place for centuries. Music was almost certainly included in the 'Olympic' contests of ancient Greece, and the public comparison of song performances played a major part in the activities of the medieval Meistersinger and Minnesinger guilds, and among the French *trouvères*. Trials of performing skill, usually arranged on a friendly and informal basis, were common in the eighteenth century: such a contest between Mozart and Clementi – both brilliant keyboard players – took place in 1781, in which both were required to improvise variations and fugues in the presence of the Emperor Joseph II; and Beethoven several times tested his skill in keyboard improvisation against rivals such as Joseph Wölffl. In 1837 the two greatest pianists of the day, Liszt and Thalberg, settled their differences by a public competition, at which the proceeds were donated to charity. Liszt played his *Niobe* Fantasy; Thalberg his *Moses* Fantasy. Honour was satisfied: a draw was declared.

But the principle of organized competitions involving many competitors is largely a twentieth-century phenomenon. The first such, the Anton Rubinstein Competition, was held at five-year intervals between 1890 and 1910. Only a handful of the great international competitions existed before the Second World War, including the Ysaÿe Competition in Brussels (later renamed the Queen Elisabeth of the Belgians Competition), whose post-war winners have included Leon Fleischer (1952), Ashkenazy (1956), and Malcolm Frager (1960); the International Competition for Musical Performers in Geneva, whose first winner, in 1939, was Michelangeli, and whose laureates have included Georg Solti (1942), Ingrid Haebler, Cécile Ousset, Martha Argerich (1957), Maurizio Pollini (second prize-winner in 1957 and 1958), Ruslana Antonowicz and Christian Zacharias; the International Frédéric Chopin Piano Competition, held in Warsaw at five-year intervals since 1927, and whose winners include Lev Oborin (1927), Yakov Zak (1937), Bella Davidovich and Halina Czerny-Stefanska (1949), Vladimir Ashkenazy (second in 1955), Pollini (1960), Martha Argerich (1965), Garrick Ohlsson (1970) and Krystian Zimmerman (1975); the Liszt–Bartók Competition in Hungary, whose first winner, in 1933, was Annie Fischer, and whose winners since have included Peter Wallfisch (1948), Lev Vlasenko (1956), and David Wilde (1961); the Marguerite Long Competition in Paris, founded in 1943, whose winners include Aldo Ciccolini (1949) and Peter Frankl (1957), and the Busoni Competition, held in Bolzano, which awarded a fourth prize to Alfred Brendel at its first event in 1949, and whose subsequent winners include Jörg Demus (1956), Martha Argerich (1957), Michael Ponti (1964), Garrick Ohlsson (1966), Ursula Oppens (1969), and Louis Lortie (1984).

The post-war period saw a sudden growth in new international competitions, among them the Robert Schumann Competition in East Germany, founded in 1956; the Munich Competition, founded in 1952, whose winners have included Ingrid Haebler (1954), Christoph Eschenbach (1962), Anne Queffelec (1968), Pi-Hsien Chen (1972) and James Tocco (1973); the Pozzoli Competition, whose first and only real winner of note was Pollini in 1959; the Alfredo Casella Competition, founded in 1952; the Jaen Competition in Spain, won exclusively by Spaniards for the first decade of its existence, but whose later winners have been more international; the Vianna da Motta Competition in Portugal, founded in 1951 and won by Viktoria Postnikova in 1967; and most importantly, the Tchaikovsky Competition in Moscow, won first – astonishingly – by an American, Van Cliburn, in 1958, and whose gold medallists have since included Ogdon and Ashkenazy jointly in 1962, Gregory Sokolov in 1966, Vladimir Krainiev and John Lill jointly in 1970, Andrei Gavrilov in 1974, Mikhail Pletnev in 1978 and Barry Douglas in 1986. In 1982 no first prize was awarded, but the silver medal was shared between Peter Donohoe and Vladimir Ovchinnikov.

The Leeds Competition followed five years later, alongside another new batch – the Beethoven Competition in Vienna, founded in 1961; the Montreal Competition in 1965, won by Pogorelich in 1980; the Casagrande Competition at Terni, founded in 1966; the Clara Haskil Competition at Vevey in Switzerland, won first by Christoph Eschenbach in 1965; and the most important American competition, founded by Van Cliburn at Fort Worth in Texas in 1962. Its early winners included Radu Lupu (1966), and Cristina Ortiz (1969), but like so many competitions, its more recent winners have not achieved such great celebrity.

By the end of the 1970s, even more competitions had been added to the list: the Sydney International Piano Competition (1977); the Géza Anda in Switzerland (1979), the Gina Bachauer at Salt Lake City (1976); the University of Maryland International Piano Competition (1971); the Paloma O'Shea Competition in Santander; and another top-league competition – the Artur Rubinstein in Israel – whose first winner in 1974 was Emmanuel Ax, and whose laureates since have included Gerhard Oppitz (1977), Gregory Allen (1980), Jeffrey Kahane (1983) and Benjamin Frith (1989).

These, together with a plethora of minor competitions, meant that by 1989 there were well over forty international piano competitions of varying degrees of importance, and the number continues to rise. Not all offer large cash prizes, or international engagements, but in general pianists are encouraged to enter with the hope of establishing a career at least in that country. Many enter more than one competition during their formative years; and some, it seems, go on and on, always with the hope of achieving the first prize in one of the handful of major competitions which will actually launch their careers.

What makes young pianists submit themselves to this gruelling ordeal? Few admit to enjoying a competition; but most seem to agree with Bernard d'Ascoli, who says:

it's still the fairest way of trying to make oneself known to the public. There are other ways – through private patronage, based often on someone's sentimental judgement – but they are not as fair. The dangers of individual sponsorship are clear: the decision is often based on the fact that someone happened to meet someone else at a dinner party. Patronage achieved through another musician's judgement may work, but not based on corporate or non-musical criteria. I would much prefer to be assessed by a group of people all looking for different things from different viewpoints: a record producer will be looking for immaculate playing, a concert promoter will want someone absolutely reliable; a teacher will be looking for someone who respects the score, and another performer will look for electricity. There are now too many performers for the available work, and competitions are the least unfair way of selecting the best players.

'I tried to get my career going in the early 1980s by acting as my own publicist,' says Hugh Tinney:

But it's a hard, long slog. I got only one or two responses from over 400 mailings. Some of the people who make it very young don't enter competitions – it would only hold them back if they didn't do well. A competition depends on the quality of its winners, and that's partly a question of luck. Pianists are not always there on demand. Competitions are there ready to elevate somebody – but that person may not be there at the time.

'Earlier in the century there were certain influential people who could help a young performer to launch a career,' says Andras Schiff,

but over the last thirty years we have seen this phenomenon of the competition appear, which now seems to be the only solution. One has to do them, but once you feel it's no longer absolutely necessary, you stop. The danger is that if you win a first prize you are offered an incredible number of engagements, and if you have little experience of performing and are suddenly pushed into learning a great deal of difficult and complex repertoire, it can easily burn you out.

'I don't like the sporting element in competitions,' says Dmitri Alexeev,

and too often, the winners are the ones with the strongest nerves and good fingers, but not necessarily the most musically talented. There are certainly too many competitions now. But on balance, I feel they are beneficial. They are good preparation for the life of a concert pianist in that, in order to win, one must develop extraordinary powers of concentration to get the best out of oneself.

'The career of a solo pianist is the loneliest in the world,' says Fanny Waterman:

It takes real grit. One is always on trial: if you make a mistake it will instantly be criticized, and you have to face those hostile reviews. And life is especially tough for competition winners: many critics have a preconceived idea that you may have a good technique, but no originality. One has to take into account the past, the present and the future. The past is the foundation on which you have built your technique and your approach to the study of music. The present requires nerves of steel – the ability to walk on to the platform and forget all the technical groundwork – what you have to be able to do is to find the inspiration to produce the magic which makes the listener listen. And you are only ever as good as your last performance. A few mediocre performances can quickly erase the memory of past good ones. It's not a glamorous life. The life of a barrister or a doctor is much easier. The strain of a competition is some kind of preparation for that life – but in some ways it is a different situation. When a competitor comes on to the platform, everybody – the jury, the organizers, the audience – wants him or her to play well.

I'm often asked if young pianists can become great artists without winning a competition. Look at Radu Lupu – he'd already won the Van Cliburn, but it didn't give him the kind of career he wanted. So he entered Leeds. And Murray Perahia had already played with the New York Philharmonic. He came to England shortly before the Leeds competition, and tried to get one of the London agents to take him on. But they weren't interested. If they had been, I'm sure Murray would not have competed. The engagements which each of those artists was offered as a result of winning at Leeds gave them the opportunity to reveal their qualities. It gives the winners a chance.

'I think competitions are a necessary evil,' says Marion Thorpe:

One doesn't want to compare them with Olympic races, but life is made up of competition. If you can't cope, especially as a performer, you're not in the right job. Bad decisions do happen of course: there are always people who are eliminated when they shouldn't have been. Democracy has its drawbacks.

Whatever they feel about the advantages and disadvantages of competitions in general, all the Leeds entrants are unanimous in agreeing that the Leeds competition is one of the best. 'It's a musicians' competition, not just for the barnstormers or the acrobats,' says Bernard d'Ascoli. 'The programme rightly places its emphasis on music, not technique. The ultimate test for any pianist has to be the slow movement of a Beethoven sonata.'

Nevertheless, the relentless growth of the competition industry in the 1970s alarmed some music educationalists, who felt that young performers were being forced into a system that would not ultimately be in their best interests. Shortly before the first Leeds competition, the critic Martin Cooper (father of pianist Imogen Cooper) issued a warning that, in his opinion, the market was already flooded with 'keyboard athletes', and that 'no more competitions are needed to discover more of them'. In 1984 a working party, set up by the European String Teachers' Association (ESTA) to look into the effect of music competitions on young people, published a sharply critical report, written by Martin Cooper, based on its findings. Under the chairmanship of Rodney Slatford, the committee – which included critics, teachers, and performers, among them Alan Blyth, Joan Dickson, Christopher Elton, Hans Keller, and Nannie Jameson – pointed out that the original meaning of the word 'competition', 'to strive or seek together for a common objective', had instead come to imply the 'confrontation of antagonistic forces, which can only achieve their objectives at another's expense. The common activity, the performance of the music, is not, therefore, the real objective of the seeking and striving, it is merely the vehicle for the true aim which is to be chosen as a winner.' While noting that the nature of society is inevitably competitive, the report pointed out that all activities cannot be transformed into contests without 'essentially altering their nature. When musical performances are asked to produce "results", to produce winners and losers, [they] become a sport . . . which exploits music for non-artistic purposes. Furthermore, the exploitation of music leads with grim inevitability to the exploitation of musicians, especially young ones.'

The ESTA report went on to discuss the impossibility of measuring achievement in terms of musical performance – 'art, like humanity, is individual and immeasurable and the conclusion must be drawn that, in the sense of "winning and losing", artists cannot compete artistically'; and drew attention to the need for a long period of sustained artistic development in a suitable environment:

Young performers need playing experience, but they need it in circumstances which will not expose them to a glare of publicity for which they are emotionally unprepared and to a flood of concerts for which they are unready and which will drain them of the time and enthusiasm for the kind of serious study which should occupy the greater part of their student lives . . . Competitions, because their sponsors usually want a single winner, tend to cultivate 'star-consciousness' . . . The constant demand for more winners means that many 'shooting-stars' will be created, whose light will vanish for ever as soon as a successor appears.

The report feared that as a result, some young musicians would suffer the 'personal and professional disaster of instant glory followed by total oblivion', while others would suffer from a decrease in opportunities. 'Too little work for most musicians means far too much for a few, subjecting those few to intolerable strain, which leaves them no time for rest, reflection and further growth, and which cannot fail to have a deleterious effect on them as musicians and people.'

Having drawn attention to the dangers inherent in mass media coverage for non-altruistic reasons, and the fact that the mushrooming of competitions meant that such events 'are in competition with each other for the limited number of available contestants, offering ever more glittering prizes', the report went on to sum up the 'pros and cons', concluding that the disadvantages outweighed the benefits – which it listed as 'playing experience', 'an objective for hard work', 'the stimulation of contact with fellow musicians', 'advice from notable teachers and performers', and 'professional advancement'.

The report reserved its most stringent criticism for the BBC's Young Musician of the Year Contest – 'a degrading musical equivalent of the Miss World Contest', in which 'young musicians are being exploited for the sake of audience ratings'; but deplored the current lack of alternative ways of advancing a career in music. While concluding that 'competition in music is not only inappropriate but can also be exceedingly harmful and therefore, ideally should play no part in musical life,' the committee accepted that that viewpoint was hopelessly idealistic under present circumstances, and offered some suggestions for damage limitation. These included a recommended minimum age-limit of twenty-four for what it termed 'senior events . . . which aim to fill the winner's diary', such as the Leeds competition.

Following the publication of the ESTA report, Fanny Waterman was moved to respond in letters to *The Times* and the *Yorkshire Post*, pointing out that the Leeds competition was 'only open to professional pianists who are ready to embark on a career and fulfil the many important engagements which follow. . . . The LIPC has no "losers" ', continued Fanny Waterman,

because each competitor benefits from participating in the event. The twenty sessions provide a platform for pianists to perform before distinguished and influential musicians . . . music critics, representatives of music clubs, orchestras, impresarios, and the BBC . . . In our competition, the 'winner does not take all' and at least eighteen pianists from the Leeds competition have had national and international careers with their names constantly before the public. If, as the ESTA report implies, competitions damage aspiring young competitors, why did artists like Artur Rubinstein, Clifford Curzon, Nadia Boulanger, Gina Bachauer, and so many great artists return again and again to sit on juries for ten hours a day, for two weeks, without fee . . . ? Surely they would not have been associated with 'media-conscious gladiatorial encounters'.

Competitors and jurors alike have strong feelings about the nature of competitions. Sir William Glock agrees with the essence of the ESTA report:

When you are twenty or twenty-two, it's very damaging to your development as a musician and an artist to be suddenly confronted with numerous engagements, requiring a large repertoire that you probably won't know, the expectancy of very high standards, and everyone pushing you. I would say 'never come first'. Why have competitions? The whole thing quickly becomes very materialistic, run for the benefit of the media. And the public loves it. It appeals to people's gladiatorial instincts. You're not competing if you're playing a Festival Hall concert. And why this rush to make a world-wide reputation? Schnabel and Serkin never won a competition. Rakhmaninov was the greatest pianist I ever heard, but he never won a competition either. If someone is profoundly good, he or she will come through anyway.

'All piano competitions are fine in their earlier, pristine years,' says Raymond Leppard,

but then some form of sclerosis creeps in. I think it comes with the invasion of publicity – once the media moves in. Leeds was originally a young competition for young players – it had a friendly sportiveness about it. Some good people came out, and had a leg up in their careers. But even by its second year, it had become the equivalent of winning the Derby. I think this has a terrible effect. Suppose you are a young British pianist, wanting to enter. You play badly in the first round, and you get thrown out. Your career may be finished. So the young British pianists – the inexperienced ones that the competition was supposed to be helping – were exposed to dangers they dared not take. So they didn't enter. I think it's self-defeating to give a lot of concerts to a young professional.

I no longer approve of competitions. I think they have entirely lost their original impulse. Their aims should be lower – the idea should be to encourage young pianists. It's sad, because the original idea is altruistic.

'Competitions are a valuable experience whether you win or lose,' says John Lill, who has experienced both triumph and disaster in such events:

If you go into them with the right motives, and with experience, they can be of help. Every performance you give is like a competition in miniature: being under continuous scrutiny from critics and the audience is part of the job. But there is a darker side to them: we live in a competitive world, and everyone gets very excited about competitions. It appeals to their basest instincts, giving them an inverted pleasure in seeing someone defeated. And competitions are destined to make a lot of money for promoters and agents who want to push the latest 'label' which will last for a couple of seasons only. They can just be a temporary passport to fame – until the next winner comes along, and the previous one finds himself dropped. If a young winner is truly prodigious, and has a large repertoire, then he may survive. But if his repertoire is limited – the demands on him may cause him to panic. You should not aim for short-term gain in this profession: you come under very great pressure from all sides; and you must be the master of your own mind. Your priorities should be the deeper, long-term aspects of music.

'Music is so much about gradual evolution, a gradual growth,' says Bryce Morrison, who has prepared many students for competitions,

that if you are to survive, that growth should not be interrupted. It is said that a competition prepares you for the tough world outside, but I think that misses the point. If you win, you are suddenly given an enormously accelerated push which thrusts you into an artificial prominence. One day you are nobody, the next, you are a great celebrity. It's very difficult to stabilize through such an experience, and that's why some winners disappear from the scene. Instead of offering a glittering list of prizes and engagements – and some competitions (the Van Cliburn, for instance) offer prizes such as a gold watch, which only encourages an atmosphere of material greed – I feel that a competition should offer its winners money to be used for scholarships or for further study with a teacher of the pianist's choice. And there should be some engagements – but not with the Berlin Philharmonic!

'The public has become lazier about making decisions,' says Peter Donohoe, who also has experienced both sides of the coin, and is now one of the most vociferous critics of the competition system:

They no longer have to use their own ears: they expect to be told what to think by the critics and the record companies. And the greatest evil of competitions is that they tell the public what to think – who is the best, who is second-best, and so on. But I think that while competitions are inevitable and inescapable – expertism is a growth industry – public awareness and that of the record companies is changing, especially over the last three years. The novelty of the rock-star image of the soloist, which a competition win can create, is dying away. And agents are becoming more cautious: they have to make a living and they can't afford to back the wrong horse. One can no longer take a name out of a hat and present it to the public on the basis of an outrageous personality, good looks, and so on. They are beginning to see that such an investment is a short-term one. The development to greatness has to be slow – a great artist must hold himself back. Competitions can suddenly thrust a young player into the limelight – then if he gets a few bad reviews, his record sales drop, and he is destroyed just as instantaneously. The really great successes are those who hold themselves down, and can remind themselves who they are. It took Arrau a lifetime to develop his artistry. Had he been treated like a rock-star, denied a proper childhood, his personality might have suffered irreparable damage.

'There's nothing wrong with competitions as such,' says Jonathan Dunsby, now responsible for the formation of young musicians' careers at the University of Reading:

Yes, there's a danger that successful youngsters will be exploited, but that's not a sufficient argument against competitions. One can't turn one's face against our competitive society. Someone who is going to be conspicuous has to be an exceptional person, and a parent or teacher should be able to identify those who are exceptional and still can enjoy it. As a teenager, I was put under incredible stress – travelling, performing, coping with academic work at the same time – but I didn't resent it. Anyone who goes in for a competition has to be competitive by nature, and you have to be prepared to take the rough with the smooth. Of course juries can make mistakes, and one can always play less than one's best. If you feel that losing will put your career in a position of great jeopardy, then you should not take the risk of entering. It's difficult to say whether losing incurs any lasting professional damage in the long term.

A competition is a highly-wrought emotional experience. It's like a bullfight – and like any bloodsport, it draws the crowds. But I do think the Leeds competition has played a large part in upgrading the British school of pianists – Shelley, Fowke, Stott and so on. Some of them have been through the competition, others have been more subtly influenced by it. If the Leeds competition can bring together Alexeev, Schiff, Uchida, then it's good that native players can say to themselves, 'This is the real thing. Well, I'm not that good.' Better that than pursuing a chimera.

Leeds is suffering the 'curse' of Perahia and Lupu. After them, everyone is waiting for the next one. They may have to wait a long time. Some of their most brilliant successors may not enter the Leeds. It's a lot for any winner to live up to. But the longer the series continues, the more likely it is that something truly spectacular will emerge.

What do the two most famous Leeds winners feel about competitions? 'It's not an essential way to start a career,' says Radu Lupu:

It's a forced way. The good thing about competitions is that one is immediately launched on the circuit, one can go through barriers which it would otherwise be difficult to surmount. If a winner is lucky enough to survive the pressure, then he will have a career. But there are far too many competitions nowadays – the whole thing seems to be on an industrial level of 'pianist-makers'. Few people now have great respect for them: there's more cynicism. The system of admittance is now so rigorous that it seems we're trying to breed a super-race of pianists. What about the unknown pianist with great talent? People like Brendel, Barenboim, Kissin, didn't have to win a competition to start a career.

But Leeds does look after all its prize-winners: many people who have won prizes there – and some who didn't – have still managed to have good careers. That's not true elsewhere. One has to be realistic, and there are many positive things about the Leeds competition. It has history and prestige, and one hopes that many more good pianists will come. But if you have such a positive asset, it must maintain its self-respect. I hope that it will not feel obliged to award the first prize every year.

Murray Perahia also has ambivalent feelings about the value of competitions:

I wish there were other ways of establishing a career. There are many kinds of artists that the public should hear who are not competition artists – but it's very difficult to be heard unless you win a competition. Competitions are useful and beneficial, but I just wish there were other opportunities.

'I hate competitions,' says Fanny Waterman (who is nevertheless known as the 'Competition Queen'), 'but what are the alternatives? I have suggested to some distinguished musicians that it would be a good idea if the main London orchestras held annual auditions for young players; then the orchestra could choose which ones they wanted as soloists. But nothing has happened, so we're left with competitions.'

'There must be alternative ways of helping young people to make careers wihout putting them through these sporting events,' says Sir William Glock. He, and several others, have suggested establishing a system based on the Hungarian Interforum, which offers a 'showcase' at which young performers are invited to play before an audience of critics, managers, record producers and so on, but without any element of competition. A similar impetus governed the Leeds National Musicians' Platform, which Fanny Waterman and Marion Thorpe tried to establish in the 1970s. But they soon found that a non-competitive event failed to attract adequate audiences and interest from the media. Similar events held in the USA have encountered the same problem – no one turns up. Anthony Phillips, a London manager who formerly ran the Van Cliburn Competition, is of the opinion that competitions are still the best way of persuading people in the 'music business' to listen to young performers at the outset of their careers.

Simply from a music business point of view, only the competition context seems to be the right one, and all the others lack the mixture of concentrated talent, showbiz, gladiatorial excitement and superheated critical evaluation . . . The winner is what sponsors, the media and the music business want, and if you take it away you are left with a much less powerful and effective machine to do the required job.

But for Fanny Waterman, the ultimate justification for the Leeds competition is contained in three letters, one written to her in 1983 by Rudolf Serkin, which reads:

Dear Fanny
Thank you for the announcement of the Leeds competition. You have me wrong – I don't disapprove of competitions at all, and

especially the Leeds has very much helped deserving artists who are now recognized for their great artistry.

I only feel sad and sorry for the young colleagues who have to go through such nervous strain, which is quite different from the rather positive tension in performance. I understand that you personally help very much to make it a wonderful human experience for many of the young artists.

I am sending you my kindest greetings, best wishes and congratulations.
Devotedly, Rudi

another which Murray Perahia sent her after his Leeds victory:

25 September 1972

Dear Miss Waterman
I wish to thank you so much for the very thoughtful and considerate way you ran and organized the competition, and for your very personal and human interest, not only in myself but, I think, in all the competitors.

I think you very much succeeded in your goal of taking the competitive part out of the competition. And as a result, both the musical motivation and direction (shown both by the choice of repertoire and also the choice of jury) of the competition, was one that I regard very highly.

It was also wonderful speaking to you & I look forward to our next meeting.
Best regards,
Murray Perahia

and the last from Clifford Curzon, after hearing a recital by Murray Perahia shortly after he had won the 1972 competition:

What greater and more touching pleasure is there in life than giving a young and beautiful talent a little lift in the direction (only, for we can never reach them) of the stars?

Chapter Ten

The Fifth Competition: 1975

Since Radu Lupu's and Murray Perahia's rapid rise to stardom as two of the world's finest young pianists, the reputation of the Leeds Competition had correspondingly soared into the top league: many aspiring entrants had now come to regard it as the premier competition. But its future in 1975 was far from secure: the cost of the next competition looked set at around £20,000, an increase of almost 30 per cent over 1972. Once more the Friends of the Competition, chaired since Lady Parkinson's retirement two years earlier by Edward Davies, helped to raise enough money to run the 1975 event. Since Lord Boyle's involvement, the competition's ties with the University of Leeds had been strengthened: the Friends had organized three fund-raising concerts in the Great Hall, two of them joint promotions with the university's Music Department, then under the professorship of Alexander Goehr. Goehr, however, was no great lover of competitions. 'Leeds would be simpler to run if you started all the competitors off together and gave the prize to the one who finished first,' he once remarked.

The Friends of the LIPC also supported a new venture of Fanny Waterman and Marion Thorpe, designed to further the careers of young musicians other than pianists. This was the Leeds National Musicians' Platform, a non-competitive event which was first held in November 1974. Although only the final rounds took place in Leeds, the preliminaries being held at the Purcell Room on London's South Bank, the idea was, as with the piano competition, to give young performers – both soloists and chamber music partnerships – the chance to perform in public under conditions that would attract potential managers and concert promoters. The participants were accommodated by Leeds families, and a distinguished panel of judges (termed assessors) was assembled by Fanny and Marion.

The National Musicians' Platform took place three times – in 1974, 1977 and 1980. Lloyds Bank offered to sponsor the second and third of these; and each performer who took part received a fee. Those who appeared in the final concert received a further fee. But although the initial idea was to give as many young performers as possible the chance to appear in public, rather than to create 'winners and losers', the competitive element could not be kept out for long. For the 1977 event, Lloyds Bank donated a 'prize' of £500 for the 'best performance in the final concert', together with a further 'prize' of £300 for a performance of outstanding musicianship; and by 1980, the event had more or less turned into a full-blown competition. Renamed the Leeds National Competition for Musicians, it rivalled the Piano Competition in scope – with a massive jury of thirty distinguished musicians under the chairmanship of Lord Boyle, semifinals in the University's Great Hall and a final involving an orchestral performance with the Philharmonia under Vernon Handley in the Town Hall; trophies and four substantial cash prizes plus an accompanists' prize for the winners; and an impressive list of engagements at music clubs and festivals all round the country.

But while the principle behind the Leeds National Competition for Musicians was sound, it became clear in 1980 that the fledgeling offspring of the piano competition was growing at such an alarming rate that it threatened to overturn the nest. Firstly, the jury was given the impossible task of selecting four finalists from among seven woodwind players, two cellists, two violinists, two piano trios and six singers; and then the introduction of an orchestral final, rather than recitals (as in 1974 and 1977) created its own problems. The 1980 finalists were the clarinettist Michael Collins (who eventually emerged the winner), the baritone Peter Savidge, the oboist Andrew Knights, and the Trio Zingara, who were obliged by the nature of the event to perform the Beethoven Triple Concerto. This irrationality attracted considerable criticism in the press: writing in The *Financial Times*, Arthur Jacobs commented that, 'unless a competition restricts itself to comparing like with like, under conditions which are openly declared and are seen to be observed, its authority cannot be strong.' Furthermore, it proved impossible to keep such a huge panel of busy judges together at Leeds for the duration of the competition, since many had concerts or other engagements elsewhere; and despite the sponsorship of Lloyds, it became clear to Fanny Waterman and Marion Thorpe that the new event was going to prove too much of a drain on the resources – both financial and personal – which were needed to maintain the piano competition. So despite the achievement of having exposed such young and subsequently successful artists as Melvyn Tan, Susan Daniel, Philippa Davies, Malcolm Messiter, Vanya Milanova, Eugene Sarbu, Michael Collins, William

Shimell, David Owen Norris and Caroline Dale, among many others, the experiment has not been repeated since.

The 1975 Piano Competition once more took place under the patronage of the Duchess of Kent, and with the assistance of Leeds City Council, Leeds University, the Arts Council of Great Britain, and the Yorkshire Arts Association. Few administrative changes had taken place since 1972, and the committee was once more chaired jointly by Fanny Waterman and Marion, by then Mrs Jeremy Thorpe.

Under Lord Boyle's chairmanship, the jury comprised Gina Bachauer, Artur Balsam, Béla Siki and Sir Charles Groves, who had all served in 1972; Charles Rosen, a member of the stormy 1966 jury; and six new members: Pál Kadosa, a Czech-born pianist who had consistently championed contemporary music, and who since 1945 had been on the staff of the Budapest Academy; Mindru Katz, the Romanian pianist; Gerald Moore, the distinguished British accompanist, partner of Schwarzkopf, de los Angeles and Fischer-Dieskau; Phyllis Sellick, a pupil of Isidor Philipp and wife of Cyril Smith (Fanny Waterman's former teacher), with whom she often gave piano duet recitals; Rosalyn Tureck, the leading Bach exponent of her generation, influential pedagogue, founder of the International Bach Society, author of *An Introduction to the Performance of Bach*, and performer on a wide range of early and modern keyboard instruments; and Mikhail Voskressensky, the USSR's chosen juror, from the Tchaikovsky Conservatoire.

As before, the 1975 competition offered a range of prizes, but this time, perhaps as a result of the experience of 1972, when so many fine players had to be eliminated at the semi-final stage, it was decided that six finalists, rather than three, would go through. As usual, the Princess Mary Gold Medal, and a cash prize of £750 (donated by Mr Charles Tapp) went to the first-prize-winner; the second prize, the George de Menasce Memorial Prize, was worth £400; the third, donated by Harry and Jacqui Hurst, £300; the three competitors placed joint-fourth would each receive £200; while the two eliminated semi-finalists would each receive £100. As before, there were twelve second-stage prizes of £50.

Apart from the spread of orchestral and recital engagements for the winners, the 1975 competition offered more international dates: concerts at the Adelaide Festival, with the Amsterdam Philharmonic, the Chicago Symphony Orchestra, and for concert agencies in Belgium, Holland, Japan, Norway, and Vienna. Leeds was clearly attracting interest from all over the world as an event of international prestige. In addition, EMI expressed interest in offering a recording contract to the winner.

The final night of the 1972 competition had taken place amid a tremendous gale. 'We could hear noises from the roof of the Town Hall,' Fanny Waterman recalls,

and although we didn't know it at the time, we had been in considerable danger. So for quite some time in the mid-1970s, the Town Hall was closed for repair. We decided, therefore, to hold the semi-final and final stages of the next competition at the Grand Theatre, which fortunately could accommodate a larger audience than the Town Hall. We all thought it would be marvellous – a great improvement.

This year, for the first time, there were to be two Finals Nights, on Friday 12 and Saturday 13 September, giving each of the six finalists the opportunity to play a complete concerto with the Royal Liverpool Philharmonic Orchestra, under Sir Charles Groves. Since the date of the final this year did not coincide with the Last Night of the Proms, BBC Television arranged to broadcast the whole of the Saturday concert live from the theatre, together with recorded highlights of the previous evening's finalists. In addition, all the semi-final recitals and the complete Friday night final were recorded for future transmission on Radio 3.

The repertoire for the 1975 competition remained similar to that of 1972, with one or two minor changes. The first stage again required three pieces drawn from a first group consisting of Bach, Haydn, Beethoven or Schubert; a second group consisting of several Chopin impromptus or scherzos, Schumann's *Papillons* or the Brahms Variations in D, Op.22 No.1; and a third group consisting of any Scarlatti sonata, any Debussy Étude or any Bartók study, Op.18. Twenty competitors would then go through to the second round, in which they would be required to offer two large-scale virtuoso pieces, one of which was drawn from an enlarged and rather more adventurous choice of twentieth-century repertoire.

This year the semi-finalists' choice was rather restricted: they had to include a specified piece selected from one of three Chopin nocturnes, three Brahms intermezzi, the Schubert Impromptu in G flat, D.899 No.3, or the Duetto in A flat from Mendelssohn's *Songs without Words*, Op.38 No.6. 'The idea was to counteract the fact that nowhere else in the competition did contestants have to play a piece of a contemplative nature,' explained Fanny Waterman. In addition, they were not allowed to repeat any piece they had played already (all previous recitals had allowed the repetition of any one piece from a former round – but presumably the jury felt that one performance of a piece was often sufficient). The final list of concertos comprised the Bach D minor, Mozart's K.466 in D minor, K.491 in C minor and K.503 in C, Beethoven's First and Fourth, the Schumann, the Grieg, the Britten and Prokofiev's Third.

The response to the competition was enormous – over 190 prospective candidates applied from 38 different countries, but were whittled down to 98. As always, there were last-minute withdrawals, but 72 competitors (rather more than in earlier years) actually arrived in Leeds. Several who had entered previous Leeds competitions re-applied: Penelope Blackie, who had reached the second stage in 1972; Daniel Epstein and Alan Marks from the USA; Erika Lux and Andras Schiff from Hungary; John O'Conor from Ireland; Alberto Reyes from Uruguay; Geoffrey Tozer from Australia, who had made such an impression as a fourteen-year-old in the 1969 competition; and Mitsuko Uchida from Japan, a semi-finalist in 1972. The Russians were back with a three-strong entry: Dmitri Alexeev, who had taken second prize at the 1969 Marguerite Long Competition in Paris, and first prize at the Enescu Competition in Bucharest, Evgeny Koroliev and Elena Kuznetsova.

Among the other entrants were Yitkin Seow from Singapore, who had studied at the Menuhin School and the Royal College of Music, won the BBC Piano Competition in 1974, and had just made his London début as a concerto soloist; Steven de Groote, the brilliant South African prodigy who was to win the 1977 Van Cliburn Competition; Michael Houstoun, from New Zealand, who had won third prize at the 1974 Van Cliburn Competition, and Myung-Whun Chung, from South Korea, brother of the violinist Kyung-Wha Chung and the cellist Myung-Wha Chung, and a silver medallist at the 1974 Tchaikovsky Competition.

The British entrants included Antony Peebles, Peter Hill, Philip Fowke (who had already made his London début, and was to become a pupil of Rosalyn Tureck the following year), and Jonathan Dunsby, who had already won the Commonwealth Cup, and a bronze medal at Geneva, and was currently studying for his Ph.D at Leeds, under Alexander Goehr. He was the only British contestant to reach the second round in 1975, and the experience decided the course of his subsequent career:

The 1975 competition was a very big turning point for me. The decision to enter at all was a major one – as a local boy and one of Fanny's more successful pupils, I couldn't do it without being noticed. I came within a whisker of getting to the semi-final. That competition was one of the best in depth. I remember listening to the German boy Gerhard Oppitz in the semi-final – he was a big player, he played Brahms – the sort of thing I was doing. I thought then – this is what these guys do all the time – they're not doing PhDs, they're totally committed to it. Afterwards, Béla Siki asked me to go to Seattle as his teaching assistant. For a young would-be pianist, that was a very exciting opportunity, something I wouldn't have got otherwise. So I was all set up to go on a Harkness Fellowship, but then I decided not to go to Seattle, but to Princeton instead, and to see whether I could do without that kind of life.

The other pianists who reached the second stage included Oppitz and his compatriot Robert Benz; the Americans Marks, Alan Weiss and Gerald Robbins; Pierre Reach and Pascal Devoyon from France; Seta Tanyel from Austria; Elza Marchand from Poland; Alexeev and Kuznetsova from the USSR; Boris Berman from Israel; Lux, Schiff, O'Conor, Houstoun, Tozer, Uchida and Myung-Whun Chung.

Charles Rosen, who was on the jury, particularly regretted the elimination of Steven de Groote in the first round: 'He was a controversial player, very individual. Some members of the jury hated his playing, but he was the kind of pianist who should have got through – the sort who puts backs up, but interests some members of the jury too.' Rosen also admired Dunsby's playing: 'He was a fine musician, and he played extremely well, but his playing didn't give the impression of real physical pleasure.'

The eight semi-finalists selected to give a recital at the Grand Theatre were Alexeev, Benz, Berman, Chung, Devoyon, Houstoun, Schiff and Uchida. Andras Schiff was the first to play in the semi-final. 'He played the Chromatic Fantasy and Fugue better than anyone else could have done,' recalls Charles Rosen. 'And his Brahms *Handel* Variations were stunning. He overstepped the time-limit in his performance of *Papillons*, but no one could bear to stop him. It was the best performance of *Papillons* I have ever heard – he followed all the directions in the score – but with imagination.' Nonetheless, some listeners – and some members of the jury – found Schiff's interpretations, especially of Bach, distinctly unconventional. Fanny Waterman, however, liked Schiff's playing:

It was authoritative – his method of starting ornaments on the beat, for example, gave a marvellous edge to the rhythm. He did certain things – like playing some passages an octave higher than written – that perhaps made Rosalyn Tureck sit up, but he was entirely his own man. His Bach interpretations combine both schools of thought – sometimes he makes the piano sound like a harpsichord, but at others he values the potential that a full-size Steinway can offer. He's a purist, yet a romantic, compassionate one. He can play staccato quavers and semiquavers with better articulation than most people I've ever heard. Hearing him was an inspirational experience.

Schiff was followed by Mitsuko Uchida, who chose an all-Chopin programme, giving an immaculate performance of the F major and A minor Etudes, the E major Nocturne and 'some moments in the B minor Sonata that held the audience spellbound with their poised serenity', according to the critic of the *Yorkshire Post*. Bryce Morrison was in the audience. 'She threw them off with marvellous, musicianly ease,' he recalls. 'It was superlative playing. Radu Lupu, who was there, said "My God, I wish I could play Chopin like that!" '
Then Alexeev – at twenty-eight the oldest competitor – dazzled the jury with a brilliant technical display in the Third Étude and Sixth Sonata of Prokofiev ('only a Russian could play them like that,' said Morrison) and – a last-minute change of programme – a sensational Liszt Sonata. Up to this point, Chung had been the bookies' clear favourite, but Alexeev's amazing semi-final round changed the situation dramatically. His 'lovely singing tone' won general praise, as did his astonishing pyrotechnics and his projection. The last to play that evening, Robert Benz, faced a more intellectual challenge in Beethoven's Op.111 Sonata.
The second batch of semi-finalists also concluded their evening's recitals with the same sonata, played in a 'brave and well-controlled' way (according to Gerald Larner) by Michael Houstoun, preceded by two accounts of the Chopin B flat minor Sonata (by Chung and Devoyon), two memorable performances of *Gaspard de la nuit* (by Houstoun and Devoyon), and a lively Prokofiev Seventh Sonata, played by Boris Berman. Rosen was extremely impressed by Devoyon's technical brilliance. 'In the first round, Michael Houstoun (a very cultivated player) played the last étude of Debussy about as well as it could have been played. Then along came Devoyon, and played the same piece about twice as fast, but still perfectly! It was not necessarily better, but it was more spectacular.'
Berman and Benz were eliminated at the semi-final stage, leaving Schiff, Uchida, Alexeev, Chung, Devoyon and Houstoun to dispute the final placings. For years, everyone had complained vociferously about the unsatisfactory acoustic of the Town Hall. Now that of the Grand Theatre came under heavy fire, from competitors and listeners alike. Andras Schiff found it very dry, while Radu Lupu, who came to listen, thought it 'terrible'. Fanny Waterman was disappointed. 'Somehow it lacked atmosphere – the semi-finals and finals of the

competition didn't sound nearly as good there as opera performances.'

At this stage, the result still hung very much in the balance: all six semi-finalists had each received no less than six votes, so a clear-cut winner looked unlikely. Once again, Schiff found himself in the unenviable position of playing first in the Friday evening final, with the Bach D minor Concerto (the only time Bach has ever been chosen at a Leeds final). And as in the semi-final, he was followed by Uchida, who had chosen the Schumann. The concluding performance of the first evening's finals would be Alexeev's Prokofiev Third Concerto. On the Saturday night, two of the finalists, Chung and Devoyon, both chose Beethoven's Fourth, while Houstoun, like Alexeev, played the Prokofiev No.3. As luck would have it, this evening, which was fully televised by the BBC, proved less interesting than the Friday night, of which only edited highlights were shown. Chung's performance, under the pressure of the occasion, failed to come up to expectations; Michael Houstoun, while possessing a 'streamlined technique' according to Joan Chissell of *The Times*, 'only read what was on the lines' of his Prokofiev, 'not between them'. Chissell found Devoyon's 'fresh, strong, buoyant' Beethoven the highlight of the Saturday concert, 'not least for the deeper undercurrents of feeling he touched without sentimentality'.

Of the previous night's performances, Joan Chissell considered that Schiff 'risked his life with this jury by transposing parts of Bach's D minor concerto up an octave', but she felt that his Bach would remain one of her indelible memories 'for characterization and colour all achieved . . . within so stylishly crystalline a sound-world'. Uchida, according to Chissell, played the Schumann with 'acute sensitivity, grace and poetry'. Gerald Larner (writing in the *Guardian*) thought her performance 'thoroughly distinctive. In spite of the surprisingly big sound, it was a very feminine, profoundly sentimental performance, too emotional for comfort, in fact, though remarkably well sustained and quite inspired in the coda of the last movement.' Bryce Morrison thought that the tension of the moment had suddenly got to her: 'I felt her Schumann was disappointing.' Fanny Waterman, however, thoroughly enjoyed Uchida's performance. 'She played with compassion and tenderness. I loved watching her. A woman can play like a man, but a man can never play like a woman.'

But Alexeev, according to Larner,

gave a quite remarkable performance of Prokofiev's Third Concerto. It was too loud at times, but usually his colouring was more remarkable for its extraordinary subtlety, for the blend and balance he achieved with the orchestra. Some of the things he attempted and pulled off were amazing, but it was no show-off interpretation: it was an exhilarating celebration of rhythm and of the many-sided character of the piano.

Larner thought that the performance would 'remain a legend at Leeds for its technical heroism and its stylistic understanding'.

For once, there were few disagreements among the jury, at least as to the first prize. Alexeev was unanimously declared the winner (indeed, he had received a unanimous vote at each stage), with Uchida second (many critics at the time, including Larner, felt that that was a surprise: 'it remains to be seen,' said Joan Chissell, 'whether she will develop matching technical strength and breadth of style to meet the demands the prize will impose'), Schiff joint-third (a great disappointment to him) with Devoyon; and Chung and Houstoun joint-fourth. 'It was fantastic to be the winner at Leeds among such good pianists,' said Alexeev, who had already encountered Chung and Schiff in the previous year's Tchaikovsky Competition, where they had both been more highly placed than he.

Although Alexeev was immediately offered many engagements, including a Festival Hall début with Antal Dorati and the RPO, as a result of his win, the political tensions which existed at that time between the USSR and the West meant that he was unable to obtain permission to fulfil many of them in the forthcoming seasons. Since *glasnost*, however, he has been able to enjoy a major career in the West. But in the early years, Uchida, Schiff and Devoyon were able to capitalize on the winner's absence, and all three, particularly Schiff and Uchida, have enjoyed international celebrity since 1975.

Chapter Eleven

The Juries

A competition is only as good as its jury. Since it began, the Leeds has been fortunate in assembling juries of international calibre, all of whom have so far given their services voluntarily – a major difference from other international competitions. The 1990 jury will be the first in the history of the Leeds to be paid.

'Leeds was the only competition that didn't pay its jury,' says Fanny Waterman:

We were always grateful to people who gave up their time, knowledge and expertise to come and listen. At first they felt it was a mission – they owed it to young people. But now there are many more competitions, and many more demands on performers' time – it is getting ever more difficult to tie people down. Gina Bachauer once turned down a tour worth many thousands of pounds because she had already committed herself to our competition and she felt she couldn't let us down. But other people have had similar offers, and have made different decisions. It's most unsatisfactory having to fill gaps at the last moment, particularly since we advertise the names of the jury in advance, unlike many other competitions. We like to let the competitors know who is going to judge them, so that they can decide whether they think they're going to get a fair hearing. We feel it's not fair if a competitor finds himself having to play for a judge who may have heard him previously, and whom he knows positively dislikes his playing.

The major criteria for selecting a jury at Leeds have remained in accordance with Marion Thorpe's early definition, of 'finding pianists one admired and enjoyed listening to, and whose judgement one could trust'. However, Fanny Waterman now aims to produce a balanced jury drawn from four categories – pianists, pedagogues, critics and the media – all of whom she feels could play an important role in supporting and developing the careers of young players. What is her starting point?

They should be fine musicians so far as piano playing and the repertoire is concerned. They should be, or have started off as, performers themselves and have lived the life of a musician so that they can understand the stresses and strains involved. A jury member who couldn't appreciate the difficulty of a young pianist coming on and giving of his or her best in the first five minutes would not be sensitive to the situation.

They must also be beyond reproach so far as integrity is concerned. We try to choose people who, if they knew a competitor personally, wouldn't let any preconceived opinion affect their judgment at the time. Naturally, now that there are so many competitions, we can't possibly guarantee that they won't have heard some of the competitors before. You do hear them saying, 'I heard so-and-so at this competition, and she's absolutely wonderful/absolutely dreadful.' However much we don't want them to, they do discuss the performances privately among themselves, and there's always the danger that the more eloquent among them might try to influence the others. In many ways, I would prefer to omit from the programme details of the competitor's previous track-records. It can influence one's judgement, to know that someone has already won prizes at major competitions.

Does she try to choose people who reflect her own pianistic preferences?

Not just my own feelings, but the accepted opinions of world-famous musicians. Privileged as I am to mix in national and international musical circles, I get the measure of who is regarded as a fine pianist or musician who would conform to certain standards. I like to think that I feel in a similar way about pianists as the great conductors and musicians with whom I am in contact. My own point of departure is always that the piano is a percussive instrument, and one must make it sing. I look for people who can make beautiful sounds on the piano, and in my discussions with fellow musicians, I sense which ones are going to be sympathetic to this approach.

However, pianists are not dependent on other pianists for their livelihood: they are dependent on teachers, critics, the media. When we're putting a jury together, we try to include people who will be of help to them in their future careers. After all, concert pianists (with some exceptions) rarely attend other pianists' recitals.

When they relax, they like to do other things. And in my opinion, famous pianists don't always make the best jury members. They have set ideas as to how performances should go, especially in their own repertoire – they are bound to feel vehemently about their own style of performance, and it's difficult for them to be objective, both in familiar and unfamiliar repertoire. The public likes to see lots of famous names on the jury, but my experience is that they're not always the best jurors. Clifford Curzon, though a great pianist, was very difficult. However, the only time we got a unanimous verdict, in 1975, we had a lot of pianists on the jury.

It's important to include some eminent professors – because, in my opinion, they are used to dealing with varieties of pianistic style and interpretation. They tend to be less dogmatic in their judgements than concert pianists.

I like to include at least one critic, because critics are professional listeners, and their impressions are valuable. A critic who goes to concerts every night gets bored with mundane performances, but suddenly he or she will sit up and listen. What makes them listen? They immediately recognize when it happens. So certain pianists will make critics listen, even if they've been sitting on the jury for ten hours a day.

We also invite one or two people from the media, particularly the BBC and from record companies, hoping that they will engage pianists afterwards. Everyone is there for a purpose. We're trying to achieve a more balanced representation of the musical profession on our juries.

Up to 1975, we also included the conductor on the jury. Sir Charles Groves, who sat on the 1972 and 1975 juries, was willing to sit in for the entire fortnight, but others are not so happy to do that, and the final verdict must depend on the performances in all four stages.

What about other instrumentalists besides pianists?

In 1969 we had Szymon Goldberg, who had played in partnership with Lili Kraus for many years. He was worth his weight in gold. Afterwards he formed a violin-and-piano partnership with Radu Lupu – they recorded all the Mozart sonatas. But I don't think he knew the piano repertoire inside out. That's the problem. I'm tempted to invite others, but I think it would be unwise. Having said that, when I was on the jury of the Young Concert Artists' Competition, run by Susan Wadsworth, in New York, which included violinists and singers as well as pianists, I did not find myself voting with the other pianists. There were three pianists on the jury, and they all disagreed!

'I think the very long hours at Leeds have made it difficult for Fanny to go on getting very good performing artists on the jury,' says Joan Chissell, a juror at Leeds in 1984:

Not everyone could give up that amount of time for a whole fortnight without being able to practise themselves. In 1984 Tatiana Nikolaeva offered to give a Bach recital during a free period. She had to miss her evening meal, because she needed to practise. She went straight from the afternoon jury session to a piano, and then on to the evening session. Some competitions start later in the day, to allow the jury members time to practise. But I do think having a broader spread of representatives from different aspects of the music profession is a good thing. Pianists always tend to see things their way.

'I think juries are carefully chosen across a breadth of approach to get a good result, and also for what they bring with them,' says Gordon Stewart, the BBC representative on the 1987 Leeds jury, and now a member of many international juries:

If there's a Russian on the jury, you will get good Soviet pianists entering. Someone from the Hanover Musikhochschule will probably attract good German pianists. You need lots of famous names, some people who are well known in the academic field, and some for media publicity. In 1987 there was a good mix of jurors at Leeds, compared with elsewhere.

For the first five competitions, the number of jurors at Leeds stayed more or less constant at eleven or twelve. Now, fifteen seems to be the norm. 'I don't know whether it's better to have more or less,' says Fanny Waterman. 'The Tchaikovsky Competition has twenty-two jurors for each discipline, while the smaller competitions have fewer. I feel we should have at least three representatives of each of the four categories. We used to ask more because some people dropped out.'

Many people, among them Marion Thorpe, feel that the present juries are perhaps not quite so collectively distinguished as formerly:

You don't get the really big names any more. People can't spare the time, especially since there are now so many more competitions, and they last longer. There seems to be a kind of 'professional juror' now – a lot of people who serve on juries keep on meeting each other all over the world – it's a kind of travelling circus. And there seem to be 'professional competitors' too, who use one competition as an entrée to the next.

Michael Roll, the 1963 winner and a juror at Leeds in 1978, also thinks that there is an increasing danger of 'peripatetic jurors who travel round the world making a living – they're not necessarily the finest musicians. How do you get the Brendels on juries now?'

Fanny Waterman disagrees with the concept of a 'professional juror', although she admits that

there is a certain nucleus of people going around the world that I meet constantly. If I think they would fit in at Leeds, I invite them – and several are the same jurors from other competitions. But you can't call them 'professional jurors' – in between competitions they are teaching or performing. There are now forty or fifty piano competitions a year, and no one could do them all. I am personally much in demand as a jury member, but I wouldn't ever do more than three or four a year. It's wearing, tiring, sometimes boring, and not very well paid. But I would agree that there are some competitors who 'do the circuit'. The prize-money in the lower-ranked competitions isn't all that marvellous, but they often get what is effectively a free holiday, with free travel. At Leeds, we've had more than one competitor going to the administrator and saying, 'I don't know how I'm going to get home; I only bought a single ticket because I thought I would win a prize'. That's the type of competitor we want to discourage: we call them 'tourists'.

Few people can agree on the composition of an ideal jury. Bryce Morrison, teacher, critic, lecturer, pianist and veteran juror (though not at Leeds) agrees with Fanny Waterman – and with Hans Keller's published opinion after the 1966 competition – that

celebrated pianists, though they confer star status on a competition, are not guaranteed to be good judges. Many great pianists are great out of fierce single-mindedness. Some great pianists only admire the qualities reflected in their own playing, and cannot empathize with other points of view. As D. H. Lawrence said of Jane Austen, 'She's a narrow-gutted spinster,' so one person's genius can lead to a restricted vision of another's. Rakhmaninov and Cortot had incredibly blinkered views of each other's playing. The great names don't necessarily lead to informed and realistic judgement. I feel there's also a danger with academics that if you're shut up in your college teaching not very brilliant students, you get the 'college mentality'. Charisma – the thing the public is aware of – has little to do with academic success. The kind of college professor who tends to appear on juries now is looking for a certain kind of academic correctness. They should be looking for attributes way beyond that – for that quality of revelation, wonder, magic, that indefinable, special something, apprehended but not comprehended, something which is beyond technique. But all too often they slip into a conditioned way of thinking. There's a danger that it's turning into a circuit of non-experts. One has heard some shocking comments on juries – of one competitor who offered the last of Liszt's Concert Studies – 'Why is he playing that? I don't know it' – 'I find it difficult to take someone who plays Medtner seriously.' Juries can be remarkably ignorant, particularly of the post-Prokofiev repertoire.

What do the competitors feel about those who sit in judgement on them? Many feel that a balanced jury is more likely to give them a fair hearing, although some would naturally prefer the imprimatur of great names. 'Complete objectivity doesn't exist,' says Bernard d'Ascoli:

Fanny Waterman chooses the jury, but she doesn't know how they are going to vote. Maybe the juries need more great performers, but it doesn't seem possible to get them any more – competitions are too long, and they can't pay them enough. The sort of jury that used to sit at Warsaw – when Pollini won, Arrau and Rubinstein were on the jury – doesn't seem to exist any more.

Peter Donohoe, who has seen both sides of the coin, having 'lost' at Leeds, and 'won' at Moscow, thinks that juries in general, whether composed of professional players or other members of the music profession, tend to have preconceived ideas:

It's difficult to find a judge who can put his own prejudices behind him. There's a lot of bigotry around – I know, because I've sat on three or four juries. A good jury should be looking for reasons to think that a player might develop into someone with something to say. The problem is how to assess an immature player who is showing signs of musical independence, even if that player doesn't conform to one's own personal ideas. A jury should be there to spot talent and help develop it. Instead, one hears comments such as 'Yes, but I didn't like the way he plays the left hand before the right in bar 223'. The key word should be 'responsibility'.

'The jury at Leeds is not there to spot talent,' says Fanny Water-man. 'That is a scholarship situation. It is there to find a new and beautiful talent, a master ready to undertake the burden of many important engagements.'

The Leeds juries have only once (in 1975) reached a unanimous decision on the winner, and there have been some well-publicized disagreements. Should these be avoided?

Some juries gel better than others,' says Fanny Waterman:

It all depends on the personalities involved. When any small group of people are thrown together – working and eating together – for so long, tempers naturally get very frayed. Listening to music is such an intense experience. People switch on and off, and come out of each session absolutely drained. You always get someone who's a troublemaker and someone who's a peacemaker. Arie Vardi, for instance, is an outstanding juror. He's a marvellous musician, and when the jury gets over-excited, he's able to calm everyone down. He has a highly balanced attitude. But really it's up to the chairman to try to unite everyone. At that time, it all seems a matter of life and death, and people get very worked up, and start threatening to resign, and that kind of thing. Then, after the explosion, it all evaporates. We like to feel we're a civilized band of people who respect each other and the competitors.

Almost all the decisions of the Leeds juries – as indeed of other competitions – have been publicly questioned. For instance, John Drummond, presently Controller of Radio 3, thinks that 'the wrong person has won three out of the last four competitions. There was some very ordinary playing in the later stages. The problem is, that having produced Lupu and Perahia, Leeds is almost under an obligation to produce a world-class winner every few years.'

'Many people in positions of power in the musical profession like to say that they didn't agree with the jury's decision – but that's based only on what they have heard or seen on television in the finals,' says Fanny Waterman:

All we can say is that at that time, having listened to the competitors for two weeks in three major recital programmes plus a concerto, we are better qualified to judge than others who only hear the two final nights on radio or television.

Each of the nine Leeds winners so far has been completely different in character and musical personality. Everyone talks of Lupu and Perahia in the same breath as if they were the same, but their playing is totally different. Orozco was a passionate, Romantic pianist with a big technique – 'a tiger', Gina Bachauer called him. Alexeev was highly intellectual with Romantic verve. Dalberto was a cool intellectual, whereas Hobson was what I would call 'a cool Romantic'. The year that Parker won, we had a message from Solomon to say that he agreed for the first time ever with all the placings, and that Parker was a very fine pianist. It's astounding what different faces these pianists present in their subsequent careers.

'The only problem at Leeds,' says Béla Siki, 'is that it feels obliged to award a first prize. I feel that that's a risky business sometimes. The problem, of course, is that if there were no first prize-winner, then maybe the engagements would not be offered again. But it does make the jury's job more difficult.' Fanny Waterman feels strongly that a first prize should be awarded, if at all possible, at Leeds; and indeed, it is part of the competition's rules:

One has to have the impression from the jury that a first prize should be awarded. The other situation has never arisen at Leeds, since the juries are usually very excited about the playing – although in 1981 and 1987, a small minority of jurors felt that no first prize had been reached. I think the worst thing would be telling the world that you'd had a disappointing show, that it wasn't up to standard. It would downgrade all the other placings. I think it would be very bad if a competition of the standard and prestige of Leeds, which attracts the cream of young players, failed to produce a clear first prize-winner who stands a chance of making a career. And it would be very difficult to persuade the donors of engagements to fulfil their obligations. We wouldn't be doing the best for the pianists. We have a duty to the competitors to say to someone, 'You were first past the post. We're opening doors for you. Now show us what you can do with all these opportunities.'

I think it's become a fashion for juries to say, 'we haven't awarded a first prize'. However, if we all genuinely felt that the standard had not been sufficiently high, then, as chairman, I would suggest to the other members of the jury that a first prize should not be awarded. I wouldn't like it, but I would do it. It is nevertheless my duty to advise the jury that a first prize should be awarded if at all possible. Personally, I think that there has always been a first prize-winner at Leeds, but each is not necessarily to be compared with the others.

Is there any correlation between the composition of the juries, and the type of winner that emerges? It has been noted that the last three Leeds winners are what might be termed 'pianists' pianists' rather than 'musicians' pianists' of the type for which Leeds was originally famous. Does a more 'balanced' – some would say 'blander' – jury tend to 'play safe' in choosing its winners, while a collection of livelier, more forceful personalities might be prepared to go for the unusual, the non-conformist?

The 1966 jury, according to Drummond, was one of 'heavyweight intellectual proportions – one of the most impressive. Now, with the proliferation of competitions, it's very difficult to get juries of that calibre together. I don't believe it's true of the Tchaikovsky or the Chopin competitions, but it's certainly true of others, including the Geneva and the Van Cliburn.' Yet the 1966 jury spent much of its time squabbling, with threatened resignations, and heated disagreements. Béla Siki, one of the most consistent Leeds jurors, recalls the 'uncomfortable fight' in 1966. 'It all became an emotional question, very politicized. Everyone was making secret phone calls, trying to influence everyone else. It wasn't really recommendable. I think it's always more difficult in years when no really great talent emerges. The jury tends to be more divided.'

Charles Rosen, who was also a member of the controversial 1966 jury, agrees:

I thought Postnikova was a very academic pianist. Orozco seemed talented, but not musically interesting. I thought Jean-Rodolphe Kars was the most interesting, and it was owing to me that he got into the semi-finals. The typical thing about competitions is that the people who do best are those who sustain a good average, rather than the ones who play very brilliantly, then very badly. I think it's better to hear someone who can play brilliantly sometimes. In the second round, Kars played like a pig, while his first round was brilliant. Annie Fischer and I agreed that anyone who could play like that should get through – but he nearly didn't get into the semi-final; he was only admitted because there were more semi-finalists than were originally planned. After his semi-final round he was voted into the final by everyone, with one exception – Nikita Magaloff – who thought he was potentially the most talented player, but that he wasn't ready. He had never played a concerto with an orchestra before. So we ended up with two contenders for the first prize, neither of whom I thought were particularly outstanding.

Just before we voted for the finalists, Maria Curcio suggested that we should discuss the situation, but Nadia Boulanger refused. 'If you're interested in discussion', she said, 'you shouldn't come to competitions. In competitions you vote.' Nadia wanted Nasedkin to win, and was very disappointed when he didn't. She didn't want either Orozco or Postnikova, who we both thought were playing as well then as they were ever going to. Should you give the prize to the one who plays best at the time, or to the one whom you think is going to go on and improve?

'One goes on achievement at the time, not promise,' says Fanny Waterman.

Sir William Glock, chairman of the 1966 jury, disagrees with Rosen:

When I heard Postnikova play, it was the first time I really listened. Her Schumann Fantasy was wonderfully controlled – it had a colouring and timing that couldn't have been learnt. Then she played the famous Schubert Impromptu with beautiful simplicity, and her Tchaikovsky in the final was equally wonderful. Orozco played Brahms in the final, and there was a feeling among some members of the jury that Brahms was more important than Tchaikovsky. Orozco played well in the previous round, like a bullfighter – it was all very lively but not always terribly convincing. I felt it lacked the subtlety of Postnikova. Kruchin [who came equal second] was good but prosaic. Nasedkin was the Russians' favourite. The fourth-prize-winner, Jean-Rodolphe Kars, played a very good *Gaspard* in the semi-final.

After the first round I was asked not to stop anyone in the Brahms F minor Sonata, even though there was a rule that we could interrupt if necessary. It's not unfair to say, 'Don't be upset if we stop you.' As a result we had to sit through innumerable performances of the same piece. The afternoon sessions were hell. I used to dread the *Hammerklavier* after lunch. It's terribly difficult to keep awake unless the playing's very good. Nadia Boulanger used to make up canons when she was bored. Keller sometimes left when the playing was poor and carried on with his German translation of one of Britten's librettos. Gina Bachauer used to pull cross-eyes at me.

There were two wings on that jury, one 'chattery' and the other dignified. Some members of the jury used to change their favourites round after round. Some jurors treat the jury as a competition in itself – you win if your opinions come through.

As the jury sat down for its final deliberations, Glock knew that Orozco's supporters were going to win the day. 'I was very annoyed about the result. Hans Keller threatened to resign. Hans and I sat up until 3 a.m. discussing it. We found the drinks cabinet, and drowned our sorrows – we thought the prize had gone to the wrong person.'

William Glock was again the chairman at Leeds in 1969, this time of a more amenable jury:

Juries are strange bodies, and choosing them is a great
responsibility. I told Fanny that I would only do it again if there
were only four pianists on the jury and no women under the age
of eighty . . . Fanny asked me who I wanted. I said Perlemuter,
but she turned him down. We agreed on the others. Siki doesn't
make a nuisance of himself; Raymond Leppard made very musical
judgements. He's one of those rare scholars who are musicians.

There were many good players that year – the standard was very
high. Lupu played the *Waldstein* Sonata in a remarkable way – it
had timing, quality, drama. He played it as if he'd never played it
before. It was fascinating. Pludermacher's playing had a poetic,
delicate quality, very light sometimes. His Ravel evoked the
eighteenth century without being precious. We had a rule that
there could be only eight semi-finalists and three finalists – and
when the votes were counted, Radu Lupu wasn't in the list of
finalists. It was inexplicable. I thought it was absurd, and I told the
jury that it would only be fair to the public to represent the true
standard of playing if more players were to be admitted to the final
– there should be five. They agreed, and Lupu was accepted. It
wouldn't have hurt Lupu, but it would have been a scandal.

'I remember Lupu as a most eccentric player,' says Raymond Leppard, who was on the 1969 jury:

He was a real oddball, but gradually he began to emerge as someone
very important. He played a Schubert impromptu extremely slowly
– but very beautifully. He was making very fine and totally
individual music. I thought Pludermacher was excellent, and Anne
Queffelec was a very interesting player. There were one or two
dazzlingly proficient Russians – very good technically, but rather
boring musically. Boris Petrushansky played excerpts from *Petrushka*
impeccably – but *Petrushka* is much better played by an orchestra.
It makes you wonder what it's all about. That year Gilels' daughter
entered. She wasn't outstanding, but the Russian judges put
enormous pressure on everyone else to let her go through to at
least one more round. They were being telephoned every night
from Moscow, with threats: 'If she doesn't get through you'll be
teaching in Kiev for the rest of your lives.'
We really had no serious disagreements that year. Everyone was
very different temperamentally, but the overall atmosphere was
harmonious. Clifford [Curzon] was rather like instant coffee – pour
on hot water and he would froth for a while, but then it would
subside – and his judgement was sound. I felt that one or two
jurors weren't prepared to say what they really thought, and some

were too easily pushed around. Fanny and Marion were very good – they were rigorous about not interfering at all.

Overt political pressure, whether in a general or personal sense, is something that Fanny Waterman has always striven to avoid at Leeds. 'Certain competitions, such as the Liszt, make you declare your votes openly at the end of each round,' says Joan Chissell. 'It can reveal some terrible things about professors marking their own pupils. It goes on especially in Eastern European competitions. And there used to be a lot of political pressure where Russians were involved – it was almost a matter of life and death if they didn't reach the final.'

'I don't like it when the pupils of members of the jury take part,' says Sir William Glock:

I was once on the jury of a major international competition, and we had to give marks out of 25. I gave one competitor 9 and my next door neighbour gave him 18. I thought that was unusually high, and I asked the reason. 'Don't you know?' came the reply. 'He's the chairman's pupil.'

'I had no impression at Leeds that anyone was touting for votes,' says Gordon Stewart. 'Fanny tries hard to be absolutely fair. Her own pupil – Benjamin Frith – entered in 1987, but was eliminated after the second round, and Fanny did not allow herself to vote for him.'

The three years that Lord Boyle chaired the jury – 1972, 1975 and 1978 – seem to have been relatively harmonious from the jury's point of view. 'I had great admiration for Lord Boyle as a man and an artist,' says Béla Siki, who was on two out of those three juries. 'He handled the situation very well: his judgement was always impartial and his remarks were pertinent and apposite. He had both artistic sense and humanity.' Fanny Waterman considered him 'a wonderful chairman. He inspired people to behave well. There were no terrible controversies under his chairmanship, but things did go on under his nose which he overlooked or was too kind to notice.'

'There was really no question over who should win in 1972,' says Siki:

Murray Perahia was ill at the time of the competition, and by the end he was worn out. So his Mozart concerto and his Chopin No. 1 in the final were not as satisfying as his previous performances. But during the jury's deliberations, Fanny reiterated that we should take into consideration the whole competition, not just the final. Only two jurors wouldn't take any notice – so the result wasn't unanimous. Craig Sheppard we thought gifted and enthusiastic. He had great ability, great stamina. The last movement of his Rakhmaninov Third Concerto was outstanding. And Eugene Indjic was also a gifted player.

'Murray Perahia won by not being a virtuoso,' says Raymond Leppard, again a member of the Leeds jury that year:

He played an innocent little Mendelssohn Sonata, Op.6 in E, and played it with such delicacy and finesse – it was impeccable. It bowled us over. He can make the Mendelssohn concertos sound divine.

Craig Sheppard was a febrile American player, with a lot of temperament. He didn't quite have Perahia's technical supremacy, but his playing was fiery, with a lot of honest emotion.

In 1975 both Charles Rosen and Béla Siki were on the jury. 'That crop of pianists all showed great promise and talent, especially Uchida,' says Siki:

But in my opinion, she wasn't quite ready. Schiff was a really gifted artist. His great forte was Bach – it was so refreshing to hear a Bach concerto played in a stylish manner. The voting was lopsided that year: each prize we voted for, except the first, seemed to produce a different crop of names. In the end we voted for the person who seemed most ready to handle 120 concerts a year.

According to Charles Rosen, Andras Schiff nearly didn't get into the final at all, owing to the determined opposition of one jury member, even though he was

clearly playing better than anybody else. His was some of the best playing we heard – but he played badly in the second round. I believe that pianists should be judged on their best performance. Lord Acton said that 'an artist should be judged on his finest work, just as a criminal is judged on his worst crime'. Pascal Devoyon was an unbelievably good pianist too. I heard him again two or three years ago – his playing of Liszt's *Années de pèlerinage* and *Sonnets* made me weep.

The trouble with competitions is that far too often only dull but worthy pianists get through. Steven de Groote, who was thrown out in the first round, was a controversial player, very individual, but the kind of player who should have got through. One Romanian competitor got everyone's vote except mine, to get into the second round. She was not so bad, so she got in. Then she didn't get a single vote to get into the next round. If you have the kind of voting system where you hear fifty pianists, and you have to pick out twelve with no grading system, then the system can go wrong. The pianists who excite the most interest – the controversial ones – can often get left out.

'The 1978 jury was very diversified,' recalls Claude Frank:

There were some disagreements, but little politicking. I really upset a fellow juror when I expressed delight after one girl's performance of Schumann's *Kreisleriana* – it was very personalized, perhaps at the expense of some of the composer's markings. But other than the expected differences of opinion, we got along. Tito Aprea had a language problem – he was the least sociable. Everyone was very discreet – it was difficult to tell what each stood for. Akira Iguchi didn't seem to understand the rules. When we had to vote at the end, she tried to vote twice for Etsuko Terada. Michael Roll was unbelievably involved. At the finals, the winner had to have an absolute majority, and the voting was very divided: the jury was fairly evenly split. Michael was so afraid that Dalberto was not going to win. As the votes were counted, he was literally on the edge of his chair. When Dalberto got his majority, Michael went wild. But I think it was a circumstantial win. Dalberto won because he played a beautiful K.503 in the final – everyone was enchanted by it – and a lovely Schumann *Humoresque* in the semi-final. That's an unusual piece – not many people play it – and if one plays it well, one can make a very good impression with it.

In my opinion, there was no obvious outstanding winner that year. Kacso played an outstanding Liszt Sonata, but then got lost in the Tchaikovsky Concerto. Unfortunately, it was very noticeable. Lydia Artymiw made a tremendous impression in the preliminaries and the finals. I thought her Brahms was a bit over the top, but she really played her best. Unfortunately, her semi-final round wasn't quite as good – she played a poor Schubert. The way to make a career is now and then to give outstanding performances, and at the same time, not to drop below a certain level.

I thought Ian Hobson had an unbelievable talent, and great facility, but his Chopin came over as very cold in the finals. His is an extreme musical intelligence. It doesn't necessarily move you, but you have to admire his technical and musical virtuosity. We did have an unofficial discussion at the last minute, and Roll wanted Hobson to be placed higher than fourth.

After the verdict, Hugo Steurer – a first-rate musician – said of Stott's performance:

'Whoever plays the *Emperor* like that at nineteen should be watched!'

After Lord Boyle's untimely death, Fanny Waterman herself assumed the chairmanship of the Leeds jury, as had been his wish. She regards it as

a responsible and arduous position. You must keep your jury happy and try to avoid lobbying. Two or three jurors will always get together and influence each other. I've heard deals made – 'If you vote for X, I'll vote for Y' – and it's very worrying when that develops during a competition. They're gambling with people's musical lives. The chairman should discourage discussion, otherwise the most eloquent advocates influence the others, especially the weaker ones, or those over the age-limit. I'm afraid to say I have been on some juries – not at Leeds – where some members were hard of hearing, or have fallen asleep after lunch.

There's no open discussion of the voting at Leeds. Boulanger would only come on condition there was no discussion, and it was reassuring to know that someone of her stature held the same view. Discussions only lead to acrimony. It becomes like a football game, with innuendos and threats thrown around. The sooner you get down to voting, the better. Once it is done, the responsibility is taken out of the jury's hands and placed in the hands of the administration. At Leeds, the counting of votes is all done in the presence of the jury, so that fair play is seen to be done.

The only time we would discuss the result is if the vote for first prize were equally divided. It could be evenly split, but it hasn't happened yet. We have rules worked out for such an eventuality.

Gordon Stewart feels that the Leeds is mistaken in not allowing discussion:

It's interesting to know what fellow jurors think. The jury never becomes a unit – you get to know each other quite well on a social level, but you never establish a common viewpoint on what exactly you're looking for. People get very fixed in their ideas. I feel you should know what there is to know about a piece from the composer's intentions, but you shouldn't close your mind to different interpretations. And I feel that with discussion, changes of mind should be permitted.

The Leeds voting system is also used at the Rubinstein and Santander competitions, but I think it can go wrong, especially if the final result is not subject to discussion. That would draw the jury together. But there's no voting system in existence which will circumvent the determined juror. [Especially not when someone like Richter sat on a jury. He was rumoured, when asked to give marks out of 20, to give everyone either 20 or 0, on the grounds that either they could play the piano or they couldn't.]

The jury's decisions in all three competitions since 1981 have been subject to some reservations, especially in comparison to the 'vintage years' of 1969, 1972 and 1975. But the jury of that controversial year, 1981 – which contained a high proportion of active concert pianists – remains generally convinced that at that time, the correct decision was made.

'I think that 1981 was a year in which the jury chose the person who could best handle the engagements,' says Béla Siki:

The others didn't have the maturity to cope with them. It was an interesting year. Peter Donohoe's talent was so evident from the very first note, but we felt he wasn't ready then. He made his real breakthrough in Moscow. I was very impressed by the concerts he played there.

Wolfgang Manz was a very young and gifted pianist, who played a brilliant Liszt in the solo recital. I liked Daniel Blumenthal's Beethoven concerto very much. Bernard d'Ascoli was very impressive. His Messiaen (*Vingt regards*) was stunning. The playing of many blind pianists can be dull, but not his. He had a beautiful range of colours. Christopher O'Riley is a good, solid player. I thought Ian Hobson's was an impressive talent. He showed an overwhelming intelligence: everything was approached with great intellect and feeling. His Haydn sonata was stunning. His choice of Rakhmaninov in the final was unexpected, but very convincing.

'I felt the placings were in the right order,' says Claude Frank:

We felt that Manz was very talented – but he didn't reach the semi-final in Tel Aviv. We certainly felt that Hobson was the most deserving of the first prize. Perhaps O'Riley should have been placed higher than Blumenthal, and personally, I wasn't terribly taken with d'Ascoli – but there is no right or wrong in these matters. Donohoe simply didn't make much impression.

Moura Lympany, also a member of the 1981 jury, and herself runner-up to Gilels in the 1938 Brussels Competition, remembers that the jury was not unanimous in its decision, but that it felt Hobson had the most experience and would best be able to handle the engagements:

We liked a lot of them, but some weren't experienced when it came

to playing with an orchestra. Manz was a splendid Beethoven
player, but I don't know why he chose Rakhmaninov's Second – it
didn't suit him. D'Ascoli was very musical, but there were one or
two awkward moments . . . People felt that Donohoe was rather
too aggressive. We thought he played brilliantly, but it was rough
at times. It was certainly bravura playing, and he has a fantastic
technique, but we were looking for musicianship, for a beautiful
touch, for interpretation. We were not voting on how a person
would be playing in ten years' time, but on his performance at
that time. One can't, for instance, give a prize to someone who has
memory slips. A young pianist who wins a competition now has
so many engagements to fulfil immediately.

Both John Lill and the critic Joan Chissell were jurors in the 1984
competition. John Lill (who was also on the 1987 Leeds and 1989
Van Cliburn juries) enjoyed his experiences at Leeds:

The 1984 finalists were all good and the winner was both highly
professional and distinguished. Personally, I felt that the one with
the most talent was Ju Hee Suh, who had great natural flair. Last
year she didn't get through the first round of the Van Cliburn. It's
very annoying, if you are a pianist with strong feelings, when some
people who are excellent don't go through, and others, who
deserve it less, do. But – juries work on majority rule. You can't
fight it.

Joan Chissell, who herself intended to become a concert pianist
until a hand injury put an end to her hopes and encouraged her to
turn to criticism as a career, was 'totally convinced' by Jon Kimura
Parker's Leeds performances:

He played really well – absolutely beautifully. Only one person on
the jury thought he was only a technician. He never let one down
– he played extremely well throughout. But I wasn't so convinced
by his Queen Elizabeth Hall recital later on – it was a bit
disappointing. The trouble is, a jury is looking for the impossible.
If you put Rubinstein, Arrau, Richter, Gilels and Ashkenazy in the
same competition, they would not all be equally good in different
styles and different music. Nobody is good at absolutely
everything. I find it easier in a way to judge at the Liszt Competition
in Budapest, or the Schumann in Zwickau. There what you're
looking for is more clearly defined. The thing about Leeds is that
because it offers so many important engagements, you have to
have someone who is ready to cope with them – you can't just look
for potential. Ju Hee Suh was only a kid, but she was absolutely

incredible. She over-acted outrageously in the concerto, but she has enormous talent. In the chamber music round, when she played with Erich Gruenberg, his whole playing changed in sympathy with hers. She was very impressive in the earlier rounds.

My own second choice would have been Louis Lortie, whose concerto was tremendous. There was only one performance of his in the last-but-one round that wasn't so convincing.

The performance I really remember from the 1984 competition was Emma Tahmisian's exquisite *Davidsbündlertänze*. It was so beautiful I actually cried.

John Lill agrees that the performance at the time is what counts: 'If you're going to be a great artist, you have to be convincing at the time. Juries are notoriously fickle.' Lill says he has rarely agreed with the first prize in any competition:

I wasn't so excited about the 1987 finalists, although the general standard was high. I liked Tinney's Beethoven; but I thought Ogawa should have been joint first.

There were fewer competitions years ago, and the winners seemed to have more personality, more character. I think people now try to play safe. Their playing is very accurate, very well-endowed, but it's not exciting – it's like making records.

John Lill considers that Kathryn Stott's unexpected elimination from the first round of the 1987 competition was the biggest upset of the whole thing:

She was an outstanding player – obviously finals material. It made me lose confidence in the jury's judgment – and the same thing happened in last year's Van Cliburn. I have given about 2500 concerts in the course of my professional life, and I feel that my experience is perhaps more relevant than that of the so-called 'professional jurors', who have had little to do with active music-making on the platform. They may be distinguished in an academic way, but they have no experience of that lonely walk on to a platform. I feel it is my duty as a performer to sit on juries, even though it's time-consuming. I find that the majority of non-active performers rarely agree with my views. Most of those who do are performing members of the jury.

'People got very hot under the collar about the "injustice" done to me in the 1981 finals', says Peter Donohoe,

but it pales into insignificance when one considers how many fine pianists get eliminated in the first rounds of competitions. Look at

Kathryn Stott in 1987 – how could such an absurdity happen? And Christian Blackshaw, Martin Roscoe – neither of them flashy players, neither 'competition winners' – but among the best British pianists of their generation. They deserved to do better – yet this sort of thing happens time after time.

'All the greatest mistakes are made in the first rounds of competitions,' says Joan Chissell:

I think the system they operate at Sydney is a good idea – everybody is allowed to play twice in the first round, not on the same day. It's better for the candidates – they can settle down – and better for the jury, and it avoids Kathryn Stott-type casualties. Of course, that means that you have to start with fewer contestants in the first place – and, of course, you can make mistakes by trying to eliminate too many people before the competition.

Like Joan Chissell, Gordon Stewart feels that there should be fewer entrants, with a more rigorous pre-competition elimination system, and that each candidate should be given a longer hearing at first: 'I feel that if someone has prepared a complete programme, it should be heard, except for the concerto round, for obvious reasons. One would then hear fewer people, but at their best.'

Bryce Morrison agrees:

I feel that there are too many competitions trying to cram too much into too short a space of time. Is one more critical when fresh, first thing in the morning? Or, by the end of the day, when one is tense and irritable, and suffering from aural fatigue, is it still possible to listen as critically as one should? Sitting on a jury from 9 a.m. to 11 p.m. is a great strain, and you feel dead at the end. You must make sure that you listen to every note, and everyone switches off sometimes.

'It doesn't matter how late it is, or how tired the jury is, when a fine player performs – even last thing at night – I have noticed that the jury always wakes up and is alert and refreshed once again,' says Fanny Waterman.

'I would prefer to see fewer people accepted,' says Morrison:

Musically speaking, there's no reason to have more than sixty people in a competition. The weeding-out process can go wrong, too – some people send in tapes not by them; others are not accurately assessed, and are not admitted. Some competitions will not admit anyone who hasn't won a previous competition. I think that's irresponsible. But the Leeds is more professionally organized than that.

Fanny Waterman does not like the idea of restricting the numbers of competitors, because she feels it is impossible to assess a pianist from his or her paper qualifications:

We take in as many as time will allow. You need a lot of milk for a little cream. If you invite forty, then perhaps only thirty would turn up, and you would have a mini-competition. The fairest way, in my opinion, would be to accept everybody, as does the Tchaikovsky, and stop them if necessary after fifteen minutes – but I realize that this would be impossible at Leeds.

'I think Leeds got it right last time,' says Gordon Stewart,

but it wasn't a hundred per cent unanimous. Berezovsky will be a fine pianist, but in the first round he played like a 'factory player' – very strong and loud. Ovchinnikov, on the other hand, is a musicians' pianist, and a fine chamber music player. Munro seemed to me a groomed competition winner – things didn't go wrong, but I liked his playing progressively less as the competition went on.

I don't think there should be limitations on what you play. I heard some terrible classical playing in Leeds, from people who had no stylistic awareness. You don't want to hear people playing rotten Beethoven. You should just say, 'You are a pianist: convince me in what you can do best.'

'We're experimenting in 1990,' says Fanny Waterman:

There is to be a much freer choice of repertoire. For example, in the first stage, there are still certain specified works by Bach, Beethoven, Mozart, Haydn – but the rest is to be largely own choice. There are no prescribed studies this year either – if pianists want to play studies, they can choose to do so. So far as the concertos are concerned, we choose them in conjunction with Simon Rattle. He stipulates that they have to be ones he has performed in the year prior to the competition, so that the orchestra knows them.

'I feel it's a shame that Leeds has never commissioned another piece since 1963,' says Gordon Stewart, 'but after Britten, who can you ask? On the other hand, I've heard some specially written pieces at other competitions that the pianists clearly haven't bothered to learn – they sounded as if they were sight-reading. But it does keep the piano repertoire alive – it's an added *raison d'être*.'

'We did ask Tippett to write us a piece,' says Fanny Waterman, 'but he could never find the time. It didn't happen.'

'One of the problems from the candidates' point of view,' says Gordon Stewart

is: do you play to win? Do you turn in a generalized performance that is going to try to please everybody, or at least a majority, or do you play the way you want to play? If you have well-known pianists on a jury, you can get hold of their recordings and style your own playing to fit what you think they will want. I'm sure it's possible to set out to be a competition winner.

'I can't believe that people can alter their playing to suit a particular jury,' says Fanny Waterman. 'I should have thought it would be a certain disaster: any such performance would sound synthetic and unconvincing, and it is impossible, in my opinion, to try to imitate another artist's performance.'

'What I look for is what I'm *not* looking for,' says Stewart. 'What I long for is a complete performance – one that makes you forget "Is this a winner or isn't it?" When I heard Louis Lortie in 1984, my faculty for criticism left me entirely. It's like lightning – but it can strike individuals without striking a jury collectively.'

'I'm looking for charisma,' says Lill:

The whole should be worth much more than the sum of the parts – it should make every heart miss a beat. It's not just a matter of playing the right notes – it needs about thirty qualities, of which only one is the ability to play the piano. You have to be physically tough, able to communicate, sincere, free from affectation. It's a very long-term thing, and you find a number of people who can't cope with the deeper aspects of it. But if you compromise your art, you'll get nowhere.

Given her forceful – even dominant – personality, and the fact that the Leeds is 'her' competition, should Fanny Waterman continue to chair the juries at Leeds?

'I think she wanted to be chairman because she felt there was perhaps room for improvement in some areas,' says Gordon Stewart:

Each competition should have a clear image, and you don't get that if you remove it too far from its prime motivator – otherwise it would be a case of 'rent-a-competition' – it would be bland and uninteresting. Leeds has a clear image. Fanny likes beauty of sound, and she wants what she believes in. It's a cause worth fighting for, although she doesn't always get what she wants. I think it's a good thing that the competition has a personal imprint.

John Lill was vice-chairman in 1987. 'I thoroughly enjoyed it,' he says:

Fanny is used to having her own way, but she is tremendously enthusiastic, and has done wonders because of her enthusiasm. She's exceptionally keen and passionate about what she believes in, and she is completely sincere. I'd rather have that than blandness. We often have tremendously different musical views – she told me last time she and I were on a 'different musical planet' – but we can still be on the same jury. She's always alert in jury sessions, always writing. She never switches off. There was no jury squabbling in 1984 and 1987 – it was all extremely professionally done, and the voting was very straightforward. People swallowed their differences.

What are the rewards of membership of international juries, particularly for those who have strong reservations about the nature of competitions?

'One owes it to the young people', says Bryce Morrison,

to go along and do your bit as honestly as you can. If the right person wins, it's wonderful, but you can suffer the agonies of the damned, wondering if that will be the case. There's also something wonderfully moving about the international nature of competitions – the idea of young people from many nations sharing a common language and learning from each other, playing to the best of their abilities. And jury members from different countries can make close and dear friends from all over the world. It's very heart-warming to find common ground.

'For me,' says Béla Siki,

Leeds is the only competition in the world. I feel it is not only fair, absolutely clean, but the greatest competition which opens the door to young talent. I have tremendous admiration for Fanny and for what she has done. None of the organizers has ever tried to influence me – and not every competition is run in that way. I was very happy to be there – it left a good aftertaste.

Chapter Twelve

The Sixth Competition: 1978

Between 1975 and 1978, the fortunes of the Leeds Piano Competition received an important financial boost with the introduction of commercial sponsorship. After a private luncheon with Sir Mark Henig, a music-lover and Chairman of the English Tourist Board, Fanny Waterman and Marion Thorpe were put in touch with Harveys of Bristol, the well-known wine importers. In contrast to many companies which preferred to pour money into well-publicized sporting events, Harveys already had an impressive record of arts sponsorship, promoting concerts and recordings by the Bournemouth orchestras, concerts at the Bath Festival, and other musical events in the West Country. Fanny and Marion asked whether Harveys would consider subsidizing part of the 1978 competition's projected expenditure of £30,000. To their delight, the request met with an enthusiastic response. At a Press conference shortly afterwards, John Squirrel, then Deputy Chief Executive of Harveys, announced, 'The Leeds International Pianoforte Competition deserves to be financially secure. We are more than pleased to provide this security and feel it is highly appropriate for an intrinsically English company to be sponsoring England's most prestigious music competition.' Apart from a substantial cash sum, Harveys also provided the Leeds with assistance towards printing costs, and supplied wine and sherry for the competition's major social events.

From 1978 onwards, Fanny Waterman took over the sole chairmanship of the competition, since Marion Thorpe now had other demands on her time. She was happy to accept the post of vice-chairman, a role she fulfilled until 1983.

Apart from Harveys, the 1978 competition also received financial assistance from the City and University of Leeds, the Arts Council of Great Britain, West Yorkshire Metropolitan Council, the Yorkshire Arts Association, and Marks and Spencer – a happy blend of civic and corporate funding. The corresponding increase in the available funds meant that the competition was able to offer a substantial increase in prize-money, which had effectively been pegged since 1966. The first prize, which continued to carry the Princess Mary Gold Medal, went from £750 to £2,000, and included the Charles Tapp Prize; while the second prize-winner received the Pierre de Menasce Prize of £1,000; the third, a prize of £500 offered by Harry and Jacqui Hurst; the other three finalists, prizes of £300 each, including the Dorothy Hess Memorial Prize; the four semi-finalists, £150 each; and the ten second-stage competitors, £75 each. The ever-expanding list of engagements included four BBC dates, including a Prom, a Radio 3 recital, and a recording with the BBC Northern Symphony Orchestra; thirteen festival recitals, including the Aldeburgh, Brighton, Edinburgh, and King's Lynn Festivals; nineteen concerts with British orchestras ranging from the CBSO, Bournemouth, Hallé, Royal Liverpool Philharmonic and Scottish National Orchestras to the Philharmonia and the LSO; twenty-three recitals all over the country, and fifteen international concert dates with major orchestras, in venues ranging from Chicago to Berlin, Amsterdam and Tokyo. As before, one of the prize-winners had the possibility of a recording contract with EMI.

The 1978 competition also received more extensive media coverage. Recognizing the somewhat unbalanced nature of its broadcasting of the 1975 competition (see Chapter 10), the BBC arranged to televise both final concerts live and in full, on Friday 15 and Saturday 16 September, together with the prize-giving ceremony; while a further programme of recorded highlights (including some of the semi-finals) would be broadcast on the following Monday evening.

The 1978 jury was also enlarged. Fifteen jurors were originally planned, under Lord Boyle's chairmanship, but Rosalyn Tureck had to cancel at the last minute. With the exception of Artur Balsam and Phyllis Sellick, it was a completely new set of faces, and reflected Fanny Waterman's desire to achieve a more balanced representation of all facets of the musical profession. Among the pedagogues on the jury were Dmitri Bashkirov, a professor at the Moscow Conservatoire; Akiko Iguchi from Japan, the Viennese Hans Graf, concert pianist, founder of a music school in Rio de Janeiro, and a professor at the Vienna Academy of Music; Hugo Steurer, a notable interpreter of Beethoven and Schumann, formerly a professor at the Leipzig Academy of Music, and then director of a master-class at the Munich Hochschule; and Arie Vardi, himself a distinguished pianist, winner of the 1961 Enescu Competition, a specialist in the music of Mozart, Debussy and Ravel, and professor of piano at the Rubin Academy in Tel Aviv. The 1978 jury included the Swiss composer André-François Marescotti, the Italian accompanist Tito Aprea, and several distinguished concert pianists – Balsam; Claude Frank, a German-born pupil of Schnabel who had pursued a successful career in the USA and Europe, recording all the Beethoven sonatas, and had also taught at the Curtis Institute, Mannes College and the Yale School of Music; the Hungarian pianist Lajos Hernádi, also a former Schnabel pupil, and a Mozart specialist; his compatriot Louis Kentner, himself a former prize-winner in the Chopin and Liszt Competitions, who had given numerous premières of important twentieth-century piano works throughout Europe, including the Bartók Second and Third Concertos and the Sonata for Two Pianos and Percussion (with his then wife, Ilona Kabos), the Tippett Concerto, Rawsthorne's First Piano Concerto, and the Walton Violin Sonata (with Yehudi Menuhin); and finally, Michael Roll, winner of the first Leeds competition.

The repertoire for the 1978 competition was also enlarged, and a chamber-music stage (but not a concerto) reinstated. For the first stage, the competitors now had to offer four works: firstly a sonata by Haydn, Mozart, Clementi or Beethoven, or one of two works by Bach; secondly a large-scale virtuoso piece drawn from a selection by Chopin, Debussy, Granados, Liszt, Mendelssohn, Schubert or Schumann; and two pieces from the third group, which comprised a selection of Chopin études, or preludes by Debussy or Rakhmaninov.

The second stage consisted of two works, one taken from the customary nineteenth-century virtuoso repertoire, the other from a twentieth-century selection which this year drew heavily on the Eastern European repertoire, including the Bartók *Improvisations on Hungarian Peasant Songs*, Prokofiev's *Sarcasms*, Kodály's *Dances of Marosszek*, and the Stravinsky Sonata.

The 1978 semi-final again offered a free-choice recital, with the proviso that it must contain the Britten *Night Piece* (the original 1963 test piece) – in memory of the composer, who had died in 1976. In addition, the semi-finalists were required to perform one of five chamber works with the Gabrieli String Quartet.

The six finalists would then be required to play a concerto, this time with the BBC Northern Symphony Orchestra under Norman Del Mar, who, as the former conductor of the ill-fated Yorkshire Symphony Orchestra, had great affection for Leeds. The list of concertos offered rather more choice than in 1978 – but interestingly, Beethoven's Fourth – with which so many competitors had come to grief – was absent. Instead, it included the Bach D minor, Beethoven's First or Fifth, the Brahms No.1, the Grieg, the Liszt No.1, four Mozarts, Chopin's Second, the Schumann, the Tchaikovsky No.1 (reinstated for the first time since its banishment after 1966) and

Bartók's Third. After the unrewarding experience of the dry acoustic at the Grand Theatre in 1975, many competitors were relieved to hear that the final would once more be held in the resonant 'bathroom' of the Town Hall.

Out of 201 applicants, 95 names appeared in the programme for the 1978 competition. Philip Fowke, by then a prize-winner at Sydney and a finalist at the 1978 Tchaikovsky Competition, re-entered; as did Ronan Magill and Yitkin Seow, by then a bronze medallist in the 1977 Rubinstein Competition. Two of Fanny Waterman's pupils entered: Paul Roberts, a semi-finalist at Geneva in 1976, and Timothy Ravenscroft. Among the competitors who had already won important international prizes were Frédéric Aguessy, from France, a silver medallist in the Casella and Liszt–Bartók Competitions, Peter Bithell, a silver medallist in the Marguérite Long Competition and third prize-winner at the 1972 Busoni Competition, Michel Dalberto, from France, who had won the 1975 Clara Haskil Competition and taken the fourth prize at the 1977 Van Cliburn; Jean-François Heisser, also French, who had come first in the Jaen Competition, John Hendrickson from Canada, a prize-winner at the 1975 Chopin and 1976 Montreal Competitions, Ian Hobson, from Britain, a tall, intellectual young man with a big technique, who had studied at Cambridge University and at the Royal Academy of Music, and then at Yale with Claude Frank, winning fifth prize in the 1977 Van Cliburn; Diana Kacso from Brazil, a pupil of Sascha Gorodnitzki, who had come second in the 1977 Rubinstein Competition, Boris Nedelchev from Bulgaria, who had won a silver medal in the 1975 Marguerite Long Competition; Alain Neveux, a pupil of Perlemuter, who won the Casella Competition in Naples in 1970 and also took a prize in the Chopin Competition; the Israeli Gershon Silbert, a silver medallist at Geneva; the Canadian Kathleen Solose, a pupil of Neuhaus in Moscow, who won the 1973 Casagrande Competition; the Americans Gary Steigerwalt, who took second prize in the 1976 Liszt–Bartók Competition, and Lydia Artymiw, who had been a finalist in the Leventritt Competition; and Etsuko Terada from Japan, who took third prize at the 1977 Rubinstein.

Although the Russians sent a jury member, no Soviet competitors turned up at Leeds in 1978: the only Russian entrant was Helene Varvarova, an ex-pupil of Bashkirov's at the Moscow Conservatoire, and winner of the 1977 Marguérite Long Competition, who had defected from the USSR two years earlier, and was officially classed as 'stateless'. Indeed, when Fanny Waterman had requested a Soviet juror, she was told, 'Why do you want a juror when you have no Soviet competitors?' No official reason was given for the Russians' absence: clearly the political tensions between Britain and the USSR were much to blame, but Fanny Waterman suspects that the real reason was that there were simply no potential winners in Moscow at that time, and the Russians chose not to send a losing team.

The thirteen British entrants included nineteen-year-old Kathryn Stott, from Nelson in Lancashire, a pupil of Perlemuter, Kentner and Kendall Taylor at the Royal Academy, and her fellow Academy student Philip Smith. Melvyn Tan, from Singapore, who had studied with Perlemuter and Boulanger, also entered.

The 1978 competition got off to a shaky start: an air-traffic controllers' dispute hit flights into London, and to the organizers' dismay, only 68 of the 95 listed competitors had arrived in Leeds the day before the competition was due to start. In the end, 73 reached the starting post. One Dutch contestant was delayed at Zurich *en route* to Leeds from the state conservatory at Budapest, and then found that British Airways had mislaid her luggage, containing her music. Louis Kentner arrived suffering from severe toothache, and grumbling that he disapproved of competitions. And the piano in the University's Great Hall was strongly criticized by the competitors – one in a radio interview – for having too heavy an action.

These irritations notwithstanding, Fanny Waterman announced at the end of the first round that the standard had been higher than ever before, and that the jury had accordingly decided to admit three extra competitors to the second round, and would be prepared to sacrifice their only free day during the competition to accommodate the 23 performances. The successful competitors included four Britons – Smith, Fowke, Hobson, and Stott together with the Americans Artymiw, Steigerwalt, Marian Hahn, Beth Levin, Kimberley Schmidt and William Wolfram; two Canadians, Paul Berkowitz and Adrienne Shannon; Michel Dalberto from France; two Brazilians, Kacso and Jean-Louis Steuermann; two Germans, Michael Korstick and the youngest competitor, seventeen-year-old Kristin Merscher (whose blonde Teutonic charm made a great impact on the more impressionable male members of the jury); Mario Patuzzi from Italy; Akira Imai and Terada from Japan; Yitkin Seow from Singapore; Janice Vakerelis from Greece; and the twenty-eight-year-old Russian Varvarova, who was hotly tipped to win.

Ten made it into the semi-final: Hobson, Stott, Smith, Shannon, Artymiw, Dalberto, Kacso, Steigerwalt, Terada and Merscher. In a competition that had not on the whole been a lucky one for female contestants, it was gratifying for some to see such a large proportion of women in the semi-final – six out of ten. Lydia Artymiw, who felt that she had made a 'strong impression' in the opening round with

Beethoven's Op.34 and the Rakhmaninov G minor Prelude, had played an outstanding *Kreisleriana* in the second round 'with the sort of beauty and insight that had observers in delight', according to *The Times*; while Kacso, a girl of striking dark looks and dramatic gestures, played a fine Brahms sonata which elicited calls of 'encore' from the delighted audience. Ian Hobson's Rakhmaninov preludes in the first round had even the jury applauding; as also did Dalberto's stylish and sensitive Schubert Sonata in D major.

But the bookies were by now predicting that Steigerwalt would win, with Dalberto as second favourite, and Kacso joint third with Hobson. Having tried out the piano in the Great Hall in preparation for the semi-final stage, Dalberto was critical of the acoustic: 'I just don't know how the jury are going to be able to hear what is being played,' he told the *Yorkshire Post*. 'I hope the quality of the hall improves when it is full of people.'

For him, it evidently did. Gary Steigerwalt, 'an intensely original, poetic and musical pianist whose recital of Schumann and Bartók was one of the high points of the semi-final, flawed, to be sure, but deeply involving, keenly intelligent', according to Dominic Gill of *The Financial Times*, was eliminated, as was Kristin Merscher, whom Gill thought 'one of the most sensationally gifted pianists ever to appear on the stage of the Leeds competition'. Out, too, went Shannon and Smith, leaving four women – Kacso, who played an impressive Liszt Sonata in the semi-final; Artymiw, whose Schubert A minor Sonata Gill thought 'piercingly original, eccentric even, but wholly gripping in its intensity'; Stott, who never expected to get as far as the final that year, and Terada (both of whom Gill considered at the time 'efficient and charming, but otherwise undistinguished'). (Geoffrey de Keyser thinks Terada was admitted to the final on the basis of her poetic semi-final playing of the 24 Chopin Preludes). The two male finalists were Hobson, whose account of the *Hammerklavier* Sonata Gill found 'strong, strange, awkward'; and Dalberto, who played a fine Brahms Quintet with the Gabrieli, but whose Sixth Partita of Bach and Schumann's *Humoreske*, though 'beautifully turned, small-scale performances', Gill found 'firm and lucid, but without either real centre or real daring.'

For once, the finals provided an interesting mix of concertos. Dalberto chose Mozart's K.503; Kacso the Tchaikovsky; Artymiw the Brahms, Hobson Chopin's Second, Stott the *Emperor* Concerto (which she had had to learn in just a fortnight), and Terada the Schumann. Stott, Terada and Artymiw were selected to play on the Friday night; Stott – 'an extremely personal pianist who invites controversy', according to Bryce Morrison – was still relatively inexperienced with an orchestra, and endured an uncomfortable middle movement which Del Mar took too fast for her liking. But Artymiw brought the audience to its feet with an 'incredibly forceful and combative' Brahms (Bryce Morrison). 'She was a tense, high-wire player.' – 'I was terrified of Artymiw,' recalls Kathryn Stott. 'She played like a tiger.' Lydia Artymiw herself felt that her playing got better and better. 'The final was really exciting. It was the first time I had played the Brahms in public, and I felt it went really well. I got a fantastic ovation.' 'She played spectacularly,' says Norman Del Mar. Fanny Waterman liked her playing enormously, but felt she was rather overpowered by the orchestra. 'No one could have played a bigger Brahms than she did, but she was swamped.'

The Saturday night final was delayed by a few nerve-racking minutes, since one of the trombonists failed to turn up on time. Dalberto's Mozart was, some felt, a disappointment: Dominic Gill found it a 'paragon of correctness and neat arrangement, fluent but oddly featureless'; but Robert Cockcroft remarked on the 'mind of remarkable sensibility' behind the 'cool, calm and classical' performance. 'He has enviable finesse, is evidently unflappable, and above all plays with clarity and a sense of style.' 'I thought he was a professional, consistent player,' says Morrison. 'He was good competition material, without exceptional qualities.'

Ian Hobson felt that he had misjudged the acoustics of the Town Hall with his Chopin – 'the critics called it "sensitive", but I felt it sounded pale and small-scale. I didn't get the measure of the projection.' Kacso's fiery and committed Tchaikovsky was undoubtedly the highlight of the evening from the audience's point of view – Robert Cockcroft, the *Yorkshire Post*'s music correspondent, felt that she suffered from some sloppy orchestral playing, but nevertheless gave a forceful account. 'Like the rest of the finalists', wrote Cockcroft, 'her technical powers were beyond dispute. But unlike some of them she had the rarer ability to communicate directly, and a capacity to excite.' Unfortunately, Kacso suffered a memory-lapse at the beginning of the last movement – which was sufficient to deny her the first prize.

'Orchestras expect a soloist to be totally reliable,' says Fanny Waterman. But Charles Groves takes a more lenient view:

I wouldn't lessen a person's marks for a memory lapse in the final, provided the rest of the playing was up to the required standard in the previous rounds. After all, Olivier was in dread of 'drying' every time he went on stage for five years – and sometimes he did – but it didn't ruin his career. Personally, I wouldn't be above stopping, going to the score, and saying 'start from there'. But they almost never do stop – the way the orchestra can pick it up is amazing – much better than a conductor.

And it was Dalberto, despite his rather colourless concerto performance, who was ultimately declared the winner, with Kacso second and Artymiw third. Like Schiff in 1975, Artymiw was bitterly disappointed: 'It was a smack in the face. I think I just missed the second place by one or two votes.' Norman Del Mar thought that Artymiw should have won: 'I felt I didn't have enough connection with the finalists – that's my only regret. The conductor is very much on the inside, and I would have liked more say in who was chosen.' The remaining places were filled by the two British competitors, Hobson and Stott, with Terada in sixth place. Stott was delighted by the result – 'I was very pleased to have got so far.'

At least one critic, Dominic Gill, felt that the jury had got the result wrong. 'The decision is more or less arbitrary, an expression of preference,' he wrote:

A glance at the list of prize-winners from the previous five competitions at Leeds, or that of any competition, and at those performers' subsequent careers, shows just how arbitrary the choice can be . . . there is even the chance that juries will play safe, and allow the evidently attractive and competent to pass in the place of real, dynamic and dangerous (but by its very nature fallible and vulnerable) talent.

With hindsight, Fanny Waterman now agrees. 'One had to make the decision at the time, but it's afterwards that the picture does – or doesn't – build up.'

In the event, Michel Dalberto was unable to take full advantage of the opportunities showered upon him by his win: immediately after the Leeds he was called up for military service in France. Diana Kacso picked up many of his engagements in the next couple of years, including some important QEH recitals. Artymiw has since vindicated Del Mar's opinion by enjoying a hightly successful career in the USA, making many records. Terada has disappeared: Hobson, as we shall see, re-entered in 1981; and Kathryn Stott found that her UK career really took off as a result of her fifth place in 1978.

Chapter Thirteen

The Sponsors

By the mid-1970s, it became clear that almost a decade of high inflation had put the financial basis of the Piano Competition under severe strain. So far it had survived mainly through the heroic efforts of 'Field Marshal Fanny' and her team of volunteers, especially the Friends of the LIPC. But in order to continue to attract competitors of the highest international quality, the prize-money had to be raised at least in line with inflation, and the cost of running the competition had continued to rise. By late 1976, the organizers decided that they must actively seek to interest a major sponsor from the business world, who could guarantee the competition's financial stability.

In the New Year of 1977, following Fanny Waterman's lunch with Sir Mark Henig, it was suggested that a suitable sponsor might be found in Harveys of Bristol, the international group of wine-merchants. Robin Frost, head of public relations at Harveys, was immediately interested. He had heard that the competition was experiencing financial problems, and here, it seemed, was a quality British event of international stature which would fit in with his current plans of enhancing his company's prestige by extending its arts sponsorship programme.

Harveys of Bristol, whose most famous product is the celebrated 'Bristol Cream Sherry', was founded nearly two centuries ago as a traditional family business in Bristol two centre. Until 1960, when the firm's rapid expansion obliged it to find larger premises on the outskirts of the city, it had occupied the same site in the warren of medieval cellars beneath Denmark Street. These had originally served as store-rooms for the thirteenth-century Hospital of the Gaunts, founded under the patronage of the Monastery of St Marks, close to the great former Abbey of St Augustine (now incorporated into Bristol Cathedral). In 1989 Harveys moved its blending and bottling business to Spain and Portugal, while the corporate headquarters returned to its original premises in Denmark Street. The cellars beneath the offices now house a fine restaurant and a wine museum.

In 1971, the year of Robin Frost's appointment as head of PR to Harveys, the business world spent far less on sponsorship generally, and on arts sponsorship in particular. The arts were still very much regarded as dependent on public funding, and of interest only to a small élite. Where money was available for sponsorship, it was spent on sporting events, particularly those widely televised. Frost, a cultured man with a strong interest in the arts, especially music, persuaded Harveys that it should put money into sponsoring the arts, rather than sport. 'We believe it is only right for successful companies to put something back into the community and help to maintain a flourishing artistic life which is beneficial to the country and society as a whole,' he says:

We regard sponsorship as a PR activity – not advertising – there are far more effective ways of advertising a company and its products then by sponsorship. The world of symphony concerts and music in general provides an appropriate setting for a traditional company with quality products such as Harveys. It is altogether a more appropriate field than sport; far less competitive and much cheaper.

Indeed, the PR budget accounts for only about 4 per cent of Harveys' total promotional expenditure, and Frost decided from the outset that the available money should be concentrated on one main sustained campaign with a clear central focus. Charity, he determined, should begin at home – so the sponsorship campaign began in Bristol itself, the city with whose welfare and community life Harveys had always been closely identified.

Since 1976, the company had sponsored the Bournemouth Symphony Orchestra, which serves the whole of the south-west of England, including the Bristol area. Had there been a resident orchestra in Bristol itself, then it would have been the favoured candidate – and indeed Harveys played a crucial role during the abortive discussions of the mid-1980s to try to relocate both Bournemouth orchestras in Bristol: the ultimate failure of the plan was a major disappointment. To begin with, Harveys sponsored the Bournemouth SO's regular concert programmes in the south-west – at the Colston Hall in Bristol in particular – subsequently adding records by both the Symphony Orchestra and the Bournemouth Sinfonietta. Feeling that it had established a solid local presence in the arts by 1977, the company then began to sponsor the Bournemouth SO's London concerts, especially at the South Bank. To these it added sponsorship of selected events at the nearby Bath Festival and the principal musical events at the Arnolfini Gallery in Bristol, including a series of contemporary music. 'That was a brave thing to do,' says Frost. 'But if we are a serious music sponsor, then that is the kind of thing we should be doing.'

Having arrived at that stage, Frost decided that Harveys' sponsorship programme should take on a more national outlook, to raise its profile. He therefore persuaded the company to put money into a season of concerts at London's Queen Elizabeth Hall by the English Chamber Orchestra – whose image as a top quality national asset fitted with the brand image that Harveys wished to project.

At much the same time, he first heard about the difficulties experienced by the Leeds Piano Competition – another national musical asset that would clearly benefit from sustained financial help, and which, in return, would wave the Harveys banner not only in Britain, but all over the world. Frost duly approached Fanny Waterman with an offer of help. It was quickly accepted, and for the next competition in 1978, Harveys provided not only £12,000 towards the prize-money (more than doubling it at a stroke) and the running costs, but also assistance with printing the brochures and programmes (from this year the plain white programmes carrying the Leeds City coat of arms were replaced by glossier and more professionally produced literature in Harveys' distinctive livery), and 'product' in the form of suitable alcoholic beverages for receptions and jury dinners. The company also agreed to host and fund an elaborate reception at the Queens Hotel after the final night.

Harveys has continued to support the competition financially: its 1990 sponsorship package amounts to well over 50 per cent of the total budget. And support is not just limited to the competitions themselves: in 1981 the company sponsored a nine-concert UK tour for the winner with the English Chamber Orchestra, including a Queen Elizabeth Hall début (Harveys also sponsored Ian Hobson's début concert with the RPO at the Festival Hall), followed by a series of piano recitals in National Trust houses by several recent prize-winners including Wolfgang Manz and Peter Donohoe.

The company takes a keen interest in the subsequent careers of Leeds prize-winners, encouraging such pianists – among them Jon Kimura Parker, Wolfgang Manz and Vladimir Ovchinnikov – to give concerts in the Bristol area with the Bournemouth orchestras, at the Bath Festival, and throughout the South-West in a Harveys-sponsored concert series. 'We encourage the whole range of prize-winners to get engagements,' says Robin Frost. 'This is particularly pleasing since it enables high-quality people to play in smaller locations – in village-halls and schools, for example.' And in 1981 Frost initiated 'The Harveys Collection', a six-record series on the Classics for Pleasure label which combined recitals by Leeds finalists (Manz, Orozco, Hobson, Blumenthal and Alexeev) with specially commissioned sleeve-paintings by six leading British artists – Graham Arnold, Peter Blake, Terry Frost, Patrick Heron, Howard Hodgkin and David Inshaw. The original paintings are owned by the company and have been exhibited at the Institute of Contemporary Arts in London and at the Arnolfini Gallery.

Harveys' enlightened sponsorship programme over the past fifteen years (also extending into the realm of theatre – it has supported several major productions at the Bristol Old Vic and initiated an awards scheme for Irish Theatre) has won it two awards from the Association for Business Sponsorship of the Arts, and the 1982 Goldsmiths' Company/Sothebys Award for services to the arts. But naturally enough, the company expects some return for its investment – and it is clear that the media's interest in the Leeds Piano Competition has proved a major factor in Harveys' continuing involvement. As Frost explains:

On TV alone the event is seen by an audience of over six million. In advertising terms, the total coverage we achieved on TV, radio and Press is worth about seven times our investment. Apart from the international publicity and pleasure provided to millions by the Leeds competition, one benefits from the knowledge that this event provides very positive help for young musicians. After becoming a Leeds finalist, a musician's career is made. This is a very big event which has lifted our arts sponsorship programme on to a much higher plane, and it is worth remembering that without sponsorship this privately run event could not survive.

However, we don't subscribe to a philosophy of secret patronage. If one is going to help an organization it is not unreasonable to be credited. Of course we do it for the publicity and to enhance the image of the company – and if, by virtue of one's financial support one is enabling an event to take place which otherwise wouldn't, or is improving the quality of that event, then that sponsor should receive adequate recognition.

Harveys is at present embroiled in a dispute with the BBC over the way it is credited in radio and television coverage of the competition. From 1978, Harveys received the credits it expected – all the relevant literature of publicity, including *Radio Times* billings, bore the title 'The Leeds International Piano Competition in association with Harveys of Bristol'. At the end of broadcasts and transmissions the company received a similar verbal credit. The trouble started after the 1984 competition, when, in recognition of Harveys' key role, the competition's official title was legally changed to 'The Harveys Leeds International Piano Competition'. The BBC was informed of the change well in advance of the 1987 competition, but shortly before it began, the organisers were informed that BBC rules on sponsorship and advertizing do not allow a commercial sponsor's name to appear as an integral part of the title of any arts event. This rule does not, of course, apply to sports events, which permit the broadcasting of titles such as The Second Cornhill Test, or The John Player Trophy. From Harveys' point of view, this meant that much of the publicity for the competition, including bulletins compiled for national and provincial newspapers from billings in the *Radio Times*, failed to mention Harveys' name at all.

Furthermore, during preparations for the televised finals of the 1987 competition, the BBC requested that display boards round the back of the stage, provided by Harveys and bearing the legend 'The Harveys' Leeds International Piano Competition' should be moved out of sight of the cameras. Afterwards, Harveys registered a strong protest to the BBC, supported by the Association of Business Sponsorship of the Arts, the Arts Council and the Minister for the Arts himself, but the BBC refused to compromise. 'We were disappointed for our own sake and on behalf of other potential sponsors,' says Robin Frost:

We feel that the BBC is doing a disservice to the arts world. It will make other companies reluctant to sponsor arts events if they feel they will not get a fair crack of the publicity whip. After all, it's not as if we were expecting the pianists to appear with the sponsors' name across their backs.

The official BBC line at present is that broadcast arts events should not be too closely identified with commercial sponsorship, particularly if there is any question of the sponsor pressing for the official title of an event to be changed for publicity purposes. Its current guidelines state:

Commercial sponsors of events wish to obtain maximum exposure, and, while the BBC seeks to credit fairly the support which made the event possible, it does not want the viewer to think it was anything other than the BBC's decision and the BBC's broadcasting resources which brought the event to the screen . . .

According to Patricia Hodgson, Head of the BBC's Policy and Planning Unit,

this is a very complicated situation, with complex ramifications.

Basically, we want to be fair to the sponsor without getting into a situation where the sponsor can buy prominence on air and get credit for the television coverage of the event. We want to avoid a situation in which these events become traded among sponsors. This has happened abroad, when certain properties have become eminently tradable.

The BBC has refused to reconsider its decision in regard to Harveys' sponsorship of the 1990 piano competition. But some change in future policy seems inevitable, particularly since the Corporation now finds itself in the position of seeking commercial sponsorship for some of its own orchestras and artistic events. Furthermore, in its efforts to avoid any taint of commercialism, such a blanket policy seems increasingly absurd. How, for instance, could the BBC cover The Benson and Hedges' Singing Competition without compromising its principles?

'We would try to avoid using the sponsor's name in the title if at all possible,' says Patricia Hodgson:

It is a difficult situation, particularly since everyone is used to seeing sponsors' names in sporting events. But for instance, when we covered the Mars London Marathon, we managed to avoid calling it that in the title of the programme. Clearly there are exceptions – the Booker Prize, for instance. What we try to do is hold the line. If not, every event would become a tradable vehicle for advertising. We have to strike a balance between trying to protect the BBC (which cannot, of course, accept advertising), while on the other hand trying to ensure that the sponsors get reasonable credits. It's the Judgment of Solomon.

As provider of the major source of income for the Leeds Piano Competition, does Harveys feel that it has any right to influence artistic or organizational policy? 'We are happy to leave the music to the experts,' says Robin Frost:

We don't seek to influence the artistic content of any of the events we sponsor. We would never say to the Bournemouth Symphony Orchestra or the English Chamber Orchestra, 'You must include a Tchaikovsky piano concerto in your programme or you won't get the money', and likewise, we would not insist on the first prize being awarded at Leeds if it was felt that no suitable standard had been reached. However, this is very unlikely to happen, especially with the Soviet Union re-entering, and the likelihood of more Eastern European competitors in the future, which will almost certainly raise the general standard. All we look for is a reasonable acknowledgement of our financial support. We help with the administration, when needed, but we don't interfere. On the financial side, we ask for a balance-sheet, and we need to be reassured that the competition is being properly run, but there is a very sound honorary treasurer in charge and the financial side is handled in a thoroughly businesslike way. We have a meeting thirty months before each competition, at which we announce our intention of continuing as sponsor – or not, which would give the competition time to find another – and then the organizers produce a budget, from which we decide how much money they will need to make up the shortfall. We certainly don't insist on our money being spent on specific areas – the organizers are free to spend it as they see fit.

Given the criticism levelled at competitions generally, has Harveys any qualms about sponsoring such events? 'We take the attitude that competitions such as the Leeds do a tremendous amount for the careers of aspiring young musicians,' says Frost.

Leeds prize-winners with the right personalities have their careers made, and if Harveys is contributing to the advancement of those careers, it must be a good thing. Any publicity for classical music, such as competitions like the Leeds which are extensively televised, is doing a worthwhile job for music in general, not just for individual musicians.

We are now one of the country's leading sponsors of the arts. We are proud of this record, and hope that our activity will help to encourage greater business help for the arts which is still much needed.

Chapter Fourteen

The Seventh Competition: 1981

Just as the 1978 Leeds International Piano Competition had been overshadowed by the deaths of two people – Benjamin Britten and Gina Bachauer – who had taken a close interest in its welfare, so the 1981 event was saddened by the deaths in the interim of a number of loyal friends and helpers, including its long-serving honorary treasurer, Cecil Mazey; both Lady Parkinson, who had played such a major role in the establishment of the Friends of the LIPC, and her husband, Sir Kenneth; the former Vice-Chancellor of Leeds University, Sir Roger Stevens; Norah Tapp; and Valerie Solti's father, William Pitts, in whose name a prize was donated.

Even more distressing personally for Fanny Waterman and her husband was the imminent death from cancer of their great friend Edward Boyle. Although gravely ill, Boyle had insisted on attending the final concert of the last of the Leeds National Competitions for Musicians, which had taken place in November 1980. In June 1981, knowing that the end could not be far off, he asked Murray Perahia if he would play the second movement of the Schubert G major Sonata at his memorial service in the university; and two months later, on the occasion of one of Fanny Waterman's visits to him in hospital, he asked her whether she would take his place as chairman of the jury of the forthcoming competition. 'This is the saddest day of my life,' he told her, 'but I know you will be a perfect chairman and will do the job admirably.' At that moment, Fanny said, she realized that he had finally given up hope.

Edward Boyle died on 28 September 1981, a week or so after the end of the piano competition. Six months later, Harold Macmillan spoke movingly of his former colleague at a reception held at St James' Palace on 16 February 1982, to launch the appeal for the Edward Boyle Memorial Trust, whose Patron was to be the Duchess of Kent. Its aim was to hold occasional concerts, with distinguished artists, to commemorate Boyle's name; and to give practical and economic help to young music students, in the form of grants to enable them to continue their studies either in Britain or abroad. Thirdly, the Trust intended to help gifted overseas students in any discipline to study at a British university. Response to the appeal was generous, and with a reserve of some £350,000, the Edward Boyle Trust (of which Fanny Waterman is a trustee, and whose honorary secretary is Professor Charles Whewell) has since launched an annual music award for young musicians. This takes the form of private auditions before a panel of judges in London: the best performer receives a sum of money for further study and a Wigmore Hall recital. All these projects would have been dear to Edward Boyle's heart, and have ensured the continuing link of his name to music education.

The brochure and programme for the 1981 competition underwent a change of format and style that has since been consistent: it now carried the distinctive grand piano logo on a glossy black background, with red lettering, thus combining the Harveys and the LIPC image. Once more Harveys provided substantial financial and practical support in conjunction with an enlarged list of private and corporate sponsors: the Arts Council, the City of Leeds, West Yorkshire Metropolitan Council, the Yorkshire Arts Association, the Gulbenkian Foundation, the Sir George Martin Trust, Marks & Spencer, Harry and Jacqui Hurst, Clifford Seed, and Majorie and Arnold Ziff. The Ziffs – Arnold is Chairman of the Barratt-Stylo footwear group, and Marjorie a keen amateur musician – have proved themselves generous patrons of the competition, and (through the Marjorie and Arnold Ziff Charitable Foundation) of many other musical events in and around Leeds.

Since 1978, a number of administrative changes had also taken place: Fanny and Marion were still respectively Chairman and Vice-chairman, while Stuart Johnson, Chief Education Officer for Leeds, had taken over as administrator from Edward Davies; there was a new treasurer, Max George; and Harry Tolson, who had succeeded Charles Tapp as printer to the University of Leeds, was now Publications Director. Harry Tolson, who had run several orchestras in the Leeds area, including the Yorkshire Sinfonia, had also been the last administrator of the Leeds National Competition for Musicians.

The Leeds competition celebrated its twenty-first birthday by offering its winners an even more dazzling array of prizes than before. In addition to a cash prize of £2,000, the first prize-winner would receive a £9,000 Model 'O' Steinway grand piano, purchased with funds largely raised by the Friends of the LIPC and other local business sponsorship; while Harveys sponsored a national tour (worth £2,500 to the winner) in October with the English Chamber

Orchestra and Sir Alexander Gibson, taking in nine different venues round Britain, including a concert at the Queen Elizabeth Hall. In addition, Harveys proposed to sponsor two recordings – one orchestral, one a recital – for EMI's Classics for Pleasure label. In all, the prize-money totalled £5,750, with a string of 120 engagements worth £60,000. These included twenty-seven dates with British orchestras, such as the LPO, the RPO, the BBC Symphony, the Philharmonia, the Scottish National, the Hallé and the London Mozart Players; and forty international engagements, including the chance to play with the Chicago Symphony Orchestra, the Leipzig Gewandhaus, the Baltimore, Minnesota, Detroit Symphony and the Israel Philharmonic Orchestras; in addition, there were to be forty-five dates at British festivals.

The 1981 jury, now under the chairmanship of Fanny Waterman (who had not previously been a jury member at Leeds) numbered fifteen and included a substantial proportion of well-known concert pianists. Both Hepzibah Menuhin and Viktoria Postnikova had been invited, but the first had died and Postnikova found herself unable to attend for political reasons. Four members – Claude Frank, Hans Graf, Hugo Steurer and Arie Vardi – had already served on the 1978 jury; while Béla Siki was, of course, an old hand. The new members included Marie-Antoinette de Freitas Branco, the French widow of the famous Portuguese conductor, a *grande dame* who had known Ravel and who in her day had been a fine pianist. Françoise Logan, who was then Fanny Waterman's personal assistant, and was later to become the honorary administrator of the competition, remembers Madame de Freitas Branco asking what 'that curious appliance' in her room at the Queens Hotel was – it turned out to be an electric kettle for making early morning tea. Having never set foot in a kitchen in her life, Marie-Antoinette – rather like her ill-fated eighteenth-century, namesake – had never even seen any kind of domestic apparatus. 'She was terribly pampered', recalls Françoise Logan. 'Everyone used to fall over themselves to fetch her cushions at the jury sessions.'

Apart from Madame de Freitas Branco, the jury included the East German pianist Rudolf Fischer, then chairman of the International Bach Competition at Leipzig; Peter Frankl, the celebrated Hungarian pianist, by then living in London, whose recordings included the complete piano music of Debussy and Schumann; Moura Lympany, a former student of Mathilde Verne, and one of the leading women pianists of her generation; Nina Milkina, a fine Mozart player; two American pianists – Daniel Pollack, a student of Rosa Lhévinne, who had played with Heifetz and Piatigorsky, as well as making

144

worldwide solo appearances, and Abbey Simon, winner of the 1940 Naumburg Competition, whose numerous recordings include all the Rakhmaninov concertos, the complete works of Ravel and Chopin, and the Beethoven sonatas; Orazio Frugoni, a Swiss pupil of Dinu Lipatti, and professor of Piano at the Cherubini Conservatory in Florence; and the Pole Viktor Weinbaum, Vice-President of the Fédération des Concours Internationaux de Musique, and for many years General Secretary of the Chopin Society in Warsaw and of the Chopin Competition. Weinbaum was a member of the Polish trade union movement Solidarity (which in 1981 was making its first bid for democracy, only to be brutally crushed by the imposition of martial law). International politics were superimposed on purely musical considerations, as Weinbaum and the East German Rudolf Fischer often found themselves in heated disagreement.

The repertoire for the 1981 competition remained much the same as for the previous one. In the first stage, competitors were asked to play three works, one drawn from the customary choice of works by Bach, Haydn, Mozart and Beethoven; the second from pieces by Brahms, Chopin, Mendelssohn and Schumann; and the third, as before, a choice of a Scarlatti sonata or a study by Bartók or Debussy with the additional choice of any Liszt *Transcendental* study.

The second-stage repertoire remained very similar to that of 1978; while the semi-final, again divided into two stages, comprised a free forty-five minute recital, together with a chamber work again played with the Gabrieli Quartet.

The final, for which Sir Charles Groves returned once more, this time with the Philharmonia Orchestra, offered the usual range of concertos: the Bach No.2 in E, Beethoven's Second, Third or Fourth, Brahms' First, the Grieg or the Schumann, the Mendelssohn No.1, Mozart K.271 or 466, Rakhmaninov's Second or Bartók's Second.

Such was the public response to the radio and television coverage of the 1978 finals, that in addition to the televised finals, the BBC undertook in 1981 to relay each of the ten semi-final recitals complete on Radio 3 during the two weeks following the competition.

And such was the attraction of the rewards that, rather to the organizers' dismay, 94 out of the 98 accepted competitors actually turned up: the anticipated 30 per cent drop-out rate had simply not occurred. Two of Fanny Waterman's pupils – Thomas Duis and Benjamin Frith – entered in 1981. Ian Hobson, who between the two Leeds competitions had won second prizes in the Maryland, Rubinstein and Beethoven competitions, re-entered – a brave decision after his fourth prize in 1978. The eleven-strong British entry also included Sally-Ann Bottomley, a student of Perlemuter and

Bishop-Kovacevic; Peter Donohoe, at twenty-eight one of the oldest and most experienced competitors and a finalist in the 1976 Liszt–Bartók Competition, who already had a concert career in Britain – having played on the South Bank, at the Proms and at the Bath Festival; Gordon Fergus-Thompson, a prize-winner at Geneva, who had given recitals at the Fairfield and Wigmore Halls and at the Purcell Room, and had recorded for the BBC; Alan Gravill, who had already made his Wigmore Hall début; Martin Roscoe, who, like his friend Donohoe, had already appeared with major British orchestras and made several BBC recordings; Philip Smith, a semi-finalist at Leeds in 1978, now also playing regularly for the BBC; and Nicholas Walker, a pupil of Neuhaus at Moscow, who was quite well known in Europe.

The opposition included Geoffrey Tozer, now twenty-six and entering Leeds for the third time, having won the third prize at the 1980 Rubinstein Competition; his Australian compatriot Piers Lane, who had been awarded special prizes at the Liszt–Bartók and Sydney competitions; Myung-Hee Chung from Korea, who had taken first prize in the 1977 Maryland Competition and fourth in the 1980 Gina Bachauer Competition; the blind French pianist Bernard d'Ascoli, who had won prizes in the Geneva, Vercelli, Barcelona, Marguerite Long, Santander, Warsaw and Leipzig competitions, and who learnt his pieces from braille; the Italians Sandro de Palma, a first prize-winner at the 1976 Casella Competition, who had already made his Carnegie Hall début, Mario Patuzzi, third at Munich in 1977, Francesco Nicolosi, third-prize-winner at Santander and second at Geneva in 1980, Pietro Rigacci, second in the 1979 Clara Haskil Competition, and Giovanni Battel, a prize-winner in the Vercelli and Busoni Competitions; the Swiss Christian Favre, who was already making an extensive career as a soloist in Europe; the Japanese Ayami Ikeba, a silver medallist in the 1977 Busoni Competition, Akiyoshi Sako, a member of the Tokyo Piano Quartet, and second-prize-winner at Geneva in 1980, and Kei Itoh, who won second prize at Leipzig in 1980; Michael Korstick of Germany, eliminated in the second round at Leeds in 1978; the Lebanese Avedis Kouyoumdjian, another Neuhaus pupil who had just won the 1981 Beethoven Competition; Panayis Lyras of the USA, winner of the 1976 Maryland Competition, and silver medallist at the 1980 Rubinstein; Wolfgang Manz of Germany, winner of two first prizes in the 1979 Cortot and 1981 Mendelssohn Competitions; the Americans Daniel Blumenthal, seventh at Sydney in 1977; Peter Orth, first at Naumburg in 1979; Cynthia Raim, winner of the 1979 Clara Haskil Competition; Vytautas Smetona, who had already performed with the St Louis Symphony, and had released a commercial record; Christopher O'Riley, second at Montreal in 1980, and Jeffrey Swann, a prize-winner at the Chopin, Montreal, Vianna da Motta, Queen Elisabeth, Dino Cianni and Van Cliburn Competitions, and a well-established US soloist; from Korea, Miryo Park, a Gorodnitzki student at the Juilliard, who was already well known as a soloist in the USA; the Frenchmen Marc Ponthus, winner of the Jaen and Paloma O'Shea Competitions in 1977 and Yves Rault, winner of the 1979 Gina Bachauer Competition; the Brazilian Eliane Rodrigues, a special prize-winner at the 1977 Van Cliburn; the Korean Hai-Kyung Suh, winner of the 1980 Busoni Competition; and the Israeli Natasha Tadson, winner of the Munich Competition.

Of this impressive list, many likely candidates – such as Roscoe – were eliminated in the first round. Out, too, went the local hope, twenty-two-year-old Benjamin Frith. 'It was a shattering experience,' says Frith. 'I was terribly inexperienced; and although it was a great disappointment, it taught me a great deal about how much harder I'd have to work.' 'Ben was not on top form that day,' says his teacher.

Ten semi-finalists eventually emerged from the second-round survivors, including Tozer, two Japanese girls – Akiko Ebi and Kei Itoh; two Americans, Blumenthal and O'Riley; Hobson and Donohoe from Britain; the German Wolfgang Manz; Liora Ziv-Li from Israel, a pupil of Arie Vardi; and d'Ascoli. Françoise Logan, who helped to interpret when necessary for d'Ascoli (who then spoke no English) remembers the tension his playing generated:

In the second round he played the Liszt Sonata. The jury held its breath all the time – would he hit the right notes? He was amazing – he took massive risks. It reduced people to tears. Marie-Antoinette de Freitas Branco found it overwhelmingly moving – he was so talented.

Bernard was also very brilliant – he was very quick to pick up English. When he went to meet Charles Groves at the hotel, to talk through his concerto, he asked me the English for all sorts of technical terms on the way in the car – and he sang when he couldn't find the right word. He's very sociable – after a while you forget his handicap. He can learn the geography of a place remarkably fast – he learns to orientate himself; and he's also very perceptive – he can pick up people's feelings without having to see their faces.

D'Ascoli – a charming, sensitive pianist who won all hearts in Leeds for his courageous musicianship – received a great deal of attention from the media, some of it unwelcome. 'I got a lot of publicity – I was asked to give interviews, and take part in a Yorkshire

TV programme, and I'll never know how much positive discrimination went on just because I was blind.'

In the semi-final round, d'Ascoli chose to play the Franck *Prélude, Choral et Fugue, La Leggerezza* by Liszt, Messiaen's fifteenth *Regard sur l'enfant Jésus*, the Chopin *Polonaise-fantaisie* Op.61 and the twenty-fourth Prelude in D minor, followed by the Schumann Quintet. 'I was very pleased to do the chamber music round with such a good quartet,' he says. 'But of course I had to learn it by heart. It would have been better in a less reverberant acoustic – the town hall is OK for an orchestra, but not for chamber music, or for a piano with orchestra. The piano gets lost.' The critic Robert Henderson of the *Daily Telegraph* found d'Ascoli's semi-final performance 'finely tempered, often scintillating and pianistically refined'.

Geoffrey Tozer coupled Bach's Fourth Partita with the Schumann *Humoresque* for his recital; while both Liora Ziv-Li and Daniel Blumenthal included several Debussy preludes from Book I. Blumenthal also played the Liszt *Dante* Sonata, and Beethoven's Op.109 – a bravura programme. Akiko Ebi coupled several Chopin works, including the Sonata in B flat minor, with *Gaspard de la nuit* – which also formed part of Ian Hobson's recital, together with two Rakhmaninov preludes. Robert Henderson thought Hobson's performance 'meticulously calculated and contrived', while Wolfgang Manz's Op.110, *Mephisto* Waltz and the Barber Sonata, Op.26, 'made an authoritative impact'. Both O'Riley and Donohoe also chose *Gaspard* for their recitals, Donohoe in conjunction with the *Wanderer* Fantasy, and O'Riley with the Chopin *Polonaise-fantaisie*, and the Scriabin Sonata No.5. The Japanese girl Kei Itoh offered Beethoven's Op.109 and twelve Chopin études.

Both Japanese girls were subsequently eliminated, together with Tozer – yet again – and the Israeli Liora Ziv-Li, leaving an all-male final. This time only four concertos were aired. Both Hobson and Manz elected to play Rakhmaninov's Second. 'It's a great favourite of mine, and a great challenge,' Hobson explained at the time: 'On the face of it, it seems to be a virtuoso piece and a crowd-pleaser, but it allows a wide range of expression.' Blumenthal was to play Beethoven's Second, d'Ascoli and Donohoe the Fourth. O'Riley chose the Schumann.

On the last day of the competition, Fanny Waterman came dangerously close to losing half her jury. The irrepressible Claude Frank was determined to go to Edinburgh on Saturday afternoon, where his favourite nephew was getting married:

But the plane was due back at Manchester Airport only fifteen minutes before the second final started. I asked Fanny if that would allow me time. 'Are you out of your mind?' she said. 'The Duchess of Kent will be there, and we all have to be on time!' So then I remembered that the Duchess had come up by plane the previous evening, and I suggested to Fanny that perhaps the Duchess wouldn't mind if I borrowed her plane on Saturday afternoon to go to Edinburgh. 'Claude, are you totally out of your mind?' she said. 'Do you know whose plane that is? It's the Queen's!' So in the end, I chartered a small plane for the afternoon, and because it was so expensive, I invited four members of the jury – single men, who hadn't brought their wives – to come with me. Fanny was horrified. 'What would happen if it crashed?' she said. 'I might lose half my jury!' But it didn't, and we made it back in time!

On finals night, Bernard d'Ascoli was on bad form:

I had only played the concerto once before, in Leipzig, and I was short-changed at the rehearsal – we rehearsed on the afternoon of the concert at three o'clock, and I only had three-quarters of an hour. I was so keyed-up that I couldn't either re-practise or sleep before the concert. I was very nervous – I heard Hobson play just before me, and it sounded brilliant.

In fact, Robert Henderson commented that the 'contrived' nature of some of Hobson's semi-final playing was now 'even more blatantly obvious', becoming in the final 'dangerously close to a caricature of the grand romantic style', while at the same time having 'the advantage of a fire and determination that immediately captured the audience's attention'. Ernest Bradbury, the *Yorkshire Post*'s often controversial critic, agreed that Hobson had turned in a 'slap-dash, not wholly accurate account' of the Rakhmaninov. Hilary Finch of *The Times*, on the other hand, thought that 'here we had an extrovert, broadly built, urgently rhetorical performance, sure of itself and its relationship with the orchestra'. D'Ascoli's Beethoven, 'in spite of its understandable nervousness and occasional miscalculations, revealed a probing beauty and finesse, and absorbing interpretative character,' according to Henderson. Finch concurred:

His discovering and cherishing of a uniquely warm-hearted voice from his instrument, an often revealingly original performance of the fourth Beethoven concerto . . . were obviously allowed to compensate for both his tendency to become stuck in over-deliberate phrasing, as his fingers searched for their place, and for some hair-raising miscalculations of execution.

The two Americans Henderson found 'dull but technically efficient', while Donohoe's playing he thought 'solid and reliable, but rather characterless'. Finch described Blumenthal's Beethoven as 'too self-absorbed and undeveloped', while O'Riley, 'a disappointing if fascinating Jekyll and Hyde of a pianist', offered a Schumann 'of overdriven, undernourished execution'. Ernest Bradbury, however, thought that Blumenthal played Beethoven's Second 'with a sense of flow and musical discernment much to my taste, while his delicate pianissimos were beautifully controlled'. Donohoe's Beethoven Fourth Bradbury thought had a 'similar but more robust approach'; while O'Riley's Schumann was 'delectably played . . . Here was a real partnership with the orchestra, the only one worth mentioning.' O'Riley's 'keen, singing tone, his total command of the music's rich style and warmth of line, his lack of exaggeration without loss of meaningful virtuosity and his obvious musicianship, so notably lacking elsewhere' made him Bradbury's personal favourite.

Both Henderson and Finch thought Wolfgang Manz the most promising finalist. Although his concerto was a 'slight disappointment', Henderson regarded him the 'most penetrating musician, the most pianistically imaginative and the most potentially gifted of all the contestants', and while Finch lamented the fact that he was 'clearly ill-at-ease in his suffocating relationship with the orchestra', nevertheless 'details like his matching of finely and rigorously controlled sonorities to structure, his inspirational accompaniment in the second movement, his tempering of the fugal rigours in the finale with an almost whimsical spontaneity' seemed to her 'just random manifestations of an unsurpassed degree of imaginatively intelligent musicianship'. Bradbury disagreed: 'Manz's brash Rakhmaninov, more braggadocio than bravura, was not for me.'

Both Finch and Henderson roundly criticized Sir Charles Groves for his handling of the Philharmonia. 'Even taking into consideration the short (50 minutes) preparation time for each soloist, it is shameful that one of our finest orchestras should have its responses stultified, its sensitivity blunted, by direction as indiscriminating and unauthoritative as we witnessed on Friday and Saturday,' wrote Finch. Henderson expressed the hope that never again in their careers will these young players 'have to battle against accompaniments as unhelpful and inconsiderate as those provided by Sir Charles Groves and the Philharmonia Orchestra'.

Sir Charles was undeniably hurt by the accusations:

I had arranged for all the finalists to visit me individually at the hotel to go through their scores – and a story started going around that I had 'summoned them there to tell them how to play their concertos'. I was only trying to save time in rehearsal. Each one only gets half a rehearsal, and it's very difficult.

The jury retired to consider its verdict; and at 10.20 p.m. Ian Hobson was pronounced the first British winner since Michael Roll. He won a standing ovation. 'Leeds has a reputation of being more interested in artistic achievement than in the technical virtuoso,' he told the *Daily Telegraph*:

The programme I chose I would not offer elsewhere. The works I played might have been ignored in other contests in favour of more flashy interpretations. I also purposely picked pieces I didn't know well. I think that lent a certain tension to many performances – the Schubert C minor Sonata for example – and also, I hope, a freshness of approach.

The second prize was awarded to Wolfgang Manz. 'I thought he gave a dazzling performance,' said Fanny Waterman. 'He was very young, very exciting and brilliant – he achieved all he set out to do. I don't think we've heard the last of him.' Bernard d'Ascoli was a popular – though by no means universally acclaimed – choice for third place. 'I was pleased with my placing,' says d'Ascoli. 'I didn't want to be sixth.' 'I thought d'Ascoli the most interesting talent,' said Fanny Waterman. 'But he couldn't win because he slipped up. It affects the audience and the jury. If you find yourself feeling sorry for a handicapped artist, then clearly his handicap is influencing your decision. It's very difficult.'

Blumenthal and O'Riley were placed fourth and fifth, with the luckless Donohoe in sixth place – a bitter disappointment. According to Hilary Finch, this controversial result confirmed the jury's 'avowed intention to set ear-catching interpretative inventiveness higher than maturity and reliability' – although Donohoe's concerto performance evidently made little impression on either critics or the jury: it has not remained in people's memories. 'It didn't come over as an authoritative Beethoven performance,' says Fanny Waterman. 'It's not what you play, it's how you play it that counts.' Only with hindsight did the placings come to be seen as eccentric.

'Standards were not of the highest,' concluded Hilary Finch:

not one of the pianists shows yet a truly distinguishing or memorable potential talent to sustain a career that the prizes mark them out for. Whether or not in the preliminary rounds there existed some hidden seeds of greater potential it would perhaps take more than a jury composed entirely of professors and pianists to judge.

'The finals come after a period of great intensity,' says Fanny Waterman. 'One is caught up in the excitement of the audience – in the sense of occasion. At the time, one doesn't compare one set of finalists with another. But it is true that we do have vintage years. One never knows who is going to develop into a great artist.'

Chapter Fifteen

———

The Runners-Up

'There are no losers at Leeds,' says Fanny Waterman:

It is not a 'winner-takes-all' competition. While the prizes are awarded to the winners, the engagements are given to the competition, and we have little influence over which pianists are selected for which engagements. We want all our competitors to capitalize on their experience at Leeds, especially from the media exposure they will receive if they get into the finals.

'Of course there are losers,' says Bryce Morrison. 'The rewards offered to the runners-up often bear no relation to what the first prize-winner gets.'

'If you do well in a competition, it helps,' says John Drummond. 'If you do badly, it doesn't necessarily hinder. But is it worth coming fourth or fifth?'

Certainly, the fortunes of the runners-up at Leeds have varied considerably: by no means all – even among the second-prize-winners – feel that their careers flourished as a result of the exposure they received, although all the second-prize-winners of the Leeds competitions are still playing.

The second prize in both 1963 and 1966 went to a Soviet pianist. Vladimir Krainiev, the only Russian competitor who insists he was put under no pressure from his teachers either to enter major competitions or to win them ('My teachers spoke only of music, art, culture, never about places in competitions'), seems to have thoroughly enjoyed the Leeds, and has since had 'a fantastic career' as a result:

The political controversy over whether the English boy should have won it or whether I should was all great publicity. I was asked to do many good concerts afterwards, in the Wigmore Hall, the Royal Festival Hall, and so on: between 1964 and 1973 I played with all the London orchestras, and in Liverpool, Manchester, Glasgow – all over the country, in fact. Of course I had a problem [with the

Soviet authorities], like everyone else – but all Russian pianists were having the same problems. I still managed to play abroad. My career really developed. There was an intermission from 1973, when I severed my relationship with Victor Hochhauser, until 1980; but since *perestroika* it's been much easier. I can now play in any city I choose, at the highest level. I have a public all over the USSR, and I play a great deal in West Germany, Switzerland and the USA. I hope I will soon once again have a better relationship with England.

Krainiev now has some sixty-four concertos in his repertoire, from Bach to contemporary works. He was the dedicatee of Alfred Shnittke's Piano Concerto, with which he has toured widely; and he has made many records on Soviet labels, including all the Mozart concertos and works by Chopin and Prokofiev. 'The Leeds competition was one of the biggest events in my life. The two major events which launched my career were Leeds and the Tchaikovsky Competition, which I entered seven years later, and won' [he shared first prize with John Lill, who had been eliminated from the first round of the 1963 Leeds].

Viktoria Postnikova, whose second placing in 1966 aroused such controversy, lacked Krainiev's insouciant temperament and found the competition rather a strain:

It was difficult. I didn't speak any English then, and there was enormous pressure on me to bring back a prize – it was horrible. After the Leeds I entered the 1967 Vianna da Motta Competition and won it; but then I was forced to go in for the 1970 Tchaikovsky Competition, even though I had had a baby only two months before. I couldn't play – but the Minister of Culture, Madame Furtsova, told me I had to enter. I came third.

But I have good memories of Leeds – I liked the way we were all invited into people's homes, and given the opportunity to practice – that was wonderful. Everyone was very friendly, and there was a nice atmosphere; after each round we could speak to members of the jury, who gave us advice.

Leeds was a major watershed in my career – I got a lot of invitations afterwards all over Britain, including important concerts at the Albert Hall [at a Prom] and the Royal Festival Hall, playing with Barbirolli, Boult, Colin Davis – it was very good for me. But it was difficult to get out to the West. The third or fourth time one asked for permission to go to England to play, it would be refused, and one would be told, 'you must go somewhere else'. But quite recently, all that has changed, and now there's no problem. I have had a good career in the West, and now I have fantastic opportunities – many engagements all over the world. I did have a problem in the UK when I broke connections with my agent Victor Hochhauser [who fell out with the Soviet authorities], and I didn't get concerts as a result – it's almost impossible, from a human point of view, suddenly to change your agent. That was a shame, because I love England and the English people. London is the musical centre of the world – it has so many wonderful orchestras and audiences.

Viktoria Postnikova is now married to the Soviet conductor Gennadi Rozhdestvensky, with whom she travels all over the world, giving concerts. She also sits on the juries of major international competitions, although she is not 'a great lover of competitions':

They're not really a musical thing, but unfortunately for most people, it's the only way to be known. Many people just move from one to another, and that's bad. I'd prefer to see another system, if there was one. A competition is only good if it gives you the opportunity to become an artist.

Postnikova's joint second-prize-winner, Semyon Kruchin, seems to have mysteriously fallen foul of the Soviet authorities shortly after his appearance at Leeds, and may have spent some time in internal exile under the former Soviet regime. Certainly he was never allowed to perform in the West. He has recently reappeared in Moscow, where he is believed to be teaching piano.

Georges Pludermacher, whom Clifford Curzon thought should win the 1969 competition, 'even if he falls down dead drunk under the piano at the final', was approached by an agent immediately after his second prize, and 'hoped it would be the start of a brilliant career in the UK':

But I was disappointed – I didn't get many engagements. I think the differences between winning first and second prize is considerable. My career developed quite slowly. I was offered some concerts in England – by the BBC and in the provinces – but then they dried up. I've done a lot of chamber music since: I formed a sonata team with Nathan Milstein, and I've gained a lot in musical experience as a result, but I'm seen now primarily as an accompanist. I don't regret it, though. I've never stopped playing in France as a soloist. I'm now working mostly in France, but I hope it will develop elsewhere.

Pludermacher has made several records for French labels, two of which (Debussy *Etudes* and the *Diabelli* Variations) have won the Grand Prix du Disque.

Craig Sheppard, who had come third in the 1968 Busoni Competition, and was eliminated in the first round of the 1970 Tchaikovsky ('I was well-prepared, but the études knocked me out – I chose the most difficult ones and played them abominably'), felt that the Leeds was 'the sort of competition I wanted to be associated with. When I saw the list of past winners, I felt that the jury had gone for the qualities I was striving for at the time.' Although Sheppard naturally hoped to win first prize, he feels that he could have done worse than come second to Murray Perahia:

Murray is unique. He's a great artist, and it was an honour to come second to him. He is so completely himself – in touch with his inner feelings. I have a very real affection for Murray: there are very few artists I feel really warm towards, but this is a feeling of appreciation from a deep artistic level. Since Leeds he and I have often got together and worked on things we found we were both playing at the same time – such as the *Hammerklavier* Sonata.

It is a great stroke of luck to be given a prize in a competition – you have a responsibility to know how to treat your talent, and you only learn the hard way. I think Murray was more mature than I was – he knew how to put his foot down. I was afraid to turn down engagements: I couldn't say no because I didn't want to disappoint people. I was very uncertain at the time. After the Leeds I was offered a great many engagements, since Murray then didn't do all the winner's concerts, and I came over to live in London. Even though I had a good agent, there was hardly anyone I felt I could talk to, who would give me advice I knew I could trust. Until 1973 I had enjoyed a good support system in the US – one person offered me their flat to practise in if he was away – that kind of thing. When I came over to England, with lots of concerts lined up, including a television appearance, I really had to twist people's arms to find somewhere quiet to practise. I was living at the London Musical Club, and all I could find was an ancient piano with its strings missing. At that stage in my life it would have been helpful if someone had kept an eye on me, as part of the learning process – but you are very much on your own.

The Leeds really gave me an entrée to the UK – but not so much to Europe. I still play in the USA, but in some years the pickings there haven't been so good – I sometimes feel like a stranger in my own country. But it's not a closed door to me; I played there recently with Solti and the Chicago Symphony.

156

Sheppard has made three solo records: one of Liszt operatic para-
phrases, made shortly after the Leeds, one of the Rakhmaninov Third
Concerto with Pritchard and the LPO, and a Chopin album. He feels
strongly that the early, rather brash image of him that the record
companies tried to project was not at all helpful ('I wasn't well
packaged'). He has also made several chamber music recordings, and
has a regular violin-and-piano partnership with Mayumi Fujikawa.
Having acquired a post-Leeds reputation as a virtuoso in the big
Romantic repertory, he now plays everything from Bach to Stock-
hausen:

For me, Bach was the greatest Romantic of all. I'm sure he would
have loved hearing his music played on a nine-foot concert grand.
I love Mozart, and I've played a lot of Beethoven. I feel a
tremendous affinity for Beethoven's volatile nature – I'd really like
to have had lunch with him! I think the *Hammerklavier* is the greatest
work. Serkin says, 'it's not difficult, it's impossible!'
As far as the future goes, I want to do more solo work, rather
than chamber music, and I'd like to fill in the gaps in my repertoire.
I regret I haven't done more twentieth-century music. I played
Berio's *Sequenza IV* at my London début; and I'm working on the
Berg Chamber Concerto – which for me is one of the greatest works
of this century. I've played quite a lot of Prokofiev – three of the
concertos – as well as the Bartók Nos.2 and 3, and I did the Copland
Concerto at the Proms.
I'm very grateful for what the Leeds competition did for me. And
it works both ways – the winners help the competition. I love
Fanny's enthusiasm and vitality. If it weren't for her, I might not
be here now. But at the end of the day, one has to take
responsibility for oneself.

For Mitsuko Uchida, now one of the world's finest Mozart players
(she is currently recording all the piano concertos with Jeffrey Tate
and the ECO) her second prize at Leeds in 1975 came during a phase
in her life when she was

good enough to win prizes [first in the 1969 Beethoven Competition,
second in the 1970 Chopin], but not clear enough in interpretation
and thoughts to be a valid musician. I was looking for an
understanding of music and the right way of expressing it – I was
also unhappy about my technique. During those years, when I was
really trying to find my own musical understanding and style, I
suffered from the syndrome so common among young people, of
'having to have a career', so I was getting small concerts to try to

make a living. It was a couple of years after the second Leeds [she entered in 1972 and made a 'fabulous mess' of it, in her own words, although she did reach the semi-final] that I finally discovered my own sound-world from outside – I listened to my tape-recordings, and thought for the first time, 'that's right'. The rest was up to me – and that's the right attitude.

On the basis of her concerto performance alone, Mitsuko Uchida thinks she may have been placed too highly at Leeds:

I played a very good *Carnaval* in the recital round, but a disastrous Schumann Concerto in the final. I felt I played very badly – I couldn't cope with the dry acoustic in the Grand Theatre . . . I didn't feel that coming second had any positive effect on my career – I had an agent already – in fact, I think it was rather negative, because of the reaction to my bad final performance. One reviewer even said of the 1975 competition, 'This year was rather dull'. It's difficult to imagine a competition with so much potential talent! Schiff played wonderfully in the final.

Not much came my way after Leeds – one or two engagements – but I have built up my career slowly. It was my series of Mozart sonata recitals in the Wigmore Hall and in Tokyo in 1982 which seemed to strike a chord with people – I had reached the stage where people were talking about my interpretations. Then, my musical life seemed to acquire a different dimension, with serious interest from record companies. But that didn't really derive from any competition – none of them meant much to me. But on the other hand, had I won no prizes at all, my life might have been even more difficult.

The winners make a competition, and Leeds was incredibly lucky to have had two great artists – Lupu and Perahia – at a time when they could cope with the pressure. Winning had a great effect on their careers, but it had little effect on mine. If you win a competition prematurely, it can be very difficult: you can just disappear. The pressure not to make mistakes is very great if you win, and you don't have the scope to experiment. I'm very happy that I didn't win the Leeds: it would have been too early for me. I had time to develop. There comes a point in your life when you have to be fairly clear about what you're doing. Some people reach it at twenty – but that's often far too early. Then you may end up playing interestingly at thirty-five – but by then no one will want you. I was lucky that some people spotted me before I got to be seventy . . .

In retrospect, it is up to you how you develop, but it's difficult to see that when you're young. You just know if you're not there yet. You must be true to yourself.

Apart from her Mozart performances and recordings, Mitsuko Uchida is performing all the Beethoven concertos with Tate and the ECO in London and has just released two further recordings, one of the Chopin Sonatas Nos.2 and 3, and the other of the Debussy études.

The Brazilian pianist Diana Kacso, runner-up in 1978, was very happy with the way she played at Leeds, but was disappointed not to have won:

Although I didn't get an offer from an agent, I did get quite a lot of engagements after the competition. Michel Dalberto had difficulties in fulfilling some of the winner's engagements – he had to do his military service shortly afterwards – and I picked up about twenty concerts over the next two or three years, mostly music clubs and societies, universities, etc. I did three QEH recitals, and played at the Festival Hall with the London Mozart Players and the Wren Orchestra. I also got some engagements in the USA as a direct result of Leeds. But I haven't performed in England at all for the last four or five years. I was with Ibbs & Tillett in the early 1980s, but the engagements fizzled out.

For the past eighteen years or so, Diana Kacso has lived in New York, where she is married to a lawyer. She plays a mixture of solo engagements in relatively minor venues in the USA, together with chamber music recitals with her regular duo partner, the cellist Nancy Green. She has released only one record, a live recital, shortly after she won second prize in the 1977 Rubinstein Competition. Her US agent thinks that her current lack of a career in England may be due to her having being 'overpriced' at an early stage in her career, and also to the fact that one set of Leeds winners is often eclipsed by the next.

The young German pianist Wolfgang Manz was still a student at the Musikhochschule in Hanover when he entered the Leeds in 1981. It was his first major international competition. He went on to take two more second prizes, at Bonn and Brussels, in the next two successive years:

I was very happy at that time. Although I missed the first prize, I was lucky to be a finalist. I got many engagements in Britain as a result, and I'm still profiting from it now. I have a British agent, and I'm still playing in the UK – though not quite so often as I used to – as well as in Western Europe: recitals, chamber music, and some recordings. Now I'm mostly playing in Germany, Belgium, and Holland. This year I'm going to Japan. Between 1983 and 1985 I was doing fifty or sixty engagements a year, but now it's nearer thirty or forty. I'm doing a little teaching, but mostly playing.

I have good memories of Leeds – we were well looked after, and the social atmosphere was good. But I don't know how fair the jury was – you can't believe anyone. I sometimes think that the nicer they are to you, the more they are against you!

Ju Hee Suh, a prodigy who made her public concerto début at the age of nine, was also still a student – at the Curtis Institute in Philadelphia – when she entered the 1984 Leeds competition at the tender age of sixteen. Leeds was her first experience of an international competition:

I heard only a few of the other competitors – I thought they were all good. You get to hear all the different styles of the different nationalities: it reflects the way each is taught. I was very happy with my placing. It helped my career a lot; it opened up Europe to me. After the finals I had many invitations to play in different European countries, from Sweden to Ireland.

I did have a manager in the USA before I came to Leeds, but afterwards many agents came to see me. My parents decided on Stephannie Williams because she's like a mother to me.

Ju Hee Suh entered the 1989 Van Cliburn competition, but failed to get through the first round. She is still only twenty-two, and could, of course, enter many more:

I don't want to think about any more competitions – but I wouldn't say no definitely. I think you gain something even when things don't go well – after the Van Cliburn, my mother was far more depressed than I. I couldn't stop laughing about it!

My career has really taken off since Leeds – I've done concerts with Zubin Mehta and the New York Philharmonic, and with Paavo Berglund in Sweden and Australia. I'm playing the second Liszt Concerto at the Proms with the Bournemouth Symphony Orchestra and Andrew Litton.

The list of concertos in her repertoire is impressive: she has recently played Mozart K.595, the Ravel G major, Rakhmaninov's Second and Third and the *Paganini* Rhapsody, Prokofiev's First and Second, the Tchaikovsky, Grieg, Schumann, Chopin, both Liszts and both Brahms – 'my favourites'. She chose the Rakhmaninov Third at Leeds because 'I like the piece so much. I played it once when I was eleven or twelve, and fell in love with it – it's so wonderful. I've since played it many times.'

In addition to her heavy concert schedule, Ju Hee Suh is currently studying for a Master's degree at the Curtis Institute:

I have to do a lot of academic work, so I haven't been taking on all the concerts I could, or else my work would suffer. It's difficult when you have to learn a new piece in a hurry – once I had to miss some of my French lessons, and when I came back to the class, the teacher told me I had a big exam the following week!

I want to do as much playing as possible, and learn more repertoire – especially the twentieth-century classics and contemporary music. I really want to learn some Tippett! My next project is the Britten concerto.

The Australian Ian Munro, Leeds' most recent second-prize-winner, originally obtained a travelling scholarship to study in Vienna, where he hoped to study with Paul Badura-Skoda. But he found that the terms of his award did not extend to the Musikhoch-schule; his British girlfriend (now his wife) brought him to London, and by the time he entered the 1987 Leeds competition, he had already settled in the UK:

My first competition was in Barcelona in 1985; then I did several more, including two just before the Leeds. I came back from the Busoni only four or five days before the Leeds, played for my brother-in-law's wedding, and had to miss the reception in order to catch a train to Leeds in time for the first round. I had met Fanny Waterman at the Vianna da Motta Competition in Lisbon, and she said she would be glad to see me in Leeds.

I'd been in the finals of my previous two competitions, and I think I'd have been disappointed if I hadn't made the Leeds final. But I was prepared for all eventualities – after a while, you have to come to the conclusion that you can be eliminated whether or not you think you've played well. I was very happy with my placing. When I heard Vladimir Ovchinnikov play, I thought, 'this is really fine playing'. I thought Berezovsky and Ogawa played really well too.'

Then a few days after the competition, I began to read some of the criticisms in the papers – they were shattering. I felt they were very unkind. John Lill, who came to my ECO concert, said some wise things about music critics, and reassured me that I had got to the final with very high marks. And I wasn't the only finalist to be criticized. At least the London papers do apply the highest standards – they equate your performance with those at the top of the profession.

I didn't get an agent until a year after Leeds, when I did my Wigmore Hall début. Some of the big agents were not even at the competition – they evidently had enough Leeds people. Leeds had a big impact on my career. Before then, I was doing six to twelve small concerts a year, but immediately afterwards the phone began to ring, and I found myself fully booked a year ahead. Then it was a bit up and down, but the 1990/1991 season looks very good. I'm touring Australia twice, and Czechoslovakia, and I'm playing with the RPO, which will be exciting. Most of my engagements have been in this country – the engagements which result from a competition do tend to come from within that country.

I feel that winning first prize in a major competition ensures an international career, but not the other prizes. A competition is one thing, a professional career is quite another. You must be able to fulfil the engagements you are offered well enough to be re-engaged. People have said to me that I must be disappointed because of *glasnost* – that Ovchnnikov has been able to take most of the engagements offered. But I think it's great.

I'm doing my first record next year – a CD of Australian contemporary piano music, including two pieces I commissioned. You have to lay time aside to learn contemporary music; but everyone has to play the Classics, and we all must develop the technique to cope with the virtuoso Romantic repertoire if we're going to do competitions. Competitions were my baptism of fire – they jolted me out of my beach-going days. I didn't spend enough time at the piano before I came to London, so I didn't learn my basic technique until I was around twenty-three. I needed the impetus of a competition to get me going. Competitions are valuable – so long as you can take the strain.

Of the ten third-prize-winners of the Leeds competition, one (Sebastien Risler, 1963) seems to have disappeared from the concert scene; another (Alexei Nasedkin, 1966) is now a professor of piano at the Moscow Conservatoire; Arthur Moreira-Lima (1969) toured Eastern Europe, North and South America, made several records on the Muza and Melodiya labels, and is now believed still to be playing, but mostly in his native Brazil; while Junko Otake (1984) started her career in Japan, but subsequently married an oboist and is presently raising a family in Tokyo. The other six are still active in Europe or the USA.

Eugene Indjic (1972) entered the 1974 Rubinstein Competition after the Leeds, and took the second prize. He now lives in France:

My third prize at Leeds didn't have much effect on my career – I didn't get an agent, or many engagements. It helped only in countries like Holland. I started to make a career only after the Rubinstein. I'm now playing in France, Holland, Eastern Europe, the USA. I mostly play the nineteenth- and twentieth-century classics – a great deal of Chopin, the Brahms concertos, and some chamber music. I've released some recordings on the Claves [a Swiss] label.

A third prize was jointly awarded in 1975 – to Andras Schiff and Pascal Devoyon. Schiff, a former pupil of Pál Kadosa and György Kurtág at the Budapest Conservatory, is currently regarded as one of the finest pianists of his generation, and perhaps the greatest Bach interpreter in the world today. He has very mixed feelings about the Leeds competition:

All my teachers agreed that if someone from a politically isolated country has talent, that person should try to achieve international recognition somehow – and entering a major competition seemed to be the only way. Leeds looked like one of the best – the emphasis was more on musicianship than technique. Kurtág was against my entering, but Kadosa was in favour.

Like Mitsuko Uchida, Schiff first entered the Leeds in 1972:

I got through the first round only. I felt that was a fair judgement. Then I came fourth in the 1974 Tchaikovsky Competition, and I thought I would have another go in the 1975 Leeds. Kadosa was on the jury that year, but of course, he couldn't vote for me. I was disappointed with my placing, but it hardly matters now. It did bother me that people said, 'If you hadn't played Bach in the final, you would have been placed higher.' If Bach is on the list, then theoretically one should have as good a chance with it as with any other concerto. I played a lot of Bach in the competition, and I don't think Rosalyn Tureck liked it. Afterwards Kadosa said to me, 'You should have won, but I couldn't say a word.'

It did give me a break, though – I had the TV exposure; I got a British and a US agent, and I made many close friendships. I also got a lot of engagements on a fairly basic level, at music clubs, and so on. I loved it, and did it for many years. It's good to build up a career (I hate this word) like that. You need an audience if you're a musician. I also played many concerts in provincial venues in

Hungary under trying circumstances – many of their pianos were out of tune, one even had a leg missing! – but it helped to build up my repertoire slowly. I wasn't rushed.

I'm trying to play less at the moment – it's a difficult and thorny path to get to the point when you can really choose your engagements, your repertoire, your partners. But in order to play good music you have to have time to study, think, and digest.

I wish there was another way to start a career – competitions aren't the last word. I'm very much against them; they're far too subjective. It's all down to personal taste, and if you talk to many 'experts', the difference of opinion is hair-raising. Music should not just be a matter of taste. And the public like competitions so much – even a mediocre performance, which under normal circumstances would be greeted with polite applause, takes on a totally different perspective when performed by a gladiator in the arena!

One has to do it when necessary, but I can't understand the people who just keep going for years, getting into the finals over and over again. I suppose they must find it a comfortable way of life! And if someone who has won three first prizes still hasn't managed to establish themselves, then clearly something is very wrong with the requirements. The jury's criterion should be 'Would I buy a ticket to a recital by this person?' Instead, they argue about points of technique and tempi.

What was very good about Leeds was the family atmosphere and the number of lifelong friends one makes. There's a large percentage of civilized people there!

Pascal Devoyon, who shared the third prize with Schiff, was finishing his third cycle of studies at the Paris Conservatoire:

We had to enter an international competition each year of the third cycle, and in 1974 I'd come second in the Busoni. I wasn't happy with my performance in the semi-final – I suffered from nerves, and it was most taxing. But I was happy with the way I played the concerto, and I was pleased to win a third prize. At the time I was still young, and I had no real concept of an international concert career. I got an agent in Holland, with a London office, but it's always the same with all competitions – there are few engagements for a lower prize-winner. Very little happened in fact until I came second in the 1978 Tchaikovsky – then I was offered engagements around the world. I now play in England, France, the USA, where I often go, Japan, the USSR – it's built up. I play a lot of French music, Schumann, the Romantic repertory. In 1990 I'm doing a

complete cycle of Beethoven sonatas in Eindhoven. I used to record
for Erato – now for Virgin, Hyperion, Classics for Pleasure.

I loved meeting people at Leeds – Andras Schiff is a good friend.
We were both football fans, and between the semi-final and the
final, instead of practising, we went to a Leeds United match! Leeds
is one of the nicest competitions in the way we were treated. I
enjoyed the social aspect.

Lydia Artymiw had only entered one competition before the 1978
Leeds – the Leventritt in 1976. She was studying with Gary Graffman
at the time, but had not played at all in Europe:

I'd met Murray Perahia in Marlboro in 1972, the year he won the
Leeds. We had mutual friends, including Irving Moskovitz, who
encouraged me to apply for the Leeds. The repertoire looked good
– it suited me. I had no money to go, but the Rockefeller
Foundation paid my air-fare.

I felt I made a strong impression in the opening round with
Beethoven's Op.34 and the Rakhmaninov G minor Prelude, Op.23
No.5, but I thought my playing got better and better. The final was
a very special occasion, one of the high points of my career. I was
very disappointed by my third placing. The judges did not criticize
my playing in a constructive way – I felt they resented the fact that
I played with freedom. I was a very emotional player then. When
you are performing, you aim to communicate something. Perhaps
you can go over the top when you're young. Now my playing is
very different.

I didn't enter any more major competitions after Leeds – I think
I was disillusioned, and I didn't want to become a war horse. But
I now have a very active career, although I never got a British agent.
I got very good reviews – my Wigmore Hall recital debut was
excellently reviewed, but it didn't generate enough interest to attract
an agent. But I did get a German manager, who used the Leeds to
orchestrate my career there.

I'm now playing a great deal in the USA, both solo dates and
chamber music, and I do five hours' a week teaching at the
University of Minneapolis. I play more concerts now than ever. I
tour Europe once or twice a year. My repertoire is mainly
nineteenth-century – the Classics and Romantics. I have a recording
contract with Chandos, with whom I've made seven records so
far.

I've played with the Scottish National Orchestra in Britain, and
given some recitals in smaller places. But a year or so after the
Leeds, my agent wanted me to do a recital in Plymouth, and the

management wouldn't pay the fee, saying I had only won a third prize at Leeds, and yet my fee was higher than the second prize winner's! The view seems to be, that if you come third, you should be paid less.

Bernard d'Ascoli was invited to Leeds by Fanny Waterman, who heard him in the 1980 Bach Competition in Leipzig:

I had won a first prize at Barcelona, but I didn't expect to get to the finals at Leeds – the gap between the standards of the two competitions was considerable. I knew it would be difficult. I was delighted to be in the semi-finals at Leeds – that was my best stage. I played very badly in the final.

Afterwards, I got an agent, and many engagements. It made a great difference. Before, I was doing three to five concerts a year; afterwards, more like fifty. I had a London date at the QEH, a *South Bank Show* appearance, a record for Classics for Pleasure, a Royal Gala Performance – all in the following year.

Bernard d'Ascoli now divides his time between London and the South of France:

The Leeds competition has been central to my career. It gave the necessary kick-start – it was going slowly and could have taken years. I am very grateful to it. Coming third was no handicap. If you win the first prize, people can say, 'You didn't deserve it.' If you come third, they can say, 'You should have been placed higher.'

Noriko Ogawa, third-prize-winner in 1987, was encouraged to enter the Leeds Competition because of its repertoire, which she found 'sympathetic – some competitions require weird pieces, but not the Leeds', and its reputation:

It left a very good impression – the organization is excellent, everyone was very kind, and there was a very special, friendly atmosphere. I was very happy with the way I played – I felt my second-round playing was my personal best. There is always a lot of gossiping about the result – but I was happy with my placing. And it had a great effect on my career, both in Japan, where it really took off, and here in England, where my work permit allows me to spend six months of each year. I now do many concerto dates in Japan, radio and TV appearances, and I play everywhere.

I didn't get so many engagements directly as a result of Leeds, but many people heard me, and offered me engagements in spite of my third prize. I got a great deal of exposure. Since then, I've played a great deal in England with Michael Collins and London Winds. I play a lot of Russian music, especially Prokofiev and Rakhmaninov; Schumann, Liszt, the Beethoven sonatas. I've started playing some Mozart. I'd like to do more new music, but it's difficult to find time to learn it. I'm playing a new piece by a Japanese composer in March. I just want to go on playing every concert the best I can.

The two weeks I spent in Leeds were the most wonderful of my life. I got so excited about the result, despite the tension. It was a fantastic experience.

The winners of the fourth prizes in the first two competitions are no longer active concert pianists. Nothing further is known of Armenta Adams; Jean-Rodolphe Kars, whom Charles Rosen thought so promising, gave up the piano to become a Trappist monk. Boris Petrushansky (1969), who went on to win the 1975 Casagrande Competition in Italy, seems to have pursued a career only within the Soviet Union. No fourth prize was awarded in 1972. In 1975, it was shared between Myung-Whun Chung, who almost immediately turned to conducting rather than playing the piano, becoming first Giulini's assistant with the Los Angeles Philharmonic Orchestra, then a regular guest conductor of several major European orchestras, and most recently, succeeding Daniel Barenboim as conductor of the Bastille Opéra in Paris; and the New Zealand pianist Michael Houstoun, who is now playing about thirty concerts a year in the Pacific region, has made six solo recordings, and is about to begin recording all the Beethoven sonatas. His book on piano technique was published in 1988, and in 1989 he was awarded the Turnovsky Prize – the highest artistic award in New Zealand.

'I have two abiding positive memories of the 1975 Leeds Competition,' says Houstoun: 'My finals performance [Prokofiev's Third Concerto] with Sir Charles Groves, which I really enjoyed; and a conversation with jury member Rosalyn Tureck, which will always stay with me. She was fully wise about the nature of competitions and totally encouraging about my approach to music.'

Ian Hobson came fourth in 1978. Three years later, he re-entered at Leeds and won. He is so far the only competitor for whom the risk has paid off.

Daniel Blumenthal, a pupil of Benjamin Kaplan, entered the Leeds in 1981 having already acquitted himself creditably at the Sydney, Busoni and Rubinstein competitions:

One enters for competitions hoping that they will be a stepping stone to a career, not because one enjoys them, or for the money.

The media interest is important, and one hopes for concert engagements. Leeds had a reputation for starting people's careers – Lupu, Perahia – but that's not true so much now that there's a glut of competitions. I thought the Leeds was a good competition; the repertoire was musicianly, and it's a musicians' contest. I didn't get any engagements from my fourth prize there, but I did get an agent. Since 1981, the number of concerts offered to the winner had declined – it's now no longer a blank cheque, and the organizers decide who they want for a particular concert. There was a time when sponsors of concerts felt they could fill halls on the strength of a Leeds prize-winner, but that's no longer true.

I felt that the order in which we played in the final was rather too arbitrary – it was for the benefit of TV. I had to play first, with the Beethoven Second Concerto. It was a good experience working with Charles Groves, even under such trying circumstances. There was a period when I thought I could adapt my playing to suit a particular jury, but I quickly realized it wouldn't work. It's not like a concert: the atmosphere's all wrong. It's a survival course – you have to go out and master your nerves. I never played my best in competitions.

After the Leeds, Blumenthal entered the Geneva Competition, coming second, and the 1983 Queen Elisabeth of the Belgians, where he won fourth prize. Rather surprisingly, that started his career.

In Belgium, the contest is a national event – it's on TV six nights a week, four hours a night. People watch it as if it's a sporting event. But it only leads to national, not international engagements. Something just happened to me there – people wanted to hear me again. A competition is only as important as its TV coverage. Without Brussels, I would be back in New York, struggling to make ends meet.

Blumenthal settled in Belgium, because he couldn't have fulfilled the engagements offered him had he still lived in the States. He is now a professor in the Flemish section of the Brussels Conservatoire, where he prepares his own students for competitions ('because there's no alternative'), and plays about a hundred concerts a year. He has released a Gershwin record for Classics for Pleasure, and several recordings on French and Belgian labels: 'One must be realistic about competitions. Even if you win first prize, you may not get anything out of it. Anyone can win a competition, unless your nerves can't take it. We need a few more Lupus and Perahias.'

Louis Lortie's fourth place in 1984 came as a disappointing anti-

climax. He arrived in Leeds on a high, having just won the Busoni Competition:

I felt I should have been placed higher. Beethoven's Fourth may not have been the right choice of concerto – but it was on the list of both competitions, and I won the Busoni with it. It's not a typical competition winner. I didn't try to adapt my playing in any way – the only time I might try that is if I were required to play at 9.30 a.m.!

I went in for the Leeds to try to get a foothold in Europe. I already had an agent, but afterwards I did have other offers – but not the 'big men'. The combination of Busoni and Leeds actually worked very well. The good thing about Leeds is its visibility. I built a public right away through the TV exposure, and afterwards, when I played in London, the halls were full. The real jury, after all, is the public. The next two or three years afer a competition are the important ones. I still haven't got a firm foothold in London, although I have played with all the London orchestras, and have made eight records so far, including one with the LSO.

I'm now doing a lot of work in Canada, more than before in the USA [where he has played with many of the top American orchestras, including the Boston, San Francisco, and Philadelphia], and quite a lot in Europe, especially Germany, Italy and Holland. I played a couple of times in France, under very bad conditions. I can live without France.

I want to diversify, to explore other musical directions. I've started to conduct from the keyboard, especially in Mozart, and to play two-piano repertoire. My solo repertoire is very diverse: I don't want to be categorized. It encompasses Mozart, Liszt, Chopin, Ravel, Stravinsky – different composers, different periods.

Unlike most of the other competitors, Lortie found the atmosphere at Leeds rather uncongenial, a recollection perhaps compounded by his disappointment:

I'd just come from the Busoni where everyone was very friendly, people were having fun together, but at Leeds, I felt that everyone was looking at each other like Roman gladiators. Some people even asked me, 'Why did you bother to come? You've just won the Busoni!' But in the long run, it benefited my career considerably – it got me a public. That's what matters.

Boris Berezovsky entered the 1987 Leeds as a complete novice:

My teacher at the Moscow Conservatory made me enter. I was only seventeen and I knew nothing about competitions. I had never entered one before. The Leeds was considered the finest in the world. I was satisfied with the way I played, but it was really too early for me to play Beethoven 4 in the final. I wasn't quite ready for it. I was disappointed after the competition, but now I realize that it was a good thing to come fourth. Over the last two years I've been able to expand my repertoire, and I'm now giving concerts – some in England, some in Germany, many in the USSR. I feel the good thing about Leeds is that the audience remember you, and I got a lot of concerts out of it. There are many competitions in which only the first prize-winners get noticed, but not at Leeds.

I thought Ovchinnikov played very well at Leeds. The Moscow audiences were indignant about the 1982 Tchaikovsky Competition result – they felt that Donohoe should have been placed higher than Ovchinnikov. I shall be entering the 1990 Tchaikovsky Competition, and I'm broadening my repertoire to prepare for it.

I'm doing a record for an American label at the moment, but I want to do more work in England. England is the best place to play now.

A fifth prize has been awarded only five times at Leeds. The French pianist Anne Queffelec was the first such recipient, in 1969:

I had finished my cycle of studies at Paris, and for me, it was the right time to enter competitions. I had the technical ability, and I was bursting with enthusiasm – I needed new horizons, and I saw competitions as part of the possibilities which were opening up for me, not as competitive events. I enjoyed playing at Leeds. Competitions are said to be anti-artistic, but it's difficult to measure. There's no absolute truth about the result, but there is a sympathetic audience, which one feels is not just there to enjoy the rivalry between pianists. There was a very warm atmosphere – everyone was trying to give their best. The standard was very high. I was surprised to get through each stage, and I wasn't expecting to get to the final. I was naturally disappointed not to win, but I just wanted to do my best. I felt my playing improved as I went along. The finalists were all brilliant.

My post-Leeds career has gone very well. There are so many talented pianists around, and sometimes the most talented ones don't do well. Nowadays, because of the increasing importance of the media, you have to have great confidence in yourself in order to inspire confidence in others. You need charisma as well as talent.

I'm very lucky to have so many engagements – about fifty or sixty a year, together with a great deal of chamber music.

I now play principally in England – and that is because of Leeds. I didn't just win a prize there – I also met a lot of people, who did a great deal for me. I was lucky that my career didn't collapse afterwards. There are always others coming up behind – you have to capitalize on your win. It's important to maintain a high profile. I've always had good contact with English audiences, and I love the atmosphere here – it's a good mixture of seriousness, high professionalism and relaxation. I've had fun playing with many British orchestras; and at the start of my career I was invited to play at many music societies. I was always accommodated in people's houses, and everyone has been so nice.

One life isn't enough for all the repertoire one would like to learn – I'll never learn all the Mozart concertos, or all the Bach preludes, for example. There are so many things to be discovered. My strong point is French music – not only Debussy and Ravel, but also more unfamiliar things – the Roussel Concerto, the Fauré Ballade, d'Indy, and so on. I've been able to play these with good orchestras and conductors. I've played about fifteen of the Mozart concertos so far, and I've done many recordings – about twenty for Erato, and now some for Virgin Classics. I love Bach and Schumann, but I prefer to listen to Schumann rather than play it. There are stages in one's life when one feels the need for different types of music.

Anne Queffelec is married, and lives near Paris with her family – a three-year-old and a new baby:

It's very difficult to combine the life of a pianist with family life – it's exhausting. But I'm very grateful to the Leeds Competition and to England. If I had listened to those people who told me not to go in for Leeds, I would have not had such wonderful opportunities and musical experiences.

The next fifth-prize-winner was Kathryn Stott, now one of Britain's most sought-after pianists, with many recordings and broadcast performances to her credit. At nineteen, she was studying at the Royal College of Music with Kendall Taylor, who suggested she should enter for the 1978 competition:

I learnt the *Emperor* Concerto for the competition. My teacher thought it would be a good one, but I didn't feel as prepared as I could have been – I had only played it with two amateur orchestras before. The final was a nerve-racking shock! But I was delighted with the result – I was pleased to have got so far. Suddenly, although I was still a student, I got about ninety concerts a year, including a Proms date, which wouldn't have happened otherwise. I also made my Festival Hall début with the LSO. I was invited to play at music clubs and festivals and with big orchestras, and the RCM let me do the engagements. My repertoire was still very small – I only knew two concertos when I entered the Leeds – and I could have done with some advice. I should have turned down more concerts. I coped well for a couple of years, and then things came to a stop. I took three months off to take stock, and realized that I had been doing too much, and hadn't had any time to learn new works.

After nine years, Kathryn Stott decided to follow in Hobson's footsteps and re-enter the Leeds. For her, it seemed an unfortunate decision: she was eliminated in the first round, to the outrage of some of the jury members:

I felt happy with my performance then – I would have known it myself if I had played badly. It seemed obvious that a Russian was going to win. There were a lot of people on the jury who weren't active players and many were coming to the ends of their careers. I was fuming afterwards. I suppose I didn't play like a competition winner – it was more personal. Some people do play in a 'competition way' but I couldn't have done it. It seemed to have little effect on my career – my work doubled in 1988. Certain people were so annoyed that they made an effort to give me work afterwards. My confidence was certainly shaken – but the effects didn't last.

I hate competitions. Young players should be very careful about them – I was lucky. They're fair in principle, but the proof comes afterwards.

Christopher O'Riley, a veteran of the Montreal, Van Cliburn and Busoni competitions, was very busy at the time of the 1981 Leeds, having just finished his studies at the New England Conservatory:

My teacher, Russell Sherman, was in favour of competitions – he thought they were still the best way of establishing a reputation. Although I didn't get a top prize at Leeds, it was still good for me – the publicity at Leeds is far better than at the Van Cliburn. There the TV coverage is 'slice of life', whereas the BBC treatment at Leeds is more serious and even-handed.

I felt the placing was odd at Leeds: every round I survived, I got more and more confused. The end result at Montreal seemed to make sense, whereas in Leeds, some big guns got knocked out in the first round. It was very quirky. We were invited to talk to the jury members, and some of the things they said were disturbing – 'You wore a watch when you played', or, 'You played the Liszt Étude too fast' – and I hadn't played any Liszt! It was frightening – I didn't know what the jury was after. I think it was a mistake to choose the Schumann as a competition piece – every pianist has an intimate relationship with that concerto, and everyone reacts differently to the way you play it. I think the personal ideas of the jury do colour the result: it is not always impartial. Competitions are treacherous things: one must not make any waves.

Very little happened to me as a result of Leeds. I was represented for three years by Young Concert Artists' Trust, and I think most of the British engagements during that period came through them. I've hardly played at all in the UK since then – one concert for BBC Radio 3 – but I have had some dates in Europe, and my concerts in the USA are sold out. I'm very happy with the way my career is developing, but I would like to play more in Europe. I've released three CDs – one of all-American music, one of Ravel, and the Busoni *Fantasia contrappuntistica*.

I think there should be a minimum age requirement for competitions. Pianistic maturity is cumulative, and should not be tried by fire. I've learned a great deal from them, but I don't think they should form a part of the learning process. They are useful in training you how to concentrate, and in trying to second-guess what the jury is going to think. Some pianists enter for their first competition at eighteen and never let up until they're thirty-one. It can be a debilitating process – and they never learn any new repertoire.

David Buechner, fifth in 1984, exemplifies this new breed of 'professional competitor' – but despite a string of prizes at major international competitions, including the Tchaikovsky, the Gina Bachauer, the Queen Elisabeth of the Belgians, the Vina del Mar and the Beethoven, he has nevertheless managed to absorb well over forty concertos, ranging from Mozart to Wuorinen, into his massive repertory. A student of Rudolf Firkušný at the Juilliard School, Buechner was studying for a doctorate when he entered the Leeds, in the hope of expanding his career in Europe and England:

I wasn't happy with my placing. I didn't think I played well until the final, but I was disappointed to receive such a low placing. I think my style wasn't what the jury was looking for. Perhaps too many people were on the jury, and in a desire to keep everyone happy, any excess of temperament was discouraged. I played in a highly personal style, but it can be better to 'play safe'. But that is meaningless, and the musical public suffers. Many young pianists suffer from a lack of distinctive personality.

I was followed in the final by Ju Hee Suh, who played spectacularly. She was sensational, and she eclipsed me. I thought she played the Rakhmaninov wonderfully, but she got a high prize because she was so young and made such a stunning visual impact.

Nothing happened after the Leeds. I had gone through that intense physical and emotional ordeal, only to get no agent, no engagements. It changed my attitude to Europe – it seemed more cut-throat than anywhere else. I got more work after the Brussels competition. My career has continued to grow in the USA and the Far East since, and I've done my first recordings, one of Busoni and Stravinsky, another of Brahms and Dvořák. I think it's just fate that I haven't got a European career.

Like Kathryn Stott, David Buechner re-entered for the Leeds in 1987, also with disappointing results: 'I was eliminated in the semi-final.' Now thirty, he remains 'tempted' by the prospect of entering further competitions, but he admits he has done all the major ones:

If you're lucky, you win, and then you can give up. One has to be realistic – maybe my playing is not destined to win a top prize. I think competitions are terrible and should be abolished. They're an unfortunate aspect of life – a pre-packaged, Spartan-style exhibition which appeals to man's basest instincts. How can you do this to a Mozart concerto? I only do them for the opportunities they offer, but I wish they would all disappear.

Hugh Tinney's career had already been launched internationally before he took fifth prize at the 1987 Leeds competition. In 1984 he had won the Paloma O'Shea Competition in Santander, which had led to over a hundred engagements in several different European countries. But his Spanish agent had little influence in getting him concerts in Britain, and he decided to enter the Leeds in the hope of launching his UK career.

Tinney is one of the few competitors who admits to enjoying competitions 'so long as I am prepared for them'. He felt that the Leeds programme didn't entirely suit his existing repertoire:

I was pushed. The first round, in which I played Beethoven and Chopin, suited me well, but the second round had a very narrow choice, and I felt constrained. I had to play works I probably wouldn't have otherwise.

I find I react differently to the various stages of a competition.

The round in which one is at one's most tired and vulnerable tends to be the semi-final. There you have to give a forty-five-minute recital, together with a chamber music piece, without a break in between. I gave an interview afterwards, and I felt totally drained. That was my most nervous round in Leeds and also in other competitions. There was a fantastic sense of occasion at the final, however. I really enjoyed playing with Rattle and the CBSO.

But I wasn't happy with my placing. I remember chatting to the other finalists behind the stage while we were waiting for the results. When the announcement was made, I felt a sense of unreality. As we walked on to the stage, I thought, 'I wonder what people will make of this?' I didn't think the final placings were very fair. The system of taking a separate vote on each place can weight the results, especially if there is a powerful pressure group within the jury. Politics does enter into the voting.

Despite his relatively low placing, the Leeds had a positive effect on Tinney's career:

I had good feedback afterwards. At 9.15 on the Monday morning after the competition, the phone rang offering me a Festival Hall engagement with the Philharmonia, and the dates poured in. One of the good things about Leeds is that they leave the offer of engagements up to the individual promoters, who are free to pick whom they want. I was approached after the semi-final stage by one or two agents, and after the final I was taken on.

Like Ju Hee Suh, Tinney entered the 1989 Van Cliburn Competition with no success; but at thirty-one he is now at the end of the competition stage of his career. He is well-established as a soloist in Britain and Europe, and has broadcast on radio and TV in over fifteen different countries. At the core of his repertoire are the nineteenth-century Romantics, especially Liszt and Chopin, but recently he has performed more of the Classics, especially Mozart concertos and the solo piano music of Schubert. He has made an all-Liszt record, but feels that recording projects are currently dominated by producers' ideas:

complete this, complete that. Balanced recitals don't sell, but music isn't like that. I don't see myself as a specialist, but I'm developing a few areas. Contemporary music isn't my scene. And I've stopped programming Bach. If one is going to play Bach, one must give it a lot of thought.

A sixth prize has been awarded in the last four Leeds competitions.

The first of these went to the Japanese girl Etsuko Terada, whom Kathryn Stott recalls 'crying for ages' at her disappointing placing. Her present whereabouts and career are unknown.

By far the most controversial sixth placing, particularly in the light of the comments of some jury members that the first prize 'went to the one most ready to cope with the engagements', was awarded in 1981 to Peter Donohoe, the Manchester-born pianist who had come third in the 1976 British Liszt Competition, and who had been a finalist in the Liszt Bartók competition in Budapest. Donohoe went on to share joint-second prize (no first being awarded) with Vladimir Ovchinnikov at the 1982 Tchaikovsky Competition. He is now constantly in demand as a soloist both in the UK and abroad; and has arguably enjoyed the most successful career of any of the 1981 finalists. Nevertheless, nine years later, the memories of what he saw as a humiliating defeat at Leeds still rankle:

In 1981 I was twenty-eight and was already making a considerable living as a professional pianist. I had given concerts with many national and regional British orchestras and had made a record for EMI. But my friends and people at the BBC told me that if I wanted to work on an international level, I would have to have the exposure of a major competition. I was reluctant to agree – I thought that a lot of the entrants would be much younger than me, and I've always been sceptical of a jury's ability to judge talent. It's difficult to find a judge who can put aside his own prejudices – anyone will tend to be more sympathetic to his own style. I think many of them look for a stereotype – someone who will conform to certain ideals in terms of presentation or style of playing.

So I treated the competition like a driving test or a job interview – I did everything I cynically could to win. Up to the finals, I was optimistic. But clearly, I miscalculated. I was already doing about a hundred concerts a year by then, and my repertoire was wide. I felt that was one of my strengths, and I wanted to show the jury that I was at home in a variety of styles. But now, they want specialists. 'He is a Mozart player / a twentieth-century specialist / a big pianist, so he should play Brahms'. So someone like Paul Crossley, who has been closely associated with the music of Tippett and Messiaen, is assumed not to be able to play Beethoven. This attitude spills over to the critics, too. Mozart is a real problem.

But I love music: I thirst for new repertoire. I had done a lot of twentieth-century music because so few people play it, but I wanted to do the standard repertory too. At Leeds, I had played a series of big virtuoso pieces in the earlier rounds – *Gaspard de la*

32 Some of the 1975 semi-finalists: (left to right) Myung-Whun Chung, Andras Schiff, Boris Berman, Mitsuko Uchida, Robert Benz.

33 Mitsuko Uchida after her finals performance with Sir Charles Groves.
© *Sophie Baker*

34 Some members of the 1975 jury with Fanny Waterman (left to right) Pal Kadosa, Artur Balsam, Rosalyn Tureck, Sir Charles Groves, Mikhail Voskressensky, Fanny Waterman, Gerald Moore, Mindru Katz, Phyllis Sellick, Béla Siki. © *Yorkshire Post*

35 Marion Thorpe and Fanny Waterman with Dmitri Alexeev, winner of the 1975 competition. © *Yorkshire Post*

36 The 1978 finalists (left to right) Etsuko Terada, Ian Hobson, Lydia Artymiw, Diana Kacso, Michel Dalberto, Kathryn Stott. © *Yorkshire Post*

37 Fanny Waterman and Marion Thorpe with Michel Dalberto, the 1978 winner. © *Yorkshire Post*

38 The 1981 jury in the early rounds: front row (left to right) Nina Milkina, Orazio Frugoni, Rudolf Fischer, Fanny Waterman (Chairman), Claude Frank, Abbey Simon; centre row: Daniel Pollack, Arie Vardi, Hans Graf, Béla Siki; back row: Moura Lympany, Hugo Steurer, Viktor Weinbaum, Marie Antoinette de Freitas Branco. © *Yorkshire Post*

39 The Leeds Competition celebrates its coming of age: the 1981 finalists with Fanny Waterman (centre), Lionel Squibb and Peter Peres (from Steinways): (left to right) Squibb, Wolfgang Manz, Bernard d'Ascoli, Christopher O'Riley, Peres, Daniel Blumenthal, Ian Hobson, Peter Donohoe. © *Yorkshire Post*

40 Ian Hobson receives his prize from HRH The Duchess of Kent, while
Fanny Waterman looks on. © *Yorkshire Post*

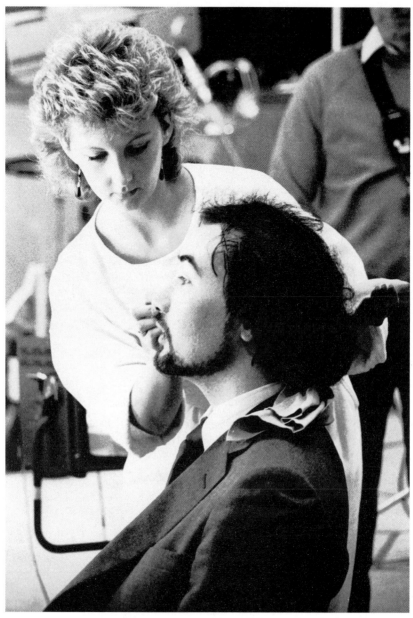

41 Jon Kimura Parker being prepared for his television appearance in the 1984 finals. © *Frank Corr*

42 The 1984 finalists with Fanny Waterman (left to right) Junko Otake, Jon Kimura Parker, Ju Hee Suh, Louis Lortie, David Buechner, Emma Tahmisian. © *Frank Corr*

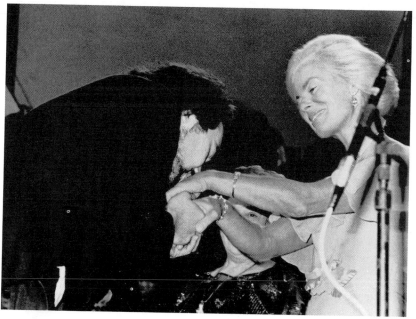

43 Jon Kimura Parker receives his prize from HRH The Duchess of Kent. © *Yorkshire Post*

44 Some members of the 1987 jury: back row (left to right), György Sándor, Takahiro Sonoda, Karl-Heinz Kämmerling, Joaquín Soriano, John Lill, Françoise Logan (administrator), Gordon Stewart, Lev Vlasenko, Rudolf Fischer, Yury Boukoff; front row: Noel Flores, Tatiana Nikolaeva, Fanny Waterman (chairman), Halina Czerny-Stefańska, Konstantin Ganev.
© *Maxwell Roberts*

45 Vladimir Ovchinnikov rehearsing for the semi-final chamber music round with Erich Gruenberg. © *Maxwell Roberts*

46 Relaxing at Tetley Hall. The 1987 semi-finalists: back row, (left to right) Marcantonio Barone, David Buechner, Eckart Heiligers, Vladimir Ovchinnikov; centre row: Ian Munro, Hortense Cartier-Bresson, Noriko Ogawa, Hugh Tinney; front row: Boris Berezovsky, Jean-Efflam Bavouzet. © *Maxwell Roberts*

47 A pensive moment for Vladimir Ovchinnikov. © *Maxwell Roberts*

48 Noriko Ogawa with David Orr (left) and Robin Frost of Harveys of Bristol.
© *Maxwell Roberts*

49 Simon Rattle with the 1987 finalists: back row, (left to right) Rattle, Ian Munro, Marcantonio Barone; front row: Vladimir Ovchinnikov, Noriko Ogawa, Hugh Tinney, Boris Berezovsky.
© *Yorkshire Post*

50 Vladimir Ovchinnikov receives his prize from HRH The Duchess of Kent. © *Asadour Guzelian*

51 Marion Harewood at the 1972 competition.

52 The manuscript of Britten's *Notturno*, commissioned by
Marion Harewood and Fanny Waterman for the first competition in 1963.

53 Murray Perahia, winner of the 1972 competition. © *Sophie Baker*

54 The first three Leeds winners at the 1972 competition: (left to right)
Michael Roll, Rafael Orozco, Radu Lupu. © *Judy Tapp*

55 Dmitri Alexeev, winner of the 1975 competition. © *Sophie Baker*

56 (*Left*) Michel Dalberto, winner of the 1978 competition. © *Yorkshire Post*

57 Ian Hobson, winner of the 1981 competition. © *Yorkshire Post*

58 Jon Kimura Parker, winner of the 1984 competition, practising at the Baskinds' home. © *Frank Corr*

59 Fanny Waterman with Françoise Logan, Honorary Administrator of the Harveys Leeds International Pianoforte Competition. © *Maxwell Roberts*

60 Fanny Waterman, 1990.

nuit, the *Wanderer* Fantasy, the Bartók and Liszt sonatas. I am a big pianist, a large-scale pianist. You have to develop the largest possible technique in order to cope with anything. But I can also be a small-scale pianist when the music requires it. I didn't want to be pigeonholed. So I chose Beethoven 4 for the final. It's a particularly difficult work to play – if you can pull it off at all, it shows you have a certain amount of talent. But I don't think it's a winning concerto. I felt I played it better than either of the Moscow concertos [Tchaikovsky 1 and Rakhmaninov 3]. The Beethoven was more of a musical challenge.

I couldn't believe the result. It seemed to me that the names had been copied down in the wrong order. People have such high expectations of the winner, and if the public is against the result, it can make life very difficult. I had played with Charles Groves many times before, and after the competition, he was quite unfairly blamed in the Press for having messed up the accompaniments of the concertos that didn't sound so good. No one could have held on to some of those concertos – the reason they didn't sound good was because the piano playing wasn't up to it, but they still got good prizes. Nobody could say that Groves is not a good accompanist.

It's difficult to be objective – I was so upset afterwards. The competitors got to hear rumours of arguments at the jury meetings – but it's all hearsay. But when we were invited to talk to the jury members at the end, no one would speak to me. Everyone excused themselves and disappeared. And afterwards I met with huge embarrassment from many of the people who had urged me to enter for the competition. I already had an invitation to play at the 1982 Proms, and Robert Ponsonby was terribly embarrassed. My agent, Howard Hartog of Ingpen and Williams, said 'You'll have to be extremely hard, and ignore the opinions of those who haven't got any opinions'.

It was a devastating blow to my self-confidence: I felt absolutely awful. If you're a sensitive artist, your self-confidence is vulnerable. Fortunately, my northern background enabled me to survive. I've always been very cynical about the media circus. And I continued to be booked afterwards by the people who believed in me. I don't think I would have survived without Moscow, though. Without that, I would probably have gone downhill as an artist. The bookings would have dried up, and I'd have stopped practising. But Moscow was on the horizon, and I was working towards it. It was a kind of revenge, and it worked well.

Ovchinnikov is a very genuine musician, not a networker. He's still young as a musician, but he has great facility. He was under enormous pressure to win the 1982 competition, and the jury couldn't allow a Westerner to beat him. So they compromised.

The Leeds is certainly better-organized than Moscow, where in the first round, out of a total of a hundred minutes of music I'd prepared I was only allowed to play thirty minutes' worth – a movement from here, a bit from there. It was a total mishmash – something one never has to cope with as a professional pianist. Then in the second round I had to play for two and a quarter hours without a break – three movements of *Petrushka*, the Liszt Sonata, a Tippett sonata, and a Soviet test-piece. For that we were given a choice of two. One turned out to be by the chairman of the jury – but I'd unwittingly chosen the other! Then we had to play the Tchaikovsky Concerto, and another of our own choice, with an unbelievably bad conductor, on only seventy-five minutes' rehearsal. The rehearsal time at Leeds is barely adequate, but it's improving.

After Moscow, all the promotors from whom I'd heard nothing after Leeds approached me, with unbelievable hypocrisy. It's a form of social climbing – but if you broke your finger, you wouldn't see them for dust. But the ones who are not like that run the best orchestras, the best concert societies. I think there are encouraging signs recently that the media circus which was in full swing in 1981 is losing steam.

On reflection it's very easy to criticize, and it's hard to run a piano competition. I think the biggest lesson of all is that nothing is right or wrong, nothing is good or bad – within certain parameters, of course. There's a shortage of people on juries who are prepared to cogitate, put their prejudices aside, and tell themselves to think fairly.

In 1984 the sixth prize at Leeds was awarded to the Bulgarian pianist Emma Tahmisian, a graduate of the Bulgarian State Conservatory in Sofia, where she had studied with Julia and Konstantin Ganev. Having won the 1977 Schumann Competition, she had subsequently won prizes at the 1980 Montreal and 1982 Tchaikovsky Competitions, and by 1984 was herself a teacher at the State Conservatory. Now resident in New York, she has given concerts and recitals in various centres in the USA, and has toured Eastern and Western Europe:

I had heard that the Leeds was one of the most serious competitions, that it was in search of real musicians, not just flashy pianists. And its prize-winners seem to have had longer artistic careers than some, who are in the limelight for a couple of years, and then come to a dead end.

I enjoyed competitions – I thought of them as concerts. One ought to be prepared to play a few recitals and concerts in a very short space of time: it rarely happens in real life, but the opportunity may arise. It's good training for the life of a concert artist, if one can put aside personal and political disappointments.

Emma Tahmisian particularly enjoyed her finals performance:

The orchestra played as if it were playing chamber music: each member played so beautifully, and established such a relationship with the soloist that it was not merely accompanying – it was an active participant in the music-making process. That was the first time I personally experienced such 'give and take' with an orchestra, and it was for me an extraordinary experience.

I prepared myself very rigorously for Leeds. I went to Paris and London to get the feel of the different atmosphere, the different culture. I have only one rather odd memory. Someone with a strange sense of humour had put a portrait of Lenin in my room at Tetley Hall. I wasn't amused. But I met some extremely nice people at Leeds: Fanny Waterman was very kind, and the people to whose homes I was taken to practise acted in a way one could never forget – they were the best possible advertisement for the city.

Emma Tahmisian was offered an engagement in England after the competition, but was unable to return to fulfil it. The next year she was invited to take part in the Van Cliburn Competition. She took the fourth prize and it changed her life:

Afterwards the competition arranged a lot of concerts for me, and people proposed that I should stay in New York. So I called my embassy, and enrolled as an MA student at the Juilliard. It took a year to adjust to the different mentality of the West, and to understand the rules of musical life. My career started little by little, but now I'm getting known through chamber music, solo recitals, broadcasts. But I would like to pursue a career back in Europe. I'm interested in doing anything – except conducting or composing – related to music-making. So far as repertoire is concerned, I eat anything!

The last of the sixth-prize-winners, Marcantonio Barone, had graduated from the Curtis Institute in 1982, where he had studied with Eleanor Sokoloff. He had only participated in one other international competition – the Busoni – before Leeds:

My decision to enter Leeds stemmed from its distinguished reputation and the track-record of its prize-winners. I already had a modest career in England, where I had an agent: I had played a début recital at the Wigmore Hall, and several other minor concerts, and I had developed a few contacts. I also had a good career in the USA.

The repertoire at Leeds was congenial, but rather narrow in that it specifies certain works. Other competitions have a broader choice. But I found works in all rounds that I was comfortable playing. Out of ten semi-finalists, three, including myself, chose the original version of Rakhmaninov's Second Sonata, which I found amusing.

My father [founder of the Bryn Mawr Conservatory in Pennsylvania] had recently suffered a stroke, and his condition worsened just before the Leeds competition. I was very torn as to whether to go, but I felt my father would want me to go ahead. The crisis gave me strength – it was far more devastating than the pressure of competing, and put it all into perspective.

I would naturally have been happier with a higher placing, but my first goal was to have the pleasure of playing with Simon Rattle. It was a great thrill to work with someone of that calibre.

I didn't get any engagements as a direct result of the Leeds. Some things did come my way, though. I was invited to play with Barry Wordsworth and the CBSO the following summer, and there were some smaller recital engagements in the north-east of England, which I don't think would have happened were it not for the competition. It gave me a boost, but not as much as I would have hoped.

My reputation at home was enhanced, but the Leeds gets little notice in the US Press. It's inexplicable – cultural events get minimal notice over there. But I'm building up my repertoire and doing more and more concerts every year, mainly recitals and chamber music, and a few concerto appearances. I made my German début in October '89, and I'm returning to Europe in the spring. I also teach at the Bryn Mawr Conservatory. I consider it's an integral part of my career – it's a great joy to pass on what one has learnt to young students.

'It is a matter of regret to us that a tiny minority of our past competitors have felt disappointed by their unexpected elimination or their placings in the final line-up,' says Fanny Waterman.

Most artists feel utterly committed to their performances and find it incomprehensible that a jury may not share the same commitment. Our aim is, and has always been, to make the Leeds competition as valuable and positive an experience as possible for all our competitors. Over the past nine competitions, some 650 pianists have played at Leeds, of whom forty-seven have won prizes, but only nine could emerge as first prize winners. Many who did not even reach the finals have gone on to major careers, and the thirty-eight 'runners-up' all had the benefit of media exposure and the opportunities of good engagements.

We feel justifiably proud of all our prizewinners, and we hope that, in spite of their disappointment at the time, they will come to look back on the Leeds as a valuable stepping stone in their careers.

In general, the young laureates are prepared to take a realistic and pragmatic attitude to their careers, and most agree with Sheppard and Uchida, who both stress that, while a competition win may give a pianist a 'leg up' on the way, 'the rest is up to you'. 'The career of a concert pianist seems to be shorter now,' says Wolfgang Manz. 'It's not like the days of Rubinstein or Horowitz. Everything changes so quickly – there are many more good players and many more prize-winners around.'

'If you don't lose, competitions help you a great deal,' says Ju Hee Suh. 'You're suddenly in the limelight, and even if you don't win first prize, you still learn a lot from the experience.'

Chapter Sixteen

The Eighth Competition: 1984

Whatever the respective merits of the 1981 prize-winners, none felt more strongly that a question mark continued to hang over the jury's decision that year than Peter Donohoe's friends and supporters. Still smarting from his disappointment at Leeds, Donohoe took his revenge the following year by occupying the second place (the first prize not being awarded), jointly with a future Leeds winner, Vladimir Ovchinnikov, at the Tchaikovsky Competition. His victory was greeted in Moscow with scenes of almost hysterical public adulation, of the kind reserved in the West only for pop-stars. 'From inflammatory and occasionally uncertain beginnings, his art has blossomed into something of exceptional ease and maturity,' wrote the critic Bryce Morrison in the *Daily Telegraph*.

Meanwhile, the 1981 Leeds winner, Ian Hobson, had decided to return to his former base at the University of Illinois, from where his multi-faceted career as performer, conductor and lecturer flourished in the States, but not so much in Britain.

'I don't think Ian Hobson was absolutely devoted to a career as an international pianist', says Sir Charles Groves, who found the 1981 competition 'a strange and uncomfortable year'. 'Peter Donohoe is a musician of extremely acute sensibilities and knowledge. He has a great grasp of the repertoire. And Bernard d'Ascoli has had a good career since 1981.'

But Fanny Waterman was determined that the 1984 competition would surmount all reservations.

The brochure attracted a record number of applicants (250), who had to be whittled down to 101 acceptances – all professional pianists:

The candidate who has carried off the prizes at his conservatoire, but has not emerged into the cold, hard, competitive musical world, is not yet ready to enter the Leeds International Pianoforte Competition, if only for the fact that he is as yet unable to carry the burden of the prize engagements.

Harveys' sponsorship package for 1984 included a massive increase in cash assistance, to £70,000, plus an important début recital at the QEH for the winner on 29 November; while the companies and individuals who had so generously supported the 1981 competition again pledged their help in 1984. This meant a substantial increase in prize-money: the first prize, now incorporating the Edward Boyle Prize and the Princess Mary Gold Medal, was raised to £3,500, with a second prize, donated by Marjorie and Arnold Ziff, of £2,000. The Calouste Gulbenkian Foundation supplied the third, of £1,200, the fourth now stood at £900, including the Dorothy Hess Memorial Prize; the fifth, incorporating the William Pitts Memorial Prize, at £700, and the sixth, the Pierre de Menasce Prize, at £500. The four other semi-finalists received £250 each, donated by the Paris fashion designers Louis Féraud (of whose British operation Fanny Waterman's eldest son Robert was a managing director); while those who reached the second stage received ten prizes of £120 each. In addition, the best performance in the chamber music round would receive £250.

The winners had the opportunity of over thirty international engagements, ranging from dates with the Chicago, Baltimore and Washington National orchestras, to engagements in Australia, East and West Germany, Israel, South Africa, Spain, Sweden, Switzerland, Eire, Malta, Italy, Belgium, Canada, France, Hong Kong, and even a P&O Annual Musical Cruise in the Mediterranean. The list of British orchestral engagements included dates with nine London orchestras, including a Victor Hochhauser concert at the Festival Hall; two with the Bournemouth orchestras, three in Scotland, one in Ulster, and one each with the CBSO, English Northern Philharmonia (now resident in Leeds), the Guildford and Hull Philharmonics, the Hallé, RLPO and Northern Sinfonia. But for the first time, no engagement with a BBC orchestra was offered. There were thirteen festival appearances, including Aldeburgh, Bath and Edinburgh; and forty-three recital dates all over the country, from Kirklees to Devon.

By 1983, Marion Thorpe had found that she could no longer devote the necessary time to the affairs of the competition, and had resigned as Vice-Chairman, while remaining Vice-President. Fanny's assistant, Françoise Logan, was now serving as Deputy Administrator to Michael Barrett, with Paul Holloway as Treasurer, and Harry Tolson as Publications Director. Since the last competition, the Friends of the LIPC, under the chairmanship of Maurice Hare, had held many fund-raising events – including three dinners with distinguished guest speakers, a recital by Bernard d'Ascoli and two post-concert receptions for Wolfgang Manz and Peter Donohoe – which enabled them to donate £1,250 to the Edward Boyle Memorial Trust, and also to assist all the competitors, not just the prize-winners, in the forthcoming competition. Prior to 1984 the competitors had been expected to pay for their own food and accommodation at Tetley Hall; but from now on, the cost was borne – for the duration of their participation – by the Friends of the Competition.

The fourteen jurors in 1984, under Fanny Waterman's chairmanship, included four – Fischer, Frugoni, Graf and Vardi – who had served in 1981. The newcomers were the long-standing music critic of *The Times* and author Joan Chissell; Dean Elder, the American writer, music journalist, editor of *Clavier* magazine and piano teacher; Ding Shande from China, a pianist, composer and deputy director of the Shanghai Conservatory; the celebrated German pedagogue Karl-Heinz Kämmerling, professor of piano at the Musikhochschule in Hanover, and Vice-Chairman of EPTA; Pierre Sancan, a former Grand Prix de Rome winner for composition, who also sustained a career as concert pianist and as a world-famous teacher (his students included Pommier, Béroff and Collard); the pianists Hans Leygraf (whose recordings included all the Mozart sonatas, and who taught at the Mozarteum in Salzburg); György Sándor, a graduate of the Liszt Academy in Budapest and one of Bartók's last living pupils, then resident in the USA, and widely acknowledged as one of the world's great virtuosos (his recordings included the entire piano works of Bartók, Prokofiev and Kodály, and he gave the world première of Bartok's Third Piano Concerto); Cécile Ousset of France, herself a veteran of many major international competitions, and much in demand throughout the world on the concert platform; Britain's John Lill, first prize-winner at the 1970 Tchaikovsky Competition, and an internationally renowned concert pianist; and Tatiana Nikolaeva, from the USSR, a professor at the Moscow Conservatoire, who had made over 150 recordings and was the dedicatee of Shostakovich's Twenty-four Preludes and Fugues. Famous for her Bach interpretations, Tatiana Nikolaeva offered to give a recital of *The Art of Fugue* during one of the jury's free days at Leeds.

The repertoire for the 1984 competition was again little changed: the Group One pieces for the first stage once more comprised a choice of sonatas by Haydn, Mozart or Beethoven; the second group was an all-Chopin list; and the third a choice of any two sonatas by Scarlatti, any Liszt or Debussy étude, or any of the Bartók studies, Op.18.

The second-stage recital again comprised two works, one drawn from a list of big virtuoso works ranging from Bach to Ravel; while the twentieth-century section, of seven works, was more restricted than in previous years.

For the semi-final, competitors were again asked to play an own-choice recital of 45 minutes' duration, together with one of four violin sonatas with the distinguished Austrian-born violinist Erich Gruenberg, himself a former winner of the Carl Flesch Competition. The six finalists would each play a concerto with the Manchester-based BBC Philharmonic Orchestra, under Vernon Handley. Only one twentieth-century concerto – Rakhmaninov's Third – appeared in the 1984 selection: the others were the last three Beethovens, the Mendelssohn No.1 (which no one had ever chosen), the Chopin No.1, the Schumann, or Brahms' First.

Several disappointed contestants from 1981 decided to return to Leeds to try their luck once more, including Sandro de Palma, who had won the 1983 Clara Haskil Competition; José Feghali, a Brazilian student at the Royal Academy of Music, who was to win the 1986 Van Cliburn Competition; Thomas Duis and Philip Smith, a semi-finalist at Leeds in 1981. Smith's seven fellow British rivals in 1984 included Paul Coker, a pupil of Louis Kentner; Clive Swansbourne, a pupil of Claude Frank and Charles Rosen; and Jonathan Plowright, who had studied at the RAM.

The Americans fielded an impressive list of candidates – twenty-seven in all. Among them were Dickrah Atamian, a pupil of Jorge Bolet and winner of the first prize at the 1975 Naumburg Competition; Jeffrey Biegel, a pupil of Adèle Marcus at the Juilliard; David Buechner, a Firkušný pupil, who had taken first prize at the 1984 Gina Bachauer Competition, and second at the 1982 Viña del Mar in Chile; Hung-Kuan Chen, a pupil of Hans Leygraf and Alfons Kontarsky, who had won the 1982 Busoni and 1983 Rubinstein competitions; Arthur Greene, winner of the Gina Bachauer Competition in 1978, who had taken third prize in the 1983 Busoni; Michael Gurt and Duane Hulbert, both Gina Bachauer first prize-winners; Norman Krieger and Alexander Kuzmin, both prize-winning students of Adèle Marcus at the Julliard; and Timothy Smith, fourth prize-winner in the 1982 Gina Bachauer Competition, and a semi-finalist at Brussels.

Canada too was strongly represented, by five pianists, among them Angela Hewitt, who had taken first prize at the 1978 Viotti Competition; Louis Lortie from Montreal, a pupil of Leon Fleischer, who had won the Busoni Competition a few days before the Leeds opened; and Jon Kimura Parker, another student of Adèle Marcus at the Juilliard School.

Parker had won the Viña del Mar competition in Chile in 1982, when Fanny Waterman had been president of the jury. 'I was very impressed with Parker's playing,' she says:

So I suggested that he applied to enter the next Leeds competition. His application was accepted, but then I heard that he had withdrawn at a late stage, apparently because he had been offered some important engagements. I was irate: he had taken someone else's chance away. I made my views known to Dean Elder, who rang him up and 'corrected his behaviour'. So Parker changed his mind – and later he was very pleased that he had!

Since Mitsuko Uchida's success at Leeds in 1975, the number of Far Eastern contestants has risen steadily. In 1984, Japan fielded nine entrants, including Junko Otake, and Mari Tsudi, winner of the 1983 Viotti Competition at Vercelli; while the Republic of China and Taiwan sent one apiece, and Korea four, including the youngest entrant, sixteen-year-old Ju Hee Suh, who was studying at the Curtis Institute in Philadelphia under Horszowski. 'I had heard about the Leeds competition – it was very famous and prestigious – but I didn't know very much about it,' she says:

So I asked my director at the Curtis, and he thought it was a good opportunity for me. It was my first big international competition, and although I came with my mother, I was worried. But I was so well looked after. When I arrived at Gatwick, the immigration officer asked me why I was coming to Britain. I told him it was for the Leeds Competition, and he seemed very pleased – he had heard all about it!

'She came with the most fabulous credentials,' says Geoffrey de Keyser. 'She'd already played with the New York Philharmonic and Zubin Mehta. Rudolf Serkin wrote to us saying she was one of the greatest talents he'd ever heard. And naturally, being only sixteen, she aroused a great deal of anticipatory interest.'

France entered a strong team of nine, all experienced prize-winners; Germany and Italy five each; Israel four – and while as in the previous two Leeds competitions, no Soviet pianists entered, there was an assortment from various Eastern European countries, including Emma Tahmisian, from Bulgaria, who had won the 1977 Schumann Competition, taken fourth prize at Montreal three years later, and seventh in the 1982 Tchaikovsky Competition. The only Russian pianist at Leeds, André Nikolsky, was (like Helene Varvarova in 1978) a defector, resident in New York.

In the event, ninety-two competitors actually arrived at Leeds – a record number. Not having expected quite so many, the jury would

have to work ten hours a day for four days, during the first stage –
and to make matters worse, it had decided to abandon its original
plan to confine each first-round recital to twenty minutes only.

The Australian Victor Sangiorgio was the sacrificial lamb selected
to open the 1984 piano competition. But his name was not among the
competitors chosen to go through to the next round. Six Americans –
Biegel, Buechner, Chen, Greene, Krieger and Paul Maillet – survived,
as did two Japanese, Hiromi Okada and Junko Otake, two Canadians, Lortie (who had arrived late in Leeds, fresh from his triumph
at the Busoni Competition) and Parker; Duis, Alexander Lonquich
and Hans-Christian Wille from West Germany; Ulrike Gotlebe from
the DDR; Sandro da Palma from Italy, Anton Nel from South Africa;
Nikolsky; Tahmisian and Ludmil Angeloff from Bulgaria; Feghali;
and Ju Hee Suh from Korea. But during the preliminary and second
rounds, the first and most serious of several disasters struck the
competition. A mysterious virus, causing severe headaches, gid-
diness and vomiting, had begun to circulate at Tetley Hall, affecting
many of the competitors and staff so severely that at least one had
to be taken to Leeds General Infirmary.

'Everyone was very frightened,' recalls Ju Hee Suh:

Everyone was talking about this thing called 'flu' – I didn't know
what it was. Someone on my floor asked me if I had it. I did have
a bad cold at the time, and I said yes. Everyone looked horrified.
But it wasn't the mystery illness, it was just a cold. One American
boy couldn't play at all – he was so ill he had to be taken to hospital.
It was very sad.

Altogether about twenty competitors and ten staff and relatives were
affected, and the Environmental Health Officer was called in to discover the cause of the epidemic. Several second-round competitors
were forced to withdraw, including Norman Krieger, who valiantly
tried to play on the Sunday evening, but was too weak. At one stage,
the organizers feared that the competition would have to close. Anita
Woolman, who was in charge of the arrangements at Tetley Hall,
told the *Yorkshire Post*:

I have been involved with the competition from the start and this
is the worst thing ever to happen. At one stage the competitors
were falling like flies. It was very traumatic because we did not
know what it was. We did not know if it was going to develop into
a raging epidemic and shut the competition, and because of the
salmonella fears [there had been an outbreak of salmonella
poisoning at nearby Wakefield] we were not anxious to make it

public. It cut right across our piano practice and transport schedules because environmental health officers said we must not send people out to private homes to practice.

Fortunately, by the second week of the competition, the illness seemed to have largely run its course. The American who was hospitalized, Jeffrey Biegel, made a good enough recovery to be admitted to the semi-finals, along with Buechner, Da Palma, Duis, Lortie, Otake, Parker, Ju Hee Suh (who throughout the competition drew attention to her extreme youth by appearing in schoolgirl dresses and white socks), Tahmisian, and Wille. Apart from Biegel, none of the semi-finalists seemed to have caught the virus. But on 18 September another calamity occurred. Vernon Handley, who was to conduct the finals, was rushed to hospital with a kidney complaint. After several hours, the BBC Philharmonic's principal conductor, Edward Downes, agreed to step in.

'As you can imagine, things were very fraught as we tried to find someone to take over what are two far from easy concerts,' said Fanny Waterman at the time, no doubt bearing in mind the barrage of criticism faced by the orchestra and conductor in 1981. 'But we rejoice that Edward Downes happened to be free and is coming to help us. Having suffered problems with the bug earlier in the competition, I can tell you we were very relieved when after some tense waiting we found ourselves with a conductor.'

To make matters worse, there was a little local difficulty in the jury. Ding Shande, the Republic of China's representative, took violent exception to the fact that the Taiwanese flag was on display at the Town Hall. 'You must take down that flag. There is no such flag as the Taiwanese.' If the offending pennant were not removed, announced Mr Shande, he was going home. Geoffrey de Keyser rang the Foreign Office. 'I'm afraid he's quite right, old boy,' said an official. 'We don't recognize Taiwan.' Down came the flag, and diplomatic relations were restored with Mr Shande.

Wille, Biegel, Da Palma and Duis went out in the semi-final, in which Ju Hee Suh had, according to Gerald Larner of *The Guardian*, 'thundered her way' through Liszt's *Prelude and Fuge on BACH*. Indeed, she 'thundered her way through most things', according to Larner, 'legitimately in the Prokofiev Toccata, alarmingly in Chopin's B flat minor Sonata where there was just the occasional line in tearful eloquence to redeem it. She has an amazing technique . . . certainly she would carry the popular vote if there were such a thing.' Jon Kimura Parker, whom Larner thought must be the favourite at this stage, and 'the pianist most likely to save the reputation of the Leeds',

is a characteristic Juilliard product in that he has a powerfully muscular and brilliantly clear technique, but he is also a highly intelligent and inspired musician. His semi-final performance of Barber's Piano Sonata, which is no easy assignment, was as illuminating as it was uncompromising. Those who thought it merely strident must surely have been won over by the poetry in Liszt's *Petrarch Sonnet* No.104 and the subtly persuasive qualities of the Rakhmaninov Prelude in G, Op.32 No.5.

Robert Cockcroft, the *Yorkshire Post* critic, also tipped Parker, who 'established his credentials as an exciting and vital artist in a remarkable performance of the Barber Sonata. His *Petrushka* movement was aggressive and overblown, but he is at least a creative and lively performer with a cheerful platform manner.'

In contrast, Larner thought that Louis Lortie 'makes his points by understatement, as he did in a beautifully controlled and yet thrilling performance of Ravel's *Gaspard*' (which Lortie coupled with the Liszt Sonata and *Les Adieux*). Cockcroft concurred. 'His *Gaspard de la nuit* was intense, inward, very delicately coloured. No great character emerged in his Beethoven, but at least he can project and colour a melodic line.'

Larner thought that David Buechner, runner up to Parker at the Vina del Mar Competition, would occupy the same position at Leeds 'as long as he insists on refining a naturally dynamic style'. Buechner, who offered the Bach B flat Partita, the Martinů Fantaisie and Toccata, and Beethoven's Op.101 as his semi-final recital, thought his own playing was not up to scratch at that stage: 'I had had a busy summer and I was tired. I didn't play really well until the final.' Cockcroft thought Buechner 'not the most exciting of the bunch', but the possessor of a formidable technique, and 'capable of dazzling things. Wonderful control and variety to his textures.'

Emma Tahmisian, 'a deeply emotional pianist who might just do as well in the Schumann Concerto as Mitsuko Uchida did in 1975', according to Larner, and Junko Otake, who was the last to be hit by the virus, just before her semi-final round, 'left a less distinct impression' on Larner; but Joan Chissell, who was on the jury, says that her abiding memory of 1984 is Tahmisian's *Davidsbündlertänze* in the semi-final, which moved her to tears. 'So did Murray Perahia's, in 1972,' says Fanny Waterman. 'I wonder if it might be the piece . . . ?' Cockcroft was most impressed by Tahmisian – 'she has the eyes of a sad cat, the spark that denotes the artist and a slightly nervy quality that commands attention' – and thought she had 'a superb technique and a soul as well'. Of Otake's performance, given under trying circumstances, Cockcroft praised her 'astonishing facility for negotiating the keyboard: her Chopin Op.58 Sonata, though emotionally and spiritually awry, was a tour de force.'

In the first final, on Friday 21 September, Lortie opted to play Beethoven's Fourth – the concerto with which he had just won the Busoni; Tahmisian the Schumann, and Parker the Brahms. 'I really messed up bits in the rehearsal,' recalls Parker:

But my friend Norman Krieger, who'd had to stop in the second round because he was ill, had stayed around, and after the rehearsal, he offered to help me. We found two pianos, and he gave me a five-hour lesson on it. It was really considerate of him.'

At the Press conference when the names of the six finalists were announced, we were all herded down to the Queens Hotel. All the jurors were there, but they weren't supposed to talk to the competitors. But at one point, Hans Graf came up to me. 'Congratulations,' he said. 'I'm glad to see you in the finals. What concerto are you playing?' – 'The Brahms D minor,' I replied. – 'Of course, you must have played it in public many times before,' said Graf. – 'Yes,' I said, without thinking – though in fact I'd never played it with an orchestra. – 'That's good,' said Graf. 'When I was young, I once played the D minor in a competition. I'd never played it in public before, and I really messed it up.'

For the finals, the BBC boasted André Previn as television co-presenter with Richard Baker. It was Previn's first involvement with the competition, although as a conductor he had often worked with previous winners: 'The thing that is so admirable about the Leeds is that the second- and third- prize-winners often go on to have very fine careers, too.'

On the first evening, Robert Cockcroft thought Lortie's playing 'refined, distinctive, tasteful but slightly boring'. Hilary Finch of *The Times* also felt it was 'a prototype competition package . . . of slick technical fluency and of bland interpretative character'. But Alan Blyth, writing in the *Daily Telegraph*, praised Lortie's 'lyricism, fluent musicality and spontaneous sensitivity [bringing to the Beethoven] an understanding of how to think a work in its entirety from a thoughtful viewpoint.' Blyth predicted that Lortie 'will have a substantial career.'

Tahmisian, according to Cockcroft, 'ruined her chances by selecting the wrong concerto for her aggressive style and then losing control of it.' In fact, she suffered a memory-slip in the last movement. But

Hilary Finch thought that Tahmisian 'highlighted in her compelling Schumann concerto many of the serious artistic drawbacks of a career shaped by such gladiatorial contests. This was a reading simmering with rich and risk-taking ideas, brought nearly to boiling point in the artificial heat of the environment.' Dominic Gill of the *Financial Times* agreed, thinking Tahmisian potentially more interesting than Otake, Buechner or Lortie. 'She came last,' guessed Gill, 'because her Schumann nearly came off the rails; but a page of her performance had more instinctive light and poetry than the whole of David Buechner's *Emperor* or Louis Lortie's Beethoven 4.'

The final performance of the Friday evening was Parker's Brahms – a scintillating, dynamic performance that earned him a rousing ovation. Some critics were unconvinced – Gerald Larner in the *Guardian* thought that 'masterful though the playing was, and as sensitive to the intimate element of the work as it was responsive to its energy, it remained on the cool side.' Dominic Gill found it 'well-made Brahms, eminently civilized, but unbuoyant, unlit, stolidly academic'; and Alan Blyth also found the account 'strong, impulsive, but also heavy-going and portentous'.

According to Hilary Finch, however, it was

marked by a strength of intellect as well as muscle . . . what he had said about the Brahms was purposeful, cumulative and authoritative if still partial. In its big-boned frame, its daring closeness to the work's emotional core and its bold dramatic pacing, his reading let in little of the radiance which also lightens the music's darkness. Instead he pursued the darkness relentlessly with all the physical strength and mental stamina so vital to this sort of success.

Robert Cockcroft praised Parker's 'strong and stylish' performance, while reserving his criticism for the 'barely adequate' playing of the BBC Philharmonic, whose horns came in a bar early at the end of the cadenza. 'I was very happy with the way my Brahms went,' says Parker. 'I really enjoyed myself.'

David Buechner opened the batting on Saturday with the *Emperor* Concerto – a 'solid, safe, respectable but dull' performance, according to Cockcroft; 'stylistically immature,' according to Finch; but which Alan Blyth thought showed a 'Kempff-like feeling for momentary inspiration and extreme refinement in his poetic yet large-scale reading'. In contrast to Cockcroft, Blyth thought Buechner's interpretation 'consistently well-considered and interesting'.

Next came Otake, still frail from her illness, a tiny and rather pathetic figure with a black cardigan over her evening dress. 'She had worn the cardigan throughout the competition,' recalls Geoffrey de Keyser. 'It was a kind of talisman.' Once again, critical opinion varied as to the merits of her Chopin No.1. 'Both idiomatic and idiosyncratic, it was astute in its listening, but stronger on earnestness of idea than imagination,' wrote Hilary Finch. 'Prettily lightweight, sensitive, orchestral in its conception, but unspecial', was Dominic Gill's verdict, supported by Gerald Larner – 'a pleasingly poetic account . . . making nothing substantial or purposeful of it but sustaining an elegantly phrased and stylishly decorative line.' Robert Cockcroft thought it 'a lovely and shapely account . . . the delicacy of the colouring and the thin tracery of the texture may owe more to the East then the West but she is an artist of rare sensibility'.

But Junko Otake was completely upstaged by the exuberant Ju Hee Suh, on top form and clearly the audience's favourite, looking as some said 'like a fairy on the Christmas tree', in a brilliant blue ballgown trimmed with white fur. With a canny eye to populist success, she had chosen Rakhmaninov's Third to round off the 1984 competition. At the end of a spectacular display of virtuosity that had the audience stamping and shouting, she leapt off the piano stool into the arms of the conductor, Edward Downes (even though she had not pleased the BBC Philharmonic by reportedly comparing them unfavourably to the New York Philharmonic at the end of the rehearsal). 'A very extraordinary individual in a very ordinary world', Robert Cockcroft described her. Though he found a 'relentless, overblown quality' to her Rakhmaninov, 'her performance was technically among the most astonishing feats that Leeds Town Hall has, or will ever, see.' 'There was nothing second-rate about her performance,' wrote Hilary Finch:

Miss Suh can swallow a Steinway whole, and what is more, digest its repertoire more thoroughly than anyone in sight . . . Her spontaneous and exuberant greeting of Edward Downes and the BBC Philharmonic at the end were the inevitable climax of an intensely integrated musical relationship which had a regenerating effect on the work itself. Whether in the gentle guiding and leading in of the lyrical opening theme . . . whether in the variations' vividly engaging repartee and freshly pondered detail, or in the massive span of her last movement, this was a reading one wanted to reflect on, assimilate, and then hear all over again.

Alan Blyth thought Suh's account 'romantic, technically flawless and often highly imaginative', though immature; while Gill thought she should have won first prize on the basis of the concerto alone, for its 'irrepressible freshness, originality and energy . . . in a finale otherwise weighed down by such a preponderance of dull and self-conscious playing, she shone especially bright'. 'Ju Hee Suh's Rakhmaninov was an extraordinary performance,' says Jon Kimura Parker. 'She played with tremendous ease and a sense of authority. It was very impressive.'

But experience, combined with technical command and exuberance, won the day. Though some jury members thought that Suh should share the first prize, Jon Kimura Parker was declared the outright winner, to his overwhelming delight. 'Winning is a great challenge and I hope am able to live up to it,' he told the *Yorkshire Post*. Ju Hee Suh was placed second, the courageous Otake third, with Lortie, Buechner and Tahmisian bringing up the rear. Lortie was perhaps the most disappointed: 'It was such an anti-climax after the Busoni. I felt I should have been placed higher. The Beethoven probably wasn't the right choice – it's not a "typical" competition winner.' Buechner, too, was unhappy about his fifth place. 'I played in a highly personal style, and obviously it was not what they were looking for. One often has to play safe to win – to avoid extremes.' – 'I was very happy with my placing,' said Ju Hee Suh. And Parker was so elated that he provided the Leeds Competition with its most memorable moment in the prize-giving ceremony – the Kiss. 'I went up to the Duchess to accept my award, he says:

She was a really great personality. Then I went up to Fanny, who was standing next to her, and gave her a big hug and a kiss. The Duchess of Kent leaned over and said to me, 'And may I have one too?' So I did – on both cheeks! 'Oh dear!' said Richard Baker – who was doing the TV commentary. And the next morning it was all over the tabloids – 'Brahms and Kissed' – 'Cheeky Canadian Pianist Breaks Royal Protocol!' A month later, when I played in Toronto in the presence of the Queen and Prince Philip, and was presented to them at the end, there was a whole battery of press photographers waiting to see if I would do it again!

Breaches of royal protocol notwithstanding, it was generally agreed that Parker was a worthy winner, and that the Leeds had triumphantly redeemed its reputation, slightly tarnished by the unhappy memories of 1981. 'There might be room for argument about the relative merits of the second, third and fourth prize-winners, but there is no doubt that Jon Kimura Parker deserved his first prize,' wrote Gerald Larner. Robert Cockcroft agreed. 'This time they got it more or less right . . . there is little doubt that 1984 rates as the most interesting and exciting in the 21-year-old history of the event.'

Chapter Seventeen

The Opinion-Formers:
Managers, Critics, the Media

Once a pianist emerges from the competition circuit a winner, he or she has to face an even more critical test – that of proving their worth on the open market to those who will constantly assess their performance, and those who will either offer employment, or persuade others to do so. 'The real competition starts the next day, when they are out there in the cold, wide world being measured against the Ashkenazys, the Perahias and the Brendels,' says Fanny Waterman. There seems little doubt that managers, critics and those in positions of influence in the media are now adopting a more cautious approach to competition winners than ten years ago.

To Fanny Waterman's list of the strengths which in her opinion are needed to make a fine concert artist, one more should be added: a good manager. 'The power of the manager has never been stronger,' says Peter Donohoe. 'One's career depends so much on which agent you get, whether you get on with them, and whether they believe in you.'

One of the prime reasons given by young pianists for entering a major international competition is to attract the attention of a top manager, who will orchestrate their careers while relieving them of the tedious and time-consuming task of promotion, deal with the delicate question of setting their fees, and provide advice, encouragement and a shoulder to cry on.

From the manager's point of view, seeking out and encouraging young talent is an essential part of his or her long-term business prospects. And the competition circuit is seen by managers not only as a talent-spotting exercise, but sometimes as a necessary step in the career of a young artist already on the books. Several of the Leeds prize-winners entered either on or against the advice of their managers.

Murray Perahia's American manager, Frank Salomon, decided that he should enter the Leeds competition, in order to establish himself in the UK. Shortly before the Leeds, Perahia had approached several London agents, including Harold Holt (which had many famous artists, including Perlman, Menuhin and Stern, on its books). He was turned down, even though he already had quite a considerable career in the USA. 'After the competition,' says Perahia, 'suddenly all the managers who didn't want me before were pursuing me with offers. Unless their own choices are backed up by the imprimatur of a jury of twelve, managers rarely have the courage of their own convictions: they tell the artist they couldn't sell him.' After a period of negotiation, Perahia eventually accepted Harold Holt's offer, and has since been managed by Martin Campbell-White.

'I wasn't at the 1972 competition,' says Campbell-White, who joined Harold Holt at about the same time as the competition,

> but I learnt that Murray had won, and that the decision was more or less unanimous. I also knew that Holt had already been offered Murray a year or so earlier, and had turned him down. As soon as a pianist wins a competition like Leeds, then that pianist immediately becomes an extremely interesting commodity in the concert world. So I said to Sir Ian Hunter that we should be interested in Perahia, and we knew that several other managements were also in the hunt. We met Murray and his American manager, and said that we would be honoured to represent him, and we were sure we could do a responsible job. We were given his European representation, with the exception of Italy, Switzerland and Germany, and there was a great deal of work to be done. In the early stages, the role of a manager is largely a secretarial one. The great strength of the Leeds competition, which marks it out from any others, is the quality and number of the engagements guaranteed to the winner. And those dates are available over a period of time, which is a very good thing if the artist is not yet physically and mentally prepared to cope with a sudden rush of engagements.

'I didn't accept all the engagements I was offered immediately,' says Perahia. 'I didn't feel ready for them. I needed to take time off to learn new repertoire. My decision was taken jointly with my manager. I was lucky to have a very sensitive and idealistic agent, so I had time to consolidate.'

'An agent would be short-sighted and self-defeating if he pushed an artist into accepting too many engagements too early,' says Martin Campbell-White:

> If the artist is tired, ill-prepared, or playing repertoire he or she

hasn't had time to learn properly, then the orchestra or the conductor will not be impressed and the artist will not be re-engaged. It is much better to keep people in anticipation than to rush in trying to earn your fee, and risk messing up the future. Of course, if you say no, you do run the risk of cutting off a career at the moment when golden opportunities are offered – you may lose dates if people think you are being too choosy – but to accept everything is dangerous. The manager must use his discretion, and encourage the artist to accept a date if necessary. The only responsible way for a manager to act is to evaluate the artist's personality, co-operate with him and the engager, and make sure that the career which is built up is based on musicianship, security of repertoire, and the ability to cope with the arduous, taxing nature of travelling and concert-giving, which a young artist will not be used to. Handling a young artist takes a great deal of time, and one sometimes makes mistakes.

Does Campbell-White still regard the Leeds competition as a major source of new talent?

The Leeds competition came to prominence through TV exposure, and Murray really captured the public's imagination. He was so poetic, so clearly in a class of his own. I don't think that Leeds has thrown up another winner of that calibre since. The major London managements are all very busy, and Harold Holt already has a group of artists with whom we work well. One should always try to find time to attend competitions, but the pressure of work and so on does tend to make one rest – rather arrogantly, I'm afraid – on one's laurels. Holt is so well known, that we tend to take the view that if an artist is going to be successful, he or she will approach us. Of course, one does then run the risk of missing a potentially great talent.

A competition is a bit of a lottery. I myself am not a musician, and I'm not sure if my judgement is sufficiently good individually to pick out the person most likely to be successful from a competition. My particular strength is not great musical discernment, and were I on a jury, I would insist on having a major musician sitting beside me. I would be looking for factors that reinforce musicianship. Had I been with Holt before 1972, I might have recognized something special about Murray Perahia – it's hard to tell.

We work on a network of contacts – we get a feel for what people are saying about a particular artist. And we are normally tipped off about people in advance. If you have a network of marvellous artists, they are often very generous about their younger colleagues. And our colleagues in managements abroad often let us know if they hear of a startling new talent.

Competitions are nevertheless important for managers. John Lill [now also under under Campbell-White's management] was one of the first artists to whom I got very close – we're the same generation. Lill's manager suggested that he should go in for the Tchaikovsky Competition, and he came back a winner. Lill said, 'I don't play any better now than I did before – why does everyone want me now?' The reason is that the imprimatur of an international jury indicates that the winner has the goods, at least for a short time. In the short term, a manager can prolong an artist's career, but if he's not successful with conductors, orchestras, and most importantly, the public, then he won't last, and there is very little a manager can do.

An artist's fee is based on supply and demand. Even if the demand is there, especially for a non-British or Commonwealth (and now a non-EC) artist, he or she is only allowed to do twenty engagements a year in this country. We couldn't even get a special dispensation for Perahia, who was in strong demand. So one is able to pitch the fee at what we think is a reasonable figure. I can't recall any organization that refused to pay Perahia's – and it wasn't low.

Competitions don't always throw up the best people. Perahia, Lupu, Roll, Alexeev – all were worthy winners at Leeds. The Tchaikovsky and the Chopin competitions have also had some fine winners. It's a short-cut to success if you have the necessary talent. Perahia's career was undoubtedly advanced more quickly than if he had just chuntered along without a prize, but he would have got there in the end. An artist – and his manager – must be pragmatic, and seize opportunities, but he must not be greedy – he must take them sparingly and not ask for too high a fee. I feel that competitions are becoming a slight anachronism these days. There are now other channels for artists – by recommendation, by watching them perform, by the grapevine. Of course, competitions are helpful, but one must keep them in context. There are too many of them now, and too many mediocre, 'consensus-vote' winners are emerging. And sometimes the wrong person wins!

Terry Harrison, another top London manager who specializes in pianists, looking after several of the Leeds prize-winners including Orozco, Lupu, and Andras Schiff, concurs with Campbell-White's

views. He, too, used to attend competitions including the Leeds
regularly, but now rarely goes:

Between 1968 and 1975 I went to a lot of competitions. At that time
I was much younger – I was just starting my company, I had more
energy, and I wanted to find artists. As it built up, I found I didn't
need to search for artists. And I basically believe that the number
of exceptionally talented artists is very small, and is not likely to be
increased by competitions – the talent will just be spread more
thinly. Over the last fifteen years, there have been more and more
competitions: before the war there were only one or two truly
international ones, and many of the top young pianists would enter
for the same competition. Look at Brussels in 1956 – the winner
was Ashkenazy, the second prize went to John Browning, the third
to André Tchaikovsky, the fourth to Cécile Ousset, the fifth to
Lazar Berman, the sixth to Tamás Vásáry, the twelfth to Peter
Frankl, and so on. Of the hundred or so pianists with international
careers, six or seven were in that one competition. That can't be
repeated now.

When Leeds started, some people thought, 'this is just going to
be an English competition with an English winner' – though Roll
is a fine pianist. Then, with the 1966 controversy over Orozco versus
Postnikova, it achieved notoriety. I started to go to it, to see if I
could recruit young talent. But its real breakthrough happened in
1969. Three people on the jury said that Lupu was a genius – others
said he played too wilfully, too personally. It was touch and go
whether he would get into the finals at all. But the final was
startling. It was obvious that here was one great artist who
shouldn't be in a competition – he was so special. That sort of
thing only happens once every ten years. The jury was out for
fifteen minutes, and came back with a virtually unanimous
decision. So by the skin of its teeth, Leeds became a truly
international competition. Then, in 1972, it was once more
incredibly lucky, in that yet another great artist appeared. When
Perahia played at Leeds, he hadn't a UK representative. I tried
hard to get him – but I tried too hard, I played a hard-sell game
and I frightened him away. Martin Campbell-White played a cooler
game, and got him.

Those two shine out like a beacon. I went to the '75 competition,
and I thought it was very strange. Alexeev is a very fine pianist,
who deserved to win a major competition, and in some respects
maybe he was a competition winner for that particular year. But
there were two talents in that competition that I thought would

ultimately become even more famous. One was Chung, who even at that stage was already thinking of taking up conducting. Within a couple of years, he was Giulini's assistant, and now he's head of the Bastille Opéra. The other was Schiff – whom I thought a greater talent than Alexeev, but he wasn't a normal type of competition pianist. He was very personal – to me, that means it's got artistry – but it doesn't necessarily win competitions. Schiff really put his head in the lion's mouth by playing Bach in the final. No one has ever agreed how Bach should be played, but after Glenn Gould's death, it quickly became clear that Schiff would be the world's greatest Bach pianist. Without that Bach, I think Schiff would have pushed Alexeev for first prize. A few years later, his manager closed her business, and I took him over.

I thought that 1975 was the first year that the decision at Leeds was open to question, because it hadn't recognized quite how special the other two were. Was it on the right road? Then, in 1978, the first real problems became manifest. There was a reasonable set of pianists, but nobody of exceptional standard. A lot of people from the music profession felt that this was not on the same level. If you are to have a competition which aspires to be a top competition, there is no way you can decide that there must be a first prize-winner every time. Of course, it couldn't go on awarding no first prize, but in my opinion, it should have done so on at least two occasions.

Leeds is still one of the major competitions. I feel it could have been the premier competition – Brussels has gone down, the Tchaikovsky has certainly had its ups and downs – if it had shown it was preserving its standards by not awarding a first prize on occasion. There haven't been talents like those of 1969, 1972, 1975 since. But the talent of Lupu, Perahia, Schiff – it's a great talent, and it's so rare. There are only seven or eight pianists of that calibre under forty-five years of age in the world today.

The difference between a fine artist and a great artist is very small, but it makes all the difference in terms of their careers – how far they will go. We're talking about someone who had a special blessing – who understands music to be a separate and very difficult language. I don't know what it is, but I know it exists, and I can recognize it when it's being delivered.

A manager has a great responsibility for a young and inexperienced artist. I nearly screwed up Barry Douglas [the 1986 Tchaikovsky Competition winner], because I was used to handling professionals who play between seventy and a hundred concerts a year. We aimed for sixty to sixty-five concerts in the first year after the competition. Well, it went to nearer eighty, and there were at least two occasions – major dates – when I booked Barry which were mistakes. It put too much strain on him, and he nearly cracked. But he came through, and three and a half years later, he's developed as an artist, he can now take things in his stride. But one can't push a young artist for money. Some unscrupulous agents on the continent are only interested in the flavour of the month, and if it doesn't work out, it's dropped. But if you take on a young artist, you know that you won't make a profit – even if they're very successful – for at least five years. The amount of time you must spend with them is disproportionate to the number of concerts they can play, and their fee.

Some teachers are now not recommending their most talented pupils to enter for competitions. There's an increasing feeling – which would have been inconceivable ten years ago – that there are now pianists who can develop their careers without winning a major competition. The competition ladder is still helpful, but it's not quite as essential. Everyone yawns now if you tell them you have another competition winner on your books.

I haven't been to the last two Leeds competitions. I have people who will go and tip me off if someone special comes along. One usually hears about exceptional people on the grapevine before they win competitions. Many managers are now asking themselves why they don't start to make and back their own judgements. But you do still occasionally get a pianist thrown up by a competition whose career goes very well. I may go to Leeds again this year if I have the time, and if I hear that there are one or two specially talented young people in. I haven't been to any competition for four or five years, and maybe I should get that feeling again.

'At the end of the day', says Craig Sheppard, 'we have to be responsible for ourselves. Managers are only human – they have to make a living. You are lucky if you get a manager who will take time over you. You have to be tough, and not allow yourself to be pushed in the wrong direction.'

'It's most disappointing that some agents do not come to Leeds and have the courage to pick their own winners, irrespective of the jury's findings,' says Fanny Waterman:

We should all be impressed by their obviously deeply felt concern if they themselves undertook to build up young performers by funding important recitals, paying for publicity and working relentlessly to secure engagements with the world's greatest conductors and orchestras. Agents already have these contacts through the great artists already on their books, such as Lupu, Perahia, Alexeev, Uchida, and Schiff – all, incidentally, presented to the world at Leeds. Why don't they put their hands in their pockets and back these fine but unknown and struggling artists – I mean really foster their careers in the way that Sol Hurok and Alexander Merovitch did for artists such as Horowitz, Milstein and Piatigorsky, and establish them with dignity – before they need to enter and win competitions? If and when this happens, the necessity for competitions will vanish, and they will wither away.

Anthony Phillips, a London manager who ran the Van Cliburn Competition for a while, deduces that the attraction of competitions for those in the music business is that the traumatic responsibility of backing their own judgement is neatly shifted on to someone else. 'It is really very convenient to be able to shelter behind a panel of approved experts.' In his opinion, that responsibility frightens many more people than would care to admit it, 'except critics, who do not have to put their money where their mouths are'.

And what of these critics, who have the power either to advance a young artist's career, or to inflict enormous damage on it? Fanny Waterman has acknowledged their influence by inviting several major critics to join the Leeds juries in recent years. Most artists loathe them. 'Some critics shouldn't be in their jobs, the way they treat some people,' says John Lill. 'Some of my best concerts have been torn apart, and others, that I felt weren't so good, have been highly praised.' – 'All artists have to face adverse criticism,' says Peter Donohoe,

but you can only cope with it if you are a fully developed person. All artists are highly strung, and it's easy, if a critic decides he doesn't like the way you play, to think about making a big public spectacle of a reply. But you can't do that: you should examine a critical review carefully to make sure that it really is unfair.'

Does winning a competition have any influence on the way a pianist is regarded by a critic afterwards?

'Critics generally have a low opinion of competitions,' says Hilary Finch, who has covered the last three Leeds competitions for *The Times*:

But although they may have a cynical attitude, they will take a performance at its face value, and one is always prepared to be pleasantly surprised. We work on an overnight basis, and we deal with the matter in hand. One's opinion is based on each performance – how someone plays at that time, regardless of how they have played before or since. But clearly, if a critic had never heard the winner of a major competition before, then his expectations may sub-consciously be higher.

Of more effect on a critic's reception of a performance is the degree of hype that surrounds competition winners – if they are being pushed by a manager or a record company, then that may generate a negative resistance in the critic, in opposition to the public's frenzy of expectation. One puts one's armour on.

I think the profession as a whole is more cautious and cynical now than it was ten years ago. EMI was very cautious about Ovchinnikov – they only gave him a temporary six-record contract. But I think that it's far less likely that a career can be destroyed by negative reviews in Europe than in the USA. I find it hard to believe that a career that's got what it takes will be destroyed in that way. People will use critics as scapegoats. Even Barenboim and Richter must have had bad reviews sometimes. I think it all depends on the artist and his manager – if they themselves are secure and confident, they are not going to be rocked by a bad review; but if the artist – or more particularly, his manager – is insecure, then it could tip the balance.

It is an enormous responsibility to be negative about a performance – I am always desperate to try to find something positive about it, if only for my own delectation. One always wants to salvage something from a poor performance, but there's no point in making out that the mediocre is anything other than that, or that people are ready for a concert career if they are clearly not.

Several of the Leeds competition reviewers have at the time offered judgements which, with the benefit of hindsight, have proved embarrassingly wide of the mark. At the semi-final stage in 1972, Gerald Larner wrote that 'the competition is not as exciting and the general standard not as high as last time'; while a reviewer wrote of the 1975 crop of pianists, which included Alexeev, Uchida and Schiff: 'this year was rather dull.'

'Looking over the reviews of the Leeds competitions, no one can fail to notice how often the views of the critics conflict, and how wrong some of their forecasts have since proved,' says Fanny Waterman. 'Many of their favourites have sunk without trace, while those whom they disdained at the time have achieved the greatest heights. The critics' constant refrain has been, "The jury has got it wrong." Sometimes the critics get it wrong!'

Hilary Finch stands by her opinions of the various Leeds performances she has reviewed, although she regrets that lack of space obliges her to cram her opinions of six performances into the slot that would normally be occupied by only one:

One has to try to distil the essence of what's important. I have only heard Ian Hobson once since 1981, and I'm afraid to say I liked his playing no better. It was technically brushed up, but still pedestrian, in my opinion. It could be that the fact that someone has won a prize means that every critic goes with preconceptions, and will come down harder on someone who doesn't deliver the goods. If someone is unwisely awarded a first prize, the slight unfairness can be compounded later by the feeling that he or she ought to be playing better than that. Reviews do count if you haven't got what it takes – you don't stand a chance.

Finch still remembers Emma Tahmisian in 1984 as having 'a real, interesting voice – but she'll never win a competition. Her playing was a genuine musical response, and the virtues necessary for a career as a competition winner are not, in my opinion, necessarily the most important pianistic virtues.' She feels that Ovchinnikov was 'clearly the winner' in 1987, a 'prize-winner of a different quality from the previous two years. I think he's potentially a great pianist. He did what he did extremely well, but he still hasn't shown since that he can do anything else. I think he still has a long way to go.'

Nicholas Kenyon, who now writes for the *Observer*, agrees with Hilary Finch that 'competitions are fundamentally anti-musical' (both are enthusiastic supporters of the Interforum idea).

Some people can make a career out of not winning a competition – look at Pogorelich in the Chopin, Donohoe at Leeds and Moscow, Christian Blackshaw at Tel Aviv. There is a valid school of thought that says that competitions put you through the sort of strain you're going to face at double quick speed – and if you can come out of that, you can come out of anything.

I think I would be less inclined to go to a concert if I knew the pianist was a competition winner. I think it would probably prejudice me against them – I would want to look beneath the smooth competition surface. One inevitably compares present and past winners, and any Leeds winner would be compared with Lupu, Perahia, Schiff or Uchida, just as any Tchaikovsky winner would be compared with Ashkenazy. But that does work to their advantage – it puts them up there in that class. They have a sort of 'Good Housekeeping' label attached which says, 'take this person seriously'. The pianists who've stuck from Leeds are those who had TV exposure in the finals – it's good that people can decide for themselves whether the actual winner is the most interesting pianist.

I would now go to a concert given by an unknown pianist only if someone I respected – even an agent – told me it would be wonderful; or if he or she was playing something interesting. If I'm reviewing a concert, I do make a distinction between well-known pianists and someone making a début. If a well-known pianist merits a bad review, then they will receive one, but I try to be constructive towards a young newcomer. Pianism is such an incredibly personal thing. Those of us who play the piano like to think we know how certain bits go.

Adrian Jack of the *Independent* points out that a competition win can get critics to a recital:

Newspaper arts editors think prize-winners' recitals ought to be reviewed. But personally I want to find out what established foreign artists are like – and of course, very often such people have won competitions. But for a British pianist, it's their reputation and whether the programme is interesting that counts. The important thing to bear in mind is that artists change constantly, in quite unpredictable ways. What I always hope to find is that indisputable authority which instantly proclaims a great artist. One can tell that Tatiana Nikolaeva is a great pianist just by the way she seats herself on the piano-stool – before she plays a note!

It would seem that the curtain key-word with record companies, too, is 'caution'. Having had their fingers burnt with one or two international competition winners who have risen on a wave of media hype to astronomical heights, only to plummet a couple of years later to total obscurity, record companies are now less likely to rush in with an immediate offer of a contract.

'Competitions are all well and good,' says Peter Alward, Vice-President, Artists and Repertoire, for EMI, which has in the past offered contracts to Leeds winners,

but they create a forced atmosphere for performers. We are very worried about this – it's how you perform under everyday conditions that counts. Of course, if some devastatingly successful artist appears at a competition, then naturally we would want to make a bid for them, but we act with extreme caution. We don't want to hype them up, or push them into doing repertoire they can't cope with. It is, of course, a *sine qua non* that a competition pianist is technically proficient, but the problems start when one comes to analyse the musical content of a performance. It is very easy to make a big impact with the Tchaikovsky B flat Concerto – but it's how they tackle things like a Bach fugue or a Mozart sonata that interests us. The last thing we want to encourage is the creation of a performing circus animal.

We will be attending the next Leeds and other competitions: every career has to start somewhere, and we act as our own talent scouts. Of course one hopes to be pleasantly surprised, to find another Lupu or Perahia – one has to keep one's eyes and ears open. But we are very aware of the havoc that the responsibility of a recording career can wreak on a young artist. Several companies have been guilty in the past of taking someone on and then dropping them.

We consider Vladimir Ovchinnikov to be an extremely promising artist: he won't allow himself to be pushed, and we feel his reputation will develop slowly and successfully. He still needs more experience, and we accept that it will be a slow process.

The public is also much more choosy now about what it buys. 'Complete sets' used to sell, but record companies are now cautious about committing themselves to large-scale series. The repertoire we wish to promote must suit both artistic and commercial enterprise.

'Competitions are important, and they have an honourable history,' says Simon Rattle.

but they're not the only way to make a career. The Leeds is marvellous – but like all competitions, one doesn't know what it's going to throw up, and at what stage. Schiff and Uchida were two of the most interesting finalists ever, but few people recognized it at the time. But there is no doubt that a competition win helps enormously – look at the difference that the Tchaikovsky made to Donohoe. It helped to make a shamefully neglected talent better known. But it's how a winner plays afterwards that matters. So far as booking artists is concerned, it really doesn't make any difference if they have won competitions. The musical grapevine is formidable, and one gets a good idea of how people will perform.

In his capacity as Controller of Radio 3, John Drummond is one of the country's major employers of young artists. He, too, is worried that the 'sifting process is currently not working' in competitions:

The kind of pianists who are emerging all too often are not ready for a career – some are pushed into competitions by their teachers. And the proliferation of competitions is not good: one simply can't absorb all the winners.

But competitions are not going to go away, and I think they're an effective short-cut to finding up-and-coming talent. And the Leeds competition is on the side of the angels – the atmosphere is very warm and supportive and it's very well run. I have every admiration for Fanny Waterman's terrific achievement in keeping the Leeds afloat by finding money, sponsors, competitors – but it does need another outstanding winner.

Of the post-Lupu and Perahia winners, Alexeev I think is a very interesting musician, who has a great following in the provinces in this country. He has a big career now; he plays everywhere. Dalberto has disappeared. Hobson went back to Illinois; Kimura Parker's fee went up too high, so few people here could employ him. The Russians are expected to concentrate on their national repertoire, so I couldn't offer Ovchinnikov a Prom because he would only play concertos he'd already played in London. Louis Lortie played at the Proms in 1986. It's the quiet talents – people like Uchida and Lortie, who are interesting – but they're not necessarily good competition pianists. I like contradictory pianists.

I do think that the Leeds competition has had a beneficial influence on the current generation of British pianists. British musical educational institutions used to have a country vicarage atmosphere – the competitive edge was not there. British pianists simply couldn't compare on a technical or intellectual level with their European counterparts. So a country like Hungary, with a population of only nine million, could go on producing great pianists and composers; and one's grades at the Moscow Conservatory determined the rest of your life. Winning a great competition abroad was a passport to a different life.

Few people in Britain were brought up to have that real need to succeed. They're all too laid back. Look at the cool intelligence of Uchida, look at Argerich – one of the best minds I know. Most British pianists just hadn't got comparable things to say. But now, I feel this country is producing better musicians. It's the influence of the Ogdon/Lill generation.

Chapter Eighteen

The Ninth Competition: 1987

Two significant events in the history of the Leeds took place between 1984 and 1987: in recognition of the major role played by its sponsors, the competition was officially renamed the Harveys Leeds International Piano Competition; and after a twelve-year absence, the Russians once more agreed to send a team of competitors to the 1987 contest. 'We opened negotiations at the Santander competition in the summer of 1984,' says Fanny Waterman:

Lev Vlasenko was on the jury, and other Soviet representatives from Gosconcert were there too. But there seemed no way we could have a private, uninterrupted conversation with them. Then we noticed that the Russians always went swimming before breakfast. So I told Geoffrey to get up and join them in the sea. After that opening gambit, we renewed the pressure in Geneva in April '85, and the deal was finally clinched a year later in Moscow. We got Vlasenko and Tatiana Nikolaeva for the '87 Leeds jury, and they agreed to send some competitors.

By 1987, the competition's executive committee – known as the Key Board – had also acquired a new Honorary Administrator, in Françoise Logan; while Robert Tebb – also in charge of advertising and looking after the jury – acted as her deputy. Harry Tolson, now Honorary Executive Director of Publications, took charge of arrangements at the Great Hall of the university; Paul Holloway remained Treasurer; while Geoffrey de Keyser continued to fulfil his usual role as Liaison Officer and Announcer. In addition, other officers were appointed to oversee specific tasks, such as box-office, catering facilities, transport arrangements, supply of pianos, the Green Room, and the arrangements at Tetley Hall.

The 1987 jury also contained several new faces, many of whom had served on the juries of other major competitions: Bulgarian-born Yury Boukoff, by then a French national, with an international career and many major recordings (including the first complete sets of

Prokofiev's piano sonatas and Chopin's polonaises to his credit); Noel Flores, born in India, but resident in Vienna, where he studied with Graf and Dieter Weber, himself becoming a professor at the Hochschule für Musik; Takahiro Sonoda from Japan, a soloist in Europe, the USSR and the USA; Joaquín Soriano from Spain, winner of the 1965 Vercelli Competition, a well-known soloist in Europe and the USA, and a professor at the Madrid Conservatory; Lev Vlasenko, the Soviet representative from the Moscow Conservatory, a former pupil of Jacob Flier, and winner of the first prize in the 1956 Liszt Competition and second prize (to Van Cliburn) at the first Tchaikovsky Competition in 1958; Konstantin Ganev from Bulgaria, a soloist and teacher, who together with his pianist wife and duet recital partner Julia Ganeva, founded a flourishing piano school in Sofia; and Gordon Stewart (the BBC representative), then a Chief Producer at Radio 3 with special responsibility for young artists.

In addition, Fanny Waterman re-invited Rudolf Fischer, Karl-Heinz Kämmerling, John Lill, Tatiana Nikolaeva, György Sándor, Arie Vardi and Halina Czerny-Stefańska. The great French pianist Aldo Ciccolini was also to have joined the 1987 jury; but, having lost his luggage on his way from Venice where he had been giving a concert, he found himself unable to face the journey, and cancelled at the last minute.

In addition to the large sum (£85,000) provided by Harveys, the 1987 competition – which took place from 14 to 26 September – also received substantial financial support from many other individuals and companies, including £15,000 raised by the Friends of the HLIPC, who again offered to pay for the competitors' accommodation at Tetley Hall. The first prize went up in cash terms by some 40 per cent, from £3,500 to £5,000, with a corresponding increase in the other prizes: Marjorie and Arnold Ziff donated a second prize of £3,000; the Calouste Gulbenkian Foundation a third prize of £2,000; the fourth-prize-winner received £1,750; the fifth, £1,250; and the sixth the Louis Féraud Prize of £1,000; while the semi-finalists each received £400; and the ten losing second-stage competitors £200 each. In addition, Harveys donated a Chamber Music Prize of £350, plus the Harveys of Bristol Medal for the most outstanding performer of the violin and piano sonata.

In 1987, twenty-five international engagements were offered, ranging from a date at the first New York Festival of the Arts at Carnegie Hall, to concerts with the Leipzig Gewandhaus, Swedish Radio Symphony, Hong Kong Philharmonic and New Zealand Symphony orchestras; together with twenty-one British orchestral concerts, ten of them with London orchestras; ten festival appearances, including

Aldeburgh, City of London, Harrogate, Swansea and York; over forty recitals throughout the UK; and a potential recording contract with EMI.

The ever-more extensive BBC coverage, under the Executive Producer Kenneth Corden (Television) and Paul Hindmarsh and Andrew Kurowski (Radio 3), this year would feature a programme presented by Michael Berkeley on the background to the Leeds competition, together with live television and radio coverage of the finals, presented by Michael Berkeley and Jane Glover; a special results programme to be broadcast on Saturday 26 September at 11.05 p.m.; and recordings for radio of highlighted performances throughout the various stages.

The repertoire for stage one again comprised a choice of a specified sonata by Haydn, Clementi, Mozart or Beethoven; plus a Chopin work (one of the first three ballades, or of the Scherzos Nos 2–4), and two études drawn from a choice of Chopin, Liszt, Bartók and Debussy. The second stage was also little changed from previous years, requiring the customary two major works.

As in 1984, the semi-final combined a free-choice recital programme with a violin sonata, played by Erich Gruenberg. And the final – this year with Simon Rattle and the CBSO – offered a choice of nine concertos, of which three – in deference to the Soviet entry? – were Russian (Prokofiev's Third, Rakhmaninov's Second and the *Rhapsody on a Theme of Paganini*). The remaining six were Mozart's K.503, the last three Beethovens, the Schumann, and the Brahms No.2 – included at Leeds for the first time. Both semi-finals and finals would in 1987 be played on Leeds Town Hall's brand new £30,000 Steinway – specially selected by Barry Douglas, winner of the 1986 Tchaikovsky Competition.

The 1987 contest attracted a record entry, of which 81 young pianists – 20 of them first-prize-winners at other competitions – were chosen to take part. Fanny Waterman's pupil Benjamin Frith (who had played unsuccessfully at the 1981 competition, but had in the meantime taken second prize in the Busoni Competition) entered once again; as did Thomas Duis (by now winner of the 1986 Rubinstein Competition); David Buechner, who had come fifth at Leeds in 1984; Eliane Rodrigues; and four Britons: Paul Coker, a pupil of Kentner, who had partnered Yehudi Menuhin; Philip Smith, a semi-finalist in the 1978 competition, Jonathan Plowright, by now enjoying a substantial career in Britain, and Kathryn Stott, returning to Leeds nine years after her 1978 fifth place. The most extraordinary re-entrant was Ju Hee Suh, second-prize-winner in 1984 – but, no doubt reflecting on the perils of not winning, she wisely decided to withdraw at a late stage.

The ten-strong British entry also included Andrew Wilde, who had already won prizes at the Naumburg and Van Cliburn Competitions, Stephen Williamson, a first-prize-winner at the Jaen Competition, and Nigel Hill, who had taken prizes at several minor European competitions. The opposition included a strong Soviet team – eighteen-year-old Boris Berezovsky and Alexander Shtarkman, one year older, both students at the Moscow Conservatory, and twenty-nine-year-old Vladimir Ovchinnikov, a first prize-winner in the 1984 Viotti Competition, runner-up to Ivo Pogorelich at Montreal in 1980, and controversial sharer of the second prize with Peter Donohoe at Moscow in 1982.

As usual, there were several good French pianists – Jean-Efflam Bavouzet, a pupil of Sancan; Philippe Bianconi, a silver medallist at the 1985 Van Cliburn; Hortense Cartier-Bresson, a descendant of the celebrated photographer, who had won third prize at the 1982 Liszt–Bartok Competition; Olivier Cazal, a second-prize-winner in the Cortot Competition; Yves Henry, a first-prize-winner at the 1981 Schumann Competition; Huillet Thierry, another Sancan pupil; and François Killian, who had won the 1985 Chopin Competition at Palma, and subsequently taken seventh prize at Warsaw in 1985.

The USA submitted the largest entry of thirteen, including Buechner; Marcantonio Barone, a pupil of Sokoloff and Fleischer, who had won fourth prize at the 1985 Busoni Competition; Ingrid Jacoby, a prize-winner in the Gina Bachauer Competition; and Edward Zilberkant, another international prize-winner. Italy sent five, among them Daniele Alberti, already a prize-winner at thirteen competitions; Mario Dalbesi, winner of the 1981 Stresa Competition; and Benedetto Lupo, who also had a string of prizes to his credit.

The West German entry included Eckart Heiligers, winner of the Viotti Competition in 1986 and the Maria Callas Competition in Athens in 1987, and Rolf Plagge, a first-prize-winner in several minor international competitions. The distinguished entrants from other countries included Pedro Burmester from Portugal, who was already enjoying an international career; Angela Cheng, from Canada, a gold medallist at the 1986 Rubinstein Competition; José Cocarelli from Brazil, winner of the 1985 Busoni and 1986 Marguérite Long Competitions; Daniel Gortler from Israel, a pupil of Vardi, who had come second at Munich and third at Geneva; Krzysztof Jablonski from Poland, third-prize-winner at the 1985 Chopin Competition; Avedis Kouyoumdjian from Austria, winner of the 1981 Beethoven Competition; the Australian Ian Munro, who had won the 1982 ABC

Concerto Competition, and come second in the 1985 Maria Callas Competition; Koji Oikawa from Japan, winner of the 1984 Viotti Competition; Jan Simon from Czechoslovakia, third-prize-winner at the 1985 Chopin Competition; Hugh Tinney, from Dublin, winner of the Pozzoli Competition in 1983 and the Paloma O'Shea at Santander in 1984; and Uriel Tsachor from Israel, second-prize-winner in the 1985 Busoni Competition.

'I think we've got a very exciting competition in prospect and I think the entry from the Soviet Union adds another dimension,' Fanny Waterman told the *Yorkshire Post*.

Apart from the non-arrival of the juryman Aldo Ciccolini, the Soviet contingent caused the Leeds organizers another eleventh-hour panic when they mistook their Aeroflot bookings, and found that the plane arrived at Heathrow too late to catch a connecting flight or train to Leeds in time to arrive for the obligatory competitors' meeting on Saturday. Françoise Logan had to send two taxis to London to collect them, and they finally arrived at Tetley Hall at 1 a.m. The French competitor Bavouzet also arrived late on Sunday, having suffered a painful tooth extraction. In all, 17 of the 87 pianists listed in the programme failed to show up, so the jury decided that – rather than shorten the competition – they would allow each of the contestants ten minutes' extra playing time in the first round.

Despite such minor irritations, the 1987 competition kicked off on time at the University's Great Hall on Monday morning, with a performance by the Brazilian José Carlos Cocarelli. Once the first stage was complete the jury, as usual, gathered all the competitors together at Tetley Hall to announce the twenty names through to the second stage. Benjamin Frith went through ('I thought I played well in the first round, but I still was under great psychological pressure'), as did Wilde, Bavouzet (despite his tooth-ache), all three Soviet contestants, Cocarelli, Buechner, Barone, Burmester, Cartier-Bresson, Heiligers, Jablonski, Killian, Munro, Plagge, Rodrigues, Tinney, and two outsiders – Noriko Ogawa, from Japan, a pupil of Iguchi and of Sacha Gorodnitzki at the Juilliard; and Lora Anghelova Dimitrova of Bulgaria.

The most spectacular first-round casualty was Kathryn Stott, whose unexpected elimination two of the jurors described as 'the greatest scandal of the competition'. What went wrong? 'I was warned not to go in for it again, but my agent persuaded me', says Stott, who after her fifth prize at Leeds nine years earlier had enjoyed considerable success in the UK. 'I felt much more experienced than in 1978, and I took it much more seriously – I was naturally hoping for a high place. But it backfired.' 'She's an excellent pianist,' says

Bryce Morrison. 'It was quite unbelievable that she was eliminated in the first round.'

Of these who did get to the second round, a further ten, including both British contestants, were eliminated, leaving two Russians – Berezovsky and Ovchinnikov, Barone, Bavouzet, Cartier-Bresson, Heiligers, Munro, Ogawa and Tinney in the running. The two Soviet competitors could not have been more different in character – Ovchinnikov intensely serious, reserved and highly strung; Berezovsky a typical teenager. 'Boris was very keen to learn English,' recalls Françoise Logan. 'He was really interested in English young people, in the pop scene – and in football results! But like all the young Russians, he was being groomed for stardom.'

Early performances in the semi-final round were briefly interrupted by a mysterious hissing noise, eventually discovered to emanate from the town hall's splendid Gothic fantasy of an organ, whose automatic humidifying equipment was found to be reacting to the heat generated by the banks of television lights. Apart from that inconvenience, the jury was obliged on one afternoon to listen to seven consecutive performances of *Gaspard de la nuit*. One of these was by Ovchinnikov, who coupled it with *Pictures at an Exhibition*, and a brilliant, barnstorming account of Liszt's *Don Juan Fantasy*. By this time, the gaunt, dark Russian, whose spectacular technique and drawn face conjured up echoes of Paganini, was widely predicted as a certain winner. Three of the semi-finalists, including Munro and Barone, chose the original version of Rakhmaninov's Second Sonata; while seven opted to play the Brahms G major Sonata with the hapless Erich Gruenberg ('Inspiration didn't seem to fly', remarked Marcantonio Barone, of his own version of the Brahms). Noriko Ogawa, however, chose the Mozart violin and piano sonata, while offering an attractive mixture of power and delicacy in her recital programme of four Debussy preludes, Takemitsu's *Rain Tree Sketch*, and the Liszt sonata. Tinney also programmed Liszt (the *Dante* Sonata) with Debussy (*Images*, Book 1), while Boris Berezovsky played a 'witty and colourful' *Islamey*, according to Bryce Morrison, coupled with the Schumann Symphonic Studies.

According to Robert Cockcroft, the *Yorkshire Post*'s music correspondent, 'safety – with three notable exceptions – appears to have been prized above originality' in the jury's choice of finalists. Many critics regretted the decision to eliminate the stylish and highly personal pianist Hortense Cartier-Bresson, together with her compatriot Jean-Efflam Bavouzet, and the talented German, Heiligers. David Buechner's failure to reach the last round also came as a shock, and a bitter disappointment. 'I was enraged,' says Buechner. 'It was a very bad experience, and came at a difficult time for me – I was just getting divorced. I was much more nervous than in 1984, but I felt I played at a much higher level.' Marcantonio Barone, one of the six finalists, was also undergoing a harrowing personal crisis – his father was gravely ill, and his condition was deteriorating throughout the competition.

While the first final – played by Tinney, Ogawa and Barone – was taking place on the Friday evening, Ian Munro – who couldn't face hearing the results of his semi-final round (he stayed in his room even during the official photographic session) – was chasing round Leeds trying to find a suitable piano to practise on:

It was the Jewish Sabbath, and I hadn't registered for a practice piano. The pianos at the college had already been returned to the shop. I couldn't find one anywhere, so I eventually gave up and went back to Tetley Hall. There I found Vladimir Ovchinnikov pummelling away on an old upright in the 'mess-hall' – but he wasn't making a sound. The piano had no strings! But it didn't worry him at all – he just grinned and waved at me. He was under enormous pressure to win – he practised all the time.

For the finals, Ovchinnikov – rather predictably – opted to play the Rakhmaninov No.2; while Munro and Ogawa both chose the Prokofiev No.3; and Tinney and Berezovsky Beethoven's Fourth (which had never yet won anyone the Leeds competition). Barone chose the Rakhmaninov *Rhapsody on a Theme by Paganini*. Though rumours of a 'fix' and of tactical voting by the Soviet juror circulated, there was never any doubt of the eventual outcome. Vladimir Ovchinnikov, who had impressed everyone by his total dedication, was declared a worthy winner, even though he had played his final under the most trying circumstances. 'He had realized the previous evening that he couldn't find his passport,' says Françoise Logan:

He'd been told – like all the Soviet competitors – to keep his identity papers together, so he was really worried about it. But he couldn't find it. After the final, he remembered that on Friday he'd gone to hire a dress suit from Dormie's, and he thought he might have left his papers there. So early on Sunday morning, we called the police, and persuaded them to open up the shop. The passport turned up in the dressing room.

Hilary Finch found a 'symmetrical satisfaction' in Ovchinnikov's win at Leeds, bearing in mind Barry Douglas's recent triumph at Moscow. Although she found him at times 'overpowered by aggressive orchestral playing' from the CBSO and Simon Rattle, Ovchinnikov's performance of the Rakhmaninov confirmed Finch's opinion of his semi-final that here was 'an artist in a class of his own'. 'It was Ovchinnikov who led the way,' wrote Finch in *The Times*, 'guiding the tempo changes of the first movement with sprung octaves, ending the adagio with the simplicity of lucid judgement and expanding the final scherzando.' Gerald Larner (the *Guardian*), confessing to being 'slightly disappointed' by Ovchinnikov's performance, also found him occasionally overpowered, but although Larner thought the slow movement 'unemotional', the whole was 'intelligently structured and unquestionably secure from the technical point of view'. Michael Kennedy (the *Daily Telegraph*) rated Ovchinnikov's Rakhmaninov 'the most mature and assured of the six concerto performances', while like Larner noting a degree of emotional detachment in the slow movement and some less than perfect ensemble playing with the orchestra. 'His daring and his feel for musical structure make him an intoxicating performer,' was the *Yorkshire Post*'s verdict.

Although few people disagreed with the winner, the other placings aroused the customary controversy. 'A very bold jury might have gambled on the exciting promise of Noriko Ogawa, whose . . . Prokofiev 3rd Concerto had a flair and brilliance which . . . offered a fuller musical experience than Ian Munro's less imaginative but no less commanding performance of the same work,' wrote Michael Kennedy. Hilary Finch thought Ian Munro's second place 'incomprehensible'. 'Diligence and delicacy' were the only qualities which impressed Finch in 'the Australian's neat, small-scale account' of the Prokofiev, while Ogawa (placed third) 'brought to it all the changes of light which were lacking in Munro's reading.' Most critics felt there was little to choose between the two accounts of Beethoven's Fourth, which won Berezovsky fourth place and Hugh Tinney fifth. Hilary Finch thought the award of the fourth prize to Berezovsky 'heartening in its decision to commend the zeal and excited responses of a daring eighteen-year-old, rather than to mark down his less than secure grasp of style', while Tinney's fifth place, despite 'a more mature and introspective interpretation . . . full of personality and imagination' (the *Yorkshire Post*), came as a severe disappointment to the competitive Irishman. After a poor showing in the semi-final, eliciting surprise that it earned him a place in the final at all, Marcantonio Barone redeemed himself with a spirited performance of the Paganini *Rhapsody*, 'well-disciplined and not unpoetic', which Gerald Larner thought was one of only three performances (the others being Berezovsky's and Tinney's) 'in which the soloist and the City of Birmingham Symphony Orchestra achieved and sustained a true balance'. This in spite of all attempts to avoid criticism, including

Rattle's insistence on extra rehearsal time and his careful evaluation of the acoustic. 'You can't play as you want, otherwise, it's too loud – you have to restrain yourself all the time,' he told the orchestra. Looking back, Rattle says:

Both the orchestra and I really enjoyed the 1987 competition. We set out to try to give the competitors the most outrageous accompaniments – to throw as much as possible at them to see what they would bat back. The problem with many competition concerto performances is that the conductor and the orchestra are often too bland and gentle. We tried to provide more than just a mere accompaniment; instead, we attempted to make very large-scale chamber music. It was fascinating to see how different people responded. I think the most complete chamber musician was Hugh Tinney. But Ovchinnikov was definitely the most ready to take on the fantastic profusion of dates that went with the prize.

I loved it, and the orchestra loved it. We decided together that we would set out to make it as positive an experience as possible. It was a very exciting – and exhausting – two days! And I'm looking forward to the next competition enormously.

The post-victory celebrations lasted until dawn, and Ovchinnikov – in true Russian style – was prostrate. 'He felt so ill he couldn't get up at all,' recalls Françoise Logan. 'So he didn't attend the meeting with the other finalists to discuss their engagements. Every time he tried to get up, he fell down again. We called the doctor – but it was just sheer exhaustion.'

A few days later, Ovchinnikov was hitting the headlines again. Pleading a back injury, he suddenly cancelled his important London début at a concert at the Barbican sponsored by Victor Hochhauser. But a determined journalist tracked him down to his Bayswater hotel, where he was found entertaining a group of well-wishers in his room – apparently in the best of health. The musical world held its breath – would this be a re-run of 1975, when the top prize at Leeds had gone to a Soviet pianist, only to have him disappear for several years from the international circuit, leaving his engagements unfulfilled? Rumours abounded: some said that the Soviet establishment had put pressure on Ovchinnikov to withdraw from an engagement sponsored by Victor Hochhauser, who was then *persona non grata* in the USSR for his vociferous criticism of Soviet treatment of Jewish citizens. The truth, according to Fanny Waterman, was less dramatic. The Barbican date specified either a Mozart or a Beethoven concerto, and Ovchinnikov would only play on condition it was the same concerto he had played at Leeds. 'I'm sorry I accepted that particular engagement,' says Fanny Waterman:

It's not fair to expect a pianist, having just won a competition, to make an important début with a different concerto that may not be in his repertoire, or which he may not have time to practise sufficiently. In 1990, Simon Rattle has offered three engagements for the winner with the CBSO – but I have insisted that it must be the winning concerto.

In fact, the spread of *glasnost* since 1987 has enabled Ovchinnikov to fulfil all his engagements – something he has done with such zeal that few have been left over for the other prize-winners. Although the narrowness of his repertoire has caused some concern – he is not prepared to venture outside his chosen late-Romantic field until he is certain that he can compete with the Western 'specialists' – the development of his European career since the Leeds seems amply to have justified critical opinion at the time that in 1987 the best man won.

Chapter Nineteen

The Winners

The nine first prize winners of the Harveys Leeds International Piano Competition have all pursued international careers on various levels. Without exception, all feel that success at Leeds opened avenues to them that perhaps otherwise would have remained closed, but each has developed along entirely independent lines.

Compared with other international competitions, the prize-money offered to the winner at Leeds is not the greatest attraction. It actually dropped from £1,000 in 1963 to £750 for each of the next four competitions: by 1978 it had risen to £2,000 as a result of the welcome injection of sponsorship, and now stands at £6,000 – not much compared with the $20,000 or so offered to the Van Cliburn winner, for example. But all the Leeds winners would doubtless agree with Ian Hobson, who says, 'The money is not the most important thing – it's the list of engagements.' The Leeds has always offered its winners an unparalleled choice of engagements, all of which are genuine. 'In some other competitions, they're listed, but they simply never materialize,' says Fanny Waterman. The Competition itself has no jurisdiction over which prize-winner is chosen to fulfil any particular engagement: the choice is up to the promoter – so theoretically all the engagements could be fulfilled by the first prize-winner. In practice, of course, this rarely happens: winning the Leeds has so far ensured a contract with one of the top London managers and a young artist can overnight find himself commanding the kind of fees that the smaller sponsors – local music clubs, for example – would be unable to afford. But it is nonetheless true that, with exceptions such as Alexeev (in whose case politics played a major role), the winner takes the lion's share of the spoils. If all goes well, the establishment of a major career in Britain as a result of all these engagements will also open doors internationally, but this is by no means a foregone conclusion. Nor does it necessarily guarantee an instant major recording contract. As Jon Kimura Parker, the 1984 winner, remembers John Lill telling the assembled competitors that year: 'for whoever ends up winning this competition, it will be an international passport for three years, but after that you're on your own'.

Having made his difficult decision after his unexpected win in 1963, Michael Roll 'was led to believe he was in the international limelight'. He was immediately signed up by a top London agent; but once the die was cast, and the emotional support he received from jury members and others in the aftermath of the competition had dissipated, he found himself very much on his own when still very young and vulnerable – a victim of the lack of educational infrastructure for the support and nourishment of young artists in the UK.

'I went on studying with Fanny for another few years, but then I felt I had to widen my own horizons,' he says:

I did a few engagements, and learnt more repertoire – and that was a blessing. If I had been subjected to the kind of excessive interest that one gets now, it would have been a disaster. Being an artist puts enormous pressure on you. You have to be as tough as old boots in physical and mental terms. Nowadays, you simply can't afford to have an off-day – it's all so media-orientated. I wasn't subjected to that kind of pressure in 1963, but on the other hand, I didn't have the opportunities either. I did a concert with Giulini in 1964, and then a recital in London. Then Hans Schmidt-Isserstedt arranged for me to do a record test for EMI. I made a complete mess of it. I just didn't have a clue what was involved. I didn't prepare it, and I ended up doing a ludicrous pot-pourri of repertoire. Looking back, I can't believe how naïve I was – it was a fiasco. I really needed a good business manager. Fortunately, Harold Holt signed me up in 1965.

I never studied with anyone except Fanny on a lengthy basis, but naturally I sought other advice occasionally. I went to live in London, and heard a lot of great artists play, and met many contemporaries. 1968 was a very important year for me – I got to hear many people play. Then I went to Paris – it was the year of the student riots – and studied conducting. When I was twenty-two I did a big Russian tour – my mother went with me to keep an eye on me. I feel I should have learnt more repertoire when I was young, but what I did learn, I learnt very thoroughly.

Does Michael Roll feel that he suffered from being so young and inexperienced when he was thrust into the concert world through winning a major competition?

Somebody might be right and ready for a competition at twenty-one, and not at twenty-five. I feel that what happens later should be taken more responsibly by those guiding the person – the worrying aspect is the outside factions, everyone who wants to make a quick killing, the 'it's good for business' aspect. That's a very bad thing. The idea should be to introduce young, gifted people to the concert scene, but it shouldn't be for the benefit of agents, TV companies, critics, etc. I think it's regrettable but inevitable to have to start your career through a competition. How else do you help young artists to get started? There's a lot of rot talked in the profession. It's very difficult to stay sane; you must trust in yourself and those close to you, and shut your ears to everything else. If you listened to everybody, you would get nowhere. Leeds was a crucial turning point in my life, but not necessarily in my development.

Michael Roll is presently living in Germany with his wife, the pianist Juliana Markova (who is virtually unknown in Britain, but who plays regularly in the States) and Max, their seven-year-old son:

I feel I have developed slowly and in a sense I have grown up very late. I feel much more positive about my playing now – I have a far greater sense of security than twenty years ago. But I was very fortunate to have that start, and to meet great chamber music partners, although I now want to concentrate again on solo playing. I feel the outlook is very good – I'm more ready now. I did go through a difficult patch, because of the lack of a recording contract, and I was dissatisfied with some of my early performances which did not make the impact they should. But I have always been busy, even without recordings.

At the moment I'm playing in England, Scandinavia, East Germany, Russia – less in West Germany. I've never played in France, and hardly at all in the USA. I do a 50/50 mixture of concertos and recitals. A big turning-point was a recital at the QEH in 1986 which I really enjoyed. It was very well received, and a number of things came out of it. As far as repertoire is concerned, my strengths are still in the Classics and early Romantics – Schubert, Schumann, the Brahms No.2 (I haven't played the D minor yet), Chopin 2. I may try Rakhmaninov 3 – I feel I'm just about ready for it now. I've also played the Britten and Stravinsky concertos, and this year I'm doing Hans Gál's Piano Concerto. My repertory is broadening out. In summer '90 I'm doing a Far Eastern tour and returning to the Proms in Mozart's K.482 – one of my party pieces. I'm also doing a Gewandhaus tour with Sanderling.

I've always enjoyed the support of the BBC Philharmonic, also the Scottish National and the other regional orchestras. There are some really interesting prospects in the pipeline. I feel I'm progressing at a steady pace and at the right time. If things had started to move earlier, it would have been the wrong time for me. Look at Bolet – he got started at sixty!

But in this business you can't afford to be asleep. You can't sit in a corner and let the world discover you. That's why we need competitions. In this profession, people are constantly making selections, deciding who to pick. The selection process goes on all the time.

At twenty, Rafael Orozco was slightly more mature than Michael Roll when he won the 1966 competition. Unlike Roll, he came from a musical background, receiving his early musical training from his father and his aunt at the Córdoba Conservatory, and then studying both piano and composition at Madrid. By the time he was seventeen he had already won prizes in several competitions in Spain and Italy, including first prize in the Jaen Competition in 1964. But it was his Leeds win that launched his international career.

'I enjoyed the Leeds competition – it was very well organized,' says Orozco:

In the 1960s and early '70s it seemed as if every international competition was being won by Russians – all the attention was focused on them and it was very difficult for a non-Russian to get noticed. I didn't expect to get into the final – I was very lucky. I felt that the jury was very special – they were looking for musical points, not just barnstormers. They were trying to find a real artist.

Immediately after the competition, Orozco moved to London, where he was able to take up the engagements offered him in the aftermath of Leeds. He was fortunate to enjoy the patronage of Carlo Maria Giulini, who offered him a string of important engagements in London, Europe and the USA. He has since played regularly with most of the major orchestras – the LSO, the RPO, the Berlin Philharmonic, and the Philadelphia, Cleveland, New York and Los Angeles orchestras – and has toured the Far East and Japan. Unlike Michael Roll, he was offered a recording contract shortly after winning the Leeds, first with EMI, and then with Philips, including a complete Rakhmaninov concerto cycle with Edo de Waart and the RPO. He now lives in Rome, and is more often heard in Europe than in Britain, although he still comes over for festival appearances and occasional recitals. 'I'm grateful to the Leeds for getting my career started,' he says. 'Through it I came into contact with a lot of people I wouldn't otherwise have met.'

Radu Lupu entered the 1969 Leeds competition a clear favourite, having already won first prizes at the 1966 Van Cliburn and the 1967 Enescu, so his success was by no means unexpected.

I was still studying at the Moscow Conservatoire at the time, and I was in no hurry to start a career. I thought my best chance would be to enter a competition that had a repertoire which reflected my own tastes – one where I wouldn't just have to show that I could play the piano by dashing off a couple of showy études. I liked the Leeds repertoire – based round the Classics and Romantics, and with the chance to play a recital of one's own choice. The Van Cliburn had a very different profile at that time – 'the greatest competition on earth' kind of thing – and I felt it leaned towards sensationalism, and put too much emphasis on the sporting philosophy. There the pieces were more 'imposed' – you had to play a certain mazurka, a certain étude. I felt it was small-minded: it seemed to me that it shouldn't be such a life-or-death issue. But it has changed recently – it's improved its repertoire, introduced chamber music. It's a good competition now.

But the Leeds suited me much more. The repertoire was modest and to the point – one was free to show one's personality, especially in the free choice recital lasting an hour. I respected the repertoire, and I believed the jury would be in sympathy with that kind of music.

I didn't feel I was the preferred candidate at Leeds. Having won one major competition doesn't really mean anything – one can have good or bad luck on the day. I never went to a competition with the aim of competing – if I'd thought that I wouldn't have been able to move a finger. I went only to play – and I played the way I wanted to play. I think it's very bad if people try to play in a way they think will please the jury. That happens much more now.

The Leeds competition started my career, no doubt about it. Afterwards, I was taken on straight away by a British agent, and I got a lot of engagements. I'd never played in England before. I know I had disappointed the organizers of the Van Cliburn because I had turned down a lot of work offered me in the USA. I had made my Carnegie Hall début in 1967, but then I turned down a European tour organized under the auspices of Jeunesses musicales. At that time, I just didn't know what a career was – and thank goodness I didn't. But after the Leeds I became a celebrity overnight, and I just had to face it. Before then, I must have felt subconsciously that I needed time to develop. I was very strong-minded, and all I felt was that I must cancel those concerts which didn't seem to fit in with my studies. I didn't want to be under pressure to learn something special for this or that concert. But after the Leeds my life changed completely. It's unknown territory, there's a lot of pressure, and one doesn't know if one will cope with it.

One year after the Leeds competition, Radu Lupu decided to leave Romania and settle in England, where he has lived ever since. The most important factor which influenced his decision, which naturally caused a political uproar in his native country, was his marriage to the daughter of the British Ambassador to Moscow, herself a talented cellist. Now divorced, Lupu lives by himself in the west London suburb of Chiswick ('it's convenient for Heathrow').

I am glad I came to England. Once one starts a career, it starts locally, and I got a lot of engagements in England. If there are any cancellations, you have to be there to take them up. In 1970 Arrau cancelled some concerts when he was in England, and I was' able to take them over. That convinced me it was necessary to be on the spot. But the English do have a slightly insular attitude – they tend to assume that if someone isn't playing so much over here, then their career is not going well, while in fact they may well be getting a lot of work on the Continent.

I have returned a couple of times to play in Romania. I was put under the greatest pressure to prove that the career I had chosen in the West was not for nothing.

Radu Lupu – the sort of pianist who, in the words of Alan Blyth, can make 'his listeners feel that he is simply sitting down and com-posing the music as he goes along' – is now unquestionably regarded as one of the finest of his generation. His early selectiveness about taking on engagements – and indeed, his insistence on cancelling them if he so wished – has characterized his later career: he now deliberately restricts himself to about sixty-five concerts a season, although he is constantly in demand all over the world. He plays regularly with all the world's great orchestras in Europe, London and the USA, and regularly tours Japan and the Far East. Two important things happened in the immediate aftermath of the Leeds competition. He signed a contract with Decca, for whom he has made over twenty records including all the Beethoven piano concertos with the Israel Philharmonic and Zubin Mehta; a Mozart/Schubert piano-duo record, the Mozart Concerto for two pianos and a two-piano transcription of the Concerto for three pianos, all with his great friend Murray Perahia; and solo recordings of Beethoven, Brahms and Schubert. He also formed a violin-and-piano duo partnership with Szymon Goldberg, who was on the Leeds jury; and together they have recorded all the Mozart violin and piano sonatas.

Lupu's repertoire has stayed more or less constant: Mozart, Beethoven, Brahms, Schubert (the sort of music which, according to the critic Bryce Morrison, 'shows Lupu's unique quality at its most luminous and subtly poetic'). He is presently branching out into Chopin and Musorgsky:

I'm trying to change. I'm lucky to have the security of a career which allows me time to experiment. I'm always looking for new horizons, but I haven't done much twentieth-century music. I feel that one should put some effort into living in one's own century, but I don't see any point in trying to prove that one is unlimited, universal. One should do oneself a favour by approaching those things which give the most personal satisfaction.

I don't teach at the moment, nor have I sat on any international juries. Those two things go hand in hand. Perhaps I'll come to them later in life. If I were on a jury, I should look for the ideal pianist – a Horowitz, a Gould. I would look for someone who was telling me a story I could believe, someone who combined presentation, technique, knowledge, culture, sincerity, projection and personality – genuine playing.

The career of a concert pianist is a very isolated one. It's a very lonely existence. Apart from the stress of performing, and the physical and mental preparation beforehand, you have to fill up every day when you don't have a concert. I do the normal things for relaxation – reading, playing bridge, chess, taking a holiday sometimes.

Murray Perahia's win at Leeds in 1972 came, like Lupu's, at exactly the right moment in his artistic development:

It was really my manager, Frank Salomon, who decided I should go in for the Leeds: he thought the repertoire would suit me. I had been attending the Marlboro Summer School for about five years, and I was interested in the idea of pursuing a solo career. I had been doing mostly chamber music – Schumann, Haydn, Brahms, the Mozart violin and piano sonatas, with a few isolated solo dates – a Mozart concerto with the New York Philharmonic, the Chopin First Piano Concerto with a pick-up orchestra, that kind of thing.

I had approached some managers with a view to becoming a soloist, and had sent some tapes, but they all said I wouldn't get started unless I entered a major competition. I didn't like the idea, but I thought it would be a good opportunity to get a couple of recital programmes and some concertos together. I thought I had better make a stab at becoming a soloist, and I was fortunate to have financial help from Irving Moskovitz, a friend of the violist in the Budapest Quartet, who wanted me to try to make a solo career. He paid for the trip to Leeds.

Winning the Leeds opened the floodgates of a massive international career:

The competition offered forty or so engagements, so I took an apartment in London, although I was (and still am) a US citizen, and I was still based in the States. My career really solidified both in the US and in England. I got a CBS recording contract the same month. I've done two records a year since: the first one was the *Davidsbündlertänze* [the performance of which was one of the highlights of the 1972 Leeds competition], and next I did the Mendelssohn concertos.

I had very mixed feelings about the idea of becoming a solo pianist – it took about two years. My first feeling after I won at Leeds was panic. Could I handle it? It's a big responsibility – to fail to live up to expectations in that situation would put you back a long way. It took me months to settle down. I didn't accept all the engagements that were offered, because I didn't feel ready for them. During the next year or two I took lots of time off to learn more repertoire – to be a concert pianist needs background, experience, breadth of repertoire.

The engagements I did take on and the repertoire I learnt was a natural outgrowth of my musical loves. The cycle of Mozart concertos with the ECO came out of my love of Mozart and of chamber music – they were the things I cherished. I did not choose the engagements in a random way, they had an inner logic. I went on to do the Beethoven and Brahms concertos, and so on. I was fortunate in that my career developed at the pace I wanted and in the way I wanted.

Murray Perahia studied conducting while he was a student at Mannes College in New York, but unlike Myung-Whun Chung, he is not interested in becoming a conductor as such: 'My conducting technique wasn't up to much; I didn't pursue it. But I also studied composition: I wanted to be a complete musician. Being solely a pianist is limiting. The advantage of directing Mozart, say, from the keyboard is that you can work out a chamber-music conception of a piece.'

For the past twelve years Murray Perahia has lived in England. When he is not touring the world, he spends his time at home in Ealing with his wife Ninette, and their two small children, Benjamin and Rafael:

The life of a pianist is very difficult. I wouldn't advise it unless the love of music is overridingly strong. There are lots of difficulties and frustrations. One's musical horizons are always changing, always growing. You never feel good about it because you are always developing.

It's physically a very difficult life – lots of travelling, the stress of being constantly up to scratch. I don't play every night – it would be impossible. One also has to have the courage to go 'away from pattern' – to branch out, do other repertoire. It's very important to grow as a musician, to have new horizons, new insights. I don't think in terms of 'career development'. There are certain things I'd like to do, more Beethoven sonatas, more Brahms, Liszt – understanding what makes a masterpiece. At the moment I'm involved with the concept of voice-leading, how it affects a piece. I'm trying to formulate my own point of view as to how one hears music. Fifty per cent of music is how you hear it. These are the subjects that occupy me.

Dmitri Alexeev – the first Soviet winner at Leeds – found that international politics played a major part in directing his career:

Like many students I wanted to make a good career as a concert pianist, and it's much easier if you win some important competition. I had already taken part in several competitions before Leeds – the Marguérite Long in Paris, where I came second, the Enescu in Bucharest, which I won, and the 1974 Tchaikovsky in Moscow. There I wasn't lucky – I came fifth, and it was a big disappointment. People have very strong competitive instincts in Russia – you have to go through a selection process just to take part. I was the favourite for that competition, but something was wrong for me – I wasn't at my best. There was a very heavy atmosphere – everyone was under a lot of pressure, and the competition was very strong – Gavrilov [the winner], Igolinsky, Andras Schiff, Myung-Whun Chung. Then I heard that the Leeds would be taking place the following year, so I decided to go in for it. I had heard a lot about the Leeds from my friends, such as Radu

Lupu, and I knew it would be good. It's not like any other competition – it's much more musical, and the repertoire was very special. It suited my own playing ideally – Schubert, Brahms, and so on.

The Leeds competition wasn't very well known in the USSR at that time. There had been no previous Soviet winner, and information about music in the West was still very sketchy. The foreign competitions that ranked in the Soviet Union then were the Van Cliburn, the Chopin, the Brussels. After I won, the Leeds got more attention, and now it's recognized as one of the really important ones.

Afterwards, although I was offered a lot of engagements, I had great difficulty in making a career in the West. I was, and still am, a Soviet citizen, and it wasn't a good time in Russia then, in the late Brezhnev era. All Soviet artists found it difficult to get permission to travel abroad. Three days after the Leeds, I was invited by Antal Dorati to play with the RPO in the Festival Hall. I finally got permission to take the engagement, with incredible difficulty – there were endless negotiations with the Embassy, Gosconcert, and so on. It was all very embarrassing. I managed to do my Queen Elizabeth Hall recital, and another concert in Vienna two months after the competition, but then it took another year to get permission to do any more engagements outside the USSR. I lost many opportunities then. That sort of thing was quite normal then – it sounds crazy now – but everyone had to be checked out. I think I probably managed to fulfil about 30 or 40 per cent of the engagements offered me. I played with the Chicago Symphony and Giulini, and in London, Vienna and Amsterdam. I was naturally disappointed not to be able to do all of them, but it was very good for me to be able to do some.

Dmitri Alexeev was taken on by the London agent Harold Holt after the Leeds, and now plays all over the world: in the USA, Canada, Japan, Hong Kong, Australia, and all the major European centres. In November 1990 he will return to the USA on tour with the Leningrad Philharmonic under Yuri Temirkanov. So far he has recorded concertos by Prokofiev, Rakhmaninov and Shostakovich, Grieg and Schumann, the Chopin waltzes and preludes, and piano works by Brahms and Rakhmaninov for EMI, Virgin, and on a Soviet label.

My engagements are increasing all the time – it has been a gradual build-up. Of course, it's much easier to organize concerts now. It has taken twelve years to develop a career which should have only taken three or four – it's been much slower than it could have been. But I did have the opportunity to consolidate my repertoire.

I've tried not to specialize so far as repertoire is concerned – I do a lot of Romantic and twentieth-century music – Russian music, Ravel, Prokofiev, Bartók chamber music, and a few contemporary works; also a lot of Mozart, Beethoven, Schubert. I don't play as much Bach as I used to.

Michel Dalberto, so far the only French pianist to have won at Leeds, was also a competition veteran by the time he entered in 1978. A prize-winner in the 1975 Clara Haskil Competition, he had taken the second prize (no first being awarded) in the Mozart Competition at Salzburg the same year; and two years later he came fourth in the Van Cliburn:

I decided to enter for the Leeds because England was clearly one of the most important countries for music. I felt it would be really good for my career if I could win at Leeds. And it did make a big difference. I got a British agent, and lots of invitations to do concerts. I did most of them, but after two or three years I felt I was playing too much. So now I play mostly in France, Germany, Italy and Japan, not so much in England. I've never really tried the USA. I hate it. I did just one recital in New York.

The core of my repertoire is Schubert – I'm recording all his piano works with Zenon, the Japanese company. I've also done eleven or twelve recordings for Erato, of Schubert, Schumann, Mozart concertos, early Beethoven sonatas, Brahms, etc. I'm now playing more twentieth-century repertoire – Debussy, the Viennese School, Boulez.

The Leeds competition was perfectly organized. I met some very nice people at Tetley Hall, and I made lots of friends, especially the Blackburn family to whose home I was taken to practise. They were very kind.

Michel Dalberto now lives in Switzerland. He is not fond of touring, and mostly restricts his concert appearances to the surrounding countries. He is probably now the least well-known former Leeds winner in the UK.

Unlike some of the earlier Leeds winners, who had entered with little previous experience of competitions, and whose unexpected success had almost taken them by surprise, Ian Hobson planned his campaign carefully. After a prolonged period of study both at the Royal Academy of Music in London and then at Cambridge University, where he took a BA degree, followed by graduate study at the

Yale School of Music, Hobson was offered a teaching job at the University of Illinois. But he still intended to pursue a concert career, and in 1977 he was a finalist in the Van Cliburn Competition. This encouraged him to enter the Leeds the following year, where he won fourth prize, the highest-placed English pianist since Michael Roll.

'I had no intention of going in for any more competitions,' says Hobson:

After the 1978 competition I got a British and a European agent, and I did some concerts in England and Europe, including my London début. But then in 1980 I was tempted to go in for the Rubinstein Competition, and I came second. There was a lot of controversy – the American winner, Gregory Allen, was booed, and there was a general feeling that I should have won. I was invited to enter the next Beethoven Competition in Vienna as a result, and someone also said, 'Why don't you go back to Leeds next year?' I got the Leeds brochure, and it offered an extremely well-endowed list of prizes and engagements, including a record contract with EMI, a new Steinway grand piano, a performance with Solti, and so on. So I decided to re-enter. I used the Beethoven Competition in June that year as a dress rehearsal, and there was a bit of a scandal when I only came second.

I regarded the 1981 Leeds competition as an opportunity to be heard again, regardless of the result. Even during the competition, people were telling me I must be crazy to take the risk – but once I got into the finals again, I wasn't so concerned. I hoped that my playing would mean something to the audience, and I welcomed the TV and radio exposure. Playing in a competition is just like doing an important engagement – there's exactly the same degree of pressure. I didn't play for the jurors – I just played my best, as I would for a concert, and I've found that to be very successful. There are competitions around in which safe playing is the best policy, but it's not true of Leeds – all the winners who have emerged are individuals. The Leeds encourages musical integrity.

After I won at Leeds, I fulfilled many engagements, including a concert with Solti and the Chicago Symphony Orchestra. I already had a concert scheduled at the Queen Elizabeth Hall, but after winning the Leeds I cancelled it, changed the programme, and did the Leeds winner's concert there instead. I also made lots of records, including the twenty-four Chopin études for Classics for Pleasure, and the Mozart concertos K.488 and 491 with the ECO for EMI, together with some Rakhmaninov transcriptions. I've since completed thirteen records for the Arabesque label in the US, such as the Hummel piano sonatas, Rakhmaninov preludes and *Etudes-tableaux* – it's been a very fruitful relationship.

Ian Hobson suffered a fair amount of adverse criticism from the British Press in the wake of the 1981 competition, particularly from those who felt that Peter Donohoe should have won. He decided to retain his professorship at Illinois, and his concert career is primarily concentrated in the USA: 'It's a flexible position, which allows me time for concertizing. I enjoy teaching – I've learnt a lot, and I'm now doing much more conducting, which I studied at Yale. I've got my own chamber orchestra – the Sinfonia da Camera – which has started to release some records.'

Hobson is a highly intelligent pianist, with wide-ranging musical interests:

I find an all-round career more satisfying, though it is more difficult from the publicity angle. My series of 'London Piano School' recitals in New York and London (three concerts of unfamiliar music by late eighteenth- and early nineteenth-century composers associated with London), were very well covered by the Press, and it's good to bring unknown repertoire to light.

As one might expect, Ian Hobson's repertoire is large. Apart from the complete cycle of Beethoven sonatas, and several Mozart concertos directed from the keyboard, it encompasses a good deal of late Romantic and early twentieth-century piano music, ranging from Rakhmaninov and Saint-Saëns to Milhaud and Ravel:

I have been identified as a pianist with a big technique, for the Rakhmaninov and so on, but actually I have a variety of styles. Now I'm getting more Classically orientated.

The Leeds competition has survived in spite of the relatively small financial rewards it offers, compared to some others. It has a very specific repertoire – which has advantages and disadvantages. On the one hand, you may end up with people of limited range and small repertoires, but on the other, it's good to include particular pieces, some of which are unusual.

I'm grateful that I was twenty-nine and experienced when I won at Leeds – I wouldn't have liked to have been nineteen or so. So many young pianists just fizzle out under those circumstances. I regard my own career in music as a long haul. I've been able to go on steadily building up my repertoire and my reputation, and I'm grateful for that.

Before the 1984 Leeds competition, Jon Kimura Parker was an

almost totally unknown Canadian pianist. He had studied with Adèle Marcus at the Juilliard School in New York, and before that had graduated from the Toronto Conservatory and the University of Vancouver:

In 1977, while I was a student in Vancouver, I had never travelled further afield than New York, except for one trip to Japan (my mother is Japanese). I remember thinking, 'If I would ever be good enough to be allowed to enter a major competition, I would like to go to Leeds', mainly because of the tremendous reputation of its previous winners as artists and musicians – people like Lupu and Perahia. In my opinion it had a better reputation than the Tchaikovsky or the Van Cliburn. I never dreamed that seven or so years later I would be accepting the first prize there.

I had good luck in competitions – I felt I had a very positive attitude towards them. I think the best way is to try to forget it's a competition, and go out there to show your stuff, as if it's a concert. Competitions serve a specific purpose. After I won at Leeds, I was so relieved that I would never have to go in for another one! They are tremendously stressful events.

I didn't enter the Leeds with any hope of winning, but I had prepared a couple of concertos, just in case. I felt very relaxed, and I had a great vote of confidence from the agent Jasper Parrott, who approached me even before the result was announced, wanting to represent me. Everyone was very supportive: after I got into the second round I got a telegram from the Canadian Cultural Attaché wishing me well – the Canada Council and the Embassy were watching me, but I hadn't been aware of it.

My parents, my girlfriend and my teacher were all very supportive. My parents just couldn't believe I'd won. Adèle Marcus was thrilled. Winning at Leeds really started my career. I was a relative newcomer, even in Canada, which suffers from a rather provincial attitude – it can only really concentrate on one pianist at a time. CBC tends to cover French Canada more, and CBC was attending the Leeds competition because Louis Lortie was playing. When I won, the Vancouver media made a great event of it – it was as if I'd won an Olympic gold medal! It catapulted me into playing with every major orchestra in the country, plus recital series, concerts with American orchestras including the Los Angeles and the San Francisco Symphony, the Mostly Mozart Festival with the Tokyo Quartet, and so on. I'm also working in Europe, especially Germany and Italy, as well as in England. I'm now doing about a hundred concerts a year in seventy different cities. I

consider myself really lucky to make a good living as a pianist –
it's something I've wanted to do since I was five years old.

Leeds ranks as a fair competition, and as a musicians'
competition. The list of engagements it offers is extraordinary, and
I'd choose engagements in preference to prize-money. The Leeds
is very fortunate to have Harveys as its sponsor – it's a privilege
to play under their auspices. One of the side benefits of having
won, was that shortly afterwards, a package arrived for me in New
York. It was a crate of sherry!

Parker's lively, outgoing personality has endeared him not only to
his acquaintances at Leeds, with whom he remains in close contact,
but also to concert promoters and record companies. He has released
two recordings for Telarc, one of the Tchaikovsky and Prokofiev
Third piano concertos with André Previn and the RPO, the other a
solo recital of works by Chopin. Since 1984 he has returned every
year to the UK, has made his European débuts in cities as far apart
as Zagreb, Lisbon and Budapest, and has toured Australia and the
Far East. So far as the BBC is concerned, however, he has run into
the problem which besets young artists who can suddenly command
astronomically high fees after a competition win: 'We can't afford
him,' says John Drummond. So at the moment, it would seem, a
Prom performance is not on the cards.

Vladimir Ovchinnikov, the 1987 Leeds winner, has also not
appeared at the Proms yet, but for a different reason: 'He insisted
on offering only the concerto which won him the competition, and
we wanted a different one,' says Drummond. Temperamentally, the
pale, quiet and intense Russian is the exact antithesis of the ebullient
Kimura Parker, but both shared the same driving ambition and will
to win.

'My career wasn't going very well before the Leeds,' explains
Ovchinnikov. 'I wanted to enter because it was important not only
in terms of prestige, but also in terms of the quality of the people
who had entered and won in the past. Many of the competitors in
1987 had already won first prizes in other competitions.'

Including Ovchinnikov himself, who had won first prize at Montreal in 1980, and joint-second prize with Peter Donohoe in Moscow
in 1982. 'That was the first competition I entered in which no first
prize was given, and I hope it will be the last,' says Ovchinnikov:

If you enter for a competition, you must expect to get the first prize.
If I had got the second or the third, it would have been a failure.

The Leeds competition is no lower in terms of prestige than the
Tchaikovsky. The main thing is that the jury members are very

respected and famous, and the selection is so careful that the best quality comes through. And it has good repertoire. The third stage – the free-choice recital – is very important. I know from experience that you can play in a fairly mediocre way during an entire competition, but if you play just one piece absolutely brilliantly, you can go through.

In contrast to Alexeev's experiences, the recent welcome thaw in East–West relations has meant that Ovchinnikov has had little trouble in fulfilling the engagements offered to him as a result of the Leeds competition. Indeed, his zeal has meant that there have been few pickings left over for the other 1987 prize-winners:

My aim was to get some engagements in England, and thanks to my English agent, I now come very often. It's the work that matters, not the prize-money. Fortunately, since Gorbachev, things have changed, and it is much easier for Russian artists to play in the West now. It's just a formality. I've been very lucky. I'm now trying to develop my career worldwide – I've played a bit in the USA, and I've visited Japan twice. I've been doing short tours crammed with good concerts.

Since his Leeds win, Ovchinnikov's limited repertoire, focusing on Liszt and the late Romantics, especially Rakhmaninov, has attracted some criticism – although his interpretations of that repertoire have recently received glowing reviews, comparing his playing to that of Horowitz or even Rakhmaninov himself. Is he in fact an example of a pianist groomed to win major competitions on the strength of a few pieces?

At Leeds I attracted attention for my playing of Russian music. The public loves Russian music, and the great appreciation I received makes me stay with it for the moment. But I also love Classical and contemporary music. There are so many specialists in the West – so many of them are at the top, and I'm in no rush to join them. I am only just beginning my career, and when I am known as a pianist and can choose what I play, then I will begin to play Beethoven – I will expand.

Apart from his many concerts, Ovchinnikov has recently released a record of the Liszt études, and has just recorded the Rakhmaninov studies. He feels that at twenty-nine, the time was ripe for him to make the most of his Leeds win:

I think it is better not to be too young for these things. In an ideal world, I wish that young musicians did not have to undergo these stressful ordeals in order to make careers. Every time you go on stage, there is stress. If I play when I am fifty or sixty I will still feel the same, but if you have enough experience, it can be used to advantage. The secret of great art is not to eliminate stress, but to know how to make use of it. Winning a competition like the Leeds is still the best way to establish a career; but you have to develop yourself from a very early age with great single-mindedness. Not every pianist can become an artist. You must also show the qualities needed to become a winner – you must feel you are the king on stage. What the public is looking for is not just technique but personality – a personal approach. That is what you have to develop, and many young kids who go in for competitions don't yet have that. There are exceptions – Evgeny Kissin, for example. He doesn't need to enter for competitions. But ones like him are very rare.

Chapter Twenty

The Future: 1990 and Beyond

The stage is set for the tenth Harveys Leeds International Piano Competition, which will take place from 7 to 22 September 1990. Just over half its estimated cost of £200,000 is being provided by Harveys; the City of Leeds has put up £20,000 to defray the cost of paying the jury; while the other major sponsors of the 1990 event are the Friends of the HLIPC, the Gulbenkian Foundation, the Leeds Permanent Building Society, the Sir George Martin Trust, the University of Leeds, and the Marjorie and Arnold Ziff Charitable Foundation. For the first time since 1963, the Arts Council of Great Britain is not involved – a sign of the times?

Fanny Waterman has asked fourteen distinguished musicians to serve under her on the 1990 jury. Claude Frank, Konstantin Ganev, Cécile Ousset, Hans Graf, Gordon Stewart (now Head of Singing at the Royal Scottish Academy of Music and Drama) and Arie Vardi have all been re-invited. New to the Leeds jury are the Italian pianist and composer Marcello Abbado, director of the Giuseppe Verdi Conservatory in Milan; José da Sequeiro Costa from Portugal, a pupil of Vianna da Motta with a major international concert career, juror at the first Tchaikovsky Competition when he was only twenty-eight, and a veteran juror of many international piano competitions since, and founder of the Vianna da Motta Piano Competition in Portugal; Sergei Dorensky, chairman of the piano faculty at the Moscow Conservatory, and another experienced international adjudicator; Dominique Merlet, concert pianist and professor of piano at the Paris Conservatoire, himself a pupil of Roger Ducasse, Nadia Boulanger and Louis Hiltbrand, winner of the Geneva International Competition in 1957, and a subsequent entrant of the very first Leeds competition in 1963; Hiroko Nakamura from Japan, a student of Rosa Lhévinne at the Juilliard, the youngest prize-winner at the Chopin Competition in Warsaw, and now a frequent jury member of major international competitions; and John O'Conor from Eire, another veteran of the Leeds Competition, and now Artistic Director of the

GPA Dublin International Piano Competition, which made its début on the international competition scene only two years ago. O'Conor's own recordings for Telarc, which include the complete Beethoven Sonatas, the Mozart concertos, the Field nocturnes and the Grieg and Schumann concertos, are currently winning critical acclaim.

In addition, two writer–critics will join the 1990 jury: Werner Felix from East Germany, author of books on Bach, Gluck and Liszt, formerly Principal of the Franz Liszt Conservatory in Weimar and Professor of History of Music at the Leipzig Conservatory, and now General Director of the J. S. Bach National Research Institute, Chairman of the International Bach Competition in Leipzig, and Principal since 1987 of the Felix Mendelssohn Conservatory in Leipzig; and the celebrated American critic Harold C. Schonberg, formerly senior music critic of the *New York Times*, and now its cultural correspondent. Harold Schonberg received the Pulitzer Prize for criticism in 1971; his thirteen books, on subjects ranging from music to chess, include *The Great Pianists*, *The Lives of the Great Composers*, and *The Glorious Ones – Superstars of Music*.

For the first time, the members of this jury will be offered a small fee for their services, in addition to their expenses. The relentless proliferation of competitions in recent years, all competing for the services of the same concert pianists and pedagogues, has made it increasingly difficult for the Leeds to continue to attract juries of international calibre on a purely voluntary basis. 'We hope that the offer of a fee will encourage jurors to think twice before they feel they can withdraw from Leeds if they are subsequently offered more lucrative engagements,' says Françoise Logan. 'We have always had problems with jury members dropping out at the last minute. They are more likely to turn up if they regard it as a professional engagement.'

The total prize-money offered in 1990 amounts to £23,500 – £6,000 for the winner, £3,500 for the second prize, £2,500 for the third, £2,000 for the fourth, £1,500 for the fifth and £1,250 for the sixth. The six semi-final prizes stand at £500 each, and the thirteen second-stage prizes at £250. In addition, Harveys are offering £500 for the best competitor under twenty.

This year, thirteen international engagements are offered, including two tours for the winner, one of Asia and the other of the USA; eighteen engagements with British orchestras, including six in London (three with the major London orchestras – Philharmonia, LPO and RPO) and twelve others with regional orchestras, including three concerts for the winner with the CBSO under Rattle; eight festival engagements, including Bath, Harrogate, Aldeburgh and the

City of London; and thirty-five recital dates at music clubs all over the country.

Several major changes to the structure and repertoire of the competition are scheduled for 1990. As in previous years, there will only be six finalists, but 25 competitors (rather than 20) will be admitted to the second stage, and 12 of these (rather than 10) will go through to the semi-finals. In addition, each competitor will be allowed to play for longer in the first stage – forty minutes instead of twenty. The competition itself will last for three extra days, and each stage will be longer.

'We're trying to improve the competition all the time,' says Fanny Waterman:

If we allocate more time to each competitor in each round, it will give them more time to settle down and enable them to reveal the architecture of a major work – something you can't do in twenty minutes. So far as the repertoire is concerned, we have decided to drop the chamber music round from the next competition. It creates an artificial situation, in which a pianist has to get together in an *ad hoc* way with other musicians, and try to do the best he or she can in a given time, with very little rehearsal. That's not really the spirit of chamber music. Chamber music partnerships take time to develop. I originally felt it was important to hear balance, accompaniment, timing. My own chamber music partnerships improved me as a player – playing the Beethoven trios and violin and piano sonatas gave me new insight into the solo sonatas, and one's own playing takes on some of the qualities of a gifted partner's. The chamber music rounds at Leeds have certainly been very enjoyable for the audience and the jury, but we feel, on reflection, that they have contributed little towards the assessment of solo pianism. So instead, we're offering the opportunity of an extra solo recital. We're also trying to improve the repertoire all the time: I want to choose repertoire that will influence what the competitors learn in the year before the competition – they should be encouraged to put together two or three complete recital programmes.

In 1990 the Leeds programme offers more free choice – a response to some criticism that it has in the past been too specific. The core of the repertoire remains intact: the first stage still prescribes a list of pieces – a choice of four works by Bach; the Mozart Fantasy and Sonata in C minor, the Haydn E flat Sonata, Hob.XVI No.52, nine Beethoven sonatas and the *Eroica* Variations. Of these, a competitor may choose one work, plus one or more pieces of his or her own choice, up to a maximum time-limit of forty minutes; while fifty-five minutes is allocated to the second-stage recital. Here, once again, the competitor is obliged to play a Romantic work – drawn from a choice of five Schubert pieces, including the *Wanderer* Fantasy, five groups of pieces by Chopin, four by Schumann, three by Brahms and the Liszt Sonata, together with one or more own-choice pieces. No studies are compulsory.

'Any professional pianist must be able to put together a good recital programme,' says Françoise Logan. 'The greater freedom of choice will allow the jury to see whether they can offer a balanced diet.'

The semi-final recital – now lasting up to seventy-five minutes – has to include a substantial twentieth-century work of the competitor's choice; while the list of concertos – to be played once more with Rattle and the CBSO – includes four twentieth-century concertos (the Bartók No.2, the Rakhmaninov No.3, the Prokofiev No.3 and the Ravel G major), as well as the old favourites – Mozart's K.467 or K.503, Beethoven's First, Third or *Emperor*, the Schumann or Brahms' Second.

'I'm worried that too much emphasis is placed on the concerto performance,' says Fanny Waterman:

We don't want it to be a concerto competition, and we have wondered whether to try to weight the first three stages. Yet any young pianist who can't give of his or her best in a concerto isn't going to get to the top. The relationship of a soloist to a conductor is one of the most important things. Conductors are very powerful, and a pianist who establishes a rapport with a conductor will get re-engaged. If not, if there are personality limitations, or a lack of charisma, they won't get on.

But while a sympathetic conductor can keep a young artist's career afloat if it begins to flag, at the end of the day, in spite of competition successes and recording contracts, we cannot underestimate the power of the box-office and the artist's ability to fill the halls. The ultimate test of a musician's ability is the listener's reaction to his or her playing. The audience has a flair for recognizing the truly great.

We don't want to stand still at Leeds. We want to do the best we can, and the rest is in the lap of the gods. Of course some years are vintage years, and others are thin on the ground. Leeds was very lucky that Lupu and Perahia entered. Many people say glibly, 'the standard of piano-playing is higher now than it's ever been.' My response is that the standard is now lower than ever before – with notable exceptions, of course. There are many more pianists of a certain level, but there's a great shortage at the very top. And it would be a bad thing if every competition kept on churning out Lupus and Perahias – there's simply not enough work to go round. I think one of the reasons for this shortage of fine young pianists is that many of the great teachers – Flier, Gorodnitzky, Oborin, Zak, Nadia Reisenberg, Dorfmann – have died in recent years, and there are too few teachers of the same calibre replacing them. To produce a really great pianist requires the support and encouragement of loving parents, and a great teacher working on the spot. One can never predict when this raw talent will emerge. Although Murray Perahia's parents were not musically educated, his father was the curator of a synagogue, and Murray as a child had the opportunity to hear the great cantors at work. New York had a tradition of great singing cantors – and many later made it at the Met. Jewish chant is richer than plain-chant – more emotional and expressive – and Murray was raised in this tradition. Radu Lupu learnt from the great Romanian teachers, such as Floria Musicescu, before he went to Neuhaus in Moscow.

The two main schools of piano playing are now Moscow and the Juilliard. I don't think France is producing as many great pianists as it once was. This world shortage of great teachers means that we may never again achieve the standards of Lupu and Perahia – either at Leeds or anywhere else.

But we should remember that it is now twenty-one years since Lupu, and eighteen since Perahia played at Leeds. Over that period each has proved himself to be one of the greatest artists of our time. The career of a great musician can only be assessed over a period of many years: some of the greatest pianists went unrecognized until middle age. Let us be fair to our more recent winners, and give them, too, the chance to prove themselves in the longer term. I don't like a musical death-sentence to be passed at any stage of a career, particularly since – as a teacher myself – I know that artists develop at very different speeds. What we try to do at Leeds is to allow artists to achieve recognition earlier in life by opening as many international doors for them as possible, with the hope that they will stay on the other side.

I feel there are now too many smaller competitions that don't offer the same degree of aftercare for their winners. Leeds, unlike many other competitions, offers genuine engagements, and takes an ongoing care and interest in its competitors. So long as the winners continue to play well, and fulfil their engagements, then we'll go on getting fine engagements for the next competition.

'Fanny Waterman has great conviction,' says Jon Kimura Parker. 'You really feel as if you can look up to her. It's an incredible achievement to have organized such a competition in Leeds, not a capital city. She had a vision, and the capacity to influence people to help her make it happen.'

On the eve of the tenth Leeds competition, almost thirty years since she had that vision, its indomitable founder celebrates her own seventieth birthday. What is her prognosis for the future of her brainchild?

It all depends on the standard of the future winners. I think I will be involved with the Leeds for ever. But things can change – Geneva once had the highest reputation – Solti, Michelangeli, de los Angeles were all laureates. But now, it is no longer in the top league. Some competitions come and go. I hope the Leeds will go on for ever.

Juries, Repertoire, Finalists, 1963–1990

The First Competition, 13–21 September 1963

JURY   Chairman: Sir Arthur Bliss, Master of the Queen's Music
Deputy Chairman: Hans Keller

Géza Anda	Paul Huband
Paul Badura-Skoda	Yvonne Lefebure
Jacob Flier	Nikita Magaloff
Barbara Hesse-Bukowska	John Pritchard

REPERTOIRE

First Stage   Candidates must offer one from each group:

Group 1   Beethoven   Sonata in C, Op. 53 ('Waldstein')
Sonata in D minor, Op. 31 No. 2
Sonata in F minor, Op. 57 ('Appassionata')

Group 2   Bach   Italian Concerto
Prelude and Fugue in E flat minor (Bk. 1 No. 8)

Group 3   Chopin   Etude No. 4 in C sharp minor (Bk. 1)
Etude No. 8 in F (Bk. 1)
Etude No. 5 in E minor (Bk. 2)
Etude No. 11 in A minor (Bk. 2)

Second Stage   Candidates must offer one from each group:

Group 1   Mozart   Fantasy in C minor, K. 475
Sonata in C minor, K. 457

                  Beethoven   Sonata in C minor, Op. 111
                  Chopin   Sonata in B flat minor, Op. 35
                  Schumann   Sonata in G minor, Op. 22
                  Brahms   Variations and Fugue on a Theme of Handel, Op. 24

Group 2   Liszt   Funérailles (Harmonies poétiques et religieuses)
Les jeux d'eau à la Villa d'Este (Années de pèlerinage, Book 3)
La campanella (Paganini Studies)

                  Debussy   Feux d'artifice (Préludes, Bk. 2)
L'isle joyeuse

                  Ravel   Jeux d'eau
Alborada del gracioso (Miroirs)

                  Albéniz   El Puerto (Iberia)

Group 3   Bartók   Suite, Op. 14
                  Prokofiev   Sonata No. 3 in A minor
                  Stravinsky   Sonata (1924)
                  Schoenberg   3 Piano Pieces, Op. 11

Group 4   Britten   Night Piece (specially commissioned for the 1963 competition)

Final Stage   Each finalist will play one of the following concertos with the Royal
                   Liverpool Philharmonic Orchestra conducted by John Pritchard:

Mozart	D minor, K. 466
	C, K. 503
	B flat, K. 595
Beethoven	No. 3 in C minor
	No. 4 in G
	No. 5 in E flat
Schumann	A minor
Liszt	No. 1 in E flat
	No. 2 in A
Tchaikovsky	No. 1 in B flat minor

FINALISTS   1 Michael Roll (GB)
             2 Vladimir Krainiev (USSR)
             3 Sebastien Risler (France)
             4 Armenta Adams (USA)

The Second Competition, 22 September–1 October 1966

JURY	Chairman: William Glock	
	Deputy Chairman: Hans Keller	
	Gina Bachauer	Nikita Magaloff
	Nadia Boulanger	Lev Oborin
	Maria Curcio	Charles Rosen
	Rudolf Firkušný	Béla Siki
	Annie Fischer	

REPERTOIRE

First Stage   Candidates must offer one from each group:

Group 1	Bach	Partita in E minor
	Haydn	Sonata in E flat, Hob. XVI No. 52
	Beethoven	Sonata in A, Op. 2 No. 2
		Sonata in C, Op. 2 No. 3
		Sonata in D, Op. 10 No. 3

Group 2	Chopin	Ballade No. 1 in G minor, Op. 23
		Ballade No. 2 in F, Op. 38
		Ballade No. 3 in A flat, Op. 47
		Ballade No. 4 in F sharp minor, Op. 52
		Polonaise in F sharp minor, Op. 44
		Scherzo No. 3 in C sharp minor, Op. 39

Group 3	Liszt	La Leggerezza (Concert Study)
		Gnomenreigen (Concert Study)
	Debussy	Étude pour les cinq doigts (No. 1)
		Etude pour les huit doigts (No. 6)
		Etude pour les degrès chromatiques (No. 7)
	Dohnányi	Capriccio in F minor (Concert Study, No. 6)

Second Stage   Candidates must offer one from each group:

Group 1	Mozart	Sonata in A minor, K. 310
	Beethoven	Sonata in E, Op. 109
		Sonata in A flat, Op. 110
	Schubert	Sonata in D, Op. 53
	Weber	Sonata No. 2 in A flat, Op. 39
	Schumann	Fantasy in C, Op. 17
	Brahms	Sonata in F minor, Op. 5

Group 2	Stravinsky	Danse russe (Petrushka Suite)
	Prokofiev	Toccata in D minor, Op. 11
	Bartók	Allegro barbaro
	Schoenberg	Piano Pieces, Op. 33a and 33b
	Messiaen	Fantaisie burlesque

**Third Stage
(Semi-Final)**

Each competitor is free to choose this programme, which may include one piece previously played by him or her in the Competition.

Final Stage

Each competitor will play one of the following concertos with the Royal Liverpool Philharmonic Orchestra conducted by Charles Groves:

Mozart	D minor, K. 466
	B flat, K. 595
Beethoven	No. 3 in C minor
	No. 4 in G
	No. 5 in E flat
Brahms	No. 1 in D minor
Chopin	No. 2 in F minor
Schumann	A minor
Tchaikovsky	No. 1 in B flat minor

FINALISTS

1 Rafael Orozco (Spain)
2 { Viktoria Postnikova (USSR)
   { Semyon Kruchin (USSR)
3 Aleksei Nasedkin (USSR)
4 Jean-Rodolphe Kars (Austria)

The Third Competition, 11–20 September 1969

JURY	Chairman: William Glock	
	Gina Bachauer	Raymond Leppard
	Clifford Curzon	Nikita Magaloff
	Szymon Goldberg	Ivan Moravec
	Peter Gould	Béla Siki
	Youra Guller	Lev Vlasenko

REPERTOIRE

First Stage Candidates must offer one from each group:

Group 1	Bach	Toccata in D
		Partita No. 2 in C minor
	Haydn	Variations in F minor, Hob. XVII No. 6
	Mozart	Fantasy in C minor, K. 396
	Beethoven	7 Bagatelles, Op. 33
		6 Bagatelles, Op. 126

Group 2	Chopin	One of the 4 scherzos
		Impromptu No. 2 in F sharp, Op. 36
		Impromptu No. 3 in G flat, Op. 51

Group 3	Liszt	One of the first 6 'Paganini' Studies
	Debussy	One of the 12 Etudes

Second Stage Candidates must offer one from each group:

Group 1	Beethoven	Sonata in D, Op. 28 ('Pastoral')
		Sonata in E flat, Op. 81a ('Les Adieux')
		Sonata in A, Op. 101
	Schubert	4 Impromptus, Op. 142
		Sonata in A minor, Op. 143
	Schumann	Carnaval, Op. 9
		Etudes symphoniques, Op. 13
		Kreisleriana, Op. 16
	Brahms	'Paganini' Variations, Op. 35
	Musorgsky	Pictures at an Exhibition

Group 2	Bartók	Out of Doors
	Britten	Holiday Diary, Op. 5
	Hindemith	Sonata No. 2 (1936)
	Messiaen	Regard de l'Esprit de joie (Vingt regards sur l'enfant Jésus)
	Stravinsky	Serenade in A
	Tippett	Sonata No. 2
	Webern	Variations, Op. 27

Third Stage (Semi-Final) Competitors are free to choose their own programmes, which may include one piece previously played by them in the Competition.

Final Stage   Each finalist will play one of the following concertos with the Royal
Liverpool Philharmonic Orchestra conducted by Charles Groves

Mozart	E flat major, K. 271
	A minor, K. 488
	C minor, K. 491
	C, K. 503
	B flat, K. 595
Beethoven	No. 1 in C
	No. 2 in B flat
	No. 3 in C minor
	No. 4 in G
	No. 5 in E flat
Schumann	A minor
Chopin	No. 2 in F minor
Brahms	No. 2 in B flat
Bartók	No. 3

FINALISTS   1 Radu Lupu (Romania)
2 Georges Pludermacher (France)
3 Arthur Moreira-Lima (Brazil)
4 Boris Petrushansky (USSR)
5 Anne Queffelec (France)

The Fourth Competition, 6–16 September 1972

JURY   Chairman: The Rt. Hon. Lord Boyle of Handsworth

Artur Balsam	Ingrid Haebler
Nadia Boulanger	Geneviève Joy
Halina Czerny-Stefańska	Raymond Leppard
Valentin Gheorghiu	Nikita Magaloff
Peter Gould	Béla Siki
Sir Charles Groves	

REPERTOIRE

First Stage   Competitors must offer one from each group:

Group 1

Haydn	Sonata in E flat, Hob. XVI No. 52
Mozart	Sonata in B flat, K. 333
	Sonata in A minor, K. 310
	Sonata in C minor, K. 457
Beethoven	Sonata in B flat, Op. 22
	Sonata in E flat, Op. 27 No. 1
	Sonata in G, Op. 31 No. 1
	Sonata in D minor, Op. 31 No. 2
	Sonata in E flat, Op. 31 No. 3

Group 2

Chopin	Fantaisie in F minor, Op. 49
	Barcarolle in F sharp minor, Op. 60
	Polonaise-fantaisie in A flat, Op. 61
	Polonaise in F sharp minor, Op. 44
	Ballade No. 2 in F, Op. 38
	Ballade No. 4 in F minor, Op. 52

Group 3

Scarlatti	One sonata
Debussy	One of the 12 Etudes
Bartók	One of the 3 Studies. Op. 18

Second Stage   Competitors must offer one from each group:

Group 1

Bach	Partita in E minor
Beethoven	'Eroica' Variations, Op. 35
	Sonata in E, Op. 109
	Sonata in A flat, Op. 110
	Sonata in C minor, Op. 111
Schubert	Sonata in E flat, Op. 122
	'Wanderer' Fantasy, Op. 15
Schumann	Davidsbündlertänze, Op. 6
	Sonata in F sharp minor, Op. 11
Liszt	Sonata in B minor
Brahms	Variations and Fugue on a Theme of Handel, Op. 24
Franck	Prélude, Choral et Fugue
Ravel	Gaspard de la nuit

Group 2

Bartók	Sonata (1926)
Copland	Variations (1930)
Falla	Fantasia Baetica
Prokofiev	Sonata No. 3
Stravinsky	Sonata (1924)
Tippett	Sonata No. 2

Webern   Variations, Op. 27

Third Stage   Competitors are free to choose their own programmes, which may
(Semi-Final)   include one piece previously played by them in the Competition.
Part 1

Part 2   Competitors must choose one of the following concertos to be
                    played with the chamber section of the Royal Liverpool Philharmonic
                    Orchestra:

Bach   D minor
Mozart   E flat, K. 449
                  A major, K. 414

Final Stage   Each finalist will play one of the following concertos with the Royal
                    Liverpool Philharmonic Orchestra conducted by Charles Groves:

Beethoven   No. 3 in C minor
                  No. 4 in G
                  No. 5 in E flat
Brahms   No. 1 in D minor
Chopin   No. 1 in E minor
Mendelssohn   No. 1 in G minor
Rakhmaninov   No. 3 in D minor
Schumann   A minor

FINALISTS   1 Murray Perahia (USA)
                  2 Craig Sheppard (USA)
                  3 Eugene Indjic (USA)

The Fifth Competition, 3–13 September 1975

JURY	Chairman: The Rt. Hon. Lord Boyle of Handsworth

Gina Bachauer	Charles Rosen
Artur Balsam	Phyllis Sellick
Sir Charles Groves	Béla Siki
Pál Kadosa	Rosalyn Tureck
Mindru Katz	Mikhail Voskressensky
Gerald Moore	

REPERTOIRE

First Stage   Competitors must offer one from each group:

Group 1	Bach	English Suite No. 6 in D minor
		Partita No. 4 in D
		Chromatic Fantasia and Fugue
	Haydn	Sonata in G, Hob. XVI No. 6
		Sonata in C, Hob. XVI No. 50
	Beethoven	Sonata in E flat, Op. 7
		Sonata in B flat, Op. 22
		Sonata in A flat, Op. 26
		Sonata in F, Op. 54
	Schubert	Sonata in E flat, Op. 122
		Sonata in B, Op. 147
Group 2	Chopin	3 Impromptus (A flat, F sharp, G flat)
		Scherzo No. 3 in C sharp minor
		Scherzo No. 4 in E
	Schumann	Papillons, Op. 2
	Brahms	Variations in D, Op. 22 No. 1
Group 3	Scarlatti	One sonata
	Debussy	One of the 12 Etudes
	Bartók	One of the 3 Studies, Op. 18

Second Stage   Competitors must offer one from each group:

Group 1	Mozart	Fantasy, K. 475 and Sonata in C minor, K. 457
	Beethoven	'Eroica' Variations, Op. 35
		Sonata in C, Op. 53 ('Waldstein')
		Sonata in F minor, Op. 57 ('Appassionata')
		Sonata in A, Op. 101
	Schubert	'Wanderer' Fantasy
	Schumann	Fantasy in C, Op. 17
		Carnaval, Op. 9
	Liszt	Sonata in B minor
	Ravel	Le tombeau de Couperin
	Musorgsky	Pictures at an Exhibition
Group 2	Bartók	Out of Doors
		Dance Suite
	Stravinsky	Serenade in A
		4 Studies, Op. 7
	Schoenberg	3 Pieces, Op. 11
	Berg	Sonata, Op. 1
	Falla	Fantasia Baetica
	Goehr	3 Pieces, Op. 18

Sherlaw Johnson	Asterogenesis
Rodney Bennett	Scena
Boulez	Sonata No. 1

Third Stage (Semi-Final)   Competitors must choose one of the following pieces:

Chopin	Nocturne in B, Op. 9 No. 3
	Nocturne in C minor, Op. 48 No. 1
	Nocture in E, Op. 62 No. 2
Brahms	Intermezzo in E, Op. 116 No. 4
	Intermezzo in E flat minor, Op. 118 No. 6
	Intermezzo in B minor, Op. 119 No. 1
Schubert	Impromptu in G flat
Mendelssohn	Duetto in A flat (From Op. 38 No. 6)

The rest of the programme is left to the competitors' own choice, but they must not repeat any piece previously played by them in the Competition.

Final Stage   Each finalist will play one of the following concertos with the Royal Liverpool Philharmonic Orchestra conducted by Sir Charles Groves:

Bach	D minor
Mozart	D minor, K. 466
	C minor, K. 491
	C, K. 503
Beethoven	No. 1 in C
	No. 4 in G
Schumann	A minor
Grieg	A minor
Britten	Op. 13
Prokofiev	No. 3 in C

FINALISTS
1 Dmitri Alexeev (USSR)
2 Mitsuko Uchida (Japan)
3 { Andras Schiff (Hungary)
    { Pascal Devoyon (France)
4 { Myung-Whun Chung (USA)
    { Michael Houstoun (New Zealand)

The Sixth Competition, 6–16 September 1978

JURY   Chairman: The Right Hon. Lord Boyle of Handsworth

Tito Aprea	Louis Kentner
Artur Balsam	André-François Marescotti
Dmitri Bashkirov	Michael Roll
Claude Frank	Phyllis Sellick
Hans Graf	Hugo Steurer
Lajos Hernádi	Arie Vardi
Akiko Iguchi	

REPERTOIRE

First Stage   Competitors must choose one work from Group 1, one from Group 2, and two from Group 3:

Group 1	Bach	Prelude and Fugue in C sharp minor (Bk. 1)
		Toccata and Fugue in C minor
	Beethoven	Sonata in A, Op. 2 No. 2
		Sonata in D, Op. 10 No. 3
		Sonata in D, Op. 28
		Sonata in G, Op. 31 No. 1
		6 Variations in F, Op. 34
	Clementi	Sonata in F sharp minor, Op. 26 No. 2
	Haydn	Sonata in E flat Hob. XVI No. 52
		Sonata in C minor, Hob. XVI No. 20
	Mozart	Sonata in F, K. 332
		Sonata in A minor, K. 310
Group 2	Chopin	Andante spianato and Grande Polonaise brillante, Op. 22
		Barcarolle in F sharp, Op. 60
		Polonaise-fantaisie in A flat, Op. 61
	Debussy	Suite 'Pour le piano'
	Granados	Los Requiebros (Goyescas, No. 1)
	Liszt	Après une lecture de Dante (Années de pèlerinage, Book 2)
		La Vallée d'Obermann (Années de pèlerinage, Book 1)
	Mendelssohn	Fantasy in F sharp minor, Op. 28
	Schubert	Impromptu in F minor, Op. 142 No. 1
	Schumann	'Abegg' Variations, Op. 1
Group 3	Chopin	Studies, Op. 10: No. 1, 4, 7, 8, 10, 11 or 12
		Studies, Op. 25: No. 3, 4, 5, 8, 10 or 12
	Debussy	Le vent dans la plaine
		Ce qu'a vu le vent d'Ouest (Préludes, Book 1)
		Feux d'artifice (Préludes, Book 2)
	Rakhmaninov	Préludes, Op. 23: No. 2, 5, 7 or 9

Second Stage   Competitors must choose one work from both groups:

Group 1	Beethoven	'Eroica' Variations, Op. 35
		Sonata in A, Op. 101
		Sonata in E. Op. 109
		Sonata in A flat, Op. 110
	Brahms	Sonata No. 3 in F minor, Op. 5
		'Paganini' Variations, Op. 35
	Chopin	Sonata in B minor, Op. 58

Musorgsky	Pictures at an Exhibition
Ravel	Gaspard de la nuit
Schubert	Sonata in D
	Sonata in B
Schumann	Kreisleriana, Op. 16
	Faschingsschwank aus Wien, Op. 26

Group 2

Bartók	Improvisations on Hungarian Peasant Songs, Op. 20
Berg	Sonata, Op. 1
Bloch	Sonata
Boulez	Sonata No. 1
Copland	Variations (1930)
Falla	Fantasia Baetica
Ginastera	Sonata
Kodály	Dances of Marosszek
Messiaen	Regard de l'esprit de joie (Vingt regards sur l'enfant Jésus)
	Fantaisie burlesque
Prokofiev	Sarcasms, Op. 17
Schoenberg	Suite, Op. 25
Stravinsky	Sonata (1924)
Tippett	Sonata No. 2

Semi-Final Stage

A recital to include Night Piece (Notturno) by Benjamin Britten. The remainder of the programme is left to the competitor's choice, except that they must not repeat any piece they have previously played in the Competition.

Competitors must choose one of the following chamber works to be performed with the Gabrieli String Quartet:

Brahms	Piano Quintet in F minor, Op. 34
Dvořák	Piano Quintet in A, Op. 81
Mozart	Piano Quartet in G minor, K. 478
Schumann	Piano Quintet in E flat, Op. 44
Shostakovich	Piano Quintet in G minor, Op. 57

Final Stage

Each of the 6 finalists will play one of the following concertos with the BBC Northern Symphony Orchestra conducted by Norman Del Mar:

Bach	D minor
Bartók	No. 3
Beethoven	No. 1 in C
	No. 5 in E flat
Brahms	No. 2 in D minor, Op. 15
Chopin	No. 2 in F minor
Grieg	A minor
Liszt	No. 1 in E flat
Mozart	D minor, K. 466
	C, K. 467
	E flat, K. 482
	C, K. 503
Schumann	A minor
Tchaikovsky	No. 1 in B flat minor

FINALISTS

1 Michel Dalberto (France)
2 Diana Kacso (Brazil)
3 Lydia Artymiw (USA)
4 Ian Hobson (GB)
5 Kathryn Stott (GB)
6 Etsuko Terada (Japan)

The Seventh Competition, 7–19 September 1981

JURY   Chairman: Fanny Waterman
Marie-Antoinette de Freitas Branco   Nina Milkina
Rudolf Fischer   Daniel Pollack
Claude Frank   Béla Siki
Peter Frankl   Abbey Simon
Orazio Frugoni   Hugo Steurer
Hans Graf   Ari Vardi
Moura Lympany   Wiktor Weinbaum

REPERTOIRE

First Stage   Competitors must choose one work from Group 1, one from Group 2 and two from Group 3

Group 1

Bach	French Overture in B Minor	
	Partita No. 4 in D	
	Partita No. 6 in E minor	
Beethoven	Sonata in D minor, Op. 31 No. 2	
	Sonata in C, Op. 53 ('Waldstein')	
	Sonata in F minor Op. 57 ('Appassionata')	
Haydn	Sonata in A flat, Hob. XVI No. 24	
	Sonata in E flat, Hob. XVI No. 45	
Mozart	Sonata in B flat, K. 570	
	Sonata in D, K. 576	

Group 2

Brahms	16 Waltzes, Op. 39
	2 Rhapsodies, Op. 79 No. 1 and No. 2
Chopin	Ballade No. 1 in G minor, Op. 23
	Ballade No. 2 in F, Op. 38
	Ballade No. 3 in A flat, Op. 47
	Ballade No. 4 in F minor, Op. 52
Mendelssohn	Andante and Rondo capriccioso in E, Op. 14
Schumann	Novelette, Op. 21 No. 8
	Fantasiestücke, Op. 12

Group 3

Bartók	One study from Op. 18
Debussy	One of the 12 Etudes
Liszt	One of the 12 Transcendental Studies
Scarlatti	One sonata

Second Stage   Competitors must choose one work from each group:

Group 1

Bach	15 3-part Inventions
Beethoven	Sonata in A flat, Op. 110
	Sonata in C minor, Op. 111
Brahms	Variations and Fugue on a theme of Handel, Op. 24
Chopin	Sonata in B minor, Op. 58
Liszt	Sonata in B minor
Mozart	Sonata in C minor, K. 457
Schubert	Sonata in A minor, D845
	Sonata in C minor, D958
Schumann	Davidsbündlertänze, Op. 6
	Fantasy, Op. 17
Prokofiev	Sonata No. 6

254

Group 2		
	Bartók	Sonata (1926)
	Britten	Holiday Diary, Op. 5
	Busoni	Sonatina No. 6 ('Carmen' Fantasy)
	Janáček	Sonata No. 1 (1905)
	Ravel	Valses nobles et sentimentales
	Shostakovich	Any two preludes and fugues
	Stravinsky	Serenade in A
	Tippett	Sonata No. 2
	Webern	Variations, Op. 27

Semi-Final Stage
Group 1

A recital programme of the competitor's own choice lasting approximately 45 minutes. The competitor must not repeat a piece previously played by him or her in the Competition.

Group 2

Competitors must choose one of the following chamber works, to be played with the Gabrieli String Quartet:

Brahms	Piano Quartet in G minor, Op. 25
	Piano Quintet in F minor, Op. 34
Dvořák	Piano Quintet in A, Op. 81
Faure	Piano Quartet No. 2 in G minor, Op. 45 (mvts 1 and 2)
Mozart	Piano Quartet in E flat, K. 493
Schumann	Piano Quintet in E flat, Op. 44

Final Stage

Each of the 6 finalists will play one of the following concertos with the Philharmonic Orchestra, conductor Sir Charles Groves:

Bach	No. 2 in E BWV 1053
Bartók	No. 2
Beethoven	No. 2 in B flat
	No. 3 in C minor
	No. 4 in G
Brahms	No. 1 in D minor
Grieg	A minor
Mendelssohn	No. 1 in G minor
Mozart	E flat, K. 271
	D minor, K. 466
Rakhmaninov	No. 2 in C minor
Schumann	A minor

FINALISTS

1 Ian Hobson (GB)
2 Wolfgang Manz (W. Germany)
3 Bernard d'Ascoli (France)
4 Daniel Blumenthal (USA)
5 Christopher O'Riley (USA)
6 Peter Donohoe (GB)

The Eighth Competition 10–22 September 1984

JURY   Chairman: Fanny Waterman

Joan Chissell	Hans Leygraf
Ding Shande	John Lill
Dean Elder	Tatiana Nikolaeva
Rudolf Fischer	Cécile Ousset
Orazio Frugoni	Pierre Sancan
Hans Graf	György Sándor
Karl-Heinz Kämmerling	Arie Vardi

REPERTOIRE

First Stage   Competitors must choose one work from Group 1, one from Group 2, and two sonatas or one étude from Group 3.

Group 1   Haydn   Sonata in E flat, Hob. XVI No. 52

                  Mozart   Sonata in B flat, K. 333
                                  Sonata in A minor, K. 310
                                  Sonata in C minor, K. 457

                  Beethoven   Sonata in B flat, Op. 22
                                  Sonata in E flat, Op. 27 No. 1
                                  Sonata in G, Op. 31 No. 1
                                  Sonata in D minor, Op. 31 No. 2
                                  Sonata in E flat, Op. 31 No. 3

Group 2   Chopin   Fantaisie in F minor, Op. 49
                                  Barcarolle in F sharp minor, Op. 60
                                  Polonaise-fantaisie in A flat, Op. 61
                                  Polonaise in F sharp minor, Op. 44
                                  Ballade No. 2 in F, Op. 38
                                  Ballade No. 4 in F minor, Op. 52

Group 3   Scarlatti   Any 2 sonatas
                  Liszt   Any study
                  Debussy   One of the 12 Etudes
                  Bartók   One of the 3 Studies, Op. 18

Second Stage   Competitors must choose one work from each Group:

Group 1   Bach   Partita in E minor
                  Beethoven   'Eroica' Variations, Op. 35
                                  Sonata in E, Op. 109
                                  Sonata in A flat, Op. 110
                                  Sonata in C minor, Op. 111
                  Schubert   Sonata in E flat, Op. 122
                                  'Wanderer' Fantasy in C, Op. 15
                  Schumann   Davidsbündlertänze, Op. 6
                                  Sonata in F sharp minor, Op. 11
                  Liszt   Sonata in B minor
                  Brahms   Variations and Fugue on a theme of Handel, Op. 24
                  Franck   Prélude, Choral et Fugue
                  Ravel   Gaspard de la nuit

Group 2   Bartók   Sonata (1926)
                  Copland   Variations (1930)
                  Falla   Fantasia Baetica

Rakhmaninov	Variations on a theme of Corelli, Op. 42
Stravinsky	Sonata (1924)
Tippett	Sonata No. 2
Webern	Variations, Op. 27

Semi-Final
Stage
Group 1

A recital programme of the competitor's own choice lasting approximately 45 minutes. The competitor must not repeat a piece previously played by him or her in this Competition.

Group 2

Competitors must choose one of the following sonatas for violin and piano, to be played with Erich Gruenberg:

Mozart	Sonata in E flat, K. 380
Beethoven	Sonata in A, Op. 47 (Kreutzer)
Brahms	Sonata in D minor, Op. 108
Franck	Sonata in A

Final Stage

Each of the six finalists will play one of the following concertos with the BBC Philharmonic Orchestra, conductor Sir Edward Downes:

Beethoven	No. 3 in C minor
	No. 4 in G
	No. 5 in E flat
Schumann	A minor
Mendelssohn	No. 1 in G minor
Chopin	No. 1 in E minor
Brahms	No. 1 in D minor
Rakhmaninov	No. 3 in D minor

FINALISTS
1 Jon Kimura Parker (Canada)
2 Ju Hee Suh (Korea)
3 Junko Otake (Japan)
4 Louis Lortie (Canada)
5 David Buechner (USA)
6 Emma Tahmisian (Bulgaria)

Chamber Music Prize: Jon Kimura Parker and Ju Hee Suh

The Ninth Competition 14–26 September 1987

JURY   Chairman: Fanny Waterman

Yury Boukoff	György Sándor
Rudolf Fischer	Takahiro Sonoda
Noel Flores	Joaquín Soriano
Konstantin Ganev	Halina Czerny-Stefańska
Karl-Heinz Kämmerling	Gordon Stewart
John Lill	Arie Vardi
Tatiana Nikolaeva	Lev Vlasenko

REPERTOIRE

First Stage   Competitors must choose one work from Group 1, one from Group 2, and two – not more than one by any composer – from Group 3

Group 1   Haydn   Sonata in C minor, Hob XVI No. 20
    Sonata in C, Hob. XVI No. 50
    Sonata in E flat, Hob. XVI No. 52

Clementi   Sonata in F sharp minor, Op. 26 No. 2
Mozart   Sonata in F, K. 332
    Sonata in B flat, K. 570
    Sonata in D, K. 576

Beethoven   Sonata in C, Op. 2 No. 3
    Sonata in E flat, Op. 7
    Sonata in D, Op. 10 No. 3
    Sonata in F, Op. 54

Group 2   Chopin   Ballade No. 1 in G minor, Op. 23
    Ballade No. 2 in F, Op. 38
    Ballade No. 3 in A flat, Op. 47
    Scherzo No. 2 in B flat minor, Op. 31
    Scherzo No. 3 in C sharp minor, Op. 39
    Scherzo No. 4 in E, Op. 54

Group 3   Chopin   Any étude from Op. 10 or Op. 25
Liszt   Transcendental Studies, Nos. 2, 5, 8, 10 or 12 or Paganini Studies, Nos. 2, 3 or 5

Bartók   Any study
Debussy   Any étude

Second Stage   Competitors must choose one work from each group:

Group 1   Bach   Partita No. 6 in E minor
Beethoven   Sonata in C, Op. 53 ('Waldstein')
    Sonata in F minor, Op. 57 ('Appassionata')
    Sonata in A, Op. 101
    Sonata in E, Op. 109

Schubert   'Wanderer' Fantasy in C
    Sonata in A minor, D784

Schumann   Carnaval, Op. 9
    Fantasy in C, Op. 17

Brahms   Fantasies, Op. 116
    'Paganini' Variations, Op. 35
    Sonata No. 3 in F minor, Op. 5

Musorgsky   Pictures at an Exhibition

Group 2	Ravel	Gaspard de la nuit
	Prokofiev	Sonata No. 7 in B flat, Op. 83
	Bartók	Sonata
		Out of Doors
	Janáček	Sonata ('October 1 1905')
	Schoenberg	3 Pieces, Op. 11
	Berg	Sonata, Op. 1
	Shostakovich	Any 2 of the 24 Preludes and Fugues
	Webern	Variations, Op. 27
	Tippett	Sonata No. 1
		Sonata No. 2

Semi-Final Stage
Group 1

A recital programme of the competitor's own choice lasting approximately 45 minutes. The competitor must not repeat a piece previously played by him or her in this Competition.

Group 2

Competitors must choose one of the following sonatas for violin and piano, to be played with Erich Gruenberg:

	Mozart	Sonata in B flat, K. 454
		Sonata in A, K. 526
	Beethoven	Sonata in C minor, Op. 30 No. 2
	Brahms	Sonata in G, Op. 78
	Schubert	Fantasia in C, D934
	Schumann	Sonata in D minor, Op. 121

Final Stage

Each of the six finalists will play one of the following concertos with the City of Birmingham Symphony Orchestra, conductor Simon Rattle:

	Mozart	No. 25 in C, K. 503
	Beethoven	No. 3 in C minor
		No. 4 in G
		No. 5 in E flat
	Schumann	A minor
	Brahms	No. 2 in B flat
	Rakhmaninov	No. 2 in C minor
		Rhapsody on a theme of Paganini, Op. 43
	Prokofiev	No 3 in C minor

FINALISTS
1 Vladimir Ovchinnikov
2 Ian Munro
3 Noriko Ogawa
4 Boris Berezovsky
5 Hugh Tinney
6 Marcantonio Barone

Chamber Music Prize: Hugh Tinney

The Tenth Competition 7–22 September 1990

JURY Chairman: Fanny Waterman

Marcello Abbado	Dominique Merlet
José de Sequeira Costa	Hiroko Nakamura
Sergei Dorensky	John O'Conor
Werner Felix	Cécile Ousset
Claude Frank	Harold C. Schonberg
Konstantin Ganev	Gordon Stewart
Hans Graf	Arie Vardi

REPERTOIRE

First Stage The competitor will play one work from the following list together with one or more works of his or her own choice to a maximum overall time of 40 minutes. The time-limit must be strictly adhered to:

Bach	Partita No. 2 in C minor
	Partita No. 6 in E minor
	Partita in B minor
	English Suite No. 6 in D minor
Mozart	Fantasy and Sonata in C minor (K. 475 and K. 457)
Haydn	Sonata in E flat, Hob. XVI No. 52
Beethoven	Sonata in C minor, Op. 13 ('Pathétique')
	Sonata in C sharp minor, Op. 27 No. 2
	Sonata in C, Op. 53 ('Waldstein')
	Sonata in F minor, Op. 57 ('Appassionata')
	Sonata in A, Op. 101
	Sonata in E, Op. 109
	Sonata in A flat, Op. 110
	Sonata in C minor, Op. 111
	'Eroica' Variations, Op. 35

Second Stage The competitor will play one work from the following list together with one or more works of his or her own choice to a maximum overall time of 55 minutes. This recital may not include a work previously performed by the competitor in the First Stage:

Schubert	'Wanderer' Fantasy in C
	Sonata in D, D850
	Sonata in G, D894
	4 Impromptus, D899
	Sonata in B flat, D960
Chopin	12 Etudes, Op. 10
	12 Etudes, Op. 25
	Any 12 consecutive Preludes, Op. 28
	Sonata in B flat minor, Op. 35
	Sonata in B minor, Op. 58
Schumann	Fantasiestücke, Op. 12
	Faschingsschwank aus Wien, Op. 26
	Davidsbündlertänze, Op. 6
	Fantasy in C, Op. 17
Liszt	Sonata in B minor
Brahms	Sonata No. 2 in F sharp minor, Op. 2

Variations and Fugue on a Theme of Handel,
Op. 24
'Paganini' Variations, Op. 35 (both Books)

**Third Stage
(Semi-Final)**   The competitor will perform a programme entirely of his or her own
choice of about 70 minutes' duration. This recital must include a
substantial work composed in the twentieth century and may not
include a work previously performed by the competitor in the First
and Second Stages.

Final Stage   One concerto from the list to be performed with the City of
Birmingham Symphony Orchestra conducted by Simon Rattle:

Mozart	C, K. 467
	C, K. 503
Beethoven	No. 1 in C
	No. 3 in C minor
	No. 5 in E flat
Bartók	No. 2
Schumann	A minor
Brahms	No. 2 in B flat
Rakhmaninov	No. 3 in D minor
Ravel	G major
Prokofiev	No. 1 in D flat

FINALISTS

Index